Find Me at Willoughby Close

Find Me at Willoughby Close

A Willoughby Close Romance

KATE HEWITT

TULE
PUBLISHING

Chapter One

*S*O THIS IS *what it feels like, when your world falls apart.* Shattered, the hairline cracks zigzagging across all the certainties she'd taken for granted. She felt numb, as if everything was suspended, waiting—but for what?

Carefully, Harriet Lang replaced her mug of tea on the coaster. It was a pottery mug from the local organic farm shop, thick and chunky, a deep, iridescent indigo with a shiny glaze. She'd bought four of them but, typically, William had broken one almost as soon as they were out of the box.

Still, she liked the remaining three, always used one for her afternoon cup of tea. The simple beauty of the mug gave her a little dart of satisfaction and pleasure, just as the coaster did—bought during their holiday in Provence, the sprig of lavender depicted on its surface a perfect match for the color scheme of the kitchen.

She glanced around the kitchen, from the large, cobalt-blue Aga gleaming against the cream walls—Farrow & Ball's Slipper Satin—to the vase of lilies, still in their peak of blossom, in the middle of the farmhouse table of reclaimed oak, releasing their heady but still pleasingly subtle scent. A cream linen sofa rested against the far wall, along with a strategically-positioned rattan basket full of lifestyle magazines. French windows overlooked the terrace and sprawling garden, the grass and leafless trees and bushes now touched with frost.

Everything looked pleasing, perfect—except for the mobile phone bill resting on the table next to the flowers. The bill that showed that her husband had, in the middle of the night, made three two-hour phone calls to his assistant over the course of the last month. And that was only December. She had no idea how many calls he'd made before that.

Listlessly Harriet picked up the bill and scanned it again even though she already knew the times and dates by heart. A ninety-seven minute call at two in the morning of December second. A one hundred and thirty-two minute call at four in the morning of the ninth. A third call at one thirty, horribly, on Christmas Eve. That one was for a whopping two hundred and twelve minutes. She'd gone online and looked at January's bill—there had been seven more calls.

The Christmas Eve one hurt the most, though. Had he snuck off to call her after he'd assembled Chloe's dollhouse, while Harriet had finished up the last touches on the stockings?

Did her husband *sleep?* How had she not woken up when he'd crept out of bed and gone—where? To his study? To make these calls to Meghan, his assistant. His young, sexy assistant, someone they'd actually joked about as having the hots for him, making fun of her kitten heels and lashings of mascara, how cringingly obvious she was.

Harriet closed her eyes, wishing she could banish the lurid images flashing in her mind. Frantic whispering. Furtive looks. Phone sex. She didn't even know what phone sex *was,* not in detail anyway, and yet perhaps Richard and Meghan had engaged in it. Repeatedly. It seemed likely.

She opened her eyes and took a deep breath. A glance at the teapot-shaped clock on the mantel told her she needed to pick the children up in five minutes. She needed to act—to pretend—that everything was normal, for their sakes as well as her own. She couldn't break down in the middle of the school yard. Then tonight she needed to talk to Richard.

After that... well, she couldn't think about an after that. The rest of her life occupied a blank white space, like a television program cut off and replaced by a screen of snow. She couldn't conceive of a future, any future, now that she was sure her husband was having an affair. Slowly, her limbs feeling wooden and awkward, Harriet rose from the table. She pushed her feet into the knee-high leather boots that were the prerequisite for the school run, along with the skinny jeans and the cashmere poncho over a ribbed turtleneck that she already wore. Chunky necklace, discreet earrings, check, check.

She was dressed as nearly as every other mum would be

as they all walked briskly to the school to collect their little darlings, chatting about the latest organic farm shop or Pilates class, or who had gained membership to the quietly elitist Soho Farmhouse. Harriet already had two years ago, along with her best friend, Sophie. They worked out there three times a week.

Except today was the children's swimming lessons, so she wouldn't walk, she'd take the car. Make the trek into Chipping Norton to sit in a damp plastic chair while her eyes itched from the humid, chlorine-saturated air for an hour. With a sigh, Harriet scooped up her keys. Tried not to think. Thinking had become dangerous.

She drove slowly through Wychwood-on-Lea, numbly fluttering her fingers at various acquaintances as she trawled the high street for a parking space. She barely noted the comfortable muddle of independent shops that had made her fall in love with the place six years ago, because it was quaint without being too upmarket or twee.

Once, she'd pictured herself poking in the antique shop, furnishing the house with local pieces, nothing too showy, but somehow she'd never found the time and, in the end, it had been easier, if not at all cheaper, to hire the interior designer Sophie had recommended.

And now she was late. Gritting her teeth as she reversed the massive Discovery into a space barely big enough to fit it, conscious of a stern pensioner glaring at her from the pavement, watching the whole, laborious process of reversing endlessly, and scowling when she hit the curb. Twice.

Harriet slid out of the car, ignoring the old woman who seemed to expect some kind of explanation or apology from her, and then hurried, half-running, towards the school at the top of the street.

It was fine to be late for Mallory and William, who, in year six and four, were old enough to leave school on their own, but not for Chloe in year one, whose teacher, Mrs. Bryson, would be checking her watch every few seconds in ostentatious disapproval if so much as a minute ticked by. She seemed like a woman who didn't actually like children, at least not Harriet's. She'd endured Mrs. Bryson twice already, when Mallory and William had gone through year one, and Harriet would be glad to see the back of the wretched woman when Chloe finished the year. Unfortunately it was only January.

Harriet strode towards the school gate, staring straight ahead, trying to avoid the other mothers, some of whom were already looking at her curiously. She was late, which was unusual enough, but Harriet suspected something of her emotions must be showing in her face. She felt brittle, ready to snap, to shatter into fragments. Surely other people could see it, sense it, and the last thing she wanted were questions she couldn't answer. Well-meaning sympathy or avid curiosity, it didn't matter which. She couldn't handle either. Her face felt as if she was wearing a hardened mask.

Ah, there was Mrs. Bryson, mouth pursed like she'd tasted something sour as she checked her watch purely for Harriet's benefit.

"Mummy, you're late," Chloe said, her high, piping voice, with all of its quivering accusation, carrying across the emptying school yard.

"Sorry, darling. I got caught up in something." Harriet kissed her daughter's plump, rosy cheek, savoring its perfect roundness, the innocent sweetness of it, before lifting her dutifully penitent gaze to the teacher. "Sorry, Mrs. Bryson. It won't happen again."

"I was," Mrs. Bryson informed her tartly, "about to send her to the office." She made it sound like Chloe had been about to be relegated to the ninth circle of hell. Maybe she had been.

"Sorry," Harriet murmured again and, taking Chloe's hand she started pulling her towards the juniors' entrance where Mallory and William would hopefully be waiting.

"Mummy, you're hurting me," Chloe complained, and belatedly Harriet realized she was squeezing her daughter's hand a little too hard.

"Sorry, darling, sorry," she said, touching Chloe's ringlets.

The last thing she wanted to do was take out her anger and fear on her daughter, even inadvertently. "Sorry," she said again because she *was* sorry. But was Richard? What on earth would he say to her—and what would she say to him? She couldn't think about that yet. She had too much to get through first.

Mallory was leaning against the brick wall by the juniors' entrance, arms folded ominously, her fringe sliding into her eyes, as Harriet approached.

"Where's William?" she asked, and Mallory shrugged.

"Nice to see you too, Mum. How was your day?"

"Sorry," Harriet said yet again. "How was your day? And where is William?"

Mallory cocked her head towards the school field, and Harriet saw her son sprinting all the way across the field, well out of shouting range. Not that she'd be so uncouth as to shout.

"Brilliant," she said on a sigh. She parked Chloe next to Mallory, who gazed down at her younger sister with disdain.

"Ew, stop picking your nose."

"I'm not picking my nose," Chloe answered indignantly, her thumb working industriously around her nostrils. "I'm itching it."

Mallory rolled her eyes and Harriet started across the field towards William, wincing as her leather boots got a liberal caking of mud.

"William," she called when she was within earshot, trying to keep her voice level and light. "It's time go. We have swimming, remember?"

William glanced over his shoulder at her, and Harriet could see the thought process racing through his nine-year-old brain just as if he'd spoken it all out loud. She was too far away to make a grab for him, and he could pretend he hadn't heard her, which was what he decided to do. He turned back and kept running, chasing another kid who was kicking a football. His clothes were filthy with mud. She stood in the middle of the field, fists clenched, boots muddy, a sudden fury pumping through her.

"William." Her voice came out in a roar of parental authority, or perhaps just anger. Her body felt as tense as a bow, arrows ready to be let loose. "We are going. *Now."*

William hesitated, and Harriet leveled him with the do-it-now-or-else death stare that she only brought out on special, or desperate, occasions. Another tension-filled pause where it could go either way, and then with a shrug of his shoulders, William started towards her, dragging his trainers through the mud so even more spattered up onto his dirty knees. At least he would get clean in the pool.

Harriet's shoulders slumped in relief at the pitched battle that had been avoided. Maybe she shouldn't have shouted, but she was holding onto her self-control by a single, fraying thread.

By the time she'd got everyone in the car and handed out the after-school snacks of yogurt-covered raisins and fruit-flavored water, they were already late for swimming. Mallory had dumped her raisins in the side pocket of her door, where they would no doubt melt and fester into one gloopy mass.

"These are so nasty."

"You used to like them," Harriet protested as she navigated back down the high street, cars double-parked on both sides. The Discovery way too big a vehicle for Wychwood-on-Lea's narrow lanes, but everyone had a four by four these days.

"Yeah, when I was like, six." Mallory blew a strand of hair out of her eyes, folded her arms, and flung herself back against the seat in a typical gesture of preteen discontent. When had her daughter developed so much attitude?

"I like them," Chloe said from the backseat.

"That's because you're a baby," Mallory returned in a bored voice.

"I am not—"

"Yes, you are," William chimed in, just because he could. "Baby, baby, baby—"

"Enough, please." Harriet held up one hand, wishing her children had the emotional astuteness to understand when she could and could not handle their bickering. "Silence until we reach Chipping Norton."

Fortunately they obeyed her for once, Mallory taking out her phone, William kicking the seat in front of him, and Chloe singing under her breath. Harriet could just about handle all of that.

Once they arrived at the leisure center, there was the usual scrum of navigating the tiny changing room with its wet floor and the center's absurd rule that you could not wear shoes in it, which meant your socks got soaked. She wrestled Chloe into her swimsuit and then the swimming cap onto her head, while her daughter screeched as if Harriet was plucking out her fingernails one by one. Finally, she sent Chloe on her way and went to take her place in the viewing gallery with relief.

A couple of other school mums were already sitting down, and Harriet wondered if she could absent herself from the usual desultory chitchat without seeming rude. She didn't think she could cope with talking healthy dinners or homework right then. She couldn't cope with talking about anything.

She smiled her hellos and then gave the necessary, apologetic grimace as she reached for her phone. "Sorry," she mouthed, "I just have to answer some texts."

She let the conversation wash over her as she stared down at her phone, everything in her going blank. *My husband is having an affair.*

It seemed impossible. It *was* impossible, surely. She and Richard were solid, always had been, since their university days. She'd never once doubted him. Never. Except... Harriet scrolled back the last few months and realized Richard didn't feature in her memories all that much. How had she not noticed that?

And how long had his affair been going on for? Weeks? Months? She hadn't looked at any phone bills before December's. Yet she must have realized something was wrong, on a subconscious level, at least—that must have been why she'd checked the mobile phone bill, something she normally wouldn't ever think to do. She hadn't *really* realized, though, not consciously. *Had she?*

What had been going through her mind when she'd picked up the bill from the day's post lying on the mat, slit open the envelope with the sterling silver letter opener that had been a wedding present, and started scanning the list of calls? What had she been looking for?

"Harriet, you're missing it!"

She looked up, blinking the world into blurry focus as she registered the tone of laughing censure. "What am I missing?"

"Chloe," Helen, another year one mum said, in censorious tone of voice that made Harriet inwardly wince. "The tadpole class is taking their polliwog test today."

"Are they?" Too late Harriet realized she should not have said that out loud.

She should have known, she *would* have known, if this hadn't happened. If a bomb hadn't dropped into her lap at one thirty that afternoon, and lay there, ticking ominously, ever since.

"Right, of course." She forced a fake-sounding laugh. "Sorry, I was spacing there for a moment."

She turned her attention to the pool, where Chloe was flailing in the water, looking as if she was about to drown. For this, she would get a little badge that Harriet would, of course, keep on proud display. Mustering a smile, she waited for her daughter to make it to the other side.

Everyone was thankfully quiet and subdued in the car on the way home, no doubt tired from the swim lessons as well as the slog from pool to car with wet hair in the freezing dark. Harriet hated swim lessons. She didn't actually think the children liked them either. Why did she do them? The answer, of course, was because everybody else did. Every mother she knew kept a schedule bristling with afterschool activities—swimming, ballet, karate, Scouts, Rainbows or Brownies, football, rugby, horse riding. Sophie's children even did some gourmet cooking class on Saturdays, with a Michelin-starred chef. To not book up every afternoon felt like falling behind or even failing.

As soon as she pulled into the drive, the children spilled from the car and into the house, eager to plug into their electronic device of choice until dinner time, when Harriet enacted the no screen time rule. For Mallory, it would be her phone; William, his DS; Chloe her kiddie tablet. Harriet trailed behind, arms full of wet towels and school bags.

The house was still and silent as she entered the utility room off the kitchen, dumping their wet, chlorine-smelling swimsuits and towels into the washer. The children had, trained in this one thing at least, put their shoes in their individual rattan baskets, each one labeled with their names in painstaking calligraphy that suddenly seemed rather absurd. She'd spent hours on those stupid baskets.

Sighing, Harriet unzipped her boots, kicked them off, and then went to decide what to make for tea.

Normally she would have put something in the slow-cooker before school pickup; normally she would have been briskly, efficiently organized. The house would be full of tantalizing smells and the table would have been set; all she would have had to do was make a salad and slide a par-baked baguette into the oven before pouring herself a glass of wine and telling the children to get their homework out. She would have texted Richard, promising him a glass of wine and a bath when he made it in from his commute. And when he had come home she would have snuggled in his arms and sighed happily. Except, when had she actually last done any of that?

Harriet opened the fridge and stared into its pristine depths, the labeled plastic containers, the wedge of very good Brie cheese, the healthy snacks, and organic milk, with blank incomprehension. Everything felt off, wrong, the simplest of movements jarring and clumsy. She no longer knew how to conduct her life. She didn't think she could even make supper.

"Mu-um, where's the charger?" Mallory's voice was a piercing whine as she stormed into the kitchen.

Harriet closed her eyes. "Check the basket where I keep all the cords."

"It's not there." Each word rang with accusation. How, Harriet wondered, was this her fault? She didn't touch the cords, ever. She didn't even like to use her phone that much, although her friends insisted on communicating by text.

"Check again, Mallory," she called. "Or, here's an idea, don't use your phone."

Mallory blinked, temporarily shocked into silence by her mother's uncharacteristic sarcasm. Except she hadn't actually meant to be sarcastic, not that her daughter would realize that. Harriet closed the door of the fridge.

"Right. Takeaway tonight."

"Is something... wrong with you?" Mallory asked cautiously, as if cornering a wild animal.

"No." Harriet took a deep breath, staving off the tidal wave of emotion that was threatening to crash over her and leave her to drown. "I'm just tired." She rummaged through the drawer of takeaway menus.

The only offering in the village was fish and chips, which her children didn't like. So that meant piling them all back in the car to go to Chipping Norton to pick up a pizza. Considering they'd only just got out of the car, that wasn't a very appealing prospect for anyone. Why did everything have to feel so *hard* all of a sudden?

Harriet turned to the walk-in pantry and grabbed a packet of pasta and a jar of sauce. She plunked both on the yawning granite island while Mallory watched sulkily.

"I thought you said we were getting a takeaway."

"I changed my mind." Harriet's tone brooked no argument and with a huffy sigh, Mallory turned back to the family room, disconsolate and cordless.

For the next few hours Harriet managed to exist on autopilot. *Make dinner, set the table, call the kids. Insist on napkins, no elbows on the table, mop up spilled milk not once but twice, load the dishwasher.* As she wiped down the kitchen counters, the children got out their homework, and then Harriet spent half an hour going over Chloe's spelling, and William's chicken-scratch handwriting before she sent them upstairs to get ready for bed.

No baths tonight, thank goodness, since they'd had showers after swimming. Pajamas, stories, Chloe's army of stuffed animals arranged just so, every inch of her body covered by something soft and cuddly, William insisting on reading *Guinness Book of World Records* rather than what Harriet deemed a proper book to read before bed, Mallory sneaking her phone under her duvet.

Harriet felt too exhausted to cope with any of it and yet somehow she did, removing Mallory's phone, turning off William's light, fishing Chloe's one-eared elephant from under her bed and positioning him next to Chloe's left arm, where he always went.

"Thanks, Mummy," Chloe said sleepily, and sudden, surprising tears stung Harriet's eyes.

Her daughter was so innocent, so unknowing. All the children were. She reached over and gave Chloe a tight hug, making her daughter squeal with surprised pleasure. What was going to happen to them? What was going to happen to her?

"'Night, darling," Harriet whispered, and tiptoed downstairs where everything was blissfully quiet.

Mallory was still awake; at eleven years old, she had the privilege of staying up half an hour later than William, as long as she was in bed reading. The other children would, hopefully, settle to sleep sooner rather than later. And then Richard would come home from his ninety-minute commute from London, only occasionally in time to kiss the children goodnight. Harriet uncorked a bottle of decent wine and poured herself a very large glass, needing the courage as well as the comfort. Now to wait.

She was, Harriet reflected as she sat on the sofa in the kitchen and sipped her wine, viewing this whole debacle from far away, as if it wasn't actually happening to her. Perhaps that was the only way to survive it—to force some emotional distance, as if she was watching it from afar, wondering what that poor, jilted woman would do. Would she be quietly dignified, taking the higher road? Would she be coldly furious, or smash dinner plates, even the Meissen twelve-piece set they'd received as wedding presents? Or, worst of all, would she dissolve into noisy tears, blubbering about all she'd given and sacrificed, how much she loved him, and now this?

The funny thing was, she really didn't know. So she'd sit here and wait for the drama to unfold, the show to start, and hope for a happy ending. Upstairs, Mallory's light clicked off. Someone went to the bathroom; Harriet heard the sound of footsteps, the flush of a toilet. A single cough, and then silence. She waited and sipped, feeling strangely, surreally calm. The wine was very good.

And then, finally, the sound of Richard's Lexus in the drive, the slam of his car door, the electronic beep of him locking the car. Footsteps, the door flung open in the utility room, a weary sigh. Harriet tensed.

"Hey." His face, his lovely, familiar face with the unexpected dimples and the cleft in his chin, the dark, floppy hair, and his warm hazel eyes, creased into a tired smile. "Sorry I'm late."

"Yes, why are you?" Harriet's voice rang out, shrewishly accusing, making her wince inwardly. So that was how she was going to play it. She wished she'd tried for something a little more dignified and composed.

Guilt flashed across Richard's face, so quick she would have missed it if she hadn't been looking, hadn't been waiting for it. Then he turned and with slow, careful deliberation, took off his overcoat and draped it over a kitchen chair, his back to her. Stalling. He was stalling.

"The usual," he said when the silence had ticked on for several taut seconds. "You know."

"No, I don't actually know, Richard." Her voice was too loud; she'd have Mallory down here, looking sulky and scared, and then Chloe and William, woken up, wondering what was going on. Harriet took a deep breath, and then a gulp of wine. "But maybe you should tell me." Another breath, and then the plunge. "Why don't you start with the phone bill?"

Richard turned around, looking so genuinely confused that for a heart-stopping second Harriet was filled with wonderful doubt. Maybe she'd got it all wrong. Oh, yes, she had, she must have. She was practically smiling with tremulous, overwhelming relief when his expression suddenly turned guarded and wary, realization settling in his eyes, in the lines bracketing his mouth.

"What do you mean?" he asked, hedging his bets. It was so *obvious* now, and she hated that. Hated that she could see through him, that there was something to see at all. Something for him to hide.

"The mobile phone bill. I had a look at it this afternoon and there were three calls this month alone to a certain number." She waited, for what she couldn't even say. For it all to come spilling out?

Richard just stared.

"Your assistant's number. Sexy Meghan." She spat the words, trying to disguise the tremble in her voice. "We joked about her, Richard, and now you're calling her at three in the morning?" Tears threatened and she blinked them back and drank more wine.

Richard stared at her for another few seconds, his expression blank. What was he thinking? She had no idea. Was he trying to come up with a credible excuse? If he said he loved Meghan, twenty-six-year-old Meghan with a thigh gap and underwear from Agent Provocateur, Harriet would scream.

Or, worse, she'd start sobbing. She felt a need to keep her self-respect in this situation, not to burst into noisy tears and show how devastated she was. Dignity was, perhaps, the only thing she had left.

"It wasn't—it isn't—like that, Harriet," Richard said. "Not... not exactly."

Not *exactly?* Was that supposed to make her feel better? Because it definitely did not.

"Then what the hell are you doing, calling her in the middle of the night? Talking to her for *hours.*" He at least had the grace to look abashed. "You're having an affair." She stated it baldly, daring him to deny it.

"No, no, not... it's not quite..."

Not quite what? She was not brave enough to ask. He sighed heavily, trailing into silence.

He couldn't deny it, then. "The truth is, Harriet," he said after a moment, "we're broke."

For a few stunned seconds she thought he meant them, as a couple, broken. Shattered beyond repair. She felt a terrible wrenching inside, as if she had just come apart. They were a couple, they had three children, they used to finish each other's sentences, he'd kissed her stretch marks. They were not broken.

"Richard..." Harriet began, trying not to cry, and he pressed his lips together.

"We might lose the house."

The house? Why was he talking about the house? With a

jolt as if she'd just mentally fallen flat on her bottom, she realized he was actually talking about money. And then she experienced a rush of relief, making her feel weak. *They* weren't broken. But wait… the house?

"What do you mean?" she asked, her voice faint, all of her self-righteous fury draining away, replaced by a dizzying incomprehension. "Broke?"

"I mean, broke." Richard poured himself a glass of wine from the bottle left near the Aga and sat wearily on the other side of the sofa, running a hand through his hair as he took a sip. "I was fired from my job six months ago."

"What?" She stared at him, disbelieving and appalled, her mind spinning with information she had not expected to receive. "How—but why—why didn't you tell me? What have you been doing all this time?" *Besides having an affair?*

Harriet had a sudden image of Meghan as she'd seen her at the Christmas party a month ago, her sly smile as she'd sipped her wine. She'd been wearing the most ridiculously inappropriate cocktail dress. It had mesh inserts on the sides that had looked trashy. Harriet had been able to see her bra, which is how she knew about the Agent Provocateur under-wear. Richard had seen it too, no doubt, and in far more detail. She felt sick.

Richard looked down at his shoes. "I kept going into London to try to find something," he admitted quietly. "Working contacts, doing business lunches, that kind of thing. Nothing's come up yet, but it will. I know it will. It's just a matter of time, and then we'll be back on our feet, just as we were."

Just as they were? How could they possibly be just as they were?

"And Meghan?" Harriet asked, the words scraping her throat.

"Meghan wasn't… that was nothing, Harriet."

"She must know you're unemployed."

"Yes… she's been… well." He sighed, smiling in only a sort-of apology.

She's been what?

"I'm sorry."

"Six months," Harriet said slowly. She could barely get her head around it all. "For six months you've been commuting to London for no good reason."

"I've been busy," Richard said, a note of defensiveness creeping into his voice. "I'm doing a lot of legwork, keeping my ear to the ground…"

He sounded like one giant cliché. "It sounds to me like you've been going to London to screw your secretary," Harriet said flatly, inwardly shocked by what she was saying.

She didn't talk like that. She didn't even think like that. And yet here she was. Here they were.

"No," Richard said, but it sounded halfhearted at best. He'd never been a good liar. Harriet remembered when he'd tried to tell her mother that he'd lost the bobble-covered Christmas jumper she'd knit for him. His face had turned beet red. And he looked more than a little flushed now.

"Save it, Richard," Harriet said tiredly. She couldn't bear to hear his stumbling excuses. She still had so much to process. "Why were you fired?"

"I got a bit too cocky." Richard sighed and rubbed his temples, not meeting her gaze. "You've got to be aggressive in this business, that's what they want. You've always got to be looking for the next big thing, the investment no one's heard of but is going to be huge. You can't imagine the pressure."

Harriet didn't respond.

And, after a pause, he continued, "But one of my sure things ended up being a bust and I lost the firm a lot of money. They decided to make me an example. That's all it was. They lost face and they decided to make me the scapegoat." He shrugged. "It happens in this business. Everyone moves on, and I will too, to something better." He lifted his chin, his eyes glinting with determination. He had, Harriet supposed, a lot of face to save.

Although the truth was, she didn't actually know what Richard did—had done—for work in recent years. Not specifically, at least. She knew he was in high-flying finance, some kind of investment management but, beyond that, the details were hazy. The important thing was he made a lot of money, and there was a big fat bonus at Christmas. At least, there used to be.

She realized she hadn't asked about it this year, had

simply assumed the money was in the bank, but presumably Richard hadn't received it. And if he hadn't received it... For a second she thought of all the Christmas presents she'd bought—the gift baskets from Harrods for friends and acquaintances she didn't actually care that much about, the remote control car for William that had cost a hundred pounds—

"How broke are we, Richard?" she asked, her voice turning shaky.

Surely not *that* broke. Maybe a bit of belt-tightening, a cheaper holiday this summer, fewer meals out, but he wasn't talking about actually anything having to *change,* was he? He'd said something about the house, but that was just a scare tactic, surely...

"Broke," Richard said flatly. He looked away, his lips compressing. "For now. Like I said, we might lose the house."

Lose the house. The words echoed through her, impossible, surely impossible. And yet... Dizziness swept over her, and Harriet closed her eyes. She thought of the dollhouse she'd bought Chloe, an enormous French chateau. She'd barely played with it. And Mallory's phone... it was brand new, the latest smartphone. Harriet had a feeling it had cost something like five hundred pounds. So much money, and all this time Richard hadn't been earning anything, not a single penny. And he'd gone along with all the spending. He'd put the dollhouse together. He'd said Mallory was old enough for a decent phone.

But surely they couldn't be *that* broke, actually, properly without any money. He would have said something. He would have had to. And how could they lose the *house?* This was their dream house, the farmhouse in the country straight off one of those property shows on the telly, the place they'd spent ages doing up, where they'd planned to have their grandchildren over for weekends. Mallory was going to come down the stairs as a bride, and the reception would be in the garden, with its stone walls climbing with roses and the huge horse chestnut with its wooden swing. They *couldn't* lose this house. Except if Richard was having an affair, they'd already lost so much more. Who even cared about the house, when her husband was cheating on her?

Except… this house was the heart of her family, her marriage. This was the house where she'd made birthday cakes and finger painted with the children and planted seeds in the gardens. Maybe she hadn't done any of that in years, but *still*. This was her dream house. Her dream life. And it looked like it was turning out really to be just that—a dream.

Harriet's fingers clenched her wineglass so hard she thought she might snap the stem. She wanted to, wanted to feel the cut, see the blood seeping out. It would be more tangible, more satisfying, than the desolation she was feeling now, empty and sweeping.

"How can we lose the house?" she asked, trying to be reasonable even though the words sounded desperate. "I mean, we had a hefty down payment. We've been paying the mortgage for six years…"

"I remortgaged it," Richard answered. "I had to. And we're three months behind on the payments already. They're threatening foreclosure and, without any real income, there's not much I can do about it. But it's temporary, Harriet, you know that—"

"I do?" She wanted to believe it was, of course she did. But in the meantime… "Why did you keep all this from me, Richard? And for so long? We could have been saving money, cutting corners—"

"We need to cut more than a few corners, Harriet."

"But surely every bit counts—"

"Maybe." Richard shrugged. "But when you're pulling in seven figures and then that suddenly goes down to zero…"

"But what about our savings?" Surely they had savings. It shamed her that she didn't actually know.

"We spent most of it in the last six months."

She stared at him, appalled. They'd spent all their savings and were behind on their mortgage? How had this happened?

"Why didn't you tell me?" she whispered. "I could have…"

What? Saved fifty pounds on the grocery bill? Bought a cheaper phone for Mallory? Richard was right; they weren't in scrimping and saving territory. And yet the betrayal of his deception, on top of the mobile phone bill and sexy Meghan… it felt like too much to bear. It was easier to focus on the money and the lies rather than the affair. A woman could only cope with so much.

"You should have told me about your job."

Richard's shoulders slumped, his gaze going downwards. He looked like a little boy, with his dark hair that held only a hint of gray, those hazel eyes that had lit on her twenty years ago at a party at university, twinkling with warmth and humor. "I know. But I was so sure something was going to come up, and I could make it all right again without you having to know. And something will come up, Harriet. I've got a promising lead…"

"But, meanwhile, we might lose our house?"

"We'll buy a bigger one."

"I don't want a bigger one," Harriet snapped. "I want this one. This life." Except it was already gone. "So you didn't tell me but you told Meghan," she said after a moment. It seemed she couldn't keep from thinking about that, as much as she didn't want to. "She gave you a shoulder to cry on, I suppose?" The words came out like the lash of a whip, but Harriet was the one feeling the scourge. It was all so much worse than she'd thought.

"I suppose she did," Richard said quietly. "She listened and understood in a way I didn't think you could—"

"So I drove you to her?" Harriet couldn't listen to anymore.

Stupid, sexy Meghan *understood?* She'd left university

three years ago. She had a nose ring, for heaven's sake. She twirled her hair.

Harriet rose from the sofa on trembling legs. "I can't talk about this now," she said. "Any of it. You've sprung so much on me…"

"I'm sorry, Harriet."

A cheap sentiment at a moment like this. Harriet doubted he even meant it. The last call to Meghan had been three days ago, for thirty-seven minutes.

Harriet turned away, unable even to look at him. "You can sleep in the spare room."

Richard nodded, accepting this as his due. "Fine, but we'll need to make some decisions about the house," he said. "And soon."

"If I hadn't found the phone bill," she asked, her voice shaking, "would you have told me any of this? Or would I have found out when—I don't know, when someone showed up at the door, asking for money?" She pictured something lurid from a television show, heartless men with bulging biceps hauling her furniture away.

"I knew I had to tell you soon. I was just hoping…"

"Hoping for what?"

He looked like a whipped puppy, all big, drooping eyes and sad frown. "That I could turn everything around. I still can, I know I can. I've been waiting for the furor to die down, and it has, for the most part. Things are looking up. I have a lunch meeting this week…"

A lunch meeting, after six months of pretending? Of lying to her? It hardly seemed like something to hang all her hopes onto, and yet what else did she have?

"And what about Meghan?" Harriet asked. Her anger had drained away, leaving a leaden, empty feeling inside. "For six months you've been cavorting with her—"

Richard's face tightened. "I have not been *cavorting.*"

"You've been pouring your heart out to her on the phone, at least," Harriet said, every word edged with bitterness. "That much I know." She shook her head, not trusting herself to say anything more, and headed upstairs. She felt numb and reeling, unable to fully realize what any of this meant. The bomb ticking in the middle of her kitchen had detonated, her life reduced to rubble. What, if anything, could they rebuild from the ashes?

Chapter Two

One month later

"SO THIS IS it." Harriet tried to inject a note of enthusiasm in her voice that she was far from feeling. "Home." As soon as she said it, she knew she shouldn't have. This wasn't home. This would never be home.

Her kids obviously agreed with her because the only response to her pronouncement was a snort of disgust from Mallory. Slowly Harriet navigated the rutted drive into Willoughby Close and parked in front of number two. She supposed the courtyard, with its four clustered cottages of golden Cotswold stone, was cute, in a holiday rental sort of way. She wouldn't have balked, perhaps, at spending a half-term in a place like this if something better hadn't already been booked.

But living? Forever? Not that this was forever. She couldn't think that way, couldn't handle any possibility of permanence. Richard kept assuring her he was going to get a job, he had some promising leads, more lunch meetings and conference calls and who knew what else, and things could change for the better at any moment. That was what he said, and she had to believe him. This was nothing more than a pit stop on a bumpy road. Everything would even out... eventually.

"Shall we have a look?" she asked in that same overly bright tone.

She couldn't seem to turn it off. She'd more or less sleepwalked through the last month, putting up a front at school, ferrying the kids around, chatting and smiling as if everything were normal. She'd thought, very briefly, about telling her friends what was going on, or at least Sophie, who was her best friend.

She and Sophie worked out together three times a week and always had protein shakes afterwards. Their kids played together, albeit a little reluctantly, and they'd all gone on holiday together, both families, to France a couple of years ago, which was better in memory than in actuality, and yet... She didn't tell Sophie. She didn't want to tell Sophie. Perhaps because if she didn't tell her, or anyone, it wouldn't be real. It wouldn't become permanent.

She hadn't told her family back in Birmingham, either. Her mother usually called once a week to chat, a warbling conversation about bridge club and noisy neighbors that Harriet usually only half-listened to while doing something else. Her mother had asked her once a couple of weeks ago, with sudden concern, if Harriet was all right since she seemed a bit quiet.

"Fine," Harriet had insisted, her bright tone as hard and brittle as glass. She'd suppressed the sudden, crazy desire to start sobbing on the phone. "Absolutely fine."

As for the rest of her family… her brother Simon lived down in Devon, pursuing a sustainable lifestyle with his wife Jessie. They rented land from a local farmer and lived in a house that had no hot water or electricity. The shower was outside and everything seemed made of hemp. Harriet only spoke to him on holidays.

Meanwhile Richard slept in the spare room and the children didn't even seem to notice. He'd tried to explain about Meghan, about how it had all happened by accident—they'd fallen into a friendship that had become so intense because of how much he was hiding, but Harriet hadn't been able to listen. She didn't want to hear about anything intense with another woman. And an affair did not happen by accident. A choice was made, and Richard didn't seem to want to own up to that.

So they'd soldiered on, Richard going to London, her managing the children and the house and meals and all the rest. Life was busy enough that she didn't actually have to think about what was happening. What had already happened, and what was yet to happen.

And then the moment had come that she'd feared most of all—the bank wanted the house back. Richard had promised her they might be able to buy it back, or at least a similar house, eventually, but, for now, they had to move, and so, stonily, she'd gone to look at rentals, and came up with number two, Willoughby Close, because it was the only three-bedroom rental going in the entire village.

When she'd signed the lease she'd felt as if bits were chipping off her heart. Soon it would be nothing but shards and fragments. Her marriage. Her house. Her life was disappearing before her eyes.

Richard wasn't moving with them. Harriet had made that clear first to him, and then to the children. He'd accepted it in a hang-dog sort of way, said he'd stay in London and look for work. Told her it was better this way, that things would move faster.

"This is the lowest part for us, Hat," he said, using her old nickname she felt he had no right to use now. "I promise. Something's going to come through and we'll be sorted, back to the way we were."

"The way we were?" Harriet had stared at him, wondering whether he was delusional or she was. "And where does Meghan fit into that picture? You're still seeing her, aren't you? Ringing her, talking to her?"

"We're not... we're just friends now, Harriet."

"What a relief," she said in a clipped voice. "That's sorted now, is it?" The sarcasm wasn't lost on him and he flinched.

Harriet wanted him to cringe, grovel, beg.

Instead he lifted his chin and gave her a direct look. "You don't have to play the martyr quite so much, you know. You almost seem as if you're enjoying it."

Harriet had been too furious to reply. *Enjoying it?* Nothing about this was remotely enjoyable. It was barely endurable. If she seemed self-righteous, it was because she hadn't done anything wrong.

A week ago she'd sat the children down and told them matter-of-factly that Daddy had to spend more time in London looking for work, and so he wouldn't be living with them in Willoughby Close.

"Why are we living in Willoughby Close?" Mallory had demanded with a scowl, arms folded tightly against her chest. "Why do we have to move?"

"I told you," Harriet replied in as patient a tone as she could manage. "Daddy lost his job and so we can't afford to live in our house anymore. We'll stay here for a while, and then, when Daddy gets work again, we'll move back."

"To our old house?" Chloe asked. She sounded more curious than anxious, as if this was nothing more than a slightly strange holiday.

"Maybe," Harriet hedged. "Or maybe an even nicer house." She'd always liked Wychwood House, a mile or two outside the village. A smallish Georgian manor with five acres and a paddock. Maybe they'd move there.

"And what about Dad?" Mallory flung at her. "If we're so poor, why is he living in London? That's expensive."

True, but Harriet could not have him living with her. Separate accommodation was an absolutely necessary expense at this point. She needed space to figure out whether they had a future. "Like I said, he's there for work."

Mallory narrowed her eyes. "That's the only reason?"

"Of course." She wasn't going to mention divorce or even separation, couldn't bring herself to yet.

She didn't know what would happen with her and Richard, and until she had a better idea she'd leave the children in the dark. The last thing she wanted to do was make them worry.

"It's going to be okay," she said quietly, gazing at each of them in turn, trying to imbue them with a self-confidence and sense of security she didn't feel herself. "I promise."

Chloe and William had nodded in acceptance of all of this, uncomprehending and obedient, but Mallory had looked at her with obvious scorn before flouncing out of the room. She was old enough to figure out what was going on, and be angry that her parents weren't telling her the truth. But sometimes Harriet felt she didn't even know what the truth was.

"Come on," she said now, as she climbed resolutely out of the car and gave them all as cheerful a smile as she could. "Let's check it out."

The movers had already come; Harriet had marked what furniture to take from their house to Willoughby Close, and it had been a depressingly small amount. The big, bespoke kitchen table wouldn't fit, and the huge dresser with all the pottery she'd collected over the years wouldn't either. In fact, at least two-thirds of their furniture was going into storage, which was expensive, but Harriet couldn't bear to lose all of it along with the house. They'd need it when Richard got his job, and they bought something bigger.

She'd spent hours and hours, weeks and months, selecting all the furniture for the house, with the help of the expensive interior decorator who had more or less held her hand through the entire process. She'd bought tasteful antiques interspersed with fresh modern pieces, carpets and kilims from various holidays, watercolors and oil paintings of places that were meaningful to them. Sophie had once said, with admiration that bordered on envy, that Harriet's house could be featured in *Country Life.*

And so it would again. This was a *blip,* damn it. Things were going to get better. Richard was going to find a job, he'd said so, and they'd get back their house or buy an even better house, and she'd live there without him, happy and defiant. Or something like that. She couldn't picture specifics yet, but she couldn't stand the thought of the rest of her life looking like… this.

The children trooped silently behind her as she fumbled with the keys and then opened the door to number two. The smell of fresh paint and emptiness hit her like a smack in the face. It was the smell of fresh starts, and she didn't want one.

She stepped inside, reaching for the lights. Although it was only four in the afternoon it was already getting dark, the skies heavy and low with gray clouds. Spring felt a long way off, despite the fact that it was mid-February, and the spattering of snowdrops interspersed with an early crocus or two that she'd seen on the drive in.

"This is it?" Mallory's voice rang through the empty space, scornful and incredulous. William kicked at the skirting board, scuffing the pristine white paint. Chloe stuck her thumb in her mouth.

"Yes, this is it," Harriet said, trying to pitch her tone somewhere between firm and bright. "It's lovely, isn't it?" And depressingly small, at least compared to their old house. Their real house. The downstairs was open plan, with a low counter separating the L-shaped living area from the kitchen, which had a tiny range compared to the Aga she'd left behind, and the bland blond wood units and black Formica countertops made her miss her distressed oak cabinets and granite counters.

There was a woodstove and French windows overlooking a tiny scrap of garden, and built-in bookshelves that were nice enough, but… it was a far cry from what they'd had, the space and luxury and elegance. But, still. A house. A place to live. And they were together and healthy and she would do her damnedest to count what blessings she had left.

Harriet took a deep breath. "Let's look at the upstairs."

Silently the children followed her up the narrow stairs to a small landing with four doors leading off it to three bedrooms and a bathroom.

"William, this is yours," Harriet said as she opened doors

and started allocating rooms. He glanced balefully in the single room with a small window. "And Chloe and Mallory, this is yours—"

"Wait, what?" Mallory's voice was an outraged screech. "I'm sharing a room... with *Chloe?*"

"There are only three bedrooms, Mallory," Harriet said patiently. At least she hoped she sounded patient. "I told you before—"

"No. You didn't."

All right, maybe she hadn't, because she was so *tired* and she'd wanted to avoid yet another confrontation. And everything with Mallory felt like a confrontation. Back at the Old Rectory, her daughter's bedroom had been enormous with an en suite bathroom and a walk-in closet that had its own window.

When Mallory had been younger she'd taken her duvet and curled up in the corner of her closet to read. Sometimes Harriet had joined her, snuggling under the duvet and reading from *The Magic Faraway Tree*. Those days seemed like a very long time ago now.

Harriet sighed. "Plenty of children share bedrooms, Mallory. I know it's different and difficult, but—"

"This *sucks,*" Mallory snapped, and stormed downstairs, the front door slamming behind her.

Harriet's body sagged. It did suck. She couldn't argue with that. She couldn't magic money out of thin air, either. This was their reality... until Richard found another high-flying job in finance. Which he *would*. He had to.

And as for them, their marriage… a pang hit her straight in the heart and she rubbed her chest. She'd been having anxiety attacks at night, when she'd climbed into bed, exhausted and yet frustratingly wide-eyed. She'd lie there, staring at the ceiling, desperate to be asleep, as her heart raced and her palms went slick. It took a huge effort of will to try to calm herself down. No, she couldn't think about her and Richard yet.

"Let me show you the bathroom," she said to her two remaining children, who stared at her in stony silence. They were all starting to realize just what this meant.

The bathtub, at least, looked luxurious, with spa jets and a handheld shower that William turned on full force, about to aim it at Chloe before Harriet snatched it from him, soaking herself.

"Sorry, Mum," William said a bit sheepishly, and she sighed and ruffled her hair. William might not emote in the same way Chloe or Mallory did, but this was hard for him too.

"It's okay, William."

After the tour Harriet ordered pizza for dinner and then started unpacking, starting with a dry shirt, while William and Chloe watched a video on Harriet's laptop and Mallory sulked outside. Harriet had occasional glimpses of her blond head from the window, shoulders hunched and hands jammed into the pockets of her puffa-parka as she kicked at the gravel in the courtyard. Harriet thought about going out there and trying to give her daughter a hug or at least a smile, but Harriet doubted either would be welcome.

And, in any case, she wasn't sure she was capable of either in that moment. She felt tired in every bone and muscle, every fiber and sinew. She felt like a very old woman. Even the prospect of a long, decadent bubble bath in the lovely tub did little to lift her spirits.

She didn't want any of this. She didn't want to unpack her things in this poky little kitchen, didn't want to figure out where her dishes or pictures or knick-knacks would go. She didn't want to make the bedrooms cozy or the one bathroom look bigger than it was, or buy a pallet of bedding plants for the weedy little garden.

She certainly didn't want to think about Richard, and wonder if he was complaining to Meghan about how henpecked he was, or perhaps he was just peeling off that slutty, red satin bra with diamante sequins she liked to wear with a white blouse. Classy, that. Harriet put a stop to the montage in her mind before she went into anxiety attack mode again.

No, all she wanted to do was rewind seven months, to before Richard had made his stupid deal, before he'd turned to Meghan, before her world had shattered.

Or, since she couldn't do that, she wanted to skip ahead to when Richard announced he had a job, handed over his signing bonus for a down payment on a proper house, and she moved in there and shut the door in his face. Or maybe, just maybe, he groveled and wept and promised a week-long holiday to… where did she want to go? Harriet paused in the middle of unpacking a box, trying to think where she'd like to travel. How to make this better.

She came empty. The only place she wanted to go was home. Her mobile rang. It was Richard.

Harriet steeled herself, squaring her shoulders as she swiped to connect the call. "Hello."

"How are you?" He sounded tired and anxious, which made her both grit her teeth and want to comfort him. Want to share something, even if it was just how sucky this all was.

"As well as we can be, I suppose."

"I'm sorry…"

"I know."

He'd apologized again and again, useless, vapid sorrys that didn't do any good. Harriet didn't want vapid apologies, especially when they were not accompanied by concrete actions, like cutting Meghan out of his life or getting a job. She moved into the kitchen area in an attempt to find some privacy, but a countertop was all that separated her from her younger two. At least they didn't seem to be listening. "Where are you?"

"I'm actually coming to Wychwood from London. I was hoping to stop by this evening, to see the kids before they started school. I'll go back to London tomorrow, maybe…"

"Where are you staying?"

"For now I booked a bed and breakfast in Witney. It's

cheap," he said quickly, as if she'd protest the expense. Perhaps she would have.

"It's fine." She pictured him at a shabby B&B, a single bed, an old TV, and her heart twisted at the words.

This was what it had come to? Custody arrangements and tatty hotels? Her eyes stung and she blinked hard and fast.

"Have you found a place in London?"

"Yes, a studio in Bexley. It's not too much."

"I'm glad you found somewhere." Then she imagined him inviting Meghan over, sharing a takeaway on a make-shift table, and pain ripped through her, savage and unrelenting. She hated this. She hated everything about this.

"Harriet…" Richard prompted when the silence had stretched on.

She was starting to breathe hard, her heart thudding, and she forced himself to sound, if not feel, calm.

"Why don't you come over after dinner?"

"Harriet…" His tone was both cautious and beseeching, the precursor to a conversation she still wasn't ready to have.

She couldn't stand for him to tell her he loved Meghan, or even that it was all a mistake and he wanted her back. She wasn't ready for either. She wouldn't know how to respond.

"I can't talk now, Richard. The children… and every-thing's a mess…"

"Okay." His voice was soft and sad, irritating and touch-ing her all at once.

She didn't know what she wanted from him, which was incredibly aggravating. "Okay. I'll talk to you later tonight, then."

"Can I talk to the kids?"

She hesitated, because a call from Daddy would have emotional ramifications she didn't have the energy to deal with. But she couldn't deny Richard his children, even in this small regard. And she couldn't deny her children their daddy.

"Okay," she said, and handed the phone to William.

She half-listened to the one-sided conversation as she continued to unpack dishes, trying to cram her sixty-four-piece set of Swedish stoneware into the kitchen's shallow, flimsy cupboards. She couldn't decipher much from William's monosyllabic answers, and when he handed the phone to Chloe she rattled off random descriptions of things Harriet hadn't even noticed—the fact that the toilet's handle was gold—*do you think it's real gold, Daddy?*—and that a dog had pooed in the garden.

"I don't like it here, Daddy," Chloe said matter-of-factly. "When will we go back to our real house?"

Harriet couldn't hear Richard's answer, but Chloe seemed marginally appeased, and went back to her mindless chatter. Eventually Harriet stopped listening; it was dark out and Mallory still hadn't come inside. She needed to get the pizza, and she wondered if she dared leave William and Mallory on their own and take only Chloe with her, something she wouldn't have considered for a moment a month ago. A lifetime ago. Back when everything felt simple and easy, when she'd been a good mother, brisk and efficient with discipline and scheduling, running their family like a small battalion, smugly sure she was on top of everything.

She felt on top of nothing now.

Mallory finally slammed inside, just as Chloe hung up the phone, shooting her sister a smug smile. "You missed Daddy."

Something dark and painful flashed across Mallory's face and she turned away. "I don't care."

Harriet put a stoneware cream and sugar set away and felt as if her life were unraveling, thread by precious thread. "It doesn't matter, Mallory," she said soothingly. "He's coming by later this evening to see you before you start back at school."

Mallory just rolled her eyes, and Harriet turned back to the china. Somehow it seemed important to get their things unpacked. If she just managed to fit their dishes in these cupboards, she'd feel... something. Carefully, she picked up a serving dish and balanced it on top of a cupboard, since it wouldn't fit inside.

A knock sounded on the door as Harriet reached for a gravy boat.

"Mu-um, someone's here," Mallory called in a bored voice.

"Can you answer it, please?" Harriet asked, because her

hands were full of china. She had no idea who it could be—the only person she'd met was the caretaker, a sexy cowboy type in faded jeans and battered boots who had made Harriet feel vaguely uneasy, he was so outside her realm of experience.

"I'm busy," Mallory snapped, and with a sigh Harriet shoved the stoneware onto the shelf and hurried to the door.

"Yes?" she said, her voice a little too impatient. She didn't recognize the woman and girl standing there, although they looked vaguely familiar. Mallory appeared behind her to inspect their visitors.

"Wait—you live here?" she said in a tone of deep disgust, and then slunk off, leaving Harriet feeling even more baffled as well as a bit embarrassed by her daughter's behavior.

"Hello, Harriet," the woman said. "I guess we're neighbors." This baffled her even more. How did this woman know her? "I'm Ellie Matthews," the woman continued. "I helped with the bake sale, although I think I was more of a hindrance than anything else." She gave a little laugh, and a memory filtered through Harriet's blurred mind. A bake sale, back in January, and this woman, this Ellie, had done something… She couldn't really remember.

"Oh, yes, of course," she said, and hoped she sounded convincing. "Sorry, I've just been manic with moving…" She trailed off, unable to think of anything else to say.

So Ellie lived in Willoughby Close? At least it was someone she didn't really know. She couldn't bear the thought of seeing someone familiar every day, enduring pity, having to explain, bracing herself for the ensuing gossip.

She hadn't explained anything to anyone yet, hadn't said a word about Richard or his job or their house, and certainly not about Meghan. No one even knew they were moving. Logically, Harriet knew she'd have to tell everyone the truth sometime, sometime quite soon, but thankfully that day had not yet arrived.

"So you moved within the village?" Ellie asked, and Harriet replastered the smile on her face.

"Yes." Was there any way she could gracefully get out of this conversation? Behind her she could hear William and Chloe starting to squabble. She forced herself to continue. "Yes, we've moved because..." Harriet reluctantly focused her gaze back on Ellie. "We're doing some renovation on our house, and moving seemed like the easiest option. Temporarily, of course. This is a temporary measure." Ellie looked unconvinced and Harriet wondered why she'd offered so much information. So many lies.

Renovation on the house? That was a bald, bold-faced lie anyone, even a stranger like Ellie Matthews, could see through almost instantly. And judging from the uncertain look on her neighbor's face, she already had. And yet Harriet had said it, because the truth was still too awful to verbalize, even to a stranger.

"Welcome anyway," Ellie said. "No matter how long you're staying. Abby and I are glad to have neighbors."

"Thanks." Harriet kept her smile with effort.

She placed her hand on the door, willing Ellie to get the message and leave. Now was not a good time. No time, really, was a good time.

"It's getting late," Ellie said, dutifully looking at her watch. Message received. "I'll let you get on. But do tell me if you need anything…"

Harriet nodded, too relieved to manage any pleasantries back, and Ellie finally stepped back.

"Bye, then," she said, and Harriet closed the door.

"Ugh." Mallory groaned theatrically as Harriet headed back to the kitchen. "Abby *Matthews.*"

"What's wrong with her?" Harriet asked. She stared down at the half-empty box of dishes. She was already running out of space to store things, and in any case she no longer saw the point.

"She's just such a loser."

"Mallory." Harriet turned, surprised by the needlessly vicious comment. "She seemed a perfectly nice girl to me." Although Harriet hadn't actually paid her any attention. "And don't call people losers. It's rude." She'd been considered a loser, once upon a time.

Such an awful word… and yet they were all losers now, in a different way. They'd lost.

"Even if they are?" Mallory returned.

"You're sounding most unpleasant," she said as mildly as she could. "How would you like it if someone spoke that way about you?"

"They never would."

Harriet shook her head slowly. "That shouldn't make a difference. Kindness never goes out of style."

"Oh, please." Mallory rolled her eyes and Harriet sighed.

"I need to go get the pizza. Can I trust you and William not to kill each other while I drive to Chipping Norton?"

Mallory folded her arms. "I don't know. Maybe."

Exasperated, Harriet reached for Chloe's hand and pulled her, protesting, up from the sofa. "Enough. I'll be back in twenty minutes." And pulling Chloe after her, she left the house.

Chapter Three

AN HOUR LATER Harriet was just cleaning up the detritus of the sauce-splattered pizza boxes when Richard knocked on the door. She felt a pang of something—an emotion caught between frustration, sorrow, and something so deep and aching she thrust it instinctively away—at the sight of him standing there, smiling uncertainly and looking tired, his hair rumpled and his khakis creased.

"Hey, guys," he said in a too-jolly voice that made Mallory and William give him death stares while Chloe squealed and tackled his knees. "How about I read you some stories?"

"Seriously?" Mallory muttered under her breath. "I'm almost twelve, not six."

"You can read me stories, Daddy," Chloe said, hugging his knees and tilting her head up to him as she batted her eyelashes.

Harriet couldn't help but smile at the sight. Her daughter was adorable and knew it, but it didn't lessen her charm.

"Brilliant." He patted Chloe's head and turned to Harriet. "Afterwards," he said in a low voice, "I was hoping we could go somewhere to talk." The words held a meaningful note that made Harriet look away.

"I don't have a babysitter…"

"The kids can fend for themselves for a bit, can't they?" Richard said with a quick, smiling glance. "Mallory's in charge." Mallory rolled her eyes at this and reluctantly Harriet agreed to walk with him to The Three Pennies for a drink and a chat. About what, she couldn't think about.

She continued to tidy up while Richard read to Chloe, Mallory sulked, and William kicked a football outside, continually thwacking it against the side of the house.

Richard ventured out there after reading to Chloe, and Harriet watched from the kitchen window as he jammed his hands in his pockets and tried to engage William, who remained stubbornly focused on his football. Was he angry at Richard, or just single-minded?

Harriet looked away. She couldn't take anymore, not when she could remember William and Richard roughhousing in the garden of the Old Rectory, their laughter ringing through the apple trees. How long ago had that been? A year? Two years? When had it stopped? When Richard had been promoted and had started spending more time in London? When William had become football mad, a sport Richard wasn't that keen on, and had stopped wanting to wrestle?

By the time all the children were settled on the sofa with a DVD so she and Richard could go out, Harriet's stomach felt knotted and her heart was starting to thud again. She'd toyed with the idea of going to the surgery to get some medication for anxiety, but she didn't want word getting out. And word would, because it always did. Someone would see the prescription bag, or think she looked tense as she left the surgery... Wychwood-on-Lea was a small place and even if she shouldn't, she cared what people thought.

"Call me if anything happens," Harriet ordered Mallory who simply nodded, her gaze glued to her phone. "I mean, anything."

"*Okay,* Mum."

Outside the night was dark, the sky inky, with a few high, cold-looking stars twinkling far above. Winter still held the world in its grip, and their breath came out in frosty puffs as they walked down the drive towards the village's high street.

"Nice place, this," Richard said with a nod towards Willoughby Close.

"It's hardly what we're used to," Harriet answered, and he looked away.

She felt a flicker of guilt, but she couldn't make it easier for him. Not yet, anyway. Not after everything he'd put her through. Was he still seeing Meghan? She couldn't ask. She didn't want to know.

"I will get it back," Richard promised in a low voice. "I promise."

"Do you have leads? Any interviews?"

"A few things on the backburner."

Harriet wished he'd stop talking in clichés. What did they even mean? She'd asked about the promising lunch meeting a few weeks ago and Richard had just shrugged.

"I'm talking to a headhunter tomorrow morning," he continued, his tone determinedly optimistic. "He says the market's been pretty quiet, but things are starting to pick up." He gave her a quick, smiling glance. "You only rented that place for six months, right? Because it won't be longer than that."

"Yes, only six months," Harriet answered.

Six months felt like a long time.

The pub was quiet on a Sunday night, only a few regulars at the bar as they stepped inside the dim warmth, ancient, blackened beams running the length of the low ceiling, a fire burning cheerily in the open grate, squashy leather armchairs on either side. The Three Pennies was the village's tony pub, bought by an ex-Londoner a couple of years ago, and the one all her friends went to. She wished for a moment that they'd chosen Wychwood's other pub, The Drowned Sailor, which the village's slightly rougher element frequented. At least no one she knew would see them there.

Richard ordered them drinks and Harriet chose a secluded booth in the back. She didn't want anyone overhearing this conversation, not even a half-cut barfly, not that The Three Pennies had many of those.

A few minutes later Richard appeared with a glass of red

for her and a pint of bitter for him. The sight of the drinks in his hands, what they both always ordered on an evening out, gave her a funny little pang, her heart turning over. This could almost have been a normal night out at the pub— although come to think of it, when was the last time they'd actually gone out alone together? Harriet couldn't remember.

The months and years had blurred together, a montage of busyness, of school days and children's activities and the occasional holiday, of Richard spending nights in London and weekends in his study, coming home too late to do anything but watch the news and drink a beer.

She couldn't actually remember conversations, or laughter, or the kind of poignant moments you looked back on with a smile. Perhaps there hadn't been any. It was an unsettling thought, as if her picture of the life she'd been building was nothing more than an empty frame and she'd never even realized.

"We should keep this quick," she said as she accepted the glass of wine. "I'm not entirely comfortable with leaving the children like that."

Richard arched an eyebrow as he sat across from her. "They'll be all right for half an hour, surely?"

"You wouldn't know, would you?" Harriet returned. "Since you usually came home when they were in bed." For six months, when he wasn't even working. Stupidly, perhaps, that stung, on top of everything else. When he could have been available, helping out, he was living a double life in

London with sexy Meghan, missing assemblies and sports fixtures and all the rest for no bloody reason. She took a large gulp of wine.

"Maybe I deserve that," Richard said quietly.

"Maybe?" Her voice rang out, too loud.

She was too angry, hadn't let go of the fury and hurt yet, hadn't even begun to process it. But now was not the time.

Harriet took a steadying breath. "So what do we need to talk about exactly?"

"Money, I'm afraid." Richard put down his glass and raked his hand through his hair.

He had lovely hands, long-fingered and surprisingly slender, elegant, pianist hands although he didn't play the piano or any other instrument. She'd noticed his hands after his eyes, at that first party. He'd handed her a drink and their fingers had brushed, and she'd thought how she'd never considered hands to look gentle before, kind.

Now Richard dropped his hand and gave her a grimacing sort of smile. "I'm sorry it's come to this, Harriet, at least for a little while."

"Come to what, exactly?" Harriet made herself ask. She didn't want to think about his hands now.

"Losing so much." Richard took a deep breath. "The house…"

"I know about the house." Harriet tried to moderate her tone. Fighting now didn't help anything. "Obviously, since we're not in it anymore. But… you've said there's still a chance? To get it back?" She sounded hopeful and scared at the same time, like a child asking if Father Christmas was real and wanting it so badly to be true. And she did want it to be true. She wanted to get back as much of their lives as they could, as quickly as possible.

"Yes, of course," Richard answered quickly. "I've told you that. Maybe not the Old Rectory, of course, but one like it. In time."

"I like Wychwood House, on the road to Burford. It has more land, and there's a paddock for Mallory's pony."

Richard nodded slowly. "It's been on the market for months, hasn't it? We could probably get a good deal."

Relief flooded through her, even though she knew this wasn't real, and at the rate Richard was going, might not ever be so. "Yes, we could."

If they lived in Wychwood House, and she could have all her furniture back, and her life, maybe, *maybe,* her marriage would come too. Maybe everything could go back to the way it was, only better.

"The thing is," Richard said after a moment, looking down as he turned a beer mat around and around between his fingers, "I don't have a job yet. And with what we owe…"

"How can we owe anyone anything?" Harriet interjected. "We lost our house."

"Your credit card bill." Richard looked up. "Have you ever actually looked at one of the statements?"

Harriet had the grace to feel discomfited by the question. "No," she said after a pause. "Should I have?" She'd arranged all the bills to go on direct debit years ago and never looked at their bank balance. She'd never thought she'd needed to.

"It's maxed out. And it has a twenty-five thousand pound limit."

"That's because I pay for everything with my credit card. For the points." They were connected to some frequent flyer program that Harriet didn't actually bother with that often, because it was such a faff. She leaned forward. "What exactly are you saying, Richard? You told me we were going to lose the house, but... do we have any money at *all?*"

"Some," Richard answered. "Of course we have some. We'll be all right, but... we need to tighten our belts, as it were, at least for a little while. Until..."

"Until you find another job, I know." Harriet took a deep breath. "Okay. So what are we talking about, exactly?"

"We need to write Ellerton," Richard said quietly. "We can't afford the fees for next year."

Harriet stared, speechless. Mallory had been accepted for year seven to one of Oxfordshire's best private schools with one of the highest percentages of A stars at A level in the country. Her two best friends were going there, she'd already sat the exam, had had her taster day. She was invited to a sleepover with a bunch of new Ellerton girls next month. And now Harriet was going to have to tell her she couldn't go? Harriet's stomach churned at the thought of Mallory's reaction.

Of course, she should have realized this. If they couldn't afford their house, they couldn't afford Ellerton. They couldn't afford anything. "What else?" Harriet asked, her voice quiet and restrained, considering she wanted to scream and kick and flail. *This wasn't fair.*

"Mallory's pony," Richard said after a moment. "She doesn't ride that much anymore, does she?"

"She rides on occasion," Harriet said defensively.

The pony was stabled nearby, and in truth Mallory *had* started to lose interest. She'd been horse-mad for a couple of years but lately Harriet had had to chivvy her along, something she found rather tedious. She'd had a solidly middle class upbringing outside Birmingham, no ponies in sight.

"Your car…" Richard continued.

Her car? The black, shiny behemoth that she complained about as being too large and ostentatious but now realized she didn't want to give up? Okay, fine. She could do that. "I need some kind of car, Richard."

"We can sell the Discovery and buy something more modest. Used."

"Right." She pursed her lips, trying to look businesslike when what she felt like doing was crying.

Sobbing like a child, as she banged her fists and drummed her heels. Not about the car or the pony or even Ellerton. If she looked at each thing separately, none of it mattered so much. It was the unforgiving whole, the relentless tearing down of their entire lives, that made her want to lay her head on the table and wail.

"I suppose the two weeks in Provence this summer are out too." As soon as she said the words, she realized how ridiculous they were.

How ridiculous she'd been for an entire month, closing her eyes to the gaping reality all around her, the unending lack. Everything about their lives was changing... for a little while, at least. They'd get it all back. They had to. And yet here they were, giving it all away. And for how long? There were no guarantees, no matter what Richard insisted. She knew that, even if she didn't want to believe it.

"Maybe instead you should tell me what I can keep," she said after a tense pause.

"The house," Richard offered. "I mean the rental."

"Brilliant." Harriet couldn't keep the bitter edge from her voice.

She took a slug of wine and stared off in the distance, trying to keep her expression neutral even as her lips trembled. Material possessions didn't matter that much, she knew that. It was all about family and health and happiness. Except at the moment she didn't feel any of those were in great shape and damn it, she wanted her things. She wanted her children to have their comforts, to feel safe and loved, not as if their world had shifted on its axis, toppled right off into black, yawning space.

"The children's things, of course," Richard continued.

"Any personal items. Although…" He paused, grimacing. "I think some of the furniture from the Old Rectory might fetch a decent price. It's designer stuff, isn't it?"

The furniture she'd put in storage because she couldn't bear to lose it. The pieces she'd picked out so carefully. Harriet pressed her lips together. It was just furniture. Sofas and tables and chairs. No big deal, not really. Some of it she hadn't even liked that much. She'd always meant to replace the hall carpet, a Turkish one that had been eye-wateringly expensive but not quite the color she'd wanted. "What happened, exactly?" Harriet asked in a low voice. "I mean, honestly. How… how did you manage to lose *all* of our money?"

Richard blinked, jerking back a little as if she'd slapped him. Maybe she shouldn't have phrased it like that, but how else could she? "I told you, I took a gamble and it didn't pay off."

"So you lost HCI Investments money," Harriet clarified. "You lost their clients' money." She couldn't even remember what HCI stood for, although she'd seen it on his pay stubs. "I get that. But *our* money. How come we're losing our house? All our things? How come we're so bloody in debt?" At the last moment she remembered to lower her voice.

She couldn't stand the thought of this conversation being whispered about and gloated over throughout the whole village.

"I haven't been working for six months," Richard said

after a moment, his voice level. "And the truth is, we spent a lot. *You* spent a lot, Harriet."

She jerked back, shocked. "That's not fair. I thought we had the money."

"Well, we didn't." Richard raked a hand through his hair and looked away. He seemed angry, but not as angry as she was.

"You should have told me earlier. I wouldn't have..."

"Are you sure about that?"

"You should have given me a chance. You never even *said*—"

"I *know* I didn't, and now we're here."

"Which is not a nice place to be." Harriet sat back and finished her wine.

They hadn't even talked about sexy Meghan yet or how *that* had happened, but Harriet didn't think she could take much more now. Her heart was skittering inside her chest already.

"Okay." She blew out a breath. "So the car and the furniture go, but the kids can keep their cuddly toys."

"And everything else," Richard replied, his voice sharpening a little.

He'd been Mr. Meek and Mild since this had all blown up, and Harriet was strangely gratified to have finally drawn a little blood.

"Their lives don't have to change that much, really. They still have their friends..."

"Except they don't have the house they were born in—"

"They were born in the hospital, Harriet and, in any case, Mallory and William were both born in London." He sighed. "But I do know what you mean, and I am sorry, more sorry than you can possibly know, that we lost the house. I wish it had never come to this. I really didn't think it would. And as I've said, it won't be long. I have a lot of experience, a lot of skills to bring to the table. I will get another job."

He looked so fiercely determined that Harriet didn't have the heart to remind him it had been six—now seven—months. Richard needed to believe. She did too.

"Okay," she said tiredly. Her body ached with fatigue and she wanted to go home and check on the kids, make sure Mallory wasn't sulking and cuddle Chloe, who at six was losing her rounded babyness, making Harriet almost feel a little broody, even though another baby was the last thing she needed right now. "Now is there anything else we need to discuss?"

"Yes," Richard said quietly. "What about us?"

Us. The word seemed to ping around the room like a ball in a roulette wheel, coming to an awkward stop on the wrong number. "There isn't an us," Harriet said unsteadily. "Not right now, anyway. Not since I discovered you were cheating on me."

Richard took a deep breath. "About Meghan…"

"I don't want to talk about Meghan, Richard," Harriet

said quickly. She drew in a shattered breath; her hands were shaking. "I definitely don't want to know any sordid details." Although she'd tortured herself, wondering about them. How had it started? Had Meghan thrown herself at him? Lent a sympathetic ear at just the right time, understanding him like Harriet hadn't been able to? Pain lanced through her and she lurched up from the table. "I need to get back, before William and Mallory kill each other."

"This is an important conversation, Harriet. I need to explain what happened with Meghan. It's not quite what you think…"

"Really? You mean you didn't talk to her in the middle of the night? You didn't go for long walks and explain how your wife didn't understand you? You didn't…" But she couldn't say it. She literally couldn't say the words sex or screw or anything else in relation to her husband and another woman. It was as if her throat was blocked; she'd swallowed a golf ball and she stood there, gulping and gaping.

"I didn't sleep with her," Richard said quietly. But he didn't deny anything she'd said. Harriet didn't know how to feel. Relief, yes, a little, and yet… "I admit, it got intense and we—we did some things we shouldn't have."

Not so much relief, then. She couldn't think about those nebulous things, not yet, and perhaps not ever. "Yet you're still talking to her, aren't you?" Harriet returned as evenly as she could. She'd been checking the mobile phone statement online rather compulsively, seen the regular calls. A necessary and agonizing form of self-torture.

Richard sighed. "We're friends, yes, but that's all it is now."

The *now* qualifier was horrible. "I don't want to hear about all that," Harriet said. "And I certainly don't want my husband being friends with the woman he was doing whatever with."

"It wasn't—"

"I don't care what you did or didn't do with Meghan, because I certainly know you did more than you should have." The crack in her voice belied that statement. Harriet closed her eyes for a second and then snapped them open. "Why don't you come back from London on Tuesday and take the kids to swimming?" Richard looked surprised and Harriet gave him a grim smile. She ought to get something out of this lousy deal, and no matter what was going on with them, the children needed to see their father.

Back at home chaos reigned, with William and Mallory screeching at each other over what to watch on the TV—the DVD they'd agreed on earlier had been tossed aside—and Chloe curled up on the sofa, her hands over her ears, her expression overly tragic.

Richard had said he'd needed to get back, and so he hadn't even come inside. Easy for him to dip in and out of their lives but he had, Harriet realized, been doing that for a while. Looking back, she realized how many nights he'd spent in London, claiming he was working late, how often he'd come home at nine or ten at night, when the children were in bed. How many Saturdays he'd spent in his study, 'catching up'—*on bloody what?*

"How about no TV?" Harriet suggested, a touch too sharply, and she turned off the television. William gave a theatrical groan and flopped on the sofa while Mallory glared at her, eyes shooting sparks of furious defiance.

"I hate you," she snapped, and then flounced upstairs, slamming the door of her bedroom so loudly the rafters shook, and an orange rolled out of the fruit bowl on the kitchen table onto the floor.

Harriet took a deep breath. She understood that her children were angry; she was angry. She got that, she really did. She wanted to allow them their feelings, their anger. She wanted this to be a safe space, blah, blah, yes, she'd read the parenting books, including several about separation and divorce and difficulty. Knowing all that, however, didn't make dealing with it any easier.

"Time for bed, Chlo," she said, gently nudging her daughter off the sofa. "School tomorrow. Why don't you get your jimjams on?"

"Daddy always said jimjams," Chloe said, speaking around the thumb she'd stuck in her mouth.

When had she started sucking her thumb again? Harriet had made her stop when she was four, coating the offending digit in some awful-tasting unguent. Stubbornly, Chloe had persisted for weeks but Harriet had won out in the end.

Except now her daughter was back at it, and Harriet couldn't blame her. Her self-soother of choice was a glass—or two—of wine. Who was she to deprive her daughter of her thumb?

"Daddy did say jimjams," she said with a tired smile. "Still does, actually. He's taking you to swimming on Tuesday. Maybe he'll put you to bed as well."

Chloe blinked slowly at her. "Why isn't he staying with us? I want Daddy to put me to bed every night."

"Daddy didn't put you to bed every night even when he was living with us," Harriet replied, trying to keep her tone light.

"But why can't he live with us now?"

"Because he needs to be in London."

"Well," Chloe demanded plaintively, "when will he live with us? When is he coming back?"

"I don't know, Chloe." The future seemed so uncertain, so impossible to divine.

Would Richard come back to Wychwood-on-Lea? And if he did… would they get divorced? *Divorced.* So awful. So final. She would be a divorcee and, horribly, she could picture herself, a terrible cliché, a caricature, alone at school functions, other women warily guarding their husbands. She'd turn brittle and hard, with glossy nails and over-highlighted hair and a sharp laugh, made bitter by loneliness and disappointment. Because of course all divorced women were like that. Harriet sighed, annoyed by the melodrama she was envisioning.

She turned to William, who had missed the whole conversation, having found his DS between the sofa cushions. "Time to unplug, darling. School tomorrow." Harriet reached over and snagged the device, earning a protesting screech from her son.

"Mu-um! I hadn't finished the level!"

"There's always another level, William." She ruffled his hair, giving him a tired smile. What would her energetic boy do without a man in the house? Richard hadn't been around much, but he'd still been a force for good when it came to William, someone to field his sudden tackles or bursts of energy. With a sigh she put the DS on the charger in the kitchen.

The plates from dinner were still stacked in the sink, and she hadn't dug out the PE kit or packed lunches for tomorrow. Most of their stuff was still in boxes. Harriet's shoulders sagged with the sheer effort of these small, mundane tasks. Tomorrow yawned ahead of her, a thousand tomorrows, each one as bleak as the last.

"Come on," she called to Chloe and William, neither of whom had moved from the sofa. "Let's get ready for bed."

Slowly she climbed the stairs, praying they would follow. She really didn't have the energy to chivvy them along, turning bedtime into some blasted game in order to get them to simply brush their teeth. Richard was the one who had been good at that.

He'd used to play a game where he'd sat at the bottom of the stairs and the children had run across, dodging a ball he threw at them. When they were hit they had to go to bed. They'd loved it, and Harriet had been both exasperated and charmed, because it was fun and cute but it also got them completely riled up right before bed. Still, she could have used some of his infectious energy now. When had *that* gone? She felt as if so many parts of her life were missing, and she hadn't even noticed their absence until now, when she looked at the whole picture and saw all the jagged, gaping holes. She'd been living in a ghost town without realizing it.

Harriet pushed open Mallory's door and peeked in the bedroom she shared with Chloe. Half the room was all soft toys and pink frills, and the other half was purple patchwork and ponies. At least, it had been ponies, back in their old house. But now Harriet saw that Mallory hadn't put up any of the pony pictures she'd torn out of magazines, and the dressage medal she'd won last year and had had pride of place on her bureau was gone. So perhaps she wouldn't mind losing the pony.

Actually, Harriet realized, Mallory hadn't unpacked anything. Her clothes were spilling out of boxes and her books were stacked in a pile by her bed, where Harriet had left them.

"Mallory, why haven't you started to unpack? I asked you this afternoon…"

"I don't want to unpack," Mallory replied in a bored voice. She was lying on her bed, her back to Harriet, her knees drawn up to her chest and her blonde hair spread out over the pillow. "I don't want to live here."

Harriet hesitated, torn between saying something sympathetic or something bracing, and not sure which was the better choice. "I'll help you tomorrow," she said instead. "It's time to get ready for bed now. Chloe's coming up and I want the lights off."

"So now I have to go to bed when my six-year-old sister does?" Mallory returned, letting out a laugh that sounded far too close to a sob. "Great."

Harriet leaned her head against the doorframe and closed her eyes. "I'm sorry, Mallory. I really am. I didn't want any of this. I know you don't either, and your father and I are both so sorry for what you're going through." Mallory didn't answer and Harriet took a deep breath. "It's not going to be forever, I promise."

Mallory snorted at that and with a sigh Harriet closed the door and went back downstairs, wondering if she'd just made a promise she had no right to make.

Chapter Four

HARRIET GAZED AT the school gates, the late February sunshine gilding everything in gold, and watched with wary trepidation as the army of children and parents trooped towards the school doors. She felt like a soldier clambering over the trenches, once more into the breach.

"Come on, guys." She aimed an encouraging smile, or what she hoped passed for one, at her children, who were uncharacteristically huddled around her on this first day back after the half-term. Even Mallory was sticking close to her, when she usually flounced off without a backwards glance.

Slowly they inched forward, heading for the gates, trying not to make eye contact, which was kind of awful. Where were her friends in her moment of crisis? Where were her children's? Why did they all feel so alone?

"Harriet." Sophie Bryce-Jones' cut-glass tones made Harriet flinch.

Here they were. Her friends, or at least one of them, but she really didn't want to see Sophie.

"How *are* you?" Sophie spoke in the hushed voice of

someone addressing the terminally ill.

"Um, fine." Harriet gave Sophie a pointed look and then gently pushed her children forward. "Come on, everybody. Before the bell rings."

Sophie dogged her like a blasted shadow as Harriet saw each child to each classroom, heartened by how a swarm of girls enveloped Chloe as soon as she entered, and William immediately began wrestling with his best friend Oliver. Just because they'd lost everything didn't mean they'd lost their friends. At least the children hadn't lost theirs. As for hers...

Resolutely, Harriet turned around to face her best friend in the emptying-out school yard. Harriet had met Sophie when she'd first moved to Wychwood-on-Lea, eight months pregnant with Chloe and overwhelmed with two small children and endless house renovations.

Sophie had regarded her with a wide smile and narrowed eyes. "So you've bought the Old Rectory," she'd said, her tone assessing, and when Harriet had nodded, that had somehow sealed it.

Harriet was 'in' before she'd even realized what that meant, and Sophie had arranged exercise classes, spa days, wine and cheese evenings. Harriet had been so grateful, so glad making friends had been easy, because it hadn't always been, not when she'd been young and shy and nerdy-looking, when a single smile had been the highlight of her lonely days.

It had felt frankly amazing to be one of the popular

mums, to have others drift closer to hear what she and Sophie were saying, to be the first to be consulted about the latest school fundraiser, or to give her opinion on the new shop/restaurant/children's activity that had appeared on the placid horizon of their smug lives.

She'd enjoyed her status, quietly reveled in it, and tried to ignore the fact that she didn't actually like Sophie Bryce-Jones all that much.

She'd certainly never questioned any of it, not even when Richard, with raised eyebrows, had asked mildly if she really wanted to spend two weeks in France with the Bryce-Joneses. Harriet had known Richard didn't really like Hugh, Sophie's husband, a beefy, red-faced man with a loud voice and an overly assured manner, who shook his hand too hard and wore red corduroy trousers and a tweed jacket with leather elbow patches for his weekend country look.

Now Sophie reached over and squeezed her arm, nails digging in even through Harriet's coat and cashmere sweater. "Harriet, my goodness, *what* has happened? I saw the foreclosure sign on your house…" She trailed off expectantly, eyes bright.

Harriet had the feeling Sophie was enjoying this, and, terribly, she wasn't even that surprised.

"I suppose you can imagine what happened," she said, gently shaking off Sophie's arm. "Richard lost his job and then we lost the house." She surprised herself with the flat truth of the statement; no lies about renovations now. There was no point.

Sophie's blue eyes widened, her lips parting. She'd had her forehead Botoxed recently, because no other expression was visible on her face. She was also tanned to a perfect golden bronze from spending half-term in Verbier. They would have gone skiing too, in their old lives.

"But you never said a *word…* "

"I didn't know."

"He *kept* it from you?" Sophie said, hardly able to hide her delighted fascination, and Harriet gritted her teeth.

Sophie was not doing a very good job of acting like a sympathetic best friend, but wasn't that why she had said nothing to Sophie for the last month?

Because she'd known Sophie was a gossip. She'd been on the receiving end of many a vicious commentary on another mum's clothing, character, husband, children, hair. Sophie critiqued everything, and Harriet sometimes contributed. It had been hard not to and, in all truth, sometimes it had felt fun, tearing other people apart just a little, not enough to really hurt. Knowing that about Sophie, why should Harriet think she'd be exempt?

They'd spent the last six years together—exercise classes, toddler groups, PTA meetings, nights out at the pub. They'd laughed and gossiped and moaned about not being able to get a decent housecleaner or the astronomical price of riding lessons, but had they actually been *friends?* Did Harriet even have any?

She'd spent all her time with Sophie, and a handful of other like-minded mothers who had orbited around them, hopeful planets to their sun. She'd felt popular, part of the in crowd, but now she wondered if it had all been a mirage… like the rest of her life, it seemed.

"No, he didn't keep it from me, not really," she said.

Why she felt the need to be loyal to Richard now, she had no idea. Perhaps it was mere self-preservation; she didn't want Sophie, and therefore the whole village, knowing that she'd lost her marriage along with her house. Or maybe she still did have a loyalty to Richard, to what they'd once had, even if they didn't have it anymore. "It just… happened suddenly. We're still adjusting."

"You poor thing." Sophie reached for her arm again and Harriet took a little step away.

She found she didn't want Sophie touching her.

"How are you coping? Where are you living?" Sophie's eyes were wide and round.

"We're renting a place for now," Harriet said stiffly. She could just imagine what Sophie would think of Willoughby Close, quaint as it was. "But when Richard gets another job…" She trailed off at the look of pity that flashed in Sophie's eyes and then she fired up. "He's got an interview today, actually. This is just temporary. But for the short term we're living at Willoughby Close."

Sophie wrinkled her nose. "Those converted stables by the manor? I suppose they're cute, as long as it's just for a little while… I went to Lady Stokeley's Christmas party years ago, did you go?"

"No," Harriet answered flatly. She could tell Sophie knew she hadn't been invited.

"Are you going to the open house, then?"

"The open house?"

"For your house. There's a viewing next week." Sophie watched her, waiting for her reaction, and even though she was trying desperately to retain a neutral expression Harriet couldn't keep from flinching.

She pictured everyone in the village parading through her house, and it felt like they'd all be seeing her naked. At least she didn't have to be present.

"I don't think so."

"What about the PTA meeting this morning? It was supposed to be at yours but I texted everyone to say I didn't think that was happening because of the foreclosure…" Sophie spoke as if this was a generous thing for her to have done, when Harriet knew she'd done it simply so she could be the first one with the gossip.

Of course, most people would have already known. The Old Rectory was in a prominent place on one side of the village green. Everyone would have driven by it, seen the foreclosure sign. During half-term, when everyone had been on their skiing or beach holidays, Harriet had been able to stick her head in the sand, pretend she could hide the truth forever, but now she had to face reality… in all sorts of ways.

"I think I'm going to have to give this PTA meeting a miss," she told Sophie with a tight smile that felt like it was splitting her face. "Too much unpacking to do."

"Are you sure?" Sophie cocked her head. "What should I tell everyone?"

"Just that I have to miss this one," Harriet said. She felt a burning need to get away; she had the urge to start sprinting out of the school yard and keep running for as long as she could. "I'll be there next month." She couldn't even imagine what next month would look or feel like. Better than this, she hoped.

Sophie pursed her lips. "All right."

Harriet nodded jerkily and started walking. It wasn't until she was halfway down the high street that she realized she'd automatically started walking towards her old house. She stopped and slowly turned around, and then she saw two mums from school coming her way, mums she knew, who had once inched closer to her in the school yard while she and Sophie held court. Their heads were bent close together, both of them whispering, and without thinking about what she was doing, Harriet walked blindly into a shop.

Bells tinkled as she hurried inside, blinking in the gloom. It was a quaint teashop with willow pattern teapots and mismatched cups in the window. She'd only been in there once before, to buy a last minute present of a box of macaroons for a teacher. A woman about Harriet's age appeared from the back room, blinking in surprise at the sight of her.

"Sorry, we're not open yet…"

It was only nine in the morning. Harriet looked around, noting the white wrought iron chairs, the spindly little tables. She'd always meant to take Mallory here for a girly chat, a proper cream tea.

"Right." She took a deep breath. "I don't want anything but do you… do you mind if I stay in here for a minute?" Her lips trembled and she pressed them together. "I just need to avoid someone out there for a few minutes."

The woman tilted her head, surprise and sympathy both visible in her expression. She had a friendly face, round and dimpled, with gray eyes and a frizz of light brown hair. "Sure. I'll just be in the back, tidying up."

"Okay."

Harriet sank into one of the chairs, her head in her hands, her legs weak. This was no way to live her life, ducking into shops and hiding from everyone she knew in a village with a population of two thousand. She knew that, but she couldn't keep herself from it. Not yet. Somehow she had to find the strength to face everyone down… or else move out of Wychwood-on-Lea completely. A fresh start for all of them, perhaps, except the children had their friends and she liked Wychwood-on-Lea. She didn't want to move.

"Here, I thought you could use this."

Harriet looked up to see the woman set a cup of tea and a pain au chocolat on the table in front of her. Tears filled her eyes at the thoughtful gesture.

"Thank you. You're very kind."

"Are you all right? Anything I can do to help?"

Harriet shook her head. "Not unless you have about a million pounds going spare," she said, "or a time machine."

"Neither, I'm afraid. I'm Olivia, by the way."

"Harriet." Harriet smiled and took a sip of tea, feeling a little cheered by this exchange.

Her life had fallen apart but people were still friendly. Some people, anyway.

She thought of Sophie's thinly disguised malice and patently false air of concern. Her alleged best friend was clearly enjoying Harriet's fall from grace. Would Sophie drop Harriet as a friend now that she'd lost her big house, her husband, and any form of income? Of course she would. Harriet felt a pang of loss, not for Sophie, but for the yawning absence her friend's defection would create. She didn't have any other friends, not real ones.

From just about the moment she'd arrived in Wychwood-on-Lea, Sophie had claimed her as her own, and, in all honesty, Harriet had been happy and relieved to be claimed. Making friends had never come easily, not since her school days. Having Sophie take care of it all, effortlessly bringing Harriet into her exalted circle, had felt like magic. A miracle.

Sighing, she took a big bite of pain au chocolat, savoring the sweetness. Olivia watched her kindly, her hands on her hips.

"Let me know if there's anything else I can do."

"I will. You've been amazing, thank you," Harriet said sincerely as she dashed pastry flakes from her chin. "I really needed a friendly face right about now."

Olivia smiled. "That is one thing I have, I think," she said, and then disappeared into the back room while Harriet sat alone, soaking in the peaceful solitude, and sipped her tea and ate her pastry, all the while letting her mind blissfully empty out. She needed not to think for a while.

Eventually she had to stir herself; with shock she realized she must have been sitting there for nearly an hour, because Olivia came out to flip the sign on the door to open, and an elderly woman with a plaid wheelie bag came in to buy some loose tea and a packet of macaroons.

"How much do I owe you for the tea and pain au chocolat?" Harriet asked after the woman had left, and Olivia arched an eyebrow.

"A million pounds? No, seriously." She waved her away. "It's on the house."

"Oh, I couldn't…"

"You could and you will," Olivia said firmly. "I was glad to be of some small service."

"Thank you," Harriet said, meaning it truly, and then she took a deep breath and stepped outside to brave the high street.

Fortunately she didn't meet anyone she knew as she walked back to Willoughby Close and let herself in. The house was quiet and still, the breakfast dishes strewn across the kitchen table—in her old house, she'd used the simple pine table as a crafts station in the family room. She lay one hand against the old, weathered wood that was covered with bits of glitter and dried splotches of paint.

It was the first real piece of furniture she and Richard had bought, back when they'd been newly married and poor. She'd had an internship in publishing and Richard had had his first job in finance, being a badly paid dogsbody to a bunch of middle men. They'd both been so proud of that table, buying it from an overpriced furniture shop in Camden Town and lugging it down crowded pavements, all the way back to their poky flat where it had been surrounded by folding chairs and plastic crates.

They'd slept on a futon on the floor, their wedding presents still in boxes because they'd had no place to put them all. What use was a twelve-piece set of fine china when they didn't have a table? Except of course they finally had one then, and now Harriet remembered how they'd ate their first meal on it using the Meissen, with candlelight and sterling silver to boot.

They'd been so *happy* then. She remembered the feeling, that shimmering, we-can-do-anything feeling, like bubbles inside her, floating up and up... when had she last felt like that? When had she lost it?

Tears sprung to her eyes, so suddenly she couldn't stop them as she'd been doing for the last month, choking everything down and soldiering on. Now she sank onto a chair and rested her arms on the table, lowering her head as the tears trickled down her cheeks and her shoulders shook with the force of her feeling.

It felt good to cry, good and bad, because while the release was cathartic, the aftermath would be awful, an emotional hangover. Still, she let it out because she needed to, she needed to grieve and not just for the house, which she missed like a lost limb, or even for her old life, which she missed like her favorite coat, the coziest blanket, but *Richard.* Richard she missed the way you missed your heart beating.

She missed him—the smell of him, aftershave and Polo mints, the feel of him, sinewy and well-muscled. When they'd first been married he'd been skinny to the point of scrawniness, a little endearingly embarrassed about it. Harriet had force-fed him enormous fry-ups and mashed potatoes made with butter and full cream, and he'd started working out at the gym and began to bulk out, at least a little.

She missed waking up in the morning with her toes tangling with his, the feel of a warm, hard body in bed next to her. She missed the sound of his hand fumbling for his phone to shut off the guitar chords of his alarm. She missed his arms snaking around her waist, and the way her chin just fit on top of his shoulder. She missed looks across a crowded room or a restaurant, wry self-deprecating looks, because they were both laughing on the inside at the same thing.

How could it be all gone? Had it meant nothing? She cried for all that and more, because the man she'd fallen in love with wouldn't have believed a twenty-six-year-old who wore a red satin push-up bra as part of her work wear understood him. The man she'd fallen in love with wouldn't have lied to her for six months.

But maybe the man she'd fallen in love with had disappeared a long time ago. She couldn't remember the last time they'd tangled toes or shared a silent, laughing look. She feared it had been years.

Eventually the full, body-wracking sobs trickled into hiccups and sniffles and then a few long, shuddering sighs. When she finally finished, one last shudder wracking her frame, she rose from the table with a big sigh and went in search of tissues.

An inspection in the bathroom mirror showed her just how indulgent she'd been, with puffy eyes, red nose, and running mascara. The face of grief. Harriet let out a hiccuppy half-laugh and set about repairing the worst of the damage, before she stopped, wondering why she was bothering.

She was going to spend the day in the house, unpacking boxes, seeing no one. She had no one to look good for, no one to impress at Pilates or a coffee morning and the catwalk of the school run was still four hours away. The realization that she had a day by herself, a day off, was a relief.

Later that afternoon, before school pick up, Harriet steeled herself to drive by the Old Rectory. After Sophie's snide comments she needed to see it, lance the wound.

It looked depressingly empty, the windows blank and curtainless, the 'Foreclosure-To Auction' sign bigger and brighter than she had anticipated, stuck right by the front gate, the branches twined above it now bare of roses.

Who would buy their house? Who would live there? The thought of seeing a family, maybe even one she knew, making the house their own caused her hands to clench on the steering wheel. She didn't think she could stand it. And what about the children? What if they were invited over?

Chloe didn't even understand that they weren't going back, not to that house at least. It was like some sort of holiday to her, and as for Mallory and William... She was worried about how angry they both seemed, especially Mallory. She wanted to say or do something to make it better, but she felt powerless and she doubted Mallory wanted to hear anything she had to say.

Harriet leaned her head against the steering wheel, her eyes closed, and wished she was coping better. Wished she was strong enough to help her children cope better. And what if this *wasn't* temporary? What if Richard never got a job, they never got together, the rest of her life unraveling like a loose thread. It felt all too possible.

With a sigh, she opened her eyes and saw it was five minutes past three. Once again she was going to be late for pickup.

"How was it?" she asked when Mallory slouched towards her, fringe in her face and school bag hitched high on her shoulder. A couple of months ago, Harriet had given her one of her old designer leather bags for school but now she wondered how appropriate that was. Mallory was eleven, but she was copping the attitude of a sulky sixteen-year-old, bulky Prada bag included.

"How was what?" Mallory asked in a bored voice, and Harriet gritted her teeth.

When had Mallory started being so rude? Was it since their lives had blown up or before? Harriet couldn't actually remember, which seemed a bit alarming.

She tried to think back to Christmas—what had the children been like then? She felt a prickle of shame to realize she hadn't actually paid too much attention to them. She'd been so busy, cooking for nine—her parents and brother and wife had all come for Christmas dinner, and Simon and Jessie were both staunchly vegan. She'd also been in charge of every single person's presents, including Richard's parents in Norfolk, because he didn't buy anything except for her. Buying presents had become a negotiation worthy of the UN, with Harriet making sure every child had the same amount of presents under the tree as well as in their stockings, and that the presents were roughly equal in terms of amount spent since Mallory and even William seemed to know how much everything cost.

Mallory had developed the irritating habit of detailing the price as the recipient opened her present—'A pair of Heelies! That's at least forty pounds!'

And then of course there was the decoration, worthy of *Country Life*, everything polished and wrapped, gleaming or glowing, and definitely perfect.

And the house *had* looked good, with candles in every window, fresh evergreen looped around the banisters and over the doorframes, interspersed with little bows of crimson velvet. Standing there, looking at her daughter's shuttered expression, Harriet wondered who had made the rule that her house had to look like a photo shoot. Who had decided that was important?

Well, she had, obviously, but the trouble was she couldn't remember when. None of that seemed very important anymore.

"How was school, Mallory?" Harriet clarified. "Was it... was it okay?"

Mallory flicked a scornful glance and then started walking out of the school yard. "Why wouldn't it be?"

Which left Harriet in an awkward position. She didn't want to say *because kids might be asking about our house. They might be teasing you.* Maybe her daughter didn't know what it was like to be teased, not like she had, and that of course was a good thing. But Harriet still felt wary. She decided to leave the question unanswered and she called to William and reached for Chloe's hand before following Mallory down the street.

Then her daughter turned left instead of right, instinctively going towards the village green and the Old Rectory instead of down the narrow lane towards Willoughby Manor and its close.

"Mallory," Harriet called gently and her daughter acted as if she hadn't heard her, striding ahead, all flying hair and far too much attitude. *"Mallory.* You're going the wrong way."

Mallory stopped mid-stride and then whirled around and started towards Willoughby Manor, her expression both anguished and furious. Harriet's heart ached for her daughter, and she reached out one hand, wanting to offer some sympathy, some understanding, but Mallory didn't want it. She shrugged off Harriet's lame attempt and kept walking, her head held high.

Sighing, Harriet pulled Chloe along, called to William again, and headed home.

Chapter Five

THE NEXT COUPLE of weeks passed in a gray fog of determined activity. While the children were at school, Harriet drove her gleaming black Discovery to a lot near Moreton-in-Marsh and traded it in for an older, battered model with a hundred thousand miles on it. She told herself she'd never liked that car anyway, and this one looked... friendlier. It also looked like it would only last a couple of months.

She arranged for an auction house to haul away all the furniture in storage, and accepted a flat and thankfully substantial figure for the lot. She tried not to flinch as moving men in blue coveralls and with bland expressions hauled everything out—the bespoke kitchen table, the antique wardrobe with beveled glass, the huge, squashy sofas that had cost far more than anyone should spend on a sofa. All of it bundled into the back of a truck in a matter of minutes, and money deposited into her and Richard's joint account.

It was probably time to get her own bank account.

When they moved into Wychwood House, she'd buy new stuff. Better stuff, and do it all herself rather than hiring an expensive interior decorator to hold her hand and reassure her that she was making the right choices. That she belonged in this world.

She went to the stables and sold Mallory's pony, Cobbler, stroking the animal's velvety nose with a pang of sorrow. She remembered a chubby six-year-old Mallory astride the pony's bowed back, looking thrilled and more than a little terrified, and she wished for those days back... in all sorts of ways.

At the time, she'd most likely been impatient and cross, balancing Chloe on her hip, a toddler-aged William running amok through mud puddles in the stable yard. Everything had felt difficult back then, so much mess and noise and lack of sleep, and yet Harriet thought she'd been happy. Happier than she was now, certainly, but that wasn't saying all that much.

"Do you want to see Cobbler?" Harriet had asked Mallory the night before. "To say goodbye?"

"No, why bother?" Mallory had said, shrugging, her expression as closed as ever, just as it had been when Harriet had, painfully, told her she wouldn't be going to Ellerton. Mallory's expression had turned stony then and she hadn't said a word, which had broken another big chip off of Harriet's heart.

"I'm sorry..." she'd begun, wretched, and Mallory had

just looked away.

Her children had accepted every incremental loss stoically, but Harriet wasn't convinced by their attitude. Underneath the silent acceptance seethed both resentment and confusion. How could it be otherwise? They were children, and their world had been ripped apart.

Admittedly not on remotely the same league as a thousand major tragedies unfolding across the globe that very minute, but they were her children, and their losses, their hurts, held the power to flay her, as well as to keep her having minor anxiety attacks at inconvenient moments.

Mallory still simmered with rage, a constant blaze in her eyes, in her stiff shoulders, and jerky movements. William had, according to his teacher, been sent to the head teacher's office several times a week for bad behavior. He'd always been a boisterous child, so much boy, but he hadn't actually acted out in a mean way. Now, according to Mrs. Wills, he'd hit a boy and called him a douche. Harriet had been appalled to realize that William even knew that word.

She'd asked him about it after school, and William had shrugged. "I'm not a baby," he said.

"I know you aren't. But even big kids don't need to rude words." Harriet hesitated, unsure how to navigate these moments. "Are you... are you angry, William?"

His response was to attempt to put her in a head lock.

And then there was Chloe, who was still sucking her thumb and looking anxious. Recently she'd also started wetting the bed. She'd shaken Harriet awake, shivering and miserable, and Harriet had spent a wretched hour in the middle of the night, washing her off, changing sheets, and disinfecting the mattress. A six-year-old, she discovered, had a lot more wee than a little baby's leaky nappy.

"I'm sorry, Mummy," Chloe had said, her voice trembling, and Harriet's heart, already battered beyond belief, had broken a little more.

She'd put her arms around Chloe's skinny shoulders and drawn her close, wee and all. "It's all right, my darling. These things happen. It's not your fault, not at all."

But it didn't feel all right. At school drop off and pickup Harriet felt adrift, anchorless, like a knobby-kneed twelve-year-old walking into the lunch room, staring at the sea of tables, no one making eye contact. Sophie had waggled her fingers at her but hadn't talked to her once, and Harriet didn't know whether she was paranoid in thinking that some of the other mums were avoiding her.

She'd had a few sympathetic smiles sent her way, a bit of desultory chitchat about the weather or the awful Mrs. Bryson, but not much more and, in truth, she wasn't seeking anyone out. She wasn't ready yet to make all that effort, summon up a jolly-hockey-sticks sort of smile, the bracing tone. *Oh, it's been tricky, but we're managing. And really it's a bit of a relief. Makes you realize what's important…*

No, she couldn't pull that off yet. Not even close.

Richard stopped by several times a week, tense, awkward

meetings that still left Harriet aching with regret and trembling at the knees. The children didn't quite seem to know what to do with him, sometimes acting hyper and overloud, sometimes sullen and uncommunicative. Richard didn't seem to know what to do either, adopting the over-jolly tone of someone who doesn't know how to act with children, which made everyone cringe, or else wandering around looking lost while the children entertained themselves, usually electronically.

He tried to talk to Harriet, but she kept the conversations brisk and businesslike, exchanging important information about school trips, parent/teacher meetings, and, of course, money. Everything seemed to be about money.

"I had an interview with that headhunter," Richard said once, sounding important. "It went really well."

"Did it?" Harriet couldn't summon the energy for either interest or hope.

Every time he visited he had some meeting or other—headhunter, contact, old friend, new lead. Nothing had happened with any of it yet, and she couldn't bring herself to ride the rollercoaster of hope and disappointment, whereas Richard was on a perpetual loop-the-loop. Everything felt like a disaster, and the only thing she felt she could do was keep blundering through.

Most of the money they'd got from selling everything had gone to paying their debts, and the rest should see them through a few months at least of careful economizing. After that… Richard's unemployment benefit wasn't going to cover their living costs, and with no other income coming in Harriet supposed she'd have to get a job. Richard said as much on one of his visits, not looking her in the eye.

"It would help," he half-muttered, "in the short term. Once I'm working again you can go back to staying at home. If that's what you want."

Harriet had no idea what she wanted. Nothing appealed. As for a job… she hadn't worked in eleven years, not since she'd had Mallory, and she didn't think there were many jobs in the marketing side of publishing in the Cotswolds. She couldn't stomach a commute to London, not with the children to think of, which left her pondering the other available choices. There were a few jobs in Oxford with some textbook publishers, but she didn't have any relevant experience in academic publishing and even that was a considerable commute.

She was clicking on various job offers online, the kids all piled on the sofa, one Saturday in mid-March, when a knock sounded on the door. The kids looked up in surprise; in the three weeks since they'd moved to Willoughby Close they'd seen their neighbor Ellie and her daughter only in passing once or twice. Jace, the caretaker, had delivered wood, shrugging off Harriet's stammering offer to pay him for it, even though she didn't think she could afford it.

"I'll get it," Harriet said, and went to open the door.

Ellie's daughter stood there, looking nervous and a little defiant.

"Abby," Harriet said after a brief pause, as she struggled to remember the girl's name. "How are you? Is everything okay?"

"No, actually, it isn't." Abby gave her a quick, worried smile. "Dorothy's ill and I was wondering if you could drive us to the doctor's."

"Dorothy?"

"Lady Stokeley," Abby clarified. "She needs to see a doctor. She's got a fever and she's shivering and I really don't think she's well."

"Oh, dear." Harriet knew Lady Stokeley by sight, although she'd never met her or been inside Willoughby Manor. "I'm sorry to hear that, but... where's your mum?"

"She's in Cheltenham visiting Oliver's parents for the weekend. Her boyfriend," Abby explained, while Harriet struggled to keep up.

She remembered Ellie saying something about being a single mum when they'd both helped out at the bake sale, but she hadn't known about the boyfriend. Why would she have? They hadn't had a long chat, and Ellie hadn't joined them for coffee afterwards, a blur of gossipy conversation that Harriet could barely remember.

"She's gone for the weekend?" Harriet said. "And she's left you all alone?" She couldn't keep a note of scandalized judgment from her voice.

"No, I'm staying with Dorothy and, like I said, she's sick. You have a car." Abby glanced at the ancient Rover parked next to her mother's equally battered estate. "So could you please drive us?"

Harriet still felt like she needed to catch up with the conversation, but she saw that Abby was impatient and worried, and so she nodded. "Okay, sure. Let me get my keys."

"What's going on?" Mallory asked without much interest as Harriet grabbed her keys.

"I need to drive Abby and Lady Stokeley to the doctor's." Harriet hesitated, reluctant to disturb her children who would no doubt moan and complain about being kicked off the telly, but she could be hours at the doctor's. "You'd better come with me."

The children, thankfully, seemed too surprised by the turn of events, as well as curious about the unknown Lady Stokeley, to complain, and so they all piled into the car, Mallory giving Abby a sniffy look, before Harriet headed up to Willoughby Manor to pick up Lady Stokeley.

She parked the car in front of the massive front doors, eyeing the place uncertainly. It was a huge house, and she couldn't imagine living in it alone. She knew Lady Stokeley's nephew, Henry Trent, was due to inherit—Richard had met him a couple of times in London, both of them working in the city. *Worked* in the city, at least in Richard's case.

She reached for the enormous lion's head knocker but Abby moved past her with another one of her quick smiles.

"It's okay, I can just go in."

"I didn't realize you knew Lady Stokeley," Harriet remarked as she followed Abby into an enormous marble-tiled foyer. "Goodness, it's freezing in here." Harriet thought it was even colder inside the house than out.

"I know, Dorothy pretty much lives in one sitting room and her bedroom," Abby explained. "Where it's warm." She started towards the ornate wooden staircase, covered in a moth-eaten crimson runner with tarnished brass rods. "You'd better stay here. I don't think she'd like strangers in her bedroom, seeing her in her nightgown and things."

"Okay. Let me know if I can help." Harriet wrapped her arms around herself, shivering in the still, icy air, as she walked around the foyer and examined the many paintings on the walls. There was barely an inch of faded, peeling wallpaper to be seen beneath all the oil paintings with their overly ornate frames.

"This place is creepy," Mallory whispered, but she sounded semi-fascinated.

"It's kind of interesting, don't you think?" Harriet pointed to an oil painting of a scowling man in an Elizabethan ruff. "Do you think that's an ancestor?"

"He doesn't look very nice," Chloe said in her high, piping voice. William, Harriet saw with alarm, was attempting to slide down the ancient banister.

"William, *don't*. You might break something and—" She stopped before she finished that unwelcome sentence. *I can't afford to pay for anything here.* "Behave yourself, please," she entreated, and William slouched down the stairs, running his hand along the banister, and causing a cloud of dust to fly up.

Mallory and Harriet both backed away, coughing and waving their hands in front of their faces.

"This place smells funny," Chloe announced, and that was when Lady Stokeley came down the stairs, managing to look regal in a tweedy twin set and Ugg boots.

"You're right, young lady," she replied in ringing, cut glass tones. "It does smell. Like old age and decay. Like me."

What a pleasant introduction. Harriet stepped forward, trying not to sneeze. Dust motes still floated in the air. "Hello, Lady Stokeley. I'm Harriet Lang."

Lady Stokeley gave a dignified nod, drawing her petite frame to all of its barely five feet. "I'm sorry not to greet you in more pleasant circumstances," she said, and then erupted into a hacking cough that sounded like she was bringing up a kidney. Mallory backed away, a look of disgust on her face.

"Ew," Chloe whispered, sidling towards Harriet. With a quick smile for her daughter, Harriet started forward, taking Lady Stokeley's arm.

"Let's get you to the doctor."

Worry niggled at her as she drove down the high street to the doctor's surgery by the school. Lady Stokeley didn't look good at all, even for a woman of eighty plus. Her face had a greyish cast and coughs continued to wrack her thin frame, making Mallory and even Abby inch away from her uneasily.

"Is she going to die?" Chloe whispered as Harriet helped Lady Stokeley out of the car.

"Not quite yet, I hope," Lady Stokeley snapped, but Harriet thought she detected a glint of humor in her faded blue eyes, and she smiled.

They had to wait an hour in the surgery's crowded waiting room, while Chloe dubiously inspected the few battered and dirty toys stuck in a cardboard box in the corner of the room. Mallory flipped through a year-old copy of *Woman's Weekly*, sighing loudly and often, and William kicked his feet against the seat repeatedly while Harriet continually asked him to stop. By the time the doctor called Lady Stokeley, Harriet was ready to scream—or have a stiff drink. Or maybe even two.

The doctor, who had treated Harriet for a bladder infection last year, listened to Lady Stokeley's chest and took her temperature and then shook his head.

"This sounds like pneumonia, I'm afraid, and at your age, I'm not comfortable with a simple course of antibiotics. I think you should go into hospital."

"In Oxford?" Harriet said, and he nodded. What other hospital was there? Harriet's heart sank, because it would take the better part of an hour to get to Oxford, and then it twisted at the look of naked fear on the elderly lady's face before Lady Stokeley stiffened, lifting her chin even as her thin frame shuddered.

"Very well."

"I'll take you," Harriet said. "Of course."

"You mean we can't go home?" Mallory hissed, and Harriet silenced her with a look, or tried to.

"No, we can't," she hissed back when Lady Stokeley was putting on her coat. "She's elderly and ill and alone, Mallory. Have some heart."

Abby watched this exchange with a shrewd, knowing look in her eyes. "She has some seriously cool clothes," she told Mallory rather suddenly. "Amazing vintage. Chanel and stuff. You should come and see it sometime."

Mallory narrowed her eyes, looking nonplussed by this information. Harriet suspected she was intrigued by the idea of clothes but wanted to blow Abby off. Her daughter chose silence, simply shrugging and looking away.

A few minutes later they were all piled into the car, heading towards the hospital in Oxford. Nobody had eaten, and the children were getting decidedly tetchy. Harriet was getting decidedly tetchy, as well as increasingly worried. Lady Stokeley was sitting semi-slumped against Abby who had put a protective arm around her shoulders. Mallory, on the other hand, had edged as far as away from Lady Stokeley as she could and was staring moodily out of the window. She wished her daughter could be a little more sympathetic, but Lady Stokeley was a stranger and old people could be scary. Still, it would have been nice to see her daughter show some compassion.

It was nearing seven o'clock before they finally got to the John Radcliffe Hospital in Oxford and Lady Stokeley was seen by a doctor and then installed in a private room. She looked frail and small and vulnerable in the huge hospital bed, her face as pale and wrinkled as a scrunched-up piece of paper.

"I do apologize for causing so much trouble," she said with dignity, and Harriet's tetchiness vanished in an instant.

"It's no trouble at all. I'm the one who should be thanking you, for converting the stables into cottages. It was the only place large enough we could find to rent in the whole village."

Lady Stokeley cocked her head, her gaze considering, and Harriet wondered how much the old lady had heard about her situation. The gossip must really be rampant if it had reached the ears of an elderly shut-in. Maybe Abby had said something.

"Do you want us to stay…" Harriet asked hesitantly, because she didn't like leaving Lady Stokeley alone, but she was realistic enough to realize she couldn't contain William much longer. He was over by a bank of important-looking medical machines, starting to push buttons.

"No, my dear, I think not. I'm tired and I very much doubt I could sleep with all of you in here." Her gaze slid to William, and Harriet found herself smiling.

"No, it's probably best for us to give you a bit of peace and quiet. We'll check on you in the morning."

"There's no need…"

"I don't mind," Harriet said, surprised to realize she meant it. It felt good, or at least better, to worry about someone other than herself, and she didn't like the thought of Lady Stokeley in here all alone. "Is there someone I should call, to let them know…?"

"No," Lady Stokeley answered, her tone firm. "Definitely not."

Okay, then. Perhaps things with her nephew were a bit strained.

"Bye, Dorothy," Abby said, giving her a gentle hug, and Lady Stokeley rested one knobbly hand against Abby's cheek.

"You'll be all right?" she asked, with a glance at Mallory.

Harriet wondered what the subtext she was missing was.

"Yeah, I think so. Don't worry about me."

Mallory blew out a loud breath and Harriet decided it was time to go. She shepherded everyone out of the room, smiling her thanks at the nurse who was hanging a chart on the end of Lady Stokeley's bed.

"I'm starving," Mallory announced with a theatrical groan as they headed towards the lift.

"Me too, Mummy." Chloe pulled on her sleeve. "I'm really, really hungry. We didn't have any tea and it's *late.*"

"I know." Harriet took a deep breath. She felt incredibly weary, and it would be another hour at least before they were home. "We'll stop on the way," she conceded, even though she knew she couldn't really afford takeaway for six.

As they navigated the endless car park in the cold and dark, Abby came up next to her. "Um, Mrs. Lang?"

"Yes?" Harriet looked at her in surprise. Abby had radiated quiet confidence all afternoon and evening, but now she looked nervous.

"The thing is, my mum is away this evening, and I really don't want her to have to come back. It's kind of an important weekend."

"Oh?" Curiosity piqued, and then the penny dropped. "Would you like to stay over at ours?"

Relief washed across Abby's face. "Do you mind?"

"Of course not," Harriet said, suppressing a guilty pang.

Why hadn't she thought of the girl's predicament earlier? Sometimes she really felt like a terrible, selfish person, so wrapped up in her own problems she couldn't see beyond her nose. Even now she was wondering where Abby would sleep, and if Mallory would behave herself. All she wanted was a hot, deep bubble bath, and she had a feeling she wasn't going to get it.

"I don't mind at all," she assured Abby, patting her arm, and she hoped Mallory wouldn't either.

The drive back to Wychwood-on-Lea, at least, was somewhat peaceful, after they'd stopped for milkshakes and burgers. Harriet couldn't believe how expensive everything was. A couple of months ago she wouldn't have even looked at the prices. She would have swiped her card with thoughtless ease, and now she was totaling the amounts in her head, insisting the children could share fries and asking the server to split the milkshakes—which were huge—into two cups.

"Seriously, Mum?" Mallory muttered under her breath. "How poor *are* we?"

"I'm being frugal," Harriet returned tartly. "And you never finish a whole milkshake anyway."

She didn't order anything for herself, finishing Chloe's burger instead. As they ate in the fluorescent-lit fast food restaurant with a handful of other people all slumped over their burgers, Harriet marveled that it had come to this. She wouldn't have even stopped at a place like this a few months ago. She would have gone somewhere more upmarket, the kind of place that offered organic food and proper coffee. She would have turned her nose up at everything about this situation, and the realization made her cringe inside, just a little.

Now, at least, she didn't feel the fury and despair she'd been battling since finding that phone bill. No, she felt a little removed from everything, or at least from her old self. She marveled at who she'd been, and she wondered if she'd ever go back to being that woman again. If she'd ever get the chance. And would Richard even want her? Did she want him? The pang in her heart told her at least part of her still did, and she had no idea how to feel about that. Self-righteous anger was so much easier, but already it was ebbing away.

Back at the house, the children slouched towards the sofa

while Abby stood uncertainly by the door.

"Mallory, why don't you and Abby go over to her house to get her stuff?" Harriet said in the brisk, officious tone she reserved for moments like this.

Cue the death stare. She hoped, she really hoped, that her daughter had enough simple human kindness not to blow off Abby to her face, in front of everyone else. She hoped her daughter hadn't turned into a mean girl, the kind of girl who had made Harriet's life a misery, once upon a time.

"Fine," Mallory said, and started towards the door without waiting for Abby to follow.

"I'll make up a bed," Harriet said, although she still didn't know where that was going to be. Chloe and Mallory's room wouldn't fit another mattress, not that they had one.

By the time Mallory and Abby came back half an hour later, she'd managed to put clean sheets on Chloe's bed for Abby, and inform a delighted Chloe that she'd be sharing Mummy's bed. William and Chloe were in their pajamas, amazingly, with their teeth brushed, reading books on the sofa. Well, William was flipping through a book, looking at the pictures, but *still*. Harriet felt as if she'd just scaled Mount Everest. Without oxygen.

To Harriet's surprise, Mallory and Abby more or less seemed to be getting along, in a monosyllabic sort of way, and they disappeared into Mallory's room while Harriet tucked Chloe into her bed.

"I like sleeping with you, Mummy," Chloe said, and Harriet kissed her cheek.

"I like it too, sweetheart," she said, even though she knew she'd be kneed in the kidneys for most of the night. Having a warm body next to hers would make for a nice change after sleeping alone for the last two months.

By ten o'clock at night everyone was in bed if not asleep, and Harriet was in the kitchen pouring herself a large glass of wine. She sipped it slowly, staring out at the darkness, battling a weird mixture of something almost like contentment, or at least satisfaction—she'd accomplished something today, she'd helped someone—and a deep, unending loneliness, an ache that went on and on.

If Richard were here, he would have poured the wine and they would have sat on the sofa, Harriet curled up on one end, her feet in Richard's lap. They would have gone over the day, laughing about the crazy moments, reflecting on Lady Stokeley and her situation. If Richard were here...

But he wasn't. And he hadn't been there, really been there, for a long time. His so-called friendship with Meghan hadn't popped up out of the blue, even if it felt like that to her. They'd been growing apart for a while, him in London making piles of money and her in Wychwood-on-Lea, spending it to make the perfect life they weren't even sharing. She took another sip of wine and then, her mood soured, poured the rest down the drain.

Chapter Six

HARRIET WOKE THE next morning to the sound of giggling and the smell of something burning, Chloe's knees firmly lodged against her lower back. She blinked sleep out of her eyes and then slipped out of bed, trying not to wake a peacefully sleeping Chloe, alarm pulsing through her brain as she half-stumbled down the stairs and skidded to a stop in the kitchen.

Mallory and Abby were making pancakes. Harriet gaped at them, taking in the burning batter, the spilled flour, and drips of milk amid broken egg shells on the kitchen counter, and the belated realization that her hair, never at the best in the mornings, was sticking up in about six different directions and she was wearing nothing but one of Richard's old T-shirts that barely covered her bottom.

"Mum." Mallory looked up from the sizzling pancakes, her expression caught between amusement and annoyance. "Put your dressing gown on."

"You're making pancakes?" Harriet said.

They obviously were, but she was still so shocked. Somehow, overnight, Abby and Mallory had become BFFs. Or something like that.

"Yeah." Mallory, to Harriet's disgust, ate an entire spoonful of golden syrup, licking the spoon with relish.

"I think it's burning," Abby said, and reached across Mallory to flip the blackened pancake.

Well. Harriet didn't know what to think. She was pleased the girls were getting along, if a little wary about it. She didn't want Abby to get hurt by Mallory whom she suspected, unfairly or not, might be a friend at Willoughby Close but a mean girl at school.

"We should head back to Oxford, to see Lady Stokeley," she said, and Abby smiled at her.

"I'm sure she wouldn't mind if you called her Dorothy."

Harriet didn't see that happening any time soon.

An hour later they were dressed and in the car, although the kitchen was still a mess of spilled batter and sticky, syrupy plates. Harriet had closed the door on it all, wanting to check in with Lady Stokeley before the day got away from them. She also wanted a large cappuccino from the Starbucks on the A40, a treat she was willing to splurge on.

When they got to the hospital, Lady Stokeley was lying in bed, looking pale and worn but composed, her hands folded on top of the blankets.

The children, hyped up on sugary pancakes, were not on their best form. Harriet collared William to keep him from kicking anything expensive or important while Chloe blew on the window and then traced patterns on the fogged-up pane.

Abby went up to Lady Stokeley. "How was your night?" she asked in a tone of such genuine concern that Harriet almost felt tearful.

Mallory, meanwhile, was in the corner of the room on Snapchat.

"I've had better and I've had worse," Lady Stokeley answered. "They're insisting on keeping me in another day, more's the pity."

"Is there anything we can do for you?" Harriet asked, and Lady Stokeley shook her head.

"Not unless you can break me out of here," she said, cracking a smile that made her face dissolve into even more wrinkles, and Harriet smiled back even as she wondered why she'd made the forty-five minute trip into Oxford for what looked to be a two-minute visit. But perhaps that was no bad thing—she didn't think she could keep ahold of William for much longer than that, and at least Lady Stokeley knew she cared.

"What about some magazines?" she asked. "I could get them from the shop. Or something nicer than hospital food…"

"I'm afraid my eyesight's not good enough for magazines, but I wouldn't mind a proper cup of tea, if this place has one."

"Of course," Harriet answered, relieved to be able to do

something. "Come on, everyone." She shepherded the children out of the room and down to the café where she splurged on hot chocolates for all of them, trying not to panic about the fifteen pounds it cost. Money, money, money. The worry was always there, a stone in her stomach, a pulsing in her head. "Keep an eye on everyone while I nip up to give Lady Stokeley her tea," she ordered Mallory, who rolled her eyes.

"Don't worry, Mrs. Lang, I'll watch out for them too," Abby offered, and Harriet gave her a grateful smile.

She was just about to knock on the door of Lady Stokeley's room when a consultant stopped her.

"Are you part of the family?" he asked, smiling, and before Harriet could explain, he continued, "We're hoping to schedule Mrs. Trent for the screening next Friday. She should be feeling better by then."

"Oh." She gazed at him uncertainly. "Right."

"But we'll call first to make sure."

"Okay."

"Thanks," he said, and continued on his rounds.

Harriet knocked once on the door and at Lady Stokeley's croaky hello, she went in. "One cup of Earl Grey," she announced cheerfully, and Lady Stokeley gave her a wan smile.

"Thank you, my dear."

Harriet placed the cup on the table next to the bed, and then spent a few minutes refreshing the jug of water and throwing away a bunch of used tissues. "The doctor mentioned an appointment for next week," she finally said. "A screening?"

It wasn't her business, but she was worried. Over the last twenty-four hours she'd become invested in Lady Stokeley's life. She wanted to make sure some kind of happy ending was in sight.

"Ah, yes." Lady Stokeley leaned her head against her pillow and closed her eyes. "I need to have some tests. When they did the Xray last night after you left they saw something a bit worrisome."

"A bit worrisome?" Harriet's stomach lurched. "What do you mean?"

"Cancer," Lady Stokeley said succinctly. "That's what they're worried about, although they haven't said as much yet. But when you've lived as long and buried as many people as I have, you can read the signs."

"Oh, no." Harriet sank onto the chair next to Lady Stokeley's bed. "I'm so sorry."

Lady Stokeley shrugged. "I'm eighty-six. I've got to go sometime. But it might not even be cancer. We'll see." Her tone was repressive.

"How will you get to the appointment?"

"Call a taxi service, I suppose. I haven't driven myself in years, not with my poor eyesight."

"I can drive you," Harriet blurted.

It wasn't as if she was doing anything with her days besides housework and scanning the want ads. The three sessions a week at the gym had disappeared along with the membership, as had the coffee mornings with Sophie, of course. The VSA was planning a quiz night but Harriet hadn't even been asked to help. Last year she'd chaired it.

She'd once been so ridiculously busy, organizing events, ferrying her children to and fro, feeling important, and now she felt as if she lived in a vacuum, but that was at least partly her own choice. She supposed, if she made more of an effort, she could make some new friends at the school gate. Some other mums would come forward. She hoped, anyway. She simply hadn't had the energy to try yet.

"That would be very helpful, thank you," Lady Stokeley answered with stiff dignity. "I don't like relying on charity, but at my age it is on occasion a sad necessity."

"It's not charity," Harriet protested. "Think of it as… as an act of friendship."

Lady Stokeley gave her an assessing look before nodding once. "Thank you." She paused, a troubled frown creasing her wrinkled face even more. "Please don't mention any of this to Abby. I don't want to worry her, poor girl. She's had enough to deal with already."

"I won't say a word," Harriet promised even as she wondered what exactly Abby had had to deal with.

Down in the café, Abby had managed to keep the peace, starting a game of table football with coffee stirrers and a penny. Unfortunately, right as Harriet arrived, William got a bit too aggressive and knocked Chloe's half-full cup of hot chocolate right into her lap. Chloe started wailing.

"It's all right, it's not burning you," Harriet said as she snagged a dozen paper napkins to mop up the mess. "The hot chocolate is *cold,* Chloe. You're not hurt, just a bit damp, darling."

"Sorry," William muttered, and then ruined his act of contrition by flicking the penny at Chloe. Thankfully it missed.

They drove back to Willoughby Close mostly in silence. It wasn't even ten in the morning and Harriet felt exhausted. Plus she had an entire Saturday to get through, with no children's activities to fill it up.

She'd had to scale back on the children's activities—everything was so expensive. She'd told them they could pursue one activity each rather than the three or more they'd been doing before. Surprisingly, or perhaps not, her children had seemed more relieved than anything.

"You mean I can drop swimming?" Mallory had exclaimed. "Thank *God.*"

"I'm quitting clarinet!" William had declared joyfully, before leveling Harriet with a look. "But I'm keeping football."

Harriet had smiled, surprised and yet not by their eagerness to shed the activities she'd once deemed so important. And she could do without driving to and fro most afternoons and Saturdays, although the day still yawned in front of her, semi-alarmingly.

The children spilled out of the car as soon as Harriet had parked. Inside the house, William and Chloe flopped on the sofa while Abby and Mallory disappeared upstairs. They'd no doubt all be on their devices but Harriet wanted a few minutes' peace to deal with the mess in the kitchen before she insisted they unplug.

She hummed under her breath as she rinsed and stacked the dishes, her mind pinging between Lady Stokeley's worrisome screening to money matters even as she kept half an ear on William and Chloe's interaction; at any moment William could start burning off that manic boy energy he always had and put his sister in a head lock, which Chloe sometimes liked but often didn't.

Mallory and Abby seemed to be getting along, at least. That was something. The dishes stacked in the dishwasher, Harriet rested her elbows on the edge of the sink and gazed out the window at the little rectangle of garden behind number two. It was nothing like the grounds of the Old Rectory, with the walled Victorian garden, an orchard of apple trees that had, admittedly, been past their prime, and a wide stretch of lawn perfect for parties or games of croquet.

This garden was a small rectangle, hemmed in by low stone walls that were probably part of the manor's original barn. There was a tree, at least—a horse chestnut, Harriet supposed, and the garden wasn't so big that she couldn't look after it herself.

The garden of the Old Rectory had been so enormous that she had, at Sophie's recommendation, hired a landscaper and then a gardener to manage it all. She'd only gone out there for parties or picnics, acting as a prop to an expensively styled set.

Which was something of a shame, as she'd once fancied becoming something of a gardener. She'd envisaged herself elbow-deep in rich soil, planting herbs and bright flowers, growing things, back when they'd been contemplating the life-changing move from London to the Cotswolds.

This garden, however, was certainly manageable. And while a few weeks ago Harriet had rebelled against the thought of putting down roots here, both literally and figuratively, now she wondered at the wisdom of planting a few seeds. She could get the kids involved. Perhaps it would make them all feel more settled, because the longer she lived here the more she realized it was probably going to be home for at least a little while. Not forever, though. That was something she still couldn't contemplate.

A screech from the living area had her straightening with a sigh. "William, let go of your sister," she called without looking, and William let out a cackle of laughter before flinging himself off the sofa, while Chloe dissolved into noisy, deliberate tears.

After a lunch of tinned tomato soup and toasted cheese sandwiches, Harriet chivvied everyone outside for a walk around Willoughby Manor. Mallory moaned as if Harriet were inflicting some rare form of torture on her, which she probably was. William took his football, managing to zigzag in front of everyone as they walked, and Harriet felt as if she tripped over the blasted ball every few minutes, but at least he was happy. She even kicked it back to him a couple of times, which made William chortle with glee.

"You're terrible, Mum," he said in delight, but then gave her a quick smile of encouragement. "But I don't mind. Kick it again."

The air was fresh and clean and the sky was a pale, fragile blue, sunlight filtering through the trees as they headed through the dense wood that surrounded Willoughby Manor. It almost felt like spring.

"How did you get to know Lady Stokeley?" Harriet asked Abby as they wound through the stark and leafless trees.

"She invited my mum and me for tea one day," Abby answered. "And then I came back and helped her organize some of her stuff. She's got masses of stuff—clothes, jewelry, everything. Mum borrowed a dress off her to go to a party in Oxford."

"Did she?" Harriet was surprised to feel a little, funny sliver of envy at hearing this.

Ellie Matthews had more of a social life than she did. But then why shouldn't she? Harriet had intentionally cut herself from everyone and everything. She'd retreated into a self-made cocoon of isolation. Maybe it was time to start emerging… if she could.

They'd walked out of the wood and now they stood on a plateau of velvety grass, overlooking the terraced lawns of Willoughby Manor. The house towered above, looking elegant and dignified with its mullioned windows and many chimneys. What would happen to the manor if Lady Stokeley couldn't live in it anymore? What would happen to Lady Stokeley?

A pang of worry assailed Harriet and she glanced at Abby who was pressing the toes of her trainers into the soft turf, watching the indentations form in the jewel-green grass. Harriet hoped the screening next week wouldn't come to anything, for Abby's sake as well as Lady Stokeley's.

"Can we go now, please?" Mallory asked. "Or are we going to stand here, like, forever?"

"It's a lovely day, Mallory," Harriet said mildly.

"It's freezing."

The wind *had* picked up a little, and the fragile blue sky was turning ominously gray. With a sigh, Harriet turned them all towards home, her arm around Chloe's little shoulders as William zoomed ahead, kicking the ball so hard that he left a deep divot through the pristine lawn.

"Sorry," he called back, and then kicked it again.

Later that afternoon Ellie came by to pick up Abby, looking slightly shell-shocked by the turn of events. Harriet couldn't blame her—they were basically strangers, after all, and she'd had her daughter for a sleepover.

"I'm so sorry," Ellie half-babbled as she stood in the doorway.

Harriet toyed with the idea of inviting her in but Ellie seemed a bit manic at the moment and, in truth, Harriet didn't possess the courage, which seemed ridiculous considering she'd been queen of the school yard, organizing everyone, for years, and now she was…

What *was* she?

"It's fine," she told Ellie. "Seriously. The girls seemed to have a good time together."

"Did they?" Ellie sounded so incredulous that Harriet frowned.

Her neighbor sounded like she had some damaging intel on her daughter.

"They really did," she answered firmly. "They made pancakes this morning."

"Wow." Ellie let out a little laugh and shook her head. "Wow."

Okay, she didn't need to sound *quite* so disbelieving. Mallory wasn't… well.

"Anyway, I'll let you get on," Harriet said. "I'm sure you want to get yourself organized before the week starts."

"Right."

Ellie ducked her head as she stepped back from the door, and Harriet felt guilty for being so dismissive. "See you soon," she said as a sort of peace offering, and Ellie waved before heading back to number one.

"You seemed to get along with Abby," Harriet said to Mallory later, as she folded laundry on the kitchen table.

Along with a thousand other things, she missed her enormous utility room with the wide slate counter for folding laundry, the huge farmhouse sink, and enough space to keep the ironing board permanently set up. There had even been a chair in the utility room, a William Morris-patterned armchair that Chloe had liked to curl up in, chattering to her about her day while Harriet had done the ironing.

Although in recent years, she'd hired someone to do the ironing, along with all the house-cleaning. She'd been so busy with responsibilities, she'd told Richard. She needed help. Now she wondered what had made her so busy. Mornings at the gym? Chairing the VSA? What had she *become?* And what could she be now?

"Whatever," Mallory said, scrolling through her phone, and Harriet tried to tamp down on the annoyance she felt.

Her daughter was trying just a little too hard to be the teen with an attitude, far older than her eleven and a half years. If she wanted to be credible, she needed to tone it down a bit.

"Why did you say she was a loser before, Mallory?"

"Because she is."

"Why do you think that?"

Mallory rolled her eyes. Again. "Because she is. I mean, look at her, Mum."

Harriet prickled. "What?"

"Didn't you see what she was wearing?"

Baggy jeans and a hoodie, Harriet vaguely recalled. She hadn't actually paid attention.

"What was wrong with what she was wearing?" she asked Mallory.

Mallory heaved a big sigh. "It's just nerdy. She barely speaks in school and she reads these stupidly big books... like, Hobbit kind of stuff. I mean, watch the film, fine, but the book?" Cue the third eye roll, Mallory's signature move.

"But you got along with her," Harriet said slowly. "Didn't you?"

Mallory shrugged. "Because I had to."

"So what about in school? Will you get along with her then?"

Mallory shrugged again. Harriet hated the thought of her daughter blowing off Abby after they'd been friendly at Willoughby Close. She didn't want her daughter to be the kind of person who blew off a friend because of what the popular crowd thought.

Kind of like Sophie had been doing to her. Maybe, like her, Abby didn't mind so much. But it still wasn't good for Mallory.

"There's nothing wrong with big books or Abby's clothes," Harriet said as mildly as she could. "You know that, right?" Mallory just shrugged. "Mallory, if Abby's a nice person and you genuinely like her, you should be friends with her. And you shouldn't not be friends with her just because some in girls think she's different."

Mallory's face closed down. There had been far too many shoulds in what she'd just said. Harriet sighed and decided to change tacks. "Have you talked to your friends?" she asked. "About our move?"

"Not really." Mallory hunched her shoulders, her fringe sliding into her face.

"Have they asked?"

"Not really."

"Do you want to have someone over?" Harriet tried again. In September, for Mallory's eleventh, she'd hosted six of her friends for a spa day and sleepover. They'd all received manicures which had, Harriet recalled now, cost a fortune. Of course she hadn't thought twice about it then. And she'd had it catered—a sleepover for a bunch of ten and eleven-year-olds, *catered*. It seemed ridiculous now. There had been a chocolate fountain and mountains of strawberries and raspberries, two different cakes, and at least three or four separate main dishes. The caterers had bustled in and Harriet had been most concerned that no chocolate spill on the living room carpet, which was a handwoven Turkish rug that had cost nearly twenty thousand pounds. She'd only got three for it when she'd sold it along with the rest of their stuff.

To think now, while she'd been planning that absurd party, Richard had been jobless. Why on earth hadn't he said anything? And why had she thought it was actually necessary to cater a sleepover?

"Well?" she asked Mallory, who had retreated into a sulky silence. "Do you? Why not have Charlotte over?"

"And where would she sleep?" Mallory demanded.

"Same as Abby, in Chloe's bed. Chloe can go in with me."

Mallory shook her head, resolute. "No way." She flounced upstairs, leaving Harriet with two loads of laundry to fold. She supposed she couldn't actually blame Mallory too much. Charlotte lived in a house the size of the Old Rectory, on Wychwood's glamorous estate of enormous new builds, each one with high walls and electric gates. The houses looked like monstrosities but they were huge.

Once again, Harriet realized what a hothouse, rarefied world they'd lived in. Overprivileged, endlessly indulged… and yet, she acknowledged with a sigh, she'd still go back if she could.

Chapter Seven

HARRIET SHIFTED ON the hard plastic seat as she tossed the worn copy of *Woman and Home* aside. Lady Stokeley had been in with the consultant for nearly an hour, and she was starting to feel anxious about both her landlady and whether she'd make pickup time at school. She didn't want to endure Mrs. Bryson's self-righteous wrath yet again.

Lady Stokeley hadn't spoken much on the drive into Oxford. She'd looked regal and remote in a two-piece ensemble of navy blue tweed that smelled rather strongly of mothballs. Harriet had tried to make conversation at first, but she'd ended up subsiding into silence. She didn't feel up for much of a chat, either.

Her anxiety attacks were persisting, and she was having trouble sleeping, with too many worries pinging around in her mind. Mallory's attitude. William's hyperactivity. Chloe's bed-wetting. And then of course money, like a time bomb ticking in the middle of the lounge. Most of the money from the sale of the furniture, car, and pony had gone to paying debts.

"How much are we in debt?" Harriet had demanded on the phone to Richard. "Actually?"

And then Richard had named a figure that had sent her staggering. It was nearly half of his yearly salary, minus the bonus.

"Like I said," he'd said wearily. "We spend a lot."

"Spent," Harriet had returned. "We spent." She certainly wasn't spending anymore.

"We'll get it back…" Richard began, but Harriet didn't want to hear that tired litany yet again, or about Richard's latest promising whatever.

"I know," she cut him off. "But not right now."

She needed to get a job, but when she'd worked up the courage to click on her CV to update it, the damned document hadn't even opened because it was too old. She'd had to install a whole bunch of software just in order to open the thing, and then she'd looked at it and realized how dismal it was. No relevant experience whatsoever in eleven years.

And the only job she'd found that was remotely suitable was as a marketing executive for an academic publisher that looked great on paper but Harriet suspected she'd be laughed out of the office, assuming she even got in the office in the first place. She'd more likely get a form rejection letter, if that.

But she needed to start making money. She'd feel better, more in control, if she was actually earning something. The trouble was, she didn't know how to go about it. Taking that first step, no matter how tiny, felt terrifying. And it made everything about this situation feel more permanent, something she hated.

"Mrs. Lang?"

Harriet looked up to see a nurse standing in the doorway of the consulting room, and her heart leaped into her throat. "Yes?"

"Mrs. Trent is ready to leave."

"Thank you." Harriet stood. "Is she… is she…"

"I'm fine." Lady Stokeley appeared in the doorway, straightening her jacket, her chin lifted. "And ready to leave."

"Okay. Do you… do you need to make another appointment?" She hadn't asked Lady Stokeley about the nature of her tests or what kind of cancer they thought she might have. She hadn't wanted to seem nosy and Lady Stokeley had definitely not been keen to offer any information.

"No further appointments are necessary at present," Lady Stokeley responded crisply. "Now shall we?"

They walked out to the car which was parked about a half mile away, and Harriet wished she'd offered to drive it round because Lady Stokeley was starting to flag. She was still recovering from the pneumonia, and whatever tests she'd had must have taken it out of her.

Gently, Harriet took the older lady's arm and it was a sign of just how fatigued she was that Lady Stokeley did not protest. They drove in silence down the A40, crawling through midafternoon traffic, while Harriet watched the minutes slipping by. She was going to be late for school pickup.

"Do you need to be somewhere?" Lady Stokeley asked abruptly. "Because you keep checking the clock."

"Sorry, it's the school pickup. The year one teacher gets rather chilly with me if I'm late."

"Can you ring?"

"Yes…" But Chloe would just be frog-marched to the office, and made miserable because of it.

"Is there someone who can pick the children up for you?" Lady Stokeley asked. "A friend?"

Harriet thought of Sophie. A lifetime ago, she would have called Sophie, no question, but then a lifetime ago she would never have been late for school pickup. She could picture it now, though—how Sophie would have taken her children home with her, and insisted they take their shoes off before they put a toe across her threshold, and then sniffily fed them organic, disgustingly healthy snacks, which was exactly what Harriet would have done in the same situation, but Sophie would have done it in a martyred way, as if Harriet was presuming and she really was the most amazing friend.

William is quite rambunctious, isn't he? She might have remarked when Harriet picked them up. *Have you had him tested?*

The whole scene unfolded in Harriet's head as if it had

actually happened. No, she most certainly could not call Sophie. And that made her realize she couldn't call anyone. She hadn't actually spoken to anyone properly in over a month and she could hardly ask for a favor now.

"Not really," she told Lady Stokeley with what she hoped was a wry smile. "Not at all, actually."

Lady Stokeley raised her eyebrows. "I thought a woman like you would have plenty of friends."

Harriet gave a huff of laughter. "A woman like me?" Who was that, exactly?

"You seem accomplished, busy." Lady Stokeley paused. "Important."

"Do I?" Harriet let out another laugh, shaking her head. "Trust me, I don't feel very important." Not anymore.

She felt a stupid lump forming in her throat and she focused on driving, switching lanes just so she could distract both herself and Lady Stokeley.

Neither of them spoke for several minutes as they crawled along in the traffic. Harriet glanced at the clock again and then gave in to the inevitable and pulled into a layby to ring the school, asking for Chloe to be sent to the office until she could pick her up.

"You know," Lady Stokeley said after Harriet had pulled back out into the traffic, "at my age one comes to realize how very long life is."

Harriet glanced at her, warily nonplussed. Was this some precursor to how death would be welcome? Because she didn't think she could handle that right now.

"So many phases and stages," Lady Stokeley continued. "And in retrospect, none of them lasts very long."

With a jolt, Harriet realized Lady Stokeley was talking about her. How much did she know about this unfortunate stage of Harriet's life?

"The trouble is," the old lady added, "when you're in a certain phase or stage it feels endless, because of course you don't know when or where the endpoint is. Pity," she mused. "It would be so much easier if we were given a detailed plan beforehand."

"Yes, it would," Harriet agreed. "Although if we knew the plan, we might run away screaming and never do anything at all." She certainly would have.

Lady Stokeley let out a sound that was halfway between a rasp and a rattle, and Harriet looked at her, alarmed. Was she having some sort of episode?

No, Lady Stokeley was actually laughing.

"Indeed," she said when she'd recovered herself and was dabbing at her lips with a lace-edged handkerchief that was yellowed with age. "If I'd known some of the things that were going to happen, I might have been tempted to admit myself to a cloister. Not," she added, "that I'm Catholic."

It made Harriet wonder what Lady Stokeley had endured, but she didn't feel bold or brave enough to ask. She drove into Wychwood-on-Lea, and Lady Stokeley waved a hand in the direction of the school.

"You're late enough. Why don't you pick up the children first and then drive back home?"

"Oh, but..."

She waved a knobby, beringed hand. "I am not as frail as I seem to appear."

Harriet couldn't help but grin at that, and she pulled into an amazingly empty space right near the school and then started jogging towards the gate.

She liberated Chloe from the school office, giving sympathetic murmurs and nods as her daughter recited her tearful litany of complaint before gathering up Mallory and William from the juniors' entrance and then hurrying back to the car.

"I've got Lady Stokeley waiting," she explained breathlessly as she chivvied them along the pavement.

"What?" Mallory looked both surprised and appalled. "Why?"

"Because I needed to take her to an appointment and there wasn't time to drop her off at home. Come on now." Harriet opened the back door of the Rover and the three children clambered in, Mallory still looking disgruntled, William more or less indifferent, and Chloe bright-eyed and curious.

"Why," she asked, "does it smell funny in here?"

Harriet closed her eyes briefly, wishing her daughter had developed something of a social filter.

It did smell funny, of mothballs and lavender water and musty decay.

"My fault, I fear," Lady Stokeley said. "It's a byproduct of aging."

"Chloe," Harriet said in a remonstrating way, and Chloe blinked at her innocently.

"What? I didn't say it smelled *bad.*"

"Even though it does," Mallory muttered under her breath, and Harriet started the car.

She let the children off at home, with strict instructions to Mallory to keep everyone in line, before driving up the sweeping lane to Willoughby Manor.

"I'll help you inside," Harriet said firmly, brooking no arguments, as Lady Stokeley began to climb out of the car. She was looking worn out, the bags under her eyes a deep violet, every wrinkle and crease seeming carved more deeply than usual.

"Thank you," she said, and took Harriet's arm as they walked towards the massive front door.

The interior of Willoughby Manor was as freezing as Harriet had remembered. Outside the damp chill of a March afternoon had been leavened by weak sunlight and a warmish breeze, but the foyer of the manor house felt as still and cold as a mausoleum. Harriet could see her own breath coming out in frosty puffs as she guided Lady Stokeley up the stairs.

"I don't actually know where your bedroom is…"

"Third door on the right."

The upstairs of the manor was as faded and over-furnished as the downstairs, with paintings vying for space on the walls whose ancient paper was peeling from damp corners. The carpet under their feet looked both expensive and threadbare.

Harriet opened the door and ushered Lady Stokeley into a large, imposing room with a huge fireplace that provided nothing but a continuous draught of cold air and a canopied four-poster bed that looked like you needed a ladder to climb into it.

"My goodness," Harriet murmured.

"This bed was here in Tudor times," Lady Stokeley informed her.

Harriet wondered if the dusty, moth-eaten hangings were original.

"I'm fine now," Lady Stokeley said, her blue-eyed gaze rather imperious.

This was a dismissal, but Harriet didn't like leaving her there alone.

"Let me turn on the fire at least," she said, stooping to fiddle with the knobs of an ancient-looking two-bar electric fire that had been placed, rather pathetically, in front of the huge fireplace. "And fetch you a cup of tea, if you'd like one."

Lady Stokeley looked both surprised and resistant, but then she gave a stiff nod. "Yes, that would be very kind. Thank you. The kitchen is towards the back of the house."

"Right." Hopefully she wouldn't get lost in this huge place.

Harriet went down the front stairs and then headed towards the back of the house, navigating a maze of corridors and walking into several empty rooms, all of them freezing cold with furniture covered in dust sheets, before she finally found the kitchen.

It was massive and looked like it belonged on the set of *Downton Abbey*, with a huge, ancient wooden work table dominating the center of the room, and an old-fashioned blackened range that looked like it should have been in a museum. A portable electric hob with two small rings had been plugged in next to it, and the sight made Harriet sad somehow.

She found an old-fashioned kettle, big and brass, and filled it up in a sink a small child could bathe in. The pipes creaked in protest as she turned the taps, and the water ran brown for several seconds before it sputtered and then turned thankfully clear.

Harriet plonked the kettle on top of one of the electric rings where it balanced precariously. Then she looked around the kitchen, curious and now more than a little saddened by it all. The cupboards were full of dusty dishes, the kind no one used anymore—chafing dishes and finger bowls and a crystal and silver condiment set. Harriet opened another cupboard and saw crystal glasses and goblets of every size and description, all of them with a fine patina of dust. Then she opened another cupboard and stared at its contents—not more crystal and silver, but a couple of tins of soup, a bag of economy tea bags, some UHT milk, and a few Fray Bentos steak and kidney pies.

Was this all the food Lady Stokeley had in the house? It was dismal, as well as sad beyond words. Harriet stared for another moment as the kettle started to whistle. She hauled it off the ring and took a teabag from the box, then searched the cupboards for a normal teacup rather than something that looked like you'd bring to the *Antiques Roadshow*.

The lumbering fridge, also antiquated, held an opened box of UHT milk and a small square of congealed butter on a saucer, and nothing else. Harriet swallowed hard. She had a strong desire to rush out and fill a trolley or two at Waitrose and bring it all back here, but she knew Lady Stokeley wouldn't countenance such a thing for a second. It would be a huge, hurtful blow to her pride.

So she took out the milk and put a splash in the tea, and then took the cup upstairs. Lady Stokeley was dozing in bed when Harriet tapped on the door, but her eyelids fluttered open as Harriet came in.

"Sorry to disturb you... tea." Harriet hefted the cup and Lady Stokeley nodded.

She looked even paler and more fragile tucked up in bed than she had in the car, and Harriet felt another hard tug of reluctance at leaving her there.

"Is there anything else I can do for you?" she asked.

"I think not," Lady Stokeley answered with some of her usual acerbity. "You've been most kind." She reached for her tea, bringing the cup to her lips with a trembling hand.

Harriet knew she should go and leave the poor woman in peace, instead of gazing at her in obvious sympathy and even pity. But it was so awful, leaving Lady Stokeley alone in this huge place, surrounded by moth-eaten carpets and moldering furniture, her only company the frowning faces of her ancestors as they stared at her from their muddy, old oil portraits.

She had a sudden, jolting thought that this was what might have become of her, in the Old Rectory, surrounded by her furniture and things, and one day entirely alone.

"Bye then," she said, trying to sound as upbeat as she could. "I might pop round tomorrow, to see how you're doing..." She made it sort of a question, and after a tiny pause Lady Stokeley nodded.

"Yes, very well."

"Right." Harriet waved and then, with no real alternative, she turned and made her way downstairs and out of the huge house, pulling the heavy wood door behind her, so it felt as if she'd just entombed Lady Stokeley inside.

She climbed in her car and started to the drive, only to slow to a stop when Jace Tucker, the caretaker, flagged her down.

Harriet rolled down her window, slightly apprehensive. Jace's impossibly good looks and simmering sexuality unnerved her. He looked like he belonged in a cologne ad, not standing in the mud holding a pair of garden shears.

"Were you up at the manor just now?" he asked, and she

nodded. "How's madam, then? Is she all right?" Something about his tone told Harriet that Jace cared about Lady Stokeley quite a lot, and the madam thing was an affectionate nickname.

"She's just had an appointment at the hospital," Harriet hedged. She didn't think it was her place to share what Lady Stokeley had been up to. "And you know she had pneumonia…?"

"Yes, but she's doing better, isn't she?" He gave her a hard look. "Or is there more?"

"I think you'd better ask Lady Stokeley that," Harriet said, and Jace gave a knowing nod.

"I see," he said, and Harriet thought he probably did.

That evening she tried to think of something more she could do for Lady Stokeley as she made supper, washed dishes, and chased children around, reminding them to put away their clean uniform, do their homework, brush their teeth. Sometimes parenting felt like one long nagging session, but perhaps that was more her fault than theirs. There hadn't been a lot of fun in their lives lately.

She couldn't think of any way to help Lady Stokeley except what she was doing, visiting on occasion and driving her places. And she wouldn't be able to do much of that once she got a job, which, she needed to figure out quite soon.

There was so much uncertainty in everyone's lives, especially her own. With a sigh, Harriet wondered if she was worrying so much about Lady Stokeley simply because it kept her from having to worry about herself.

Chapter Eight

"**I** JUST WANTED to say thank you."

Harriet stared at Ellie in surprise. Her neighbor stood on her doorstep at nine o'clock on a Saturday evening, brandishing a bottle of wine.

"Sorry I haven't come before. Life's been a bit manic..." She gave a slightly strained smile, making Harriet wonder.

It was the last week of March, only a week left until the end of the school term, and Harriet had spent the last two weeks managing children and house as well as visiting Lady Stokeley a couple of times, who had been polite but a little chilly. She hadn't offered any information about the results of her screening and Harriet hadn't asked. Sometimes she wondered why she went, and yet she knew she'd keep going.

She'd also been trying to tidy up her CV and make herself sound far more important and productive than she really was. The deadline for the academic publishing position was in three days, and she was still dithering about whether she should even apply. It would be a lot of work for probably nothing, and yet if she didn't apply... that seemed like a cop out.

"Here." Ellie thrust the bottle of wine towards her, looking awkward. "Sorry, this isn't a great time, is it? Anyway, I just wanted to say thanks for having Abby over the other weekend. It was really kind."

"Oh." Harriet took the bottle, realizing she had been standing there looking gormless. Ellie probably thought she'd been trying to get her to leave. "Do you want to come in?" she asked, and Ellie practically did a double take.

"What? You mean…"

"Come in," Harriet said, really meaning it now.

The kids were asleep except for Mallory, who was reading in bed, and she hadn't had a proper chat with anyone in months.

"I'll open this," she added, hefting the bottle. "You don't have to drive, so…"

"All right." Ellie smiled shyly and Harriet stepped aside so she could come in.

"Will Abby be all right on her own?" she asked, realizing she probably should have thought of that earlier.

"Yes, she's just reading. I'll text her to let her know I'm staying for a bit." Ellie got out her phone while Harriet went in search of a corkscrew.

It was a proper posh bottle of wine, with foil and a cork. Harriet hadn't had anything but occasional plonk from Tesco's in months. Briefly she reminisced about the wine club she and Richard had belonged to with bottles costing a hundred pounds or more. They'd been good, but she wasn't enough of a wine connoisseur to tell a ten-pound bottle from a hundred-pound one. Now it just seemed like a big waste of money, even if she'd enjoyed their evenings in front of the telly, with a bottle of wine, a wedge of really good cheese, and some nice biscuits.

"Wow, this place is miles bigger than mine," Ellie said as she tucked her phone back in her pocket. She ducked her head, giving an embarrassed smile. "Sorry, I don't know if that sounded..."

"It seemed small to us at the start," Harriet admitted. She felt the need to be frank. "But we've got used to it. I think." Sort of, not really. Mallory still moaned about having to share a bedroom, but not quite as loudly as at the start.

"What was your house like, before?"

"Oh." Harriet let out a gusty sigh and handed Ellie a glass of wine. She tossed another log onto the wood fire and then they both moved to the sofa, curling up on either end. "It was my dream house," Harriet admitted quietly. She took a sip of wine, savoring the velvety way it slipped down. "Our dream house." A stupid lump formed in her throat and she choked it down.

She really didn't feel like getting emotional right then. It was so much easier to focus on the loss of the house rather than the loss of her husband. The loss of her life.

Ellie cocked her head, her smile both sad and kind. "So what happened? Or should I not ask?"

"A lot of bad stuff. I'm surprised you haven't heard through the school grapevine."

Ellie raised her eyebrows. "There's a school grapevine? Because if so I don't know anything about it."

"Oh." Harriet felt a curdling of guilt inside that she didn't completely understand, until a memory slotted into place of Ellie helping out at that bake sale. A fuss had broken out over the cookies, and Harriet had relegated her to making tea for her and the other mums.

Harriet had a sudden, piercing memory of Ellie sitting by herself and drinking her tea while Harriet had talked to Sophie and the other mums. She cringed now at the thought.

"I'm sorry about the bake sale," she blurted. Ellie leaned back, looking surprised. "I have a feeling I acted like a... like a prat, I suppose."

"It's okay," Ellie said, not denying it. "I made a hash of the whole thing, anyway."

"Maybe, but I didn't have to be so..." Harriet shook her head. "You know, it's not until everything went pear-shaped that I've realized how annoying I was sometimes." She grimaced, and Ellie raised her eyebrows, clearly waiting for more.

"We lost the house," Harriet explained, her tone turning flat. "Richard, my husband, lost his job. And he also..." She stopped, physically unable to continue.

The lump in her throat had grown bigger and she *really*

didn't want to cry right now. She was sick of crying. She'd already had her big crying jag, had got it all out weeks ago. She wanted to move on now. She *needed* to move on now, at least in some small way, but the pain of Richard's betrayal, of losing him, still cut so deep she felt like she could bleed out from it if she said so much as a word.

"You don't have to talk about it," Ellie said when the silence had stretched on for several uncomfortable moments. "Sorry, I'm being incredibly nosy barging in here asking you to spill your guts." She smiled wryly. "Go on and ask me something."

"Okay." Harriet let out a wobbly laugh. "How long have you been with your boyfriend?"

"Oh." Ellie blushed. "How did you…"

"Abby."

"Oh. Right." She laughed, the sound as wobbly as Harriet's had been, and looked away. "Well, actually, I'm not sure we're together anymore."

"What? Why not? Abby was acting as if you were both really keen."

"We were, but then… oh, but it's complicated."

Harriet tucked her knees up to her chest. "I've got time to listen."

Ellie sighed. "It's all gone wrong somehow, and so quickly. We went to his parents' place… Endsleigh House…" She shook her head as if to dismiss the memory.

"And what happened?" Harriet asked, genuinely curious

now.

"He told me as we're pulling up the drive that he's a blooming baronet!" Ellie let out a hiccuppy laugh. "At least his father is, and he will be one day. And his parents were so snooty and disapproving because I obviously don't have the makings of a baronetess or whatever—I grew up in a three-bedroom semidetached in Oldham, for heaven's sake. And then Oliver went all chilly like he used to do and then he just disappeared. He's up in Yorkshire somewhere, doing research for his next book."

"Hmm." Harriet rested her chin on her knees. "It doesn't necessarily sound like it's over. Maybe he just needs a little space to think things through."

"And maybe I need more wine."

"I think we both do."

Ellie drained her glass and Harriet uncurled herself from the sofa to give her a top up.

"I suppose I've got a case of once bitten, twice shy," Ellie said after Harriet had sat back down and they were both sipping their wine again.

"You've dated a baronet before?"

She laughed. "No, far from it. But I've been in a relationship—with Abby's dad—where I had to do all the heavy lifting, you know? And after a while I got tired of being the only one who was trying to make things work."

"And that's how things seem with Oliver?"

"Sort of, because he just left." Ellie made a face. "I suppose I should admit here that Nathan—my ex—put in an appearance at exactly the wrong time."

"Ah."

Ellie's life had the makings of a soap opera.

"But Oliver didn't have to beat such a fast retreat, you know? And now I don't even know where he is, not really."

"You could find him."

She bit her lip. "And if he doesn't want to be found?"

"Then you'd know, at least, and could move on."

"Hmm." Ellie took another sip of wine. "Maybe," she allowed. "What about you? Are you moving on?"

Harriet grimaced. "I already have, haven't I, since I'm here?"

"Yes, but emotionally, I mean. It's been a month, right?"

"Two months since I found out about Richard." The longest two months of her life. Harriet's throat went tight again. "The truth is... not only did he lose his job, but he was—is, probably—having an affair." She gasped out the last word.

It still had the power to stun her, and it really shouldn't, considering how long it had been and how much she'd thought about it.

"Oh, Harriet." Ellie's face softened with sympathy. "I'm so sorry."

"That's what I found out first. A mobile phone bill with a record of long calls to his assistant in the middle of the night. He didn't even try to hide it."

"How long had it been going on?"

"I don't know." Harriet stared down into the ruby depths of her wine. "I didn't ask. I haven't learned many of the details, and Richard hasn't volunteered much. We're separated, informally anyway, and the only things we talk about are the children and money, or lack of it."

Ellie sighed. "Well, I'm afraid I've been there. My ex cheated on me, although he claimed it wasn't proper cheating, since they didn't actually, well, you know. But I found a bra in the pocket of his trousers, so…"

"I haven't found anything like that." The thought of finding some of Meghan's no doubt sexy underwear in Richard's things was truly horrifying.

The calls had been bad enough. Yes, he'd said he hadn't slept with her, but could Harriet believe him? And what *had* he done with her? She really wasn't ready to know.

"Is he sorry?" Ellie asked. "Do you think… could you… forgive him? In time?"

"I don't know." Harriet leaned her head back against the sofa and closed her eyes. "It all feels so mixed up, the money and the house and then the infidelity. My entire life exploded and I don't have the first clue about how to rebuild any of it." She opened her eyes and gave Ellie a wry smile. "I've just been slogging through the days, avoiding everyone and trying to survive."

"That's no way to live."

"I know." And the truth was, Harriet was starting to feel

almost unbearably lonely. Talking to Ellie felt good, healing in a way—and it made her realize she hadn't had such a frank and friendly conversation in years, maybe since her London days.

Briefly, she thought about her best friend from London, Shelley, who worked part-time as a barrister and was funny and self-deprecating and not at all precious about organic food or too much screen time for her kids. She'd felt herself with Shelley—normal and laidback. She hadn't been that way in a long time.

They'd lost touch a year or two ago—they were both busy, and their lives had become so separate and different, with Shelley still juggling work and city life while Harriet had become a rural housewife.

"So," Ellie said, her tone turning purposeful and brisk. "Let's get you back on track to the land of the living."

"What is that supposed to mean?" Harriet asked warily.

"Are you looking for a job?"

"Yes, but I haven't worked in eleven years."

"What did you do before?"

"Publishing, the marketing side. But there isn't much going at the moment."

"So you have looked?"

"Yes… there is one job," Harriet admitted, a little shyly. "I've filled out an application but I haven't sent it. It feels… risky."

Ellie nodded sagely. "It's so hard to put yourself out

there. That's how I felt when I applied for the job at Oxford."

"What do you do, anyway?"

"I'm an admin assistant to the history department. I know it doesn't sound like much, but…"

"No, it's brilliant," Harriet said quickly.

Who was she to judge? She hadn't brought in a salary in over a decade. And she might end up doing something similar if she couldn't get the kind of job she'd trained for.

"I'd love to work in Oxford, although the commute is a pain, I suppose…"

"Yes, I can do it because Abby is a bit older now, but I wish it were closer. Still Wychwood-on-Lea is lovely."

"Yes." Except, she felt as if she was avoiding most of the village's population.

She needed to get over herself. Bad things happened, and you soldiered on. What else could you do? She had to start facing people down, and figuring out a way to move on.

"So you're going to apply for this job," Ellie said and Harriet gave a start.

"I didn't say—"

"Why not? What have you got to lose?"

"My dignity?"

"A small price," Ellie answered with a grin. "I'm not sure I have any left. And who knows, maybe you will get the job, and it will be absolutely brilliant."

"Maybe," Harriet said, unconvinced.

"Promise me you'll apply."

"Promise me you'll go find this Oliver," Harriet returned. "I'm not the only one who needs to be dragged kicking and screaming into the land of the living, I think."

Ellie looked startled, and genuine fear flashed across her face before she lifted her chin. "Fine. Lady Stokeley said much the same the other week, so I suppose I need to listen."

"You're friends with Lady Stokeley?" Harriet asked in surprise, although why this should be news she didn't know. Abby was friends with Lady Stokeley, so why shouldn't Ellie be as well?

"I wouldn't call us friends exactly," Ellie answered, "although she and Abby are practically BFFs. But she scares me more than a little."

Harriet let out a little laugh. "Yes, I know what you mean. I feel sorry for her, though, alone in that big house."

"Yes, it does seem rather lonely. I'm glad Abby goes up there regularly."

"Yes." The fire in the wood stove had burned down and it was past ten o'clock. Harriet stretched out her legs towards the fire as she let out a groan. "Two glasses of wine and I feel tiddly."

"So do I," Ellie said with a giggle. "Hopefully the kids won't notice."

"Hopefully." The thought of tomorrow, another long day with the children no doubt bickering and moaning, made Harriet wince.

Perhaps when the weather turned things would be better. They'd get out in the garden, muck about, plant some seeds… start making an effort.

"I should probably go," Ellie said as she rose from the sofa. "Before it gets too late."

"Yes…" Harriet rose as well, taking their empty glasses to the sink.

"I'm glad we did this," Ellie said suddenly. "Truth be told, I was a bit intimidated by you."

"Were you?" Harriet rinsed the glasses out, her back to Ellie. "I think I intimidated myself."

"What do you mean?"

"I don't know, exactly." She turned around, leaning against the sink and folding her arms. "Just that I don't feel like the person I was anymore. I can't be that person, because… well, because she was rich and successful and popular. And now I'm none of those things."

Ellie frowned as she reached for her parka and shrugged into it. "What about all your friends? You were surrounded that day of the bake sale."

"My best friend, if I could even have called her that, dropped me." Harriet let out a humorless laugh. "But the truth is I'm almost relieved. If I'm honest, I miss feeling important, but I don't miss the people, at least not many of them." She knew she couldn't tar everyone with Sophie's brush, but she definitely didn't miss the nosy, gossipy, bustling about that she and the other mums had done as a matter of course. But she did miss having friends.

"Maybe this is a chance to make new friends."

"Present company included." Harriet smiled, feeling both encouraged and weary.

Yes, she could view this all as a fresh start, and she was trying, whether it was making a new friend, applying for a job, or planting some seeds. But it was *hard,* an exhausting slog with no end in sight. And if she had a choice, right now, she'd still go back to her old life and have everything as it was.

Wouldn't she?

The fact that she had a moment's doubt startled her. Of course she would, in a heartbeat. This wasn't living. But perhaps it needed to be. Richard still hadn't had a job, and he hadn't mentioned any so-called promising leads in a while. Maybe this *was* her future, and she needed to accept that.

Harriet was still mulling it over after Ellie had left and she'd gone up to bed. The double bed seemed too big, too empty, as she slid between the cold sheets. If Richard had been here, she would have placed her freezing feet on his calves. He would have shivered but he never complained; he'd always just brought her closer to him, to imbue her with his heat. She missed that. She missed him, but she wasn't sure if she missed the him of the last few years, or an older, faraway version. Or maybe she was viewing the early years of their marriage with rose-tinted glasses. Maybe the cracks had been there all along, and she hadn't noticed.

They must have been, for him to have some kind of affair. That didn't spring out of nowhere. As she snuggled down under the covers, she wondered if she should ask for the full story on sexy Meghan, or if she should just leave it all behind. That was the trouble—she still didn't know whether she wanted to, or even could, forge ahead, or if she should keep looking back because maybe, just maybe, there was something worth saving.

Chapter Nine

"WHY ARE YOU getting dressed up?"

Harriet turned from where she'd been scrutinizing her reflection in the mirror to see Mallory standing in the doorway of her bedroom.

"Because I want to look good."

Last week Richard had called, asking if they could talk, and Harriet had decided to bite the bullet and say yes. A conversation about Meghan was overdue, and hopefully now she was ready for the truth... even if she didn't feel ready. She felt sick.

"Does this dress make me look fat?" she asked. "Be honest."

Mallory arched an eyebrow, and Harriet braced herself. She'd been taking a risk asking Mallory for the unvarnished truth.

"You've had three children," Mallory said diplomatically, and Harriet groaned.

She *was* fat. Or at least, her poochy belly was fat. Three children and no more sessions at the gym had forced her to don control-top tights and suck in her stomach for the next three hours.

"But that's not a bad thing," Mallory continued. "Dad liked you a little rounder." She made a face. "Which makes me want to hurl, actually, but whatever."

"How on earth do you know that Dad likes me a little rounder?" Harriet demanded.

"Because he always used to say you didn't need to go to the gym."

"He was just being nice." She'd forgotten how he'd said that.

Whenever she bustled around wearing a lot of expensive Lycra, Richard would put an arm around her much skinnier waist and say she looked perfect just as she was. Harriet hadn't paid attention, not really—she'd been too busy running around after everything, except now she couldn't quite remember what that everything was. Dinner, and the kids' endless activities, and keeping the house looking like it came out of a magazine. Keeping everything about her life looking shiny and perfect.

"Whatever," Mallory exhaled on a bored sigh. "You look fine."

"Thank you."

The kids were going over to Ellie and Abby's while Harriet met Richard at the local pub—she'd chosen The Drowned Sailor rather than The Three Pennies. She didn't want to risk seeing Sophie or someone similar. And, she was coming to realize, she didn't even like The Three Pennies, with its slick yet countrified air, as if it was only pretending at being a pub.

Harriet took a deep breath and let it out, and then wished she hadn't when her stomach pooched out even more. The control-top tights were not doing their job. Or perhaps she wasn't. Sucking it all in again, she turned to Mallory.

"Right. We ought to get going."

Harriet brought the children over to Ellie's, giving her a look of immense gratitude. After their shared bottle of wine the other week, Ellie had become a surprisingly firm friend. They hadn't had any more long heart-to-hearts, nothing more than a few quick chats, but just the complicit smiles they gave each other as they headed in their houses was enough for Harriet to know she had someone living next door she could count on.

She decided to walk to The Drowned Sailor, because the sun was still shining, the evenings turning longer as a wintry March came to a close. Spring really was on the way. Besides, she didn't want to drive because she thought she might want a glass of wine, or three. Her insides were quivering like a plateful of jelly. It almost felt like a first date. A first date with Darth Maul, perhaps. She had a feeling it was dread, not excitement, that was curdling her insides.

Unlike The Three Pennies, The Drowned Sailor was full of rowdy patrons on a Friday night, most of them looking like they intended on having a very good time. Harriet wished she could say the same.

She caught sight of Richard at a table for two tucked in the back and she started to weave her way through the hot press of bodies standing by the bar waiting to be served.

Nerves tightened in her belly as she approached and Richard stood up. He had dressed up for the occasion, just as she had, and was wearing a blue button-down shirt and pressed khakis. He needed a haircut, she noticed with a pang of reluctant and unexpected affection. His dark hair was curling about his ears, wayward wisps that made him look a little bit like a mad professor.

"Hello." He smiled, and now there was a whole, new, surreal kind of awkwardness, because this was the man whose head she'd held over the toilet when he'd been violently sick from food poisoning. He'd seen her giving birth three times, and had cut the cord at every one.

She'd picked up his dirty boxer shorts and used tissues, had heard him fart in the bathroom, had lain in his arms night after night after night. She knew the sound of his snore, his laugh, the way he breathed. And now he felt like a stranger. Or perhaps she was the stranger.

"Hello," Harriet said, and sat down.

"I ordered us a bottle of wine." Richard cleared his throat. "I hope that's all right."

"Fine, thanks." She'd take the bottle by the neck and glug it as soon as it came.

Harriet smiled tightly, half of her amazed at how strained and formal everything was, and the other half not surprised at all. This was what it came to, when they had six months of lies and two months of separation. This, and it was awful.

"So." Richard laid his hands flat on the table. "Shall we order first, and then talk?"

Harriet couldn't keep from grimacing. "You make it sound as if it's some medical procedure that has to be got over."

Richard gave her one of his old, wry smiles, the kind that had her smiling back even when she was annoyed, usually annoying her further. "That's how it feels to me, I'm afraid. I know we have to have this conversation, and it's been a long time coming, but… I want to get it over with. And then move on."

As did she. She'd rather have a cervical smear than go through the next few hours… which was kind of depressing. *Very* depressing, actually.

"Order first," Harriet decided, and reached for the laminated menus that had been left on the table.

She scanned the offerings, which were far simpler than anything on The Three Pennies' menu. Not a toasted walnut or puy lentil in sight.

"I'll have the fish and chips," she said. She felt like something hot and greasy and delicious.

Richard went up to the bar to order, and when he came back there was nothing to keep them from talking… or at least staring at each other.

"Right." Hands on the table again. "So." Richard let out a breath through his nose. "Let's talk."

"Okay." Harriet wished the wine would arrive. She could really use a drink. Her stomach was clenched so hard she no longer needed the control-top tights. Well, almost.

"So do you... do you want to ask me questions? Or should I..." Richard licked his lips nervously. "Should I just... ah, start speaking?"

They'd barely started and it was already excruciating. She didn't want to hear the story, from the first late night where they shared a Chinese takeaway and Meghan fingered a button on her blouse as she said huskily, *You know, you look kind of adorable with your hair mussed up and soy sauce on your chin.* And Richard swallowed and tried not to look at her red push-up bra but then did. Or something like that.

"You first, I suppose," Harriet said, her voice coming out in something of a strangled squeak. "And I'll ask questions if... if I need to." Questions she already knew she did not want the answers to.

"Right. So." Richard looked down at his hands. "I'm not sure where to begin."

"How about at the beginning?" Harriet quipped humorlessly. Not that she wanted to go there. "It's the very best place to start."

"Right."

He needed to stop saying that. Nothing was right. *Noth-*

ing.

"I told you about the investment bit…"

"Yes, but how did that come about, anyway?" Far better to talk about the money than their marriage. Than the betrayal that still felt like a punch to the stomach, every single time. "Why did they make an example of you, do you think?"

Richard shrugged. "Because they could?"

"But surely it isn't that simple, Richard," Harriet protested.

She didn't know much about HCI, not even what the initials stood for, but she knew her husband, or at least she'd thought she did, and she suspected there was more to the story.

"I suppose," Richard said after a pause, his gaze sliding away from hers, "that I was more than a bit cocky. I suppose I was… arrogant." He looked down at his hands. "Handling those huge sums of money… trading in millions every day… you start to feel like you're, well, like you're some sort of money god. Which sounds ridiculous, I know, but I felt invincible. Omnipotent. And like no one knew as much as I did." He grimaced. "Which makes me sound like a complete prat, I do realize."

It did, but Harriet couldn't point any fingers. In a different way, she'd been just as bad. "Go on," she said quietly.

"There was a lot of pressure to outperform everyone else. To know what the next big deal was, before anyone else. And

I thought I did. I thought I was above it all… and I wasn't."
He swallowed hard. "I wasn't at all. I picked a stock everyone
said was dicey and I put a lot of money into it. I was so sure
it was going to turn around. I was living off the thrill, I
suppose, and then the whole thing went bust… and I had to
admit I'd lost the company millions of pounds." He closed
his eyes briefly, his face pale as he remembered what was
obviously a terrible moment.

"That must have been incredibly difficult," Harriet said.

She couldn't imagine the sick, sinking feeling of knowing
he'd just lost everything. Oh wait, she could.

She tried to keep the bitterness from her voice as she
asked quietly, "But why didn't you tell me, Richard? We
could have been in this together, but instead you acted as if
nothing had changed. I don't think I could even tell anything was different." She'd tried to remember what had been
going on in June last year, when Richard had been fired.

It had been William's birthday, and of course she'd
thrown a ridiculously over-the-top party. Richard had been
spending several nights a week in London, and she'd been
equal parts relieved and annoyed, which was how she'd liked
being, if she was honest. Superior and martyred at the same
time. But she felt now she should have seen something,
sensed something. How could Richard have possibly come
home after suffering the worst setback of his entire career,
and Harriet hadn't even known something was amiss? How
could two people who loved each other be so completely out

of sync?

"I didn't want to disappoint you," Richard said. "And I didn't want it to be true. It felt like a nightmare I could wake up from if I just let myself. If I tried hard enough."

Which was how the present reality felt, or had been feeling. It was, strangely and surprisingly, starting to feel the tiniest bit better. Maybe.

"And you told it all to Meghan," Harriet said.

The words felt thick in her throat. A waitress arrived with wine and Richard poured them both two large glasses.

"She knew what was going on, yes."

"We laughed about her, Richard." It was hard to get the words out. Her face felt tight, her eyes dangerously full. And her throat... her throat was like a vise, closing up. In a few seconds she'd be squeaking. "I'm not saying it was a nice thing to do, but how did she go from sexy Meghan who tries too hard to your confidant? Your lover?" The dangerously full eyes started to overflow.

Harriet blinked hard, but it was too late. Two slipped down and with a muttered curse she grabbed a napkin and started dabbing.

"Harriet..." Richard looked anguished.

"Don't. Just answer the question." She didn't want his sympathy now, and definitely not his pity. She wanted to choose fury, not grief. It felt stronger.

"She was never my lover. I told you that."

"Maybe not technically. You said you didn't sleep with

her. But… but something happened. Too much of something. You said as much. So what was it?" A question she really hadn't wanted to ask yet now that she had, Harriet realized she wanted—needed—to know.

Rip the plaster off the wound and assess the damage. How much blood? How deep the cut? Maybe, just maybe, it wasn't quite as bad as she'd thought.

Richard drew a careful, even breath and let it out slowly. "Yes, something happened. But we never… we never had sex. We never even came close, really."

Harriet reached for her wine. "Why don't you just tell me exactly? First base? Second base? I might as well know than not at this point. Hopefully my imagination is worse than the reality."

Richard was starting to look haggard. "We kissed," he said, "a couple of times."

Harriet blinked. Okay, her imagination had been *way* worse. She'd been thinking… well, never mind what she'd been thinking. And yet they'd kissed. It still hurt, mingled with a weird kind of relief.

"When was that?" she asked.

"The first time was in June."

"When you were fired."

"A little while after. I left the office in disgrace and Meghan kept in touch. She was genuinely concerned. We started spending time together. She… she was there for me when I needed her to be."

"She's a saint," Harriet said sourly and Richard flinched.

"I don't mean that. I don't expect you to understand, but—"

"You didn't expect me to understand anything," Harriet burst out. "You didn't even *try* to let me understand." She wanted to shake him by the shoulders. She wanted to say, *"Look, I know I might have seemed kind of consumed with our life and kids, but if you'd said wait, this is serious, I would have waited. I would have listened."*

At least she hoped she would have.

"I was ashamed," Richard said quietly. "And Meghan was right there, she understood about the tension and pressure, she'd lived through it with me at the office…"

"And I didn't? You didn't let me," Harriet finished.

She realized it wasn't the physical side of things, which seemed like it was, in the end, fairly minimal, that hurt so much.

No, it was the *emotional* stuff that cut so deeply. The knowledge, hard and frankly unbearable, that Richard had, in moments of crisis or desperation or genuine fear, chosen to find comfort in his secretary rather than his wife. Sexy Meghan with her stupid heels, one button too many undone, the overdone cat-flick eyeliner. Why hadn't Harriet seen the danger? Because she'd been so smug and certain of herself— and also because she'd been so certain of Richard. Certain of *them*.

And she wasn't at all certain anymore.

"Are you still… seeing her?" she asked after a moment,

when she trusted herself to sound normal.

Richard looked aggrieved. "I was never seeing her. Not like that."

"Richard, come on. The two of you *kissed.*" She hated saying the words.

"It was impulsive and stupid," Richard said, "and I'd been drinking. Honestly, Harriet, I'm being as honest as I can. It didn't *mean* anything."

"But the conversations meant something. Two hours in the middle of the night! What did you even talk about?"

"I don't know." Richard looked down, a sulky little boy. "Stuff."

Harriet leaned forward. "No, actually, I really want to know now. What on earth did you talk about with a twenty-six-year-old tart for two whole hours? Many times?" Her voice was shaking.

"That's not fair. She's not a tart."

"She kissed my husband. I think I'm allowed to call her a tart."

"I kissed her," Richard returned. "If you want to get technical."

"I *don't.*" That little bit of information hurt even more.

He'd initiated it? In her mind she'd painted Meghan as the seductress, unbuttoning her blouse, slithering over to a somewhat oblivious Richard, but maybe it hadn't been that way at all. Which made her feel sick, even if they had only kissed.

"So tell me what you talked about," Harriet insisted. "Did you tell her how lonely you were? How your wife was obsessed with money and didn't listen to you? How you hadn't had sex in ages?" The words rang out, accusing, scornful, and also filled with hurt.

When *had* they last had sex? Harriet couldn't remember. And she hadn't been obsessed with money. She'd just assumed they'd had a lot of it.

But all right, yes, she could see she hadn't been totally present. She'd been focused on the children and the house and her life as VSA chair and Stepford wife. A husband had started to feel like a somewhat needless accessory. But she still hadn't expected an affair.

Richard looked away, shifting in his seat. He was squirming. "Do we really have to do this?"

"Yes." Even though she really didn't want to. She needed to hear. Needed to know.

"I don't remember everything I said, Harriet, but you're on the right track, I'm sure. I said a lot of things. I was miserable, anxious, frustrated…" He turned back to her, spreading his hands. "I'm not excusing it, just explaining. There was probably something of a mid-life crisis thrown in. Having a young, beautiful woman be interested in me felt… affirming."

Affirming. She could just imagine how firm he'd been. "Maybe you should stop talking."

"I wasn't the one who wanted to go in to all the details,

Harriet."

"I know." She felt nauseous, and the gulp of wine she took didn't help. "I'm sorry. I thought I wanted to know but I realize now I don't." Her heart was starting to thud, her palms turning clammy. Perfect, an anxiety attack in the back of The Drowned Sailor.

"Are you still in contact with her?" she asked when she'd caught her breath.

Silence. Awful, awful silence.

"We're friends," Richard said finally. "Only friends now. I've made that clear."

Jealousy was a terrible emotion, like some poisonous vine twining its way around every organ she had, choking it. "Is that supposed to make me feel better?" Harriet asked.

"We didn't... Harriet, I admit I was spending time with her. A lot of time. But it wasn't... it wasn't what you were thinking. I wasn't envisioning some kind of future with her at all..."

"But she might have been. You talked to her. You called her on the phone. No doubt you went out to dinner, went for walks..." She stopped, because he wasn't denying any of it and the image she was forming in her head, the image she was painting with her words, was too terrible for her to continue. In an awful, twisted way she'd have preferred Richard to have had a one-night stand than this. "And you kissed her," she finished flatly. "Several times."

"I admit, I turned to her when I should have turned to

you. It felt… easier, I suppose, and with less risk. And she was there."

"Risk? How on earth was it risky to share this kind of thing with your *wife?*"

"Because you would have been angry with me, Harriet!" Richard leaned forward, his eyes glittering, his expression suddenly furious. "You would have been angry and disappointed, and you would have blamed me. And the truth is I didn't even know who you were anymore. Who you'd become. You spent my money like it was water—"

"*Your* money?" Harriet felt as if someone had just injected her with ice water. "Is that how you've seen it all this time?"

"No, not like that, not really," Richard said tiredly. "We had money and I wanted you to spend it. I wanted to give you nice things. I still do. It was more about… about who you were than how much you spent."

Ouch. Harriet tried to school her expression into something neutral. "Who I was?"

"You've been so consumed with image since we moved out here. Where we went to dinner. Who we were seen with. What people thought of us."

Harriet flinched. She didn't think she'd been *that* bad. Had she?

"You were turning into your friend Sophie," Richard said, and Harriet drew back. Now *that* was unfair. "So cutting about everyone. So shallow and determined that everything looked good all the time. At Christmas all you cared about was the blasted decorations! And you told me about the hair place in Chipping Norton you went to, and how celebrities went there. As if I'd be impressed." He shook his head, his mouth curling, and Harriet felt as if she'd been flayed.

He was lambasting her over some throwaway remark she'd made about a hairdresser's? About the decorations she'd spent hours on? *What did he want from her?*

"I was afraid that if I told you what had happened," he continued more quietly, "you'd be ashamed of me, as well as angry. And you'd be more concerned about what people thought of us than anything else."

Harriet swallowed. Her mouth felt dry. "I was never ashamed of you. But it almost sounds as if you were ashamed of me."

"No," Richard said tiredly. "Just… frustrated, I suppose."

"You never said anything."

"Maybe I should have."

And maybe you should have tried to see the good parts of me, instead of just focusing on the bad. "I just wish," Harriet said, drawing a shaky breath, "you'd given me a chance before you turned to someone else for support."

"I should have," Richard agreed. "I wish I had."

But he hadn't. He'd chosen not to. And he was still seeing sexy Meghan. And, perhaps worst of all, he didn't seem to like who Harriet was anymore. He'd spoken with such disdain just now, such contempt. It made everything inside her shrivel.

In that moment, Harriet felt as far away from him as ever, worse than before because it wasn't a distance brought on by the hot rush anger and emotion. It felt like a yawning, frozen wasteland that they were both too weary and wounded to cross.

"Well, you don't need to worry now about how much I'm spending now," she said at last, because as always it seemed easier to talk about money than marriage. "I'm spending as little as I possibly can, and I'm looking for a job." A job she most likely wouldn't get, but Richard didn't need to know that right now.

Their meals arrived and Harriet stared at her fish and chips, the battered cod glistening with grease, with revulsion. She couldn't eat a thing. Her stomach was seething. Her chest hurt. She wished she hadn't started this conversation. She wished she hadn't come here tonight. She'd known this conversation was going to be hard, but it had been even worse than she'd been bracing herself for.

Hearing about Meghan. Hearing about her own flaws and faults. She knew she wasn't perfect, of course she did. But she felt as if, when Richard looked at her, all he saw were the bad and broken bits. He didn't see the Harriet who was trying hard, who loved her children, who kept her chin up and had wanted a lovely home for her family. Because that was who she really was... wasn't it? Who was anyone, she wondered wearily. The person they were trying to be, or the fall back? And shouldn't the person they loved, the person they spent your life with, see the good parts first? The best parts?

"I'm sorry," Richard said quietly. "I feel like I've hurt your feelings."

Which made her feel worse. *But I was just telling the truth* was the silent message.

"I didn't realize how much you didn't like me," she said with a hard little laugh.

Richard looked pained. "I like you, Harriet. I love you. But I must admit I didn't like who you were becoming."

Harriet stared at him. *Am I different enough now?* She almost asked but didn't. Because she didn't want to earn back Richard's love. That didn't feel fair. He was the one who had lied, who had cheated, at least emotionally. He was the one who had turned away first. And if he'd had a problem with who she was *becoming,* he should have damned well said so.

She realized as she sat there in front of her congealing cod that she'd been hoping and holding out for more from him. For a full-on, proper grovel. That was what she'd needed tonight, what she craved after everything she'd endured, and instead she's received a truckload of guilt and a single muttered sorry.

No thanks.

Yes, she needed to shoulder some of the blame. She needed to own up to her mistakes. But she didn't need Richard pointing the finger at her and saying how she'd practically driven him to it. Harriet pushed her plate away and then rose from the table. Richard looked up in surprise.

"Where are you going—"

"Home. I think… I think we're done here."

His face paled, his eyes widening. "Done…"

Did she mean *that* done? The question was in his eyes, in her heart. Harriet shook her head. "I don't know, Richard. But this… us… isn't working, is it?" She stumbled on, not actually wanting an answer to that question. "It hasn't been working for a long time. Obviously, since you didn't like who I was becoming."

"I only meant…"

"You never would have gone to Meghan if you had felt you could go to me."

"That might be true, but that doesn't mean things can't be different now."

"Can they? You're living in London and I'm in the Cotswolds. We're both unemployed."

"For now. Harriet, I can get it all back." A light entered Richard's eyes, bright and fierce. "I didn't like all the showy stuff, I admit it. But I want our lives back. The house and the school and even the damn pony. We can get it all back. We can be who we were, only better. I have a few promising leads…"

"You always have a few promising leads." And what happened if one of them finally panned out?

He'd get a job, they'd buy another big house, and then they'd go back to being exactly who they'd been. Richard hadn't liked that Harriet, apparently. Who knew whether he would like the new one? And she didn't even know if there *was* a new one. She had no idea who she was yet, who she could be, when it had all been taken away—the house, the status, the charmed life. She was trying to find out, taking baby steps, and maybe she needed to do that alone.

"I think we need a little space."

"Space?" Richard looked wary. "It's been two months. We've both had loads of space."

"Yes, but it was two months of just coping. A holding pattern, because we both knew this conversation had to happen. And now it has, and I think... I think we should give each other some breathing room. Maybe... make a more finalized arrangement."

Pain flashed across Richard's face. "Are you talking about an actual divorce?"

"I don't know." She wasn't ready to take that big of a step, and yet right now she couldn't imagine getting back together.

There was still too much hurt, too much blame, too many unresolved issues. And at the end of the day, maybe they were just too different.

"I don't know," she said again. "But we need to do something, Richard. Something more permanent. We've been living in limbo these last few months, and it's not good for us or the children."

"And separation or divorce is?"

"I don't know. But do you really think we can get back together that easily?" She was both curious about and dreading the answer.

Richard rubbed a hand over his face. "I don't know."

His weary admission disappointed her, stupidly. Harriet suddenly felt incredibly tired, as if she could curl right up there on the floor and go to sleep. "I need to go home," she said. "We both need to think more about everything, but, in the meantime something more formalized might be good for everyone." And without waiting for him to answer, she turned and made her way through the crowded pub.

Outside the night was peaceful and cool and she walked home slowly, letting her mind empty out. She couldn't think anymore. She certainly couldn't make any decisions.

She went over to Ellie's first to get the kids, who were all piled on the sofa watching a DVD.

Ellie frowned as she opened the door. "You're back early."

"Yep." Harriet couldn't quite summon a smile. "In the end we didn't have a lot to say to each other." And what had been said had been plenty.

"Do you want a little time on your own? The kids can finish watching the DVD. There's still an hour left."

She didn't know what she wanted. Nothing appealed. "Okay," Harriet said after a moment. "Send them back when it finishes."

Back in number two the house was quiet, if not precisely peaceful. Harriet stared at the downstairs for a moment, noticing the wet washing draped over every piece of furniture, the toys crammed into a corner, the DVDs spilling out of their basket. In that moment she hated it all, the smallness and the mess, the sadness of it, *everything.*

Turning away, she reached for her laptop and typed in legal separation.

A few minutes later, she had all the information she needed to file a legal separation with the nearest divorce court. It cost three hundred and sixty-five pounds, an amount that was nothing to sneeze at. But worth it, perhaps, if it meant she could start figuring her life out. Figuring herself out. She printed out the documents and filled them in with a grim sense of purpose.

It was nearly nine and her stomach rumbled. Harriet went into the kitchen to make the ultimate comfort food, cheese on toast. She reached up for a plate and the teetering pile of Swedish stoneware serving dishes and platters on top of the cupboard shifted and then, seeming in slow motion, started to topple.

Harriet had a split second to decide whether to try to catch as many of the dishes as she could or get out of the way. She got out of the way, and watched as two platters and three serving dishes toppled to the floor and shattered with an almighty crash. She took a deep breath, her heart thudding from the near-miss. Those dishes had cost about eighty pounds each, if she remembered correctly.

She turned back to the cupboard and looked at the stacks of plates and bowls and cups. She couldn't remember how much each piece cost, she hadn't cared when she'd bought the set two years ago, but now she had a sudden, clear memory of Richard looking at the credit card bill.

"Fifteen hundred pounds at the Burford Garden Centre? What on earth did you buy?"

"Dishes," Harriet had replied with a shrug.

She'd spent fifteen hundred pounds on a new set of kitchen dishes. Because Sophie Bryce-Jones had a similar set, and Swedish stoneware was *on trend*.

She reached for a plate and then, without even thinking what she was doing, she hurled it to the ground where it shattered with a satisfyingly loud crash. Then she threw another one. She should stop. She should really stop, because these dishes were expensive and she was making a mess and, on a more practical note, they wouldn't have anything to eat off tomorrow.

But she didn't stop. She hurled every plate, cup, and bowl to the floor, rejoicing in each resounding crash, the sheer, senseless destruction of it, because at least she was in control of this one disaster. And then there were no more dishes to break and she was surrounded by broken stoneware. She let out a long breath and stared in appalled realization at what she'd done.

"Mum?"

Harriet looked up, even more appalled, to see her three children standing in the doorway, staring down at the mess of broken dishes around her. Chloe stuck her thumb in her mouth. Mallory folded her arms.

"Can I break something?" William asked.

Chapter Ten

HARRIET WOKE UP the next morning feeling hungover even though she hadn't even finished her one glass of wine at the pub. She lay in bed as lemony sunshine spilled through the curtains and felt as if she had a stone in her stomach.

Memories from last night played through her mind in an uninspiring reel. The conversation with Richard. The separation documents she'd filled out. The dishes.

There had been no easy way to explain to her children the sudden and hopefully temporary lapse in judgment and perhaps even sanity that she'd experienced in willfully destroying fifteen hundred pounds of Swedish stoneware. So she hadn't.

"Sorry," she said, giving them a tired sort-of smile. "Sorry, loves, I'm so sorry. I was just being... stupid."

"You're not meant to say the s-word," Chloe said, and Harriet smiled properly.

"No, no, absolutely, you're right."

"That is so not the s-word," Mallory said in disgust.

"What is, then?"

Thankfully Mallory just shook her head. Harriet stepped around all the broken dishes, the shards and fragments littering the floor, to give them all quick hugs; Mallory didn't even squirm.

"I'll clean it up tomorrow," Harriet said. Her children still looked rather nonplussed. "Everything's all right," she assured them. "I'm fine. Daddy's fine. I just…" She gazed down at the dishes. "I didn't really like these dishes."

"That doesn't mean you should break them," Chloe said, speaking around her thumb, and Harriet nodded in vigorous agreement.

"No, it does not. It most certainly does not."

She swept the mess into an untidy heap and told the children she'd clean it up in the morning. Then she'd chivvied them all up to bed and fallen into her own, as heartsick as she'd ever been and completely exhausted.

Now she lay in bed and wondered how she could get up and drag herself through another day. She kept replaying the conversation with Richard in her mind. The way he'd basically said he didn't like her anymore. The emotional affair—because what else was it, really?—he'd been having with Meghan. The fact that she could no longer see a way ahead, at least not an easy one. Even if she forgave Richard for Meghan, did he want to be with her? He seemed more fixated on making it all right with their financial situation than their marriage, but then she'd felt the same way.

Because maybe their marriage couldn't be fixed.

Harriet turned onto her side, tucking her knees up to her chest and closing her eyes. Perhaps she'd just stay in bed for the rest of her life. Chloe would bring her food. Mallory could do the laundry.

But no, the familiar thud and thump of William catapulting himself out of bed forced her downstairs. She needed to clean up all the broken pottery before someone sliced open an artery.

But when she came downstairs, still in her pajamas and with a serious case of bedhead, the broken dishes had all been swept up. The kitchen was completely clean. Harriet blinked at the pristine space in surprise. Then she saw Mallory out in the garden, sitting hunched on the steps, arms wrapped around her knees, and Harriet opened the French windows and stepped out into the sunshine.

"Hey."

Mallory looked up, her expression a little guarded. "Hey."

"Did you clean up the broken dishes?"

"Yeah." Mallory looked away, her hair sliding into her eyes.

"Thank you." Harriet was quiet for a moment, trying to gauge her daughter's mood as well as her own. "That was really kind of you. I'm sorry about all that." She nodded back towards the house. "The dishes."

"Yeah, I couldn't have any cereal because we don't have

any bowls. Or anything." There was the tiniest lilt of humor to Mallory's voice that made Harriet smile, despite the dishes. Despite everything.

"I'll buy some new ones. Cheaper ones."

"I never liked those ones, anyway. They always looked dirty."

Harriet laughed, because now that she thought about it, Mallory was right. The dishes were a greenish brown that *did* look dirty. "You can help me pick out the new ones if you want."

"Okay." They were both silent, the air full of birdsong and with a hint of warmth, the fresh earth smell of spring. Then Mallory asked, "So you and Dad aren't getting back together?"

Harriet tensed. "Why do you ask that?"

"The broken dishes kind of gave it away, Mum."

Harriet sighed and sat down on the steps next to Mallory. "I don't know, Mallory. I really don't know what's going to happen. Nothing feels simple at the moment."

Mallory nodded slowly. "Well, it could be worse, I guess."

"Could it?" Harriet let out a sad, little laugh. "Sometimes I feel like you got the worst deal. No pony, no Ellerton…"

"I was kind of done with the pony. And as for Ellerton…" Mallory shrugged. "Lea Comp might not be so bad."

Harriet had to keep herself from doing a double take. *Who are you and what have you done with my daughter?*

"I'm glad you think so," she finally said. "Really glad. I know it hasn't been easy."

"It's not like the Ellerton girls were really my friends, anyway." Mallory schooled her face into a determinedly bored expression as she kicked at the grass with one foot. "So it seems, anyway."

"Did you lose your friends because of this, Mallory?" Harriet asked quietly. It was what she'd been afraid of. Chloe and William had been fine; their friends hadn't even noticed, not really. Boys still tackled each other and played football and Chloe and her friends barely knew what money was.

But Mallory... all those in-girls she'd been pals with. All those rich, tanned, blonde girls who were going to Ellerton next year, who linked arms and bent their heads together and looked down on everyone else. Mallory had been popular, and if Harriet was painfully honest, she'd been glad and even a little bit proud that her daughter's experience of school was so different from her own.

"Not all of them," Mallory answered after a moment. "Not everyone's like that. But yeah, some. When they learned I wasn't going to Ellerton... and the rest." She bit her lip, her gaze turning shadowed.

Harriet longed to pull her daughter into a hug but she knew how prickly Mallory seemed. How prickly Mallory always seemed.

"It's my own fault, though," Mallory said with an attempt at a shrug. "So I can't really get angry with them."

"How," Harriet asked, an ache in her throat, "is any of this your own fault?"

Mallory didn't look at her as she answered. "Because I acted like I was all that and then when I wasn't..." She shrugged, still not meeting Harriet's eyes. "They were just waiting for me to fall, weren't they? And I probably would have done the same if it had been someone else." She let out a shaky laugh. "You know? We were all friends but we also kinda... weren't."

I know the feeling. Harriet didn't say the words. This was about Mallory, not her. "But not everyone, you said?" she asked. "Not everyone was—is—like that?"

"No, not everyone." Mallory gave her one of her usual looks and rolled her eyes, making Harriet smile. Even now her daughter had spirit. Strength. "I'm not a complete loser, Mum."

"Okay. Good to know." Harriet paused, wondering how much to say. How much more emotional Mallory was willing to go. Then she decided to take the plunge and blurted, "But you know, that's pretty much what I was, back in secondary school."

Mallory's baby-blue eyes widened almost comically. "What?"

"I was a loser. A nerd. What have you. I had awful teeth and frizzy hair and I was terribly shy. School was kind of a misery for quite a while." She laughed a little, even though the memory still stung, if only a bit.

"So you mean you didn't have any friends at all?" Mallory sounded both fascinated and horrified.

"I had a few," Harriet allowed. "But we weren't together by choice. It was more like we were survivors of a shipwreck. The lowest on the totem pole that is secondary school, if you know what I mean."

"And so what happened?" Mallory's eyes narrowed. "Because that didn't last, right? I mean, your hair's not frizzy anymore, and you have, like, mum friends."

"I got my hair straightened and I also got braces and when I went to uni I decided to be a new person." She'd still had that debilitating shyness, but then she'd met Richard, and she'd started to grow into herself, at least a little, and then… well, then she'd met Sophie. And she'd finally felt like one of the popular girls, to her shame. "The whole experience made me realize how shallow people can be. How you can be judged lacking solely because of your looks, or just because you don't have the right shirt or shoes or even pen. There were these silver glitter pens that were big in primary school and I didn't have one. Ever."

Mallory gave her a disbelieving look. "So you're saying you were a loser because you didn't have the right kind of pen?"

"No, I'm saying those things matter to a lot of people and I wish they didn't. I hate that people don't even give you a chance sometimes." Harriet sighed. "It all kind of sucks."

And she felt as if she were experiencing it all again, in a

way. She'd thought she'd figured out who she was and what she wanted a long time ago. She'd gone to uni determined not to be overlooked, but also just as determined not to overlook anyone. She knew what it was like to be on both sides. And yet, somehow, in the midst of everything, she'd forgotten what that other side looked like. Felt like.

She'd become so caught up in money and house and status she'd lost sight of the old Harriet, the real Harriet. The Harriet Richard had fallen in love with, back during those heady university days, when they'd stayed up half the night drinking cheap wine and setting the world to rights.

She'd been so thrilled at being one of the popular girls. Being *in*. And that had started to matter more than anything else, along with having the right house, car, clothes, everything. The right life.

And Richard, it seemed, had noticed. Anger still burned at the way he'd blamed her. Maybe she'd become a different person, but so had he—working all the time, obsessed with his job, turning to sexy Meghan. Why couldn't he see his own fault as well as hers?

"Mum?" Harriet blinked the world back into focus, and saw Mallory giving her a funny, lopsided sort of smile. "It's going to be all right."

The fact that her eleven-year-old daughter was the one to reassure her made Harriet feel a rush of love, gratitude, and guilt all bundled together. Motherhood, in a nutshell.

"Thanks, love," she said, and with a shrug Mallory rose

from the steps and headed inside.

As she slipped through the doors, Harriet heard William's bellow of outrage. "There are no bowls for my cereal!"

A WEEK LATER Harriet stood by the school gate as a balmy breeze ruffled her hair. It was the last day of term, and spring had come just in time for the holidays. Over the last week daffodils and tulips had exploded into bloom, and the cherry trees lining the lane into Willoughby Close were dripping with giant pink puffballs of blossom.

After the seemingly endless winter, when absolutely everything in her life had felt cold and dark, Harriet welcomed the change. The children did as well; William had torn up a good part of the garden kicking his football, taking full advantage of the lighter evenings. Even Mallory seemed less prone to moaning, and had sloped over to Abby's several evenings this week. Harriet didn't ask what they did; she was just glad her daughter was connecting with someone.

They were more than surviving, if only just, and for that she was grateful. A little over two months on from her personal ground zero and they were making it. Looking ahead, even. Harriet had taken the plunge and, as Ellie had encouraged, sent her CV off to the academic publishing house in Oxford. She hadn't heard anything, and suspected she might very well never hear, but simply sending it out had been a step for her. An important step.

Ellie had taken a step too, and gone up to Yorkshire in search of Oliver. Abby had stayed at theirs and she and Mallory had spent the entire weekend closeted in Mallory's room, giggling. Ellie had come back grinning from ear to ear, and she and Oliver were now a firm item.

Harriet told herself she was not the tiniest bit envious, not at all. No, she was just lonely. After fourteen years of married life, living as a singleton again was hard. The empty bed, the long, lonely nights, the lack of a proper grownup to talk to or to be able to hand off a kid when she were about to blow a gasket.

She missed Richard simply as another adult in the house, as much as she missed Richard her husband. Her friend. But she tried not to miss Richard-her-husband too much, because he obviously didn't miss her in the same way.

She had, after some deliberation, taken the plunge and sent off the legal separation documents to court; when she'd told Richard he'd been tight-lipped and silent, simply giving a nod. Harriet had fought the urge to shake him by the shoulders and say, *What? What objection could you possibly have, when you're still seeing sexy Meghan and you told me you didn't like me very much anyway?*

The children had accepted it stoically; it wasn't really much change from the current usual, and Harriet had gone to great lengths to explain how this wasn't a divorce, wasn't permanent. Baby steps for all of them.

She and Richard had agreed on an arrangement of him

coming to Willoughby Close twice a week—on Tuesday nights, when he took them out for pizza, and Saturdays, when he spent the day with them. Even though it all seemed grown-up and reasonable, it still felt like a rather miserable arrangement, and she found herself both dreading and looking forward to Tuesdays and Saturdays in equal measure.

Richard always asked how she was and seemed as if he really wanted to know the answer, but then he'd look away and she thought about the fact that he was still friends with Meghan, still going on about his promising leads, and she felt like they'd never make up old ground. Never find a way to meet in the middle. She didn't even know where the middle was, or what it might look like.

When he'd dropped them off last Saturday, he'd asked to have the children for one week of the Easter holidays, shocking her.

"Where will you take them?" she asked, thinking of his small studio in London.

"I'll take them up to Mum and Dad's." His parents lived in a rambling Georgian farmhouse in Norfolk, near the sea. The children would love it, they always did, and Harriet wouldn't be part of it at all.

"All right, then," she said because she couldn't exactly say no.

She couldn't invite herself along either, and she didn't even want to. She didn't know what she wanted. She never seemed to, when it came to Richard. She wanted to stop feeling hurt, but that one was harder to come by.

"Should be fun," she added with an attempt at brightness and Richard gave her one of his old lopsided smiles.

"Yes, they always like it up there, don't they? Remember when we used to spend the whole day at the beach with them? They never got tired of it—building sandcastles, drippy ice creams, the lot."

"Yes." She remembered gritty sand in the sandwiches, and lugging tons of kit the half-mile walk to the beach, and trying to rock a baby to sleep while crouching under a sun shade. But, despite all that, right now it all possessed a rose-tinted glow. It *had* been fun. Crazy, exhausting, overwhelming, but fun. And she missed it.

She thought about taking the children to her parents for the second week of the holidays, but her mum and dad's semidetached on a slightly dilapidated housing estate was a far cry from Richard's parents' idyll by the beach. It wouldn't go well to throw them up in stark contrast, one week after another. The children would just complain.

"Have you told your parents?" she asked, curious. "About... well, everything?"

Richard's expression turned guarded. "I've told them about losing my job, of course," he said. "You've told yours, haven't you?"

Harriet waited a moment too long to say anything, and a look she couldn't quite decipher flashed across Richard's face before he turned away to unlock his car. "You really are ashamed, aren't you?" he said in a low voice, and Harriet went rigid with shock.

"Ashamed? Why should I be ashamed?" she snapped, still stung from their discussion at The Drowned Sailor. "I'm not the one who did anything."

"Exactly," Richard said, and got into the car.

She hadn't meant it quite like that, but somehow the bitterness kept seeping out, like acid from an old battery, corrosive, toxic. Maybe if he'd cut all ties with Meghan, maybe if he admitted he was to blame too…

Maybe if she just finally moved on.

Now, standing at the school gate waiting for her children to tumble out, liberated for an entire two weeks, Harriet tried to banish all the worries and uncertainties tumbling around in her mind.

On the plus side, she had an entire week to herself, something she hadn't had in just about ever. Certainly not since she'd become a mother. She almost didn't know what she'd do with herself. Almost.

Harriet had vague visions of splurging on a spa day, sleeping in, going for coffee with Ellie. Lovely long lie-ins and a proper sort out of the house. If she was feeling really motivated, she'd brave the storage unit in Witney that held the last of their boxes of stuff and a few bits of furniture she hadn't been able to bear to give away. Since the storage unit cost a fair bit of money to rent, it made sense to empty the thing.

"Mummy!" Chloe came flying out, ringlets bouncing in a blond halo around her flushed face. "No school for two weeks, and we're going to Daddy's!"

"Granny and Grandad's, actually," Harriet corrected with a small smile.

She felt a twinge of unease that her youngest child had adapted so quickly to having separate abodes for her mother and father. Was divorce that easy? Children adjusted, they moved on. Simple. It didn't feel that easy for Harriet. Not yet.

"It's going to be so boring there." Mallory huffed as she joined them at the infants' entrance, flipping her hair behind her shoulder and perfecting the sulky look that seemed just a little too put on.

"You love it at Granny and Grandad's," Harriet answered mildly.

There were ponies in the field next to the house, and her in-laws were not rigorous about enforcing screen time limitations or sugar intake. In other words, kid heaven.

"When I was six," Mallory replied, flipping her hair yet again. "They don't even have mobile phone reception."

"Might be a good thing," Harriet murmured.

Mallory's attitude definitely seemed a little suspect, especially since she'd overheard her and Abby talking about their favorite Barbies a few nights ago. Admittedly it had been in a reminiscing sort of way, but still. It was reassuring to think that Mallory's sulky teen attitude might only be skin-deep.

William came catapulting towards them, trailing school books and papers that Harriet stooped to pick up while he attempted to put Chloe, who promptly screeched, into a headlock. Harriet rolled her eyes at their theatrics as she started shepherding them along.

"Maybe you should teach Chloe how to get out of a head lock, William," she suggested. "More challenge."

William looked intrigued by that idea, as did Chloe, and Harriet exchanged a smile with Mallory.

"Harriet."

She tensed at the sound of Sophie's voice. They hadn't talked properly in over a month, although Sophie had subjected her to several overly tragic looks and talon-edged hand squeezes in the school yard, asking in a sotto voce, "How *are* you?" as if Harriet must be suffering very terribly.

"Sophie," she said now, forcing a smile. There was a glitter in her ex-friend's eyes that she didn't like.

"Have you *heard?*" Sophie asked, her voice carrying across the still-heaving school yard.

Several mothers shot looks in their direction, and Harriet had the prickly, uncomfortable feeling that everyone already knew what this conversation was about, that it had somehow been staged, a drama about to enfold and she was the unfortunate main actor.

"Heard what?" she asked dutifully, because what other response was there?

"The Old Rectory," Sophie said, "your old house." As if

Harriet didn't know. "It's been bought."

"Has it?" She'd avoided that part of the village, hadn't wanted to see her empty home with the awful foreclosure sign in front of it. She'd known about the open house, thanks to Sophie, but she'd deliberately tried not to find out about any auction or sale.

Now she glanced at Mallory's stony expression and Chloe's confused face and wished this conversation could have happened anywhere else, at any other time.

"I suppose it was bound to happen," she said, trying to make her voice sound normal rather than strangled.

Her chest felt tight. Even after all this time, it hurt to think of her house belonging to someone else. Her house, her happy memories, her life.

"Do you know who bought it?" Sophie wasn't even hiding her relish.

Harriet felt a flash of disgust, and even pity, for how obvious her old friend was. Did she realize? Or perhaps she simply didn't care. Perhaps Harriet had become so unimportant that Sophie could be obvious and it didn't matter.

"No, I obviously don't," she answered, her tone taking on a distinct edge, "since I didn't even know it was sold." Sophie smiled, and Harriet realized she was winding her up on purpose. "Who is it, then?" she asked because Sophie wouldn't leave Harriet alone until she'd delivered this coup de grâce.

"Cheryl Dennison." Sophie practically crowed.

Cheryl Dennison, the latest London transplant to Wychwood-on-Lea, an uppity city girl, who drove far too fast down the high street, and flashed her bling and had two whiny and clearly spoiled children. Other mothers discreetly rolled their eyes at Cheryl; Harriet had, once upon a time. Now she didn't feel she had the right to roll her eyes at anyone.

"How very nice for her," she managed. "Now we really need to get on. Richard's picking up the children at five."

Sophie's eyes rounded, her mouth curving in transparent delight. "Are you two not together anymore?"

Harriet mentally cursed herself for making such a stupid slip. She'd forgotten she was maintaining the fiction that she and Richard weren't separated; he was simply spending more time in London to look for a job... which was technically true.

"I've got to go," she said.

Sophie didn't deserve any explanations. Grabbing Chloe's hand, she hurried from the school yard. No one spoke until they were back at Willoughby Close, the privacy of the sweeping drive and sheltered courtyard feeling like a balm.

Harriet breathed a big sigh of relief as she unlocked the front door, grateful to be home. Yes, home, even if she hadn't asked for any of this. Even if she still had no idea what the future looked like.

"So this isn't temporary." Mallory's voice was both flat

and accusing. "Like you said." Harriet tensed and then turned.

"I said I hoped, Mallory," she said carefully. "I hoped. I hated losing our house. Our home. But we couldn't afford it and the bank chose to auction it off. You knew that."

And the Dennisons had bought it. She pictured Cheryl decorating everything in gilt and leather and chrome and mentally shuddered.

"You mean we're not going back?" Chloe sounded confused, with the threat of tears.

"No, of course we're not, stupid," Mallory snarled. "Didn't you hear anything? The stupid Dennisons bought *our* house." And without waiting for a reply she stormed upstairs.

Cue door slamming, rafters shaking. Harriet let out a long, weary sigh. She should have prepared her children better for this moment. For a lot of moments like this. But she'd been so overwhelmed with keeping herself together that she hadn't. She hadn't wanted to disappoint or hurt them, had still been hoping that they could claw back some of their old life back. Richard was still so intent on getting a new job, but even if he did…

Their old life was gone. They could never go back, not really, not even if they moved into Wychwood House and Mallory went to Ellerton and everything else. It would still be different. They would be different. And there was nothing she could do about that.

"Mummy." Chloe tugged on her sleeve. "Are we not going back? I thought we were going back. I thought we were just staying here for a little while, until Daddy got a job again."

Harriet managed a smile and then drew Chloe to the sofa, hauling her onto her lap in a way she hadn't in a long time. "No, darling, I'm sorry." She pressed her cheek against Chloe's soft hair and closed her eyes. "We're not going back. Not to our old house, anyway."

Chloe stuck her thumb in her mouth and burrowed her head, rather painfully, into Harriet's chest. She gathered her more closely against her, rocking her a little as if she were a baby. "I'm sorry," she whispered against Chloe's hair. "I'm sorry, but we can be happy here, can't we?" She knew she was asking herself as much as she was asking her daughter. Chloe just burrowed harder.

A gust of air made her look up, blinking—William had thrown open the French doors and was now kicking his football against the wall with savage intensity, probably the best thing for him.

Sighing, Harriet leaned back against the sofa. "This place isn't so bad, is it?" she asked Chloe.

"It's not home," Chloe said, sounding tragic, and Harriet kissed the top of her head.

"Then perhaps we need to make it home."

"How?"

"Well… we could plant some things in the garden. We

could paint." Every room in the house was painted a bright, clean white, which was a bit boring and sterile.

"Can I have elephants on my walls?" Chloe asked eagerly and Harriet was about to demur when she thought suddenly, why not? *Why the hell not?*

"Of course you can. We'll paint them ourselves." And they would probably look like great gray blobs, but who cared? *Who cared?*

Chloe's eyes narrowed. "Why wasn't I allowed elephants in our old house?" she asked, and Harriet thought of Chloe's old room, with its high ceiling and sashed windows and fireplace. Harriet had had the walls painted pale pink and the curtains and upholstery done in matching pink gingham. Very expensive pink gingham, as she recalled. The interior designer she'd hired had insisted it was just the thing. She'd said no to elephants because they hadn't matched the decorating scheme, which seemed both absurd and sad now.

"Things are different now," she told Chloe.

In all sorts of ways. Bad, yes, but also, maybe, just maybe, good.

By the time she'd appeased Chloe, Richard was almost due, and Harriet spent the next twenty minutes hurrying around, making sure suitcases were packed, devices charged, and the crucial soft toys packed for Chloe's nighttime ritual of surrounding herself with them. After kicking the ball for twenty minutes William had worked out his anger and most of his energy, and Mallory was looking surprisingly calm.

Maybe it would all be okay. At least, it could be okay. Eventually.

Still Harriet wondered how Richard would cope with the three of them on his own. Admittedly his parents would be around, but her in-laws tended to retire from grand-parenting duties after supper, preferring to relax in the kid-free sitting room with a stiff drink. Not that she could blame them, really, but would Richard manage? Harriet couldn't remember the last time he'd done a complete bedtime, from bath to stories to the long, long goodnight.

He'd learn, she supposed. He'd survive. She didn't have to worry about it, anyway, even though she felt anxious about leaving the children when they'd just learned about the house.

Then Richard rang the doorbell and Harriet didn't have time to worry anymore. She called William in from the garden and, in exasperation, ordered him to change his trousers; he was filthy with mud.

Blowing out a breath and patting her hair to check its frizz levels, she opened the door. The sight of Richard standing there, dark hair a little mussed, uncertain smile spreading across his face like sunshine breaking through the clouds, made her heart flip over with both sorrow and longing, even now. She was going to have to do something about that. Very soon.

"Hey." Harriet stepped out of the way so Richard could come in. "I'm afraid no one's in the best of moods."

"Oh?" He aimed a smile at Mallory and Chloe, who were both standing by the stairs.

Mallory was doing her best to look bored and Chloe was clutching an armful of cuddly toys Harriet had forbidden her to take. One carrier bag of stuffed animals was surely enough.

"It's the first day of the holidays and the sun is shining," Richard said. "No one's allowed to be grumpy then."

Mallory scowled and Chloe thrust the bag of soft toys towards her father. "Can I take these?"

"Sure you can, sweetheart."

William thundered down the stairs having changed his trousers but not his socks, and the next few minutes of commotion kept Harriet from having to make chitchat.

Richard, however, wasn't so easily put off. As the children loaded their stuff in his car—he'd traded in his Beamer for an old estate he kept parked at the train station in Charlbury—he turned to her.

"What are you going to do this week?"

"Relax, mostly," Harriet answered. "And sort out the storage unit if I'm feeling up to it."

"By yourself the whole time?"

"Yes, and looking forward to it," Harriet said firmly. The last thing she wanted was Richard feeling sorry for her. "You don't know what it's like, managing these three by yourself all the time." She tried to moderate the faint note of accusation in her voice and failed.

"I guess I will now," Richard said with deliberate mildness. "For a week, at least." The kids were now squabbling about who got to sit in the front seat, but Richard was ignoring them, his gaze intent on her. Harriet had forgotten how serious he could look, as if she was the most important thing in the world in that moment. It had been a long time since she'd felt important.

"I'm sorry about the other week," he said. "At the pub. I handled that all wrong. I didn't mean to sound as if I was blaming you."

Harriet swallowed. "This isn't the time, Richard."

"It's never the time."

"That's because we have three kids. Life's busy."

"You could come with us," he said suddenly. "If you wanted."

Shock had her speechless for a few seconds. Come with them? To his parents' house? When he'd had an affair, emotional or otherwise, and when they'd been living apart for over a month? When he didn't even like her anymore?

And yet a part of her, a larger part than she would have liked, was tempted. Tempted to climb in the front seat and act as if they were a normal family again. A normal couple. To sweep the last three months under the rug and start over. But that would only be pretending, and she didn't think she could pretend for that long. And in any case, she'd already realized that they couldn't go back. None of them could.

"I don't think so," Harriet said, and took a step back for

good measure. "But thanks anyway. It's... it's a nice thought."

"Okay." Richard nodded, looking wistful, and Harriet didn't know whether she wanted to shake him or throw her arms around him. *Make up your damn mind! One minute you don't like who I've become and the next you're looking like you lost your best friend. Which is it?*

"Da-ad," Mallory called. "I'm the oldest so I get the front, right?"

"You can take turns," Richard replied equably. "It's one hundred and sixty-five miles to Granny and Grandad's, so you can each sit in the front for fifty-five miles."

"Even Chloe?" Mallory demanded, outraged, and Richard gave Harriet one last wistful smile before turning towards the kids and the car.

"Even Chloe."

Harriet had forgotten how good he could be with the children. He diffused an argument with seemingly effortless ease, never losing his temper or getting ratty the way she did. It was something she'd always admired, but right now she found it somewhat annoying. She didn't want confused feelings when it came to Richard. She wanted to move on. She needed to, for her own sanity's sake. Because the other option was to keep looking back, and wishing for things that weren't happening.

She stood by the door while they all got in the car, and then Richard honked the horn once, rolling down the window to wave as he headed down the drive.

Harriet stood in the courtyard for a moment more. It felt very empty, with Ellie and Abby gone to Manchester for the weekend, and number three and four still unoccupied. It felt lonely. A warm breeze blew over her and she told herself to enjoy this, the peace and solitude and the lovely, lovely quiet.

But as Harriet went back into the house all she felt was the emptiness.

Chapter Eleven

Harriet spent Friday night bingeing on a DVD box set and drinking wine, trying to stave off loneliness. She couldn't believe she actually missed the constant squabbling, Mallory's huffy sighs, William's constant energy, but she did. She missed Mallory's persistent eye rolls, and William's relentless wrestling, and Chloe's snuggles. She missed it all.

She tried to sleep in on Saturday morning but by eight o'clock she gave up and went downstairs, making herself a coffee and taking it out into the garden. It was a lovely spring morning, all lemony light and fresh, dewy grass—sadly they didn't have any garden furniture. The enormous wooden set from the Old Rectory had been sold along with everything else, but as she perched on the steps by the French windows, Harriet wished they'd kept a few things. Unfortunately in late January, with everything bleak and frozen, she hadn't considered that she might one day need garden furniture. That she might want it.

She sipped her coffee and tried to ignore the fact that her

bum was getting wet, wondering if she could rouse herself to do some gardening or if she should wait until the children returned so they could do it all together, a proper family activity with Chloe scattering seeds willy-nilly, William trampling over everything, and Mallory complaining the whole while. She smiled at the thought.

Eventually, she went inside and showered, and then spent the next few hours tidying up and doing laundry. By lunchtime she was ready for a change of scene, and she pulled on her welly boots and headed out, away from Willoughby Manor, towards the Lea River.

She hadn't explored much of the immediate area since moving to Willoughby Close, but when the children had been small she'd taken them for walks along the river; she had a distinct memory of William splashing in the shallows and getting soaked while she stood on the banks, Chloe strapped to her chest in a baby carrier, feeling thoroughly fed up.

Now she picked her way along the muddy footpath, enjoying the stillness, the twitter of birdsong and the gentle quacks of a few ducks paddling happy in the water. It was perfectly peaceful, and Harriet tilted her head to the sunlight, wanting only to enjoy this moment to the full. To live in the present, not the mirey past or the uncertain future.

She ended up at the top of the high street, above the school, having crossed the river on a rickety little footbridge she'd forgotten existed. Wychwood-on-Lea had emptied out over the holidays as people went in search of sunshine elsewhere, and so she meandered down the high street, almost feeling like a tourist in her own town.

On impulse she popped into the teashop; it felt like a lifetime ago when she's stumbled in there to avoid a couple of gossipy mums. Olivia was standing at the till, and she smiled as Harriet came in.

"Hello! I haven't seen you in a while."

"I know." Harriet smiled back as she shed her jacket. "Sorry, I'm tracking mud in, aren't I? You are open, I hope?"

"Yes, absolutely."

"Lovely." Harriet sat down at one of the spindly little tables and perused the laminated menu that had been stuck between the salt and pepper shakers. "I'll have…" She was about to order the sensible carrot and coriander soup when she changed her mind. This was her holiday, after all. "I'll have the full cream tea, please."

Olivia grinned. "Coming right up."

Harriet sat back in her chair, feeling strangely satisfied with her decision. Gone were the days of gym workouts and protein shakes and no desserts, the endless chasing after some ideal that she never quite managed to attain. She might have a bit of a poochy tummy, but at least she didn't have to starve herself in order to replicate the thin, ropy look of the well-worked out mum.

Sitting there enjoying the sunshine she realized she hadn't been aware of how she'd changed over the last few years, only the sense that she always had to keep up—whether it was workouts, diet, clothes, cars, or childrearing. Everything had turned into a competition—often silent, implicit, but nevertheless threatening and toxic. Was that thanks to friends like Sophie, or to her own ambition to be part of the in-set? To feel important? Was that what Richard hadn't liked?

If she was different now, would he love her again? Did she want to take that risk?

Olivia brought her the cream tea—two scones piled with cream and jam, a pot of tea and a cup, and plenty of milk and sugar.

"Thank you," Harriet said, and dug in.

"You seem in a better mood this time," Olivia offered a little while later, as Harriet polished off her second scone, feeling quite replete.

"Do I?" Harriet let out a laugh and then covered her mouth as a little burp escaped her. "I suppose I am in a better mood. Mostly." Which was odd, in a way, because so much in her life was still wrong, or at least uncertain. And yet she was starting to feel surer of who she was, or at least who she could become. Again.

Olivia propped her elbows on the counter. "What does that mean?"

"Well, nothing's really changed," Harriet admitted on a sigh. "Life is still pretty dismal in a lot of ways. But…" She blew out a breath. "I feel better, at least a little. Readier to face whatever comes. I think." She let out a laugh. "That doesn't sound very good at all, does it?"

"Seems pretty decent to me." Olivia shrugged. "Can't ask for more, can you, really?"

"No," Harriet said reflectively. "I suppose not."

She spent the rest of the day cracking on with the housework, and then that evening she finished both the box set and the wine. Loneliness was starting to creep in, like a morning mist, obscuring everything, cold and damp. She missed her kids. Amazingly, already.

Then Richard rung at half past eight, and Harriet fell on the phone like the lifeline it had become. "You could have called before," she said, no hello, and then she winced at how accusatory she sounded. She needed to start building bridges, but she was still finding it so hard. "It would have been nice to know how everyone was," she said in a more moderate tone. "I've been worried."

"They're fine," Richard said. "I'm sorry I didn't call. We were at the beach all day, at Holkham. It's gorgeous out, sunny and warm."

"Is it?" She pictured the endless blue sky, the stretch of near-white sand, the placid sea, and felt a shaft of longing. "And the children are behaving themselves?"

"Yes, more or less." Richard gave a little laugh. "Mallory has some attitude and William has some energy, but it's nothing I can't handle. It's good to be together."

"Oh. Well. Good." Was she disappointed that Richard

seemed to be coping?

Had she wanted him to complain and moan about how difficult everything was, and how on earth Harriet managed it every day? Well, yes. Maybe a little. Maybe a lot. Maybe she wanted to be needed, in this at least, because he damn well hadn't needed her in anything else.

"How have you been?" The note of concern in his voice rubbed her raw. Goodness, but she was prickly.

"I'm fine. I had a very productive day, sorting the house out and then I went for a lovely, long walk and had an enormous cream tea in the village."

"Did you? That's brilliant." Richard sounded genuinely pleased. "Where did you go?"

"That little teashop on the high street. I've always meant to go in there but never did." Except for that one time, when she'd been avoiding the other mums.

"I'm glad you finally found the time. And," Richard continued, "I'm glad you're having a proper rest. You deserve one, after everything."

"Oh." Harriet cleared her throat, unsure how to respond. This was a change from the blame back at the pub. But perhaps she shouldn't judge Richard from that one heated exchange. "Well," she said, for lack of anything better to say.

"Do you want to talk to the children?"

"Yes, please." She spent the next few minutes trying to draw out more than monosyllabic answers from Mallory, and then trying to keep track of Chloe's breathless monologue about everything they'd done since getting in the car yesterday afternoon, starting with the huge bag of wine gums Richard let them eat in the car, the fact that William was very nearly sick because of said wine gums, and that Chloe really didn't like the green ones.

"But after the car journey," Harriet said patiently. "How are things in Norfolk? Did you enjoy the beach at Holkham?"

"Oh, yes," Chloe said, and then launched into another long description of the beach and all of its wonders.

Harriet tried to ignore the pang of homesickness she felt at hearing all about it, and wishing she was there. It had only been twenty-four hours and she missed her children rather desperately. She missed Richard too, but she wasn't going to think about that.

By the time she got off the phone with Chloe, the pang had become a physical ache. She had no appetite anymore for either the boxed set or the wine, and she went to bed, curling up on her side, leaving space for Richard even though it had been months since they'd shared a bed and he was nearly two hundred miles away.

The next morning she tackled the garden, raking up dead, damp leaves and pulling weeds in preparation for the fun stuff she planned to do with the children—planting seeds and putting in bedding plants.

It felt good to be outside; the day was warm and balmy, the sun shining down, the birds twittering in the trees.

Stupidly she missed the thwack of William's football against the wall.

"Hey."

Harriet looked up from the patch of elder weed she'd been trying, without much success, to uproot, and saw Ellie smiling over the wall that separated their gardens.

"Hello," Harriet said. "I thought you'd gone up to Manchester."

"We got back this afternoon. A quick trip. I thought you'd all gone, actually. I haven't heard the children at all."

"They really are that noisy, aren't they?"

"I don't mind. It's nice to have some noise, after we'd been on our own here. It felt a bit lonely before."

"Yes, I know what you mean." Harriet straightened, wincing at the crick in her back. She was forty next September and she was feeling it. "I wonder if anyone will ever move into numbers three and four."

"Jace says someone has been looking at number three, at least," Ellie replied. "But he won't tell me any details."

"He's a bit of a dark horse, isn't he?"

"He knows how to be discreet. He wouldn't tell me anything about you before you came except that you were a single mum."

"Ah." Harriet wasn't sure how she felt about that.

"Sorry, should I not have said?"

"No, it's fine." She was a single mum, more or less. "The kids are with Richard though, actually, for the entire week."

Ellie cocked her head. "Is that a good thing?"

"Yes, of course." Harriet spoke a little too quickly. "It's good for them to see him and I could certainly do with a bit of a break." And she'd had her bit, and now she was done.

The realization was galling. It seemed she couldn't be happy either way… with the kids or without them.

"If you're on your own this week, you ought to come out," Ellie said. "We could get a group together—Anna is visiting Colin on the weekend. What if we all had dinner?"

"I'm afraid I don't know Colin and Anna."

"Oh, you'll love them," Ellie assured her. "Colin did the renovations on Willoughby Close, and his girlfriend lives in New York. She stayed here, before anyone moved in, I think. Anyway, I'll try to arrange it."

Ellie seemed so pleased about the idea that Harriet felt she had no choice but to agree—and really, why not? It wasn't as if she had much of a social life anymore. She needed to make some new friends, even if the thought filled her with trepidation.

She spent the rest of the day mucking about the house, trying not to feel lonely. She looked at some nearby spas online, but the treatments she'd once booked without a care in the world now seemed ridiculously expensive.

"Seventy-five pounds for a facial," she exclaimed aloud. "What do they even put on your face? Gold dust?"

When the phone rang she jumped on it, but it wasn't Richard as she'd expected. It was her dad.

"Hello, love," he said, and the familiar, affable sound of his voice had a wave of homesickness crashing over her so hard and fast she felt as if she were drowning, which was strange, because she hadn't been homesick for Birmingham, for her parents, in years.

"Hey, Dad." Her voice sounded small and tight.

"We were just thinking about you, as it's the holidays. We usually come down and see you round Easter, don't we? And I realized we hadn't planned anything because... well, because you've been so busy, I suppose."

She hadn't been that busy. She'd been avoiding her parents because she hadn't wanted to tell them anything. She hadn't even told them she'd moved, for heaven's sake. Just updated the phone number and evaded any questions, not wanting her mother to ferret out any information. Not wanting them to worry or wonder what went wrong, or God help her, to pity her.

"Sorry, Dad," she said now, curling up in a corner of the sofa.

"Don't be sorry, love. But what about if your mum and I come down this week, see the kiddos for a bit? Are you busy? Going skiing or anything like that?"

Skiing. Harriet wondered if they'd ever ski again. "No, we're not going skiing. But... the kids are in Norfolk, with Richard and his parents."

There was a small, telling pause. "Oh," her dad said, "oh, well, then..." Bless him, he didn't want to ask if anything was wrong. That was her dad to a tee—always willing to listen, never pushing. The gentlest man Harriet had ever known, and yet in recent years she'd found both her parents a bit exasperating.

They never changed. They'd lived in the same three bedroom semidetached since they'd been newlyweds, hadn't changed so much as the wallpaper in all that time, as far as Harriet could tell.

She hadn't actually been back to the house in Birmingham in years—probably since before Chloe was born. The place was so tiny and William kicked around so much—the last time they'd gone, he'd torn apart one of her father's little model airplanes, the kind he spent hours putting together and painting. As William had torn the wings off, her father had looked stricken, but he hadn't said a word.

And as for Harriet… she'd been annoyed, she remembered now with a prickling of shame. Not at William, who had only been three, but at her *father*—for having the planes, for strewing them about, for simply being him.

She'd been annoyed with her mother as well, for the way she bustled about, always fussing with lace doilies and little bowls of stale crisps and nuts nobody wanted. Everything about her old home had felt suffocating and small, and as they'd driven away, clearing the sprawl of Birmingham suburbs and traffic, she'd let out a huge sigh, feeling as if she could breathe properly for the first time all weekend.

She'd escaped that life, its cramped limitations, her old,

sad, nerdy self. She'd escaped it—but to what?

"Well," her father said now, "what about you coming here, then? I know it's a long way but we've got the space and if you're kicking about…" He trailed off uncertainly, no doubt because Harriet had not accepted such an invitation in years.

"I'd love to," Harriet said firmly, surprising both of them. Her father let out a little laugh.

"That's settled, then. When can we expect you?"

Harriet left early the next morning, with dew still glittering on the grass. As she drove out of Willoughby Close, she threw a worried glance back at the manor, looking dark and gloomy against a brilliantly blue sky. She hadn't visited Lady Stokeley in a week, and she decided then that she'd visit her as soon as she returned, make sure she was hanging in there.

It was only an hour's drive to the suburban street in Edgbaston where Harriet had spent the first eighteen years of her life. It was strange, driving there by herself—she couldn't remember the last time she'd done so.

An hour-long drive gave her time to reconsider whether she really wanted to come home. Her mother would be anxious, her father droopy-eyed and sad-smiling, and the house would feel as claustrophobic as it ever did. Besides, what would she *do?* She'd lost touch with her few friends from secondary school and the neighborhood was now filled with pensioners like her parents, whose primary interests seemed to be crosswords and gossip.

But no, that was mean. She didn't even know her parents' neighbors. She certainly couldn't say whether they gossiped.

Harriet parked her car on the street in front of her parents' house, and the front door opened before she'd even got out.

Her parents stood framed by the doorway, looking exactly as she'd imagined—her mother's forehead furrowed with concern, her hands twisted in the pinny she wore over her pressed jeans—she ironed everything—and her father giving her that sad-eyed smile, like a basset hound in a checked shirt.

"You made it," he called out, as he always did, and her mother gave her a quick smile before bustling back inside, no doubt to put the kettle on. A cup of tea and a piece of Battenburg cake cured all ills in the Stephenson household.

Harriet gave her father a hug, breathing in the familiar scent of Old Spice and mothballs. Her mother insisted on mothballing every item of clothing in the house. It was practically an extreme sport for her. Harriet had gone through school smelling like she was eighty years old, which had not helped her social status one bit.

But now Harriet breathed in the smell gladly as she pressed her cheek against his shoulder and her father's arms tightened around her in a way they hadn't since she was a little girl. Hugs had been little more than a brushing of bodies for decades, air kisses on occasion.

He stroked her hair, causing a lump to rise in her throat. "You all right, my girl?" he asked softly, and the tenderness in his voice made her want to cry.

"I… I think so," Harriet answered her voice muffled against his shoulder as tears burned under her lids. "I'm trying."

"You know we're always here for you, no matter what?"

"Yes." She did know that, absolutely, and the knowledge humbled her, because she hadn't been there for her parents much at all.

Why had she seen them as an exasperating inconvenience for so long? All right, she knew why—because they *could* be exasperating, with her mother whisking dishes away before she'd taken more than a bite, and her father's obsession with model airplanes, and the worried way they looked at everything. All parents became somewhat exasperating to their children, Harriet suspected, but it still made her feel petty and mean. They loved her. That was all that mattered.

She took a step back, sniffing, and her father stepped aside so she could come in.

By the time she'd gone into the lounge her mother had made tea, and came in with a tray complete with pot, cups, sugar, lemon, milk, and hot water. Harriet sank into the armchair by the gas fire that was still in the atrocious pattern Harriet remembered of large pink cabbage roses.

Her mother pressed a cup of tea in her hands and Harriet took it with murmured thanks. It was milky and sweet, just as she'd liked it as a child.

"Well, then," her father said once they were all seated with their teas. "How can we help?"

The simple practicality of the question, the openness of his expression and the obvious love in her mother's worried face, all conspired together to undo Harriet completely.

"I…" she began, and then found she couldn't say anything more.

With trembling hands she put her teacup and saucer on the table, and with her parents looking on in concern, she burst into tears.

Chapter Twelve

HARRIET WOKE UP to weak sunlight filtering through the pink floral curtains of her childhood bedroom. She rolled onto her back and blinked up at the ceiling with its brown, rabbit-shaped stain from a leak years ago still visible. Nothing, it seemed, had changed—except her own life.

Last night she'd told her parents the bare bones of what had happened over the last few months, omitting, somewhat to her own surprise, any mention of Richard's doings with Meghan. He'd always got along well with her parents, especially her dad—in part because his own was a little remote, the quintessential stiff upper lip always in place.

She couldn't quite understand why she kept such a major part of her life's falling apart to herself, but it didn't feel fair to rubbish Richard's reputation with her parents when he wasn't there to defend himself. And, in any case, what would she say? He had an emotional affair? He kissed someone else? It felt far too complicated for her to tell her parents.

Her parents had been all sympathy, in any case, the perfect mixture of compassionate murmurs and practical questions. When her mother had gone to refresh the tea, her father had taken the opportunity to lower his voice and ask, "Do you need money, Harriet? Because I've got some set aside. Not a large amount, mind, but it might make a difference to you."

"Oh, Dad." Harriet had felt tears threatening again.

Her parents did not have a lot of money. Her mother had been a housewife for her entire adult life and her father had taken voluntary retirement at age fifty-seven when his job in middle management of a large supermarket chain had been cut. Yet she knew his offer was entirely genuine, and that he would go to the bank that very moment if she asked him to.

"We're okay. I'm looking for a job, actually."

"Any luck?"

"No, but I'm still waiting to hear on an application." Not that she'd be holding her breath on that one.

After they'd finished another pot of tea they'd gone to the local pub for lunch, and Harriet had tucked into the very standard fare—a far cry from The Three Pennies' gastro-pub offerings—with gusto. Everything tasted and felt better somehow, even greasy chips.

They spent the afternoon in her parents' tiny garden, and Harriet had found herself noticing and admiring it in a way she hadn't before. It was barely bigger than a postage stamp, but her parents had considered every square inch with care.

There was a veg patch, a rockery, a few rosebushes, and a little apple tree. Harriet had a sudden, piercing memory of her father going to take the bins out and then stooping to carefully pluck a weed from a flower bed. It was a tiny gesture, but one that perfectly encapsulated her father—always trying to improve things in some small way.

They'd had a quiet dinner at home, one of her mother's turgid roasts, with everything boiled to within an inch of its life. Harriet had gone to bed soon after, exhausted and yet strangely happy.

Now she lay in bed and listened to the sounds of her parents moving around downstairs, her father's cheerful, tuneless whistling. She wondered what she would do today. She couldn't stay at her parents for too long; it had been a much-needed respite, coming here, but she wanted to get back to her own life, whatever that looked like. Whatever it was going to look like.

Harriet grabbed her phone on the table next to her bed and sent a quick text to Richard saying where she was. Then she showered, dressed, and headed downstairs to greet her parents.

They were sitting at the little round table in the kitchen, drinking coffee, a toast rack of now-cold toast between them, along with little dishes of marmalade and butter, which made Harriet smile somehow. Everything was exactly as it had always been, and while that had once been irritating, she now found it a comfort. Some things didn't change, and that was a good thing.

"Did you sleep all right, darling?" her mother asked in a too-bright voice that made Harriet suspect they had just been talking about her. Not that she was surprised. She'd offloaded a lot of information on them yesterday.

"Yes, actually, I did." She pulled out a chair and plucked a piece of toast from the rack.

"I can make more..." Her mother protested, already rising from her chair.

Harriet shook her head. "This is fine." And it was. "What are you both doing today?" she asked, and her parents exchanged looks.

"Well... I was going to go to my gardening club," her mother said cautiously. "But since you're here, of course I won't."

"Don't change anything for me—"

"I was going to work on a new model airplane," her father interjected. "You can help me."

Harriet stared at him in surprise. Her father had been making model airplanes since she was a child and she'd never helped him. She'd always found the work too fiddly and, really, what was she supposed to do with the things? She couldn't fly them. She couldn't even play with them; they were too fragile, or so her father had said.

Now Harriet noted her father's seemingly mild expression, yet with a rather unfamiliar determined glint in his eyes.

"Okay," she said as she swallowed her toast. "Sure."

After she'd helped clear the breakfast dishes away, she followed her father up to the third bedroom which he'd turned into a little workshop. Harriet stood in front of a glass-fronted display case filled with dozens of planes.

"Wow, you've made a lot," she said.

"And yet I'm always excited to start another. Look at this beauty." He tapped the box on the table he'd set up, and Harriet glanced down at it somewhat dubiously.

"The Bristol Beaufighter," she read.

"Developed over eight months using sections of the earlier Bristol Beaufort. It had a more powerful engine, along with some other modifications."

"Right," Harriet said, half-wondering why her father was sharing all this. As if she had the first clue about model airplanes.

"It was a night bomber," he continued as he carefully opened the box. "The modifications made to it allowed it to carry bombs, torpedoes, rockets, cannons, and machine guns."

"Right," Harriet said again, because she couldn't think of anything else to say.

Her father was emptying out the contents of the box— what looked like a thousand little pieces and the tiniest screwdriver Harriet had seen.

"How long does it take you to put one of those together?" she asked, and her father looked up with a boyish smile.

"Hours," he said happily. "Hours and hours."

Harriet sat and watched in silence as her father began to screw tiny bits together. Occasionally he'd asked her to look for a piece he couldn't find, describing it in terms of color or shape. Very occasionally Harriet actually found it.

Her father worked mostly in silence, but once in a while he would offer some titbit of information—how the bomber was so much improved from its original, how mechanics had taken the best bits of the first plane and adapted it to new challenges and situations.

It took about an hour of this for the penny to drop. Here was her father's life lesson—about adapting to difficult circumstances, about using the best parts of yourself to learn and change and grow. He didn't talk about anything but the plane, but Harriet got it.

A few months ago, she would have been fairly exasperated, finding the whole thing rather ridiculously twee and sentimental and a bit boring, but now she just smiled and briefly touched his arm.

"That's pretty amazing, Dad," she said quietly, and he looked up from the barely-started plane and gave her a smile of such love that Harriet's heart squeezed painfully in her chest.

That evening she took her mum and dad out to dinner, brushing aside their concerns that she couldn't afford it—she couldn't, not really, but some things were more important than money, or the lack of it. They ate at an Italian place near the city center that wasn't at all posh but which her parents marveled at all the same, exclaiming over the antipasti and the standard house wine.

Harriet's heart was full of love as well as a deep affection she couldn't remember ever having before for them, at least not as an adult. For how long has she turned her nose up, discreetly, at her parents' small ways? Now she felt a tender sort of protectiveness, along with a fierce pride. They'd had had some difficult times—her father's redundancy, a late miscarriage when she was a preteen and pretty clueless. But they'd soldiered on, determined to find happiness in the small things, and so would she.

Harriet drove back to Wychwood-on-Lea the next morning, full of determination. She stopped at a DIY store in Chipping Norton and bought a dozen paint samples, a bag of compost, a tray of bedding plants, and several packets of seeds.

She spent the afternoon dabbing paint samples on various walls, trying to decide between a sunny yellow and a cheerful blue—no modish neutral colors she'd paid a fortune for from Farrow & Ball now.

In the late afternoon, she decided to head up to Willoughby Manor to check on Lady Stokeley. It had been nearly a month since she'd driven her to Oxford for her tests, and Harriet still didn't know what the results were, but she thought Lady Stokeley must know by now.

The walk up to the manor was lovely, with everything in

full bloom. Petals of cherry blossom fluttered down like pink confetti, and a blaze of red tulips waved their regal heads proudly from the deep borders on either side of the lane.

Harriet stopped mid-stride, the manor house ahead of her, the sun shining down, the world full of flowers and birdsong. She stood still, wanting to savor it to the full, because she'd done so little of that since January the twenty-first, when her life as she'd known it had ended. She was just starting to realize, in a very unexpected and backward sort of way, that might have been somewhat of a good thing.

The front door of Willoughby Manor was ajar, and so Harriet tiptoed in, calling out cautiously, "Lady Stokeley?"

She received no answer, and so she ventured further into the house, poking her head into the small drawing room downstairs that she knew Lady Stokeley used, and then heading upstairs as all the other rooms in the house were closed off or shut up.

"Lady Stokeley?" she called again, the stairs creaking under her. "It's Harriet. Harriet Lang. I've just come to see how you're doing…" Her voice trailed off as she heard Lady Stokeley's acerbic reply.

"I'm fine, but you might as well come up since you're here."

Harriet suppressed a little smile as she headed towards Lady Stokeley's bedroom. "Okay," she called back, and then skidded to a halt in the doorway, her mouth dropping open in shock.

"Don't worry," Lady Stokeley called from in front of the full-length cheval mirror. "I haven't lost my marbles yet. Not all of them, anyway." She turned to give Harriet a brittle smile. "What do you think?"

What did she think? Lady Stokeley seemed to be invoking Miss Havisham, dressed in an ancient, yellowing wedding dress that gaped at her bosom. "It's... it's your wedding dress?" Harriet ventured, which was essentially a no-brainer. What else could it be?

"From 1953. The year of the queen's coronation." She turned back to the mirror, gazing at herself critically. "I had a much better bosom back then."

The off-the-shoulder style emphasized Lady Stokeley's now-scrawny frame, her collar bone sticking out sharply, and Harriet wondered how the dress had fit sixty-odd years ago.

As if reading her thoughts, Lady Stokeley nodded towards a heavy silver frame on the top of her bureau. "Have a look."

Harriet moved over to the bureau, bending down to peer at the black and white photograph. "Oh, Lady Stokeley," she exclaimed, "you were beautiful."

"Well, you don't have to sound quite so surprised."

"Sorry." Harriet tore her gaze away from the photo of Lady Stokeley with shining dark hair and creamy skin, a tall, serious-looking man in naval uniform next to her, to give her an apologetic smile. "I didn't mean to. What... what made you decide to try the dress on now?"

Lady Stokeley let out a huff of laughter. "Still worried I might have lost the plot a bit? No, my dear. I am quite knowledgeable of all salient plot points, including those most recently developed."

"Ah." Harriet sat down on a stool shaped like a powder puff while Lady Stokeley perched on the bed, the yellowing dress flaring around her.

"Today is my wedding anniversary," she said quietly. "Sixty-four years. Of course he died thirty years ago, but still." She shook her head. "Time is so strange, how slow it sometimes seems, and then how it speeds up the older you get, until you get really quite old, and then it slows right down again. The trouble is, there's never enough of it." She sighed and with effort rose from the bed. "Would you mind unbuttoning me? The day nurse did it up but I didn't think about getting out of it again. I would have been in a bit of a quandary if you hadn't come along."

"I'm glad I did." Harriet eyed the incredibly long row of hook-and-eye buttons that went from Lady Stokeley's nape to her tailbone. This was going to take a while.

"Did you have a happy wedding day?" she asked as she slipped the first hooks from their eyes.

"Happy enough, I suppose. My mother was tipsy and my sister was positively green with envy. She was older than me by three years but I married first." Even all these years later, Lady Stokeley sounded a little smug about this fact.

"And your marriage?" Harriet dared to ask.

It was easier when she didn't have to look into Lady Stokeley's autocratic face with its shrewd blue eyes.

"What about my marriage?" Lady Stokeley's voice was frosty, and Harriet decided it wasn't actually easier.

"Was it happy?" she asked, her fingers practically shaking as she undid another few buttons. Lady Stokeley's back was emerging, her shoulder blades like chicken wings.

"Happy enough," the old lady returned after a brief pause. "I do not believe you can be happy all the time, and certainly not in a marriage."

That didn't sound all that hopeful. "Maybe not," Harriet agreed.

She'd been happy with Richard though, hadn't she? At the start they'd been deliriously happy. Working all hours, lying in bed on Saturday mornings with the sun spilling in and their feet tangled up together, late nights with a bottle of wine, a bag of crisps, and the telly—their lives hadn't been particularly exciting, but Harriet remembered loving those days. So what had happened? How had it all gone wrong, so slowly and slyly that she hadn't even noticed until it was, perhaps, too late?

"There." Harriet did the last eye and hook and Lady Stokeley reached down to hold the dress up to her front.

"If you'll excuse me," she said stiffly, and went into her dressing room.

Harriet tidied up a little bit, hanging up Lady Stokeley's dressing gown and arranging the cut crystal perfume bottles on her bureau that looked as if they were antiques. She looked at the photograph of Lord and Lady Stokeley again, taking in his dark, fathomless eyes and stiff expression. They both looked as if the camera had caught them a moment too soon, before they'd had a chance to smile.

Lady Stokeley emerged from the dressing room in her usual twin set and tweed. "The weather's so warm today," she said. "Why don't you join me on the terrace for tea?"

"Oh." The invitation was unexpected; Lady Stokeley usually acted as if she suffered Harriet's occasional visits with great forbearance. "That would be lovely. Thank you."

Harriet made the tea in the kitchen and brought it out on a tray to the huge terrace in back of the manor. Lady Stokeley was sitting on a wrought iron chair with a rug over her knees, her wrinkled face tilted towards the sun.

"It's lovely out here," Harriet said as she set the tray down. The lawn was jewel-bright and perfectly smooth, kept in much better condition than the interior of the house.

"I have cancer." Lady Stokeley spoke flatly, her eyes closed, her face still tilted upwards.

Harriet stilled in the pouring of the tea. "I'm sorry," she said quietly.

"Lung cancer. The irony, I suppose, is that I never smoked a cigarette in my life, even when it was all the rage. Never did like the taste." She let out a little sigh. "Gerald did, though. Smoked like a chimney, poor man. That's what killed him. Not cancer, but a heart attack. At least it was quick."

"Yes," Harriet agreed. Her heart ached for Lady Stokeley but Harriet didn't think she'd appreciate any gushing sympathy or commiseration.

Harriet put her teacup and saucer on the table next to her and with a gusty sigh Lady Stokeley opened her eyes and straightened in her chair.

"What are your treatment options?" Harriet asked after a moment.

"Apparently I'm too old for the proper chemotherapy," Lady Stokeley said. "The kind that fries you like a piece of bacon."

"Oh." Harriet suppressed a shocked laugh at her plain speaking. "What kind, then?"

"Oh, some pill or other. I'll have to go in five times a week for three weeks, and then I get a blessed week off." She took a sip of tea. "I should have started last week, but I can't make my mind up about whether I want to bother with it all. It seems such a palaver and for what?"

"Oh, but you should," Harriet said impulsively, and then realized she had no right to tell Lady Stokeley what she should or shouldn't do. "If there's even a chance..."

Lady Stokeley turned to give her a stern look. "I am eighty-six years old, young lady, and I am not at all sure that I want to spend my remaining days feeling even more feeble and ill than I already do." She took a steadying breath. "Besides, I do not relish the thought of losing my hair. It is the one thing of which I remain vain."

Harriet glanced at Lady Stokeley's snow-white cap of fluffy curls and could understand why she was reluctant. And yet to simply give up? To sit and molder in this lonely old house until she died?

"I can't tell you what to do, of course, Lady Stokeley, but I do hope, for all our sakes, you'll try. Willoughby Close wouldn't be the same without you."

Lady Stokeley's lips twitched in a small smile. "Thank you, my dear," she said quietly. "I'll think on it."

Harriet felt heavy-hearted as she walked back to Willoughby Close, oblivious to the beauty all around her that she'd enjoyed on the way to the manor. She hadn't even asked Lady Stokeley how she would get to and from the hospital in Oxford—what if she worried about that, about being a burden?

She should have offered to drive her, although if she was going to get a job she couldn't actually do it. But someone needed to step up. Had Lady Stokeley told anyone else about her diagnosis? Harriet had the feeling that she hadn't.

As she came into the courtyard of Willoughby Close, Ellie was getting out of her car.

"You're back," she said with a delighted smile. "I'm so pleased. I spoke to Colin and Anna and they're having a little dinner party on Friday. You will come?"

"Oh, I…" Harriet trailed off uncertainly. She didn't even know this Colin and Anna, and at the moment she wasn't in the mood to make small talk with strangers.

"Please come," Ellie begged. "Everyone will be laidback and friendly, I promise."

She *did* need to get a social life, and friends would certainly be welcome. "All right," Harriet agreed, wondering just what she was getting herself into. "I'll come. Thanks for the invitation."

Chapter Thirteen

H ARRIET STOOD ON the threshold of the quaint, tumbledown cottage by the river, a bottle of cheapish wine in one hand, wondering if she could quietly tiptoe away. A burst of raucous laughter emerged from the house and she seriously debated whether anyone would notice if she slunk off.

It was three days since Ellie's invitation, and Harriet had kept herself busy cleaning the house, painting the downstairs, and scouring want ads. She'd staved off loneliness with plenty of activity, but she missed the children quite desperately. She'd spoken to them every night, as well as to Richard, who sounded cheerful but definitely more tired as the week wore on. It had rained the last few days in Norfolk, and apparently William had been driving Richard's parents a bit mad, and so he had taken them all back to his studio flat in London.

Harriet could only imagine how that had gone. When she'd asked, Richard had remained upbeat, determined, it seemed, not to moan even though Harriet half-wanted him to so she could then tell him how easy he actually had it.

Instead she found herself offering ideas. "The Natural History Museum might be fun for them," she'd said last night, when they'd been having their nightly chat, which had somehow become kind of a thing. "If it isn't heaving over the holidays. Or the cinema, but I know that's expensive…"

"We went to the Princess Diana Playground in Kensington Gardens," Richard said. "And William nearly broke the mast of the pirate ship."

Harriet laughed at that. "Only William."

"I'm trying to remember if I had that much energy at his age," Richard said. "I must have done. I must have driven my parents round the bloody bend."

"But you were in boarding school, weren't you?" she knew he'd been sent to boarding school when he was seven.

"Ah, yes. That's what kept me in line. I'd almost recommend it for William, if I hadn't hated it so much."

"He will grow out of it," Harriet said. "That's what everyone tells me, anyway."

"Then we'd better keep believing it."

They'd lapsed into silence then, but it hadn't felt awkward. At least not *too* awkward. Harriet had had the sudden, desperate impulse to ask him about Meghan. *Are you still friends? What did you find with a twenty-six-year-old secretary that you couldn't have with me?* She'd wanted to ask, but thankfully didn't. She wasn't at all prepared to hear the answer yet.

In the end, Richard had asked if she wanted to talk to the children, and she'd said hello to them all, laughing at Chloe's usual flood of trivial information, hearing the affection beneath Mallory's bored-out-of-my-mind routine, and managing to get a few more-than-monosyllabic answers from William. Then she'd hung up, everything in her aching for when she'd see them again.

She was driving to London to pick them up on Monday, and she was practically counting the minutes. But first she had this dinner party to get through. Another burst of laughter sounded from the kitchen. They were all clearly having an absolutely fabulous time, and Harriet didn't really feel in the mood to join in. She was still worried about Lady Stokeley, and two more visits to the manor had not yielded any positive steps forward. On both occasions she'd found Lady Stokeley in the garden enjoying the sun, and remaining tight-lipped about whether she'd start treatment. Not that Harriet had worked up the courage to ask her point-blank. She'd more hinted at it, until Lady Stokeley had given her a particularly quelling look.

She *had* mentioned the possibility of helping with lifts, and Lady Stokeley had given her a shrewd look. "You seem quite determined to keep me alive, my dear, but people age. Things change. It's a fact of life you must accustom yourself to at one point or another, more's the pity."

Harriet had a feeling Lady Stokeley wasn't just talking about her own situation, and she had not been able to think of a suitable reply.

Now, resolute, she knocked on the front door. She couldn't slip off as much as she was tempted to. It would be rude and Ellie would be so disappointed. Harriet knew she was really looking forward to introducing her to her crowd of friends.

And so Harriet braced herself for several hours of excruciating small talk as the door was thrown open by a gorgeous woman with silky, dark hair and a wide smile.

"You must be Harriet! Come in, come in." She ushered Harriet in to a kitchen that was cozy and cluttered and filled with people. Harriet blinked, feeling absurdly shy, as a dog sniffed about her knees and a huge bear of a man took the bottle of wine off her.

"Thanks for this, I'm Colin."

"And this is Emma, Colin's sister, and Rose, his other sister, and Jane, his other sister," Ellie said with a laugh.

"I'm surrounded," Colin declared affably, and Harriet managed a small smile.

She felt overwhelmed by everything and everyone—the banter that was flying around, the press of people, the easy way everyone was relating to each other, as if they'd known each other for years while she was the odd one out, the cautious stranger.

It was a bit ridiculous considering how many social occasions she'd navigated over the years, with deft aplomb and sparkling self-confidence, but that had been an act of sorts, and now without the house, the friends, the life, she was back to the gawky teenager she'd once been, the only difference being that at least her hair and teeth were better.

"And this is Tom Roberts, the local vet," Anna finished the introductions. "Do you know him? Do you have a dog?"

Harriet looked at the man standing by the Aga, a pint of beer in one hand. He had slightly longish light brown hair and glinting brown eyes. And dimples, when he smiled, which he was doing now. He wore a rugby shirt and a pair of battered jeans and there was something that was both relaxed and sexy about him. Disconcerted, she looked away.

"No, I don't think so."

"You don't think you have a dog?" One of Colin's sisters, a severe-looking woman in a trouser suit, interjected with a rather sharp laugh.

"No, I don't think I know him," Harriet returned a little stiffly. "You," she amended, with an apologetic look towards the man in question. "And I'm quite certain I don't have a dog."

Everyone laughed at that, and someone thrust a glass of red wine into Harriet's hands, and she started to relax a tiny bit as the flow of conversation moved on and over her.

It was a cheerful, rambunctious crowd, she discovered, as Anna served up platefuls of beef bourguignon from on top of the Aga, and everyone moved into a sitting room that looked as if it had only been half-completed; one wall was covered with daubs of different colored paint and another wall was nothing but joists and insulation, a few two by fours tucked out of the way.

"Sorry, it's a work in progress," Colin said.

His severe-looking sister quipped, "And always will be."

No one seemed to mind the mess, though, and soon everyone was sprawled over the two overstuffed sofas and several squashy armchairs around a lovely fireplace, digging into the mountains of beef and rice Anna had dished out. Somehow Harriet found herself next to Tom.

"So you don't have a dog," he stated with a wry, glinting smile as Harriet tried to balance her plate of food on her lap.

"No, three children are plenty enough for me," she replied with an answering smile.

She saw a flicker of acknowledgement in Tom's eyes, and she realized she'd mentioned the kids on purpose. This had the slightly surreal feeling of a set-up, and judging from Ellie's occasional, darting looks of avid interest, Harriet could guess who the instigator was. Her friend wanted her to move on in life, in all sorts of ways.

"What ages are your children?" Tom asked dutifully, and Harriet cringed at the thought of boring him with motherhood stories. Why not just launch into potty training or something equally dire? A single man hardly wanted to hear about that, and Harriet was definitely getting the vibe that Tom was single.

"They're all fairly young," she returned, "but don't worry, I won't get out the photos, and I won't bore you with war stories of motherhood from the trenches."

"I wouldn't mind, as long as they're cute," Tom teased back. "My best mate from uni just had a baby, and it's the ugliest thing I've ever seen. I did my best to say how adorable I thought the little guy was, but I'm not sure he's convinced."

"He thinks his son is beautiful and that's all that matters," Harriet replied. "But newborns tend to look rather ugly, in my opinion. All red, mashed up faces and scrawny limbs. They look like little old men."

Tom gave a genuine laugh at that, and Harriet felt as if she'd scored a point. Was this flirting? What was she doing here, exactly?

"And do you work?" he asked. "Outside of the home, I mean?"

Harriet smiled at that gallant caveat. "I'm looking for a job. I was in publishing before I had children but I've been out of the game for a while." She hesitated, wondering if she should mention Richard, and if so what she would say.

"Ellie told me a little bit about your situation," Tom said in a low voice. "I'm sorry."

Harriet stared at him in shock. So maybe she didn't need to mention Richard after all. He already knew.

"What did she say?" she asked as a cold, prickly feeling spread over her body.

She knew plenty of mums at the school gate were talking about her, of course she did. She tried not to think too much about what they were saying, but the gossip was surely flying.

But *Ellie*… Harriet hated the thought that some stranger was hearing her sob story secondhand, wincing in sympathy or even pity…

"Sorry, should I not have said?" Tom said, looking apologetic. Clearly she was not hiding her feelings very well.

"No, I'd like to know what people are saying about me." Her voice came out stiffly, and Tom looked even sorrier. This was so not going well.

"All she said was that you'd had a hard time of it lately," he said, clearly trying to backtrack as best as he could. "Not much more than that, honestly. You lost your house and you're living in Willoughby Close. That's all, I promise."

Harriet wasn't convinced that was all, but she could hardly interrogate him now.

"Sorry, I shouldn't have said anything. I was trying to commiserate and failing badly." Tom grimaced. "All this was a precursor to my own story, which is that I got divorced last year."

So it sounded as if he did know something of Richard, then. She hated the thought, and yet why should she? It was the reality. She'd filed the separation documents herself. She needed to start telling people the truth, or at least not kicking up a fuss when they knew it. This was a village. People talked.

"I'm sorry," Harriet said. "That must have been tough."

"Look…" Tom laid a hand on her arm and they both

gazed down at it.

He had strong, muscular fingers and a square palm—attractive hands, but they weren't elegant. They weren't Richard's, with his long, lean fingers.

Tom removed his hand. "I realize I shouldn't have said anything. This has all become rather awkward and that's the last thing I wanted. I was just trying to... I don't know, commiserate, I suppose. Like you said, life can be tough."

Harriet gave a stiff little nod. "Ellie meant well," Tom continued. "And so did I."

"I know." She took a quick, steadying breath.

She needed to stop having fits about people knowing things. So Ellie had mentioned a few details. It didn't have to be the end of the world.

"Sorry, it just took me by surprise. I've been keeping quiet about things and I must admit I hate the thought of anyone talking about me."

"We weren't talking about you," Tom assured her. "Not in that way. Not gossiping."

"All right." It was time to let it go. Harriet took a slug of wine and then gave Tom what she hoped passed for a smile. "So tell me your story. Have you lived in Wychwood-on-Lea a long time?"

"No, just over a year."

"Since the divorce," Harriet surmised, and he smiled wryly.

"Got it in one. I moved here from Cheltenham afterward

and set up my own practice off the high street. I met Colin when he was renovating the surgery."

"And Ellie?"

"I only met her tonight," Tom admitted. "Before you came. We got to chatting, and…" He shrugged the rest away.

So Ellie was blurting out her story to strangers? Harriet fought a desire to be furious with her friend with the sure knowledge that Ellie had only been acting in her best interests. Misguidedly, but still.

"And how do you find Wychwood-on-Lea?" she asked, knowing she sounded too formal but unable to keep from it now. The conversation was struggling to regain its footing. Soon it would be floundering.

"Good. A bit lonely sometimes, but I've met a few friendly people. Colin's a great bloke." He cocked his head, smiling almost shyly, and Harriet looked away.

Tom was attractive, funny, and seemingly interested, but his obvious intent soured her stomach. She wasn't ready to date. She wasn't even ready to flirt.

He must have guessed that because he changed the topic to a recent film that Harriet hadn't even heard of, although she asked a few dutiful questions about it.

As soon as she could do so politely she excused herself, taking her plate and glass out to the kitchen where Colin's black lab, Tilly, was sniffing around for scraps. Harriet rinsed her plate in the sink and then, because she didn't want to go back into the sitting room, she started tidying up the kitchen.

Ellie came and found her a few minutes later. "What are you doing, hiding in here?" she exclaimed. "I thought you were enjoying yourself out there."

Then Ellie had been viewing her exchange with Tom with a pair of extremely rose-tinted glasses. "I was, a bit." Harriet took a deep breath, her gaze focused firmly on the soapy plates in the basin before her. "Ellie, how much did you tell Tom Roberts about me?"

"What?" Ellie sounded surprised, and then guarded. "Is that what... hardly anything, Harriet, honestly." Harriet didn't answer and then Ellie said in a rush, "Oh no, have I messed everything up? I'm sorry. I just told him you'd had a hard time of it lately, that's all, I promise. He seemed so nice and he is cute and single..."

Harriet turned around, her arms folded as she leaned against the sink. "Did you tell him about Richard?"

"Only that you guys were separated." Ellie looked truly miserable now. "I'm so sorry, Harriet. I shouldn't have said anything. The last thing I want to be doing is blurting out someone else's story. I just got excited by the prospect of a single guy and I want you to be happy..." Ellie trailed off, biting her lip, and Harriet's anger left her in a rush.

Ellie looked so repentant and Harriet knew she hadn't meant to gossip. And she was separated from Richard. It was a fact.

"I know you meant well," she said. "And I also know I'm overreacting. Actually I'm amazed Tom didn't already know my whole story. Sophie has a schnauzer."

"Sophie?"

"My former so-called best friend. If she could, she'd have taken an ad out in the parish magazine telling everyone about what happened."

"Some best friend."

"Exactly." Harriet sighed. "I know I have to get over this. Wychwood-on-Lea is a small place. Everyone knows everything, Tom Roberts included, eventually anyway, and that has nothing to do with you."

"Why," Ellie asked slowly, "do you mind people knowing so much?"

It was a good question, and one Harriet decided she needed to answer honestly. "Because it feels like I've failed," she said after a moment. "As if everything I built my identity on has been taken away. Everything people liked me for, all the things that made me *me* in this village, is gone… which makes either me shallow or everyone I know shallow." Maybe both. Probably.

"I like you, and it has nothing to do with your house or who you were before you came to Willoughby Close," Ellie said robustly.

"Yes," Harriet answered, "but that's exactly it. Who I *was*. Because I'm not that person anymore, and I don't know if that's a good or bad thing." Richard might think it was a good thing. New and improved, Harriet 2.0. Would he take her back if she told him she'd changed? Did she want him to take her back on those terms?

Love is not love which alters when it alteration finds. Shakespeare might have had something, there.

Ellie grinned wryly. "I'm going to go out on a limb and say it's a good thing."

"Maybe," Harriet allowed. She was certainly glad of some of the strides she made, but on the other hand… She still felt lonely, and more than a little lost. And she still missed Richard. If she could turn time back, would she? Maybe not in a heartbeat, but yes. She still wanted things—everything—to be different than it was.

"I'm going to go," she said as she pushed off from the sink. "I'll thank Anna and Colin, but then I'm heading home."

"Oh, please stay, for dessert and coffee at least," Ellie begged, looking unhappy again. "I really am sorry…"

Harriet shook her head. "I'm fine, Ellie, honestly, but I just need to be by myself right now." Even if she'd been by herself all week. "Thank you, though. You're a good friend."

She made her slightly awkward goodbyes, with Tom giving her an apologetic and unhappy smile from the sofa, and then she headed out into the night. The lane Colin's cottage was on was pitch-dark, and Harriet used the torch on her phone to navigate the rutted track. She felt calm and quiet, as if a storm that had been raging inside her had finally broken. It felt like the eerie aftermath of something big, all gray early morning light, a still, windless dawn of the soul.

What was going to happen next, she had no idea. But she wanted to rest in this moment, just as she'd savored the sunshine the other day. To enjoy it for what it was before she moved on… to wherever she was going.

Chapter Fourteen

"MUMMY!"

Harriet let out a startled *oof* as Chloe plowed into her stomach, wrapping her skinny arms around her waist. "I missed you."

Love and gratitude poured through her in a warm, sweet rush. "I missed you too, darling." She looked up to smile at William and Mallory, who were hanging back. "I missed all of you."

Mallory snorted but Harriet caught her small smile and felt another rush of thankfulness. Then she caught Richard's warm smile, his hazel eyes glinting, and something in her lurched, as if she'd missed the bottom step on the staircase.

She straightened, taking hold of Chloe's hand as she avoided Richard's eyes and looked around the studio flat where he'd been living for the last two months. It was tiny, little more than a bedsit, a rectangle of a room with a wedge of a kitchen and a tiny bathroom tacked on, above a chip shop on Bexley's high street.

Guilt niggled at her as she saw how he was living—a

cheap sofa, a futon on the floor, a card table with two folding chairs. Willoughby Close was homier by miles. But then Richard had wanted to stay in London, so he could continue to network. The last time Harriet had asked about the job search had been weeks ago, and Richard had spoken vaguely yet again about promising leads and some freelance work he was doing.

"Freelance?" Harriet had asked. "Who does freelance investment management?"

"It's not investment management," Richard had said.

His tone had been repressive and Harriet had decided not to ask just what it was he was doing freelance. Maybe she didn't want to know.

"Have you had a good time?" she asked the children now.

"We saw dinosaurs," Chloe said. "And stuffed animals!" She shuddered theatrically. "Like, real ones that were dead and then *stuffed.*"

"You went to Natural History Museum?" She was still talking to the children rather than Richard, but she could *feel* his presence.

She could smell his aftershave, not the expensive one she'd bought him every Christmas for the last few years, but a cheap version he used to buy at Boots that she remembered from their university days.

And this flat… it reminded her of their first flat as newlyweds in Camden Town—the cheap furniture, plastic crates and shelving from Ikea that had seemed like a step up, once upon a time. Once upon a very long time ago.

"Mummy," Chloe said in a tone of great impatience, "you're not listening."

"Sorry." Harriet looked down at her. "Tell me again." And this time she listened avidly as Chloe told her all about the dinosaurs.

"Do you want to stay for dinner?" Richard asked when Chloe finally paused to take a breath. "I could get us all a couple of pizzas."

"Oh, well…" Harriet glanced between him and the children and tried to gauge their expressions. Did they want to stay? Did she?

"Avoid some of the traffic," he added.

"Please stay, Mummy," Chloe begged.

Mallory and William remained silent, watching her.

"All right, then," Harriet said. "I wouldn't mind relaxing for a bit before I get back on the road." She picked her way through the children's bags which littered the floor to the sofa. "Goodness, how did you all manage in here? You must have been packed in like sardines."

"We were," Mallory interjected. "And Chloe snores."

"I don't," Chloe retorted indignantly.

"And William farts," Mallory added, to which William just grinned.

Harriet laughed, having missed them all and enjoying them now, even with their bickering. She glanced up and caught Richard looking at her again, unsettling her. "Ready for a break?" she asked.

"No," he answered. "Not really."

Harriet didn't know what to say to that. She turned to Chloe, saying something mindless to cover the awkward silence.

"I'll ring up the pizza place," Richard said after a moment.

Fortunately, the children's natural chatter covered any more awkwardness, and then Richard left to get the pizzas, and Harriet listened to William and Mallory bicker back and forth while Chloe continued her lengthy description about the dinosaurs.

"And how was Granny and Grandad's?" Harriet asked Mallory when Chloe had lapsed into satisfied silence.

"Okay." Mallory paused, shrugging. "Good."

High praise from her oldest daughter. "Good," Harriet returned lightly.

"Why didn't you come, Mum?" William asked, grinding his elbow into her hip as he clambered closer to her.

"Well—"

Before Harriet could formulate a reply Mallory answered her brother's question. "Because she and Dad are separated, stupid."

"Separated?" William frowned. "What does that mean?"

Mallory rolled her eyes and retorted, "It means they're going to get divorced."

"That's not true, Mallory," Harriet interjected.

Chloe looked stricken.

"You're not getting divorced!"

"No, we're not," Harriet said calmly. "But we are separated. I told you that, remember?" In a vague sounding way that had clearly gone over both William and Chloe's heads.

"*Why?*" Chloe gave her an accusing look. "I thought Daddy was in London for work!"

Or lack of it. "It's complicated, Chloe, and not something I'm willing to discuss with you right now, but I can say—"

"Discuss what?"

Everyone turned to look at Richard, who was smiling, his eyebrows raised in expectation, pizza boxes stacked in his arms.

"Whether you and Mum are getting divorced," Mallory answered, and then flounced out of the room.

The only other room she could go to was the bathroom, which she did, slamming the door and locking it behind her. Harriet cringed inwardly to see the smile wiped from Richard's face. He moved to the tiny kitchen and began opening the pizza boxes. Harriet felt as if she should apologize, but for what? It wasn't her fault the children had asked about divorce. Really, it was amazing they hadn't asked sooner.

They ate dinner in tense silence; Mallory thankfully came out of the bathroom after a few minutes and helped herself to a slice. Harriet began to feel wretched. She'd been so hopeful earlier, so determined to start moving forward, but now she felt stuck in a swamp of emotional uncertainty, wondering whether she was messing up her children's lives along with her own.

After dinner, Richard turned the TV on for the children and looked meaningfully at Harriet. "Coffee?" he asked.

"Yes, thanks." She was going to get a proper scolding now, wasn't she?

Harriet picked up the paper plates littered with pizza crusts and brought them into the kitchen. There wasn't much privacy from the rest of the tiny studio, but she could tell that Richard was determined to have as discreet a conversation as he could.

He switched on the kettle and then moved towards the fridge, where they couldn't be seen from the sofa where the children were all slumped together. Feeling she had no choice, Harriet followed him.

"Why did you tell the children we were getting divorced?" he asked in a low whisper.

"I didn't. Mallory said it, not me."

"And where did she get the idea?"

"Where do you think?" Harriet fired back, trying to pitch her voice as low as Richard's. "We haven't been living together, Richard. We're separated. Legally, now. Mallory's old enough to put two and two together."

"And come up with five, clearly." Richard raked a hand through his hair. Harriet was standing so close to him she could see the stubble on his jaw, the gold flecks in his hazel eyes. She couldn't remember the last time she'd been this close to him. When had they last kissed? Months and months ago, even before the mobile phone bill discovery. And why on earth was she thinking about that now? The last person *he'd* kissed was no doubt sexy Meghan.

"I didn't intend on having that conversation," she said quietly, determined to stay even-tempered. She understood Richard's ire—he'd gone out for pizza and come back to what looked like her telling the children they were getting divorced. "It sprang up out of nowhere and I did my best to diffuse it. I'm sorry."

"Okay." Richard took a deep breath and then nodded. He looked a little less angry, but still unhappy. "I feel like I botched my one chance to have a proper discussion with you, Harriet. Can't we talk again?"

The kettle switched off and Harriet hesitated, torn between wanting to cut off the possibility of such a conversation and yet knowing it wasn't fair. Tempted to have it too, even though it would be hard. They'd been married for fourteen years. They'd had three children together. They needed to have a conversation, even if it was just to end things officially, something she didn't feel at all ready to do.

"I know," she said. "I just… I haven't been ready for a proper dissection of us and all that went wrong, Richard. It was hard enough to hear about Meghan. To hear you didn't even like me anymore."

"I didn't mean it like that—"

She pressed her lips together, trying to keep her emotions in check. "Then how did you mean it?"

"I just felt like, in the last few years, we both got off track somehow."

"Both?"

"I admit, I was too tied up in work." He didn't sound convinced, more like he was spinning her a line. He didn't look at her.

"Why do you even want to get back together with me?" Harriet pressed, before she realized he hadn't actually said that he did.

"You're the mother of my children. I don't want to be a divorced dad. I don't want to live in a place like this." He gestured to the little flat.

She knew what he meant, but it still hurt. Where was the love and affection? The I-can't-live-without-you declaration? Not forthcoming, apparently.

Richard was gazing at her steadily now. "I promise you, nothing happened between me and Meghan—"

"You mean nothing physical, besides a couple of kisses." Which was bad enough. "That's not even what hurts, Richard. It's the emotional…" She took a gulping sort of breath. "That hurts, almost more, if I'm honest. Can you understand that?"

He looked away, and she couldn't tell if he was considering her statement or simply annoyed by it. "So you'd rather I slept with her?" he finally said, sounding exasperated, and Harriet flinched.

"No, of course not, but… when's the last time you saw her, Richard?"

Richard didn't answer for a moment, which was all the confirmation she needed. She felt a spasm of pain flash through her, like a knife in the chest.

"She's a friend," he said at last, and Harriet shook her head. "That's all."

"I need to go."

"Harriet—"

"You can't have it both ways, Richard. You can't hang out with Meghan in London and then make your droopy dog-eyes at me. I'm going." She couldn't believe how much it hurt, that he was still seeing Meghan.

Still looking to her for emotional support, for friendship, and who knew what else, because his wife had turned into someone he didn't like. Was she being absurd, to feel so betrayed? She felt breathless with pain.

She turned away from Richard, managing to compose herself. Just. "Come on, everybody," she called. She thought she sounded normal but she must not have because Mallory gave her a strange look. "Time to go home."

She stood by the door, her arms folded tightly, as the children gathered their things.

"Can I have my phone back?" Mallory asked Richard

sulkily, and Harriet looked at her in surprise.

"You didn't have your phone?"

"I took it off her for the week," Richard explained. "She was on that thing all the time."

"Oh." So Richard had become proactive in his parenting. A good thing, of course, and yet… everything tonight was making her feel out of sorts. "Come on," Harriet called again, and Richard hugged each of the children in turn before they all trooped out to the car. Harriet didn't say goodbye. She didn't trust herself to sound or act normal.

They were all subdued on the car ride home, crawling through London traffic, while Harriet gave herself a stern mental talking-to. So she really did need to move on with her life. She'd started to do that over the last week, but the minute Richard had entered the picture she'd had a major wobbly. They were legally separated. He was still seeing Meghan in some form. He sounded like he wanted to figure out how to get back together and yet Harriet couldn't envision it. Couldn't see how they could turn the rubble of their wrecked lives back into a solid foundation.

As she drove into Willoughby Close, Harriet felt a little calmer. She was making a life for herself here. Making friends, taking small steps. Those were all good things. So she'd just keeping inching forward, and things would start to feel better eventually. She had to believe that.

She unlocked the door to number two and the children pushed past her, eager to get home to their own beds and all of their stuff.

"You painted!" Mallory exclaimed, and Harriet couldn't tell if her daughter sounded enthused or accusing. With Mallory it was often impossible to tell.

"Yes." She scooped the post up from the mat by the door. "Do you like it?"

Mallory narrowed her eyes as she studied the light blue walls. "I guess it's okay."

"Good. I bought some different paint samples. I thought we could paint the bedrooms this week. And do some stuff in the garden."

Mallory's eyes were still narrowed as she looked at her. "So we're staying here?"

"Where else would you go?" Harriet asked lightly.

"I don't know." Mallory hunched a shoulder. "When we moved in here, it seemed like it wasn't going to be forever."

"I suppose it wasn't meant to be." Harriet hesitated. "I don't know what's going to happen, Mallory," she admitted. "But while we're here, this is home, and I want to treat it as such. Okay?" She smiled, raising her eyebrows, hoping her daughter wouldn't descend into a sulk.

To her relief Mallory didn't. "Okay," she said quietly, and then went upstairs without, thankfully, slamming the door.

Harriet walked towards the kitchen as she sorted through the post. Bill, circular, a reminder she needed to have her eyes checked, and then—

A letter from Oxford University.

It had to be a rejection. Rejections came by letters, interviews by phone calls. With a dull, leaden feeling in her stomach, Harriet opened the letter.

Dear Ms. Lang, We would like to invite you to interview…

Harriet let out a shriek, and the children came running downstairs.

"What is it?"

"Are you okay, Mum?"

"Yes." Harriet beamed at them all. "I got a job interview!" The children looked at her, nonplussed. Harriet laughed. "Oh never mind, I know it doesn't seem like a big deal, but I'm quite chuffed." Still smiling, she went to press play on the answering machine with its red blinking light.

"This message is for Harriet Lang," a cheery voice chirped. "I'm pleased to say the puppies have been born, and are ready for pick up this week."

Puppies…? From behind her the children began to screech in excitement and Harriet leaned closer to the machine, straining to hear the rest of the message.

"Please call Wold View Farm to confirm when you'll be picking up your springer spaniel puppy." The woman rattled off a number that Harriet didn't have time to take down.

"We're getting a puppy!" Chloe screamed, jumping up and down.

"Yes!" William fist-pumped the air.

"No, no, we're not." This had all got out of hand very quickly. Harriet looked at her children in mounting desperation. "We can't get a puppy…"

"We can," Mallory shot back fiercely. "We put our name down for one at a breeder's last spring, don't you remember?"

"No, I don't," Harriet retorted, but it was starting to come back to her.

The children had been begging for a dog for ages and she and Richard had put it off. Harriet knew who ended up walking and training and cleaning up after the dog. Her.

But last spring they'd all sat down and had a big discussion about responsibility. Mallory had promised to walk the dog every day. With Chloe in reception, it had seemed like the right time. And she'd liked the idea of a dog at the Old Rectory, in a vague sort of way. She'd pictured some noble hound sprawled on the grass under the old apple tree, the perfect way to complete their idyllic family life. Ha bloody ha ha.

"I remember," she told Mallory. "But things are different now—"

"I know things are different!" Mallory looked ready to work herself up into a full-blown rage. "Trust me, Mum, I know. I don't have my house or my pony or my friends."

"Wait, your friends—"

"And I'm not even going to Ellerton! So I *know*. But you

did promise us a puppy, and you paid for it already."

She'd paid a deposit of a couple hundred pounds, Harriet recalled. Pocket change back then.

"Are we not getting a puppy?" Chloe asked in a tragic whisper, tears trickling down her face. William kicked the skirting board for good measure, leaving a black smudge from his trainer.

Harriet sighed, recognizing imminent defeat. "All right, I'll call the farm back," she said. "And we can see. But I need to work, and a puppy at home all day…"

"You don't have a job yet," Mallory pointed out, a note of gleeful triumph in her voice. "And we're getting the puppy this week, when we'll *all* be home."

It seemed, Harriet thought in resignation, a done deal.

Chapter Fifteen

"**A**REN'T THEY ADORABLE?"

Harriet gazed at the wriggling, squirming mass of puppies cavorting in their pen and her heart softened a little. They *were* adorable. She still couldn't see how a puppy was going to fit into their lives, though.

Over the last two days her children had battered at her resistance. When Harriet had complained about the cost, Mallory had gone on eBay and found everything they'd need for a puppy for what really was pocket change. Chloe had borrowed a book on puppy training from the library. They'd even, when she'd come downstairs for breakfast yesterday morning, worked together on a poster that read *Please, Mum. We Love You*, surrounded by blobby-looking puppies.

How could she resist? And really, she didn't even want to resist. She'd already had to deprive her children of so much. She didn't want to deprive them of this.

So they'd worked out a schedule of walking and training, and she'd called Wold View Farm and arranged to pick up their new puppy. And now they were, the children gazing in rapture at the tangle of brown and cream springer spaniel puppies, and Harriet was wondering yet again what she'd got herself into.

"I think this one was earmarked for you," the breeder, a cheerful woman in her forties wearing mud-splattered wellies and a lot of tweed said as she scooped up one of the puppies. "A girl with more brown than cream, you said."

"Did I?" Harriet murmured. She couldn't believe she'd been so particular about, well, everything.

"Isn't she darling?" The puppy wriggling in the woman's arms was adorable, with liver-colored splotches on her back, white paws, and a white stripe down her dear little brown face. "Who wants to hold her?" the woman asked, and three children shrieked their yeses.

"Mallory first," Harriet ordered. "Show them how it's done."

Mallory stepped forward, practically quivering with officious importance, and took the puppy in her arms. The puppy wriggled and whined and then licked Mallory's face. Mallory laughed, the kind of pure, clear sound that Harriet couldn't remember when she'd last heard.

"She's the sweetest thing *ever.*"

Of course William and Chloe wanted to hold her as well, and Harriet arranged them all to have turns before she was returned to the pen and Harriet went inside to get the Kennel Club certification and settle up what was owed.

"Don't mind the mess," the woman called as she led

Harriet through an enormous utility room to a huge kitchen. The puppy's mother was sprawled in front of the enormous Aga, and Harriet felt a pang of homesickness for the familiarity of the room, so like her own kitchen at the Old Rectory, if a little more worn and less interior decorated, and no worse for either of those things.

"Here's the certificate," the woman said, "and that will be five hundred pounds, please."

"Five hundred pounds?" Harriet tried not to gape.

Once she might not have batted an eyelid at such an amount, but now she knew it would put a serious dent in her bank account, if she had five hundred pounds in there in the first place.

The money left over from the furniture sales was dwindling, and the need for her to get a job was greater than ever. Her interview in Oxford was on Thursday, and Harriet couldn't keep herself from putting all her hopes on it. Couldn't keep from thinking that if she got that job, the rest of her life might just fall into place.

She smiled weakly at the round-cheeked farmer's wife. She couldn't back out now. "Do you take checks?"

Fifteen minutes later they were back in the Rover with the puppy yipping and whining, curled up on an old blanket at Mallory's feet. The children still looked rapt.

"So what do you think we should call her?" Harriet asked.

"Ruby," Chloe suggested. "After the Ruby Princess."

"Ew," William said in deep disgust. "Who's the Ruby Princess?"

"That stupid cartoon Chloe watches," Mallory returned. "How about Lucy?"

"How about Darth Maul?"

"Hmm. Darth Maul, the springer spaniel." Harriet suppressed a chuckle. "Maybe we could keep brainstorming."

They all threw out names as she drove back to Willoughby Close, with none of the suggestions seeming quite right. Meanwhile, their unnamed puppy curled up into a little ball of brown fur and fell asleep. Harriet scooped her up gently and brought her inside, her heart squeezing as the puppy stirred and looked up at her with melted-chocolate eyes.

"You are too cute for my own good," she murmured. "Especially since I know you are going to wee on everything, and probably chew my last pair of decent shoes to pieces."

Gently she placed the puppy down on the floor, and everyone watched in breathless anticipation as she sniffed around, yapped a couple of times, and then promptly did a wee.

"*Ew!*" Mallory jumped back as if the poor little puddle of wee was flesh-burning acid. Chloe wrinkled her nose. William lost interest and went outside with his football. And Harriet went to get a roll of paper towels and a bottle of cleaning spray. It looked like her initial assessment of the situation was exactly right.

Their poor unnamed puppy yipped and whined all night long, so Harriet ended up sleeping with a pillow over her head and her finger in her ear. It was like having a baby, only worse.

The next morning she came downstairs to discover their angelic little puppy had weed all over her blanket, despite Harriet having got up to take her out twice, and gnawed on her plastic crate. Harriet let her out of the crate and the puppy weed on the floor. Again. This was getting old fast.

"Mallory!" Harriet yelled up the stairs. "It's your turn to take care of this bloody puppy."

"Why are you so grouchy?" Mallory complained when she finally roused herself fifteen minutes later and came downstairs.

"I got very little sleep last night and my job interview is tomorrow," Harriet replied. "I have a right to be a bit grouchy. This really wasn't the best time to get a puppy."

"But she's so cute." Mallory scooped up the puppy and cuddled her, kissing her on her chocolate button of a nose. Harriet sighed.

"Yes, she is rather cute, I know."

Mallory glanced up, leveling her with a direct and unsettlingly adult look. "So *are* you and Dad getting divorced? William and Chloe aren't here. You can tell me the truth."

"No, Mallory, we're not. We're separated, and we're trying to..." She paused. *Were* they trying? She didn't even know.

"Did Dad cheat on you?" The question was so bold and bald-faced that Harriet felt winded.

"What…"

"I'm not *dumb*. I overheard you guys arguing. And it sounded like there was someone else involved. Phone calls and stuff."

Harriet stared at her daughter helplessly. When had Mallory becomes so mature, so *jaded*? She was only eleven, for heaven's sake. She should still be playing with dolls, not smartphones. Not sneaking onto Instagram and Snapchat, getting up to God only knew what. She wanted her daughter to get back her innocence. This time Harriet took a big, deep breath, letting the air buoy her courage.

"I don't know exactly what happened between Dad and me," she said quietly. "There were some things… some issues… that are unresolved. We need to talk about them. We need to figure out…" Everything.

"And then?" The question rang out, a demand.

"And then I don't know. But whatever happens, Mallory, we both love you and Chloe and William and—"

"Oh yeah, blah, blah, you love us, nothing changes, spare me." Mallory sounded tired rather than angry. "I really don't need the we're-getting-divorced-but-we-love-you spiel. It's in every kid's book in the library, and on every single show on CBBC."

"Okay," Harriet said after a startled pause. "Well, as long as you know."

Mallory didn't answer but took the puppy out to the garden. Harriet watched her from the window above the kitchen sink as she crouched down in the grass as the puppy sniffed around, her long blond hair flying about her shoulders, a smile softening her usually scowling features. Maybe the puppy would be worth it, for Mallory's sake at least.

TWENTY-FOUR HOURS LATER, Harriet was perched on a plastic chair in the waiting room of the academic publishing company on an industrial estate outside Oxford. It was all a lot less glamorous than she'd expected, but she was still incredibly nervous.

With Ellie at work, Harriet had worried about who to leave the kids with, and had been surprised when Jace Tucker had offered.

"I'm around and they don't look like too much trouble," he'd said with a shrug when he'd stopped by for a maintenance check on the boiler. "Plus I like puppies."

"Even ones that chew your shoes and wee everywhere?" Harriet asked.

Jace had given her one of his slow, laughing looks. He really was the most ridiculously good-looking man she'd ever met. It felt unfair somehow. "Even those."

With childcare sorted, she'd moved on to choosing an outfit. She'd never been that into fashion and her wardrobe for the last eleven years had been smart casual—mainly skinny jeans and cashmere jumpers—with the odd cocktail dress thrown in. Nothing that seemed remotely suitable for a job interview.

She'd ended up enlisting Ellie's help, and she, Ellie, Abby, and Mallory had all gathered in Harriet's bedroom to go through her wardrobe.

"Wow, this jumper is the softest thing I've ever touched," Ellie had exclaimed as she'd stroked a gray cashmere jumper that had cost around six hundred pounds. "Amazing."

"But I can't wear it to a job interview." Where were the pencil skirts and button-down blouses from her old working life? She'd got rid of them years ago, because they'd been cheap and in any case they no longer fit.

"You could borrow something of mine," Ellie had suggested. "But none of it is this kind of quality."

"I don't care about quality," Harriet had returned. "As long as it's suitable."

So she'd ended up wearing a straight black skirt and boring white blouse from Ellie's collection, livened up with a chunky necklace. Harriet had the sneaking suspicion she looked like a waitress, but there was nothing she could do about it now.

"Harriet Lang?" The man standing in the doorway was kindly-looking, in corduroy trousers, a pink button-down shirt, and a tweed waistcoat.

Smiling, trying to wipe her palms discreetly on the sides

of her borrowed skirt, Harriet rose from her chair. "Yes."

"Why don't you come through?"

She followed him into a large, square room with a conference table and several plastic chairs. Three people were sitting there, all looking bored and faintly disapproving. Harriet swallowed hard.

"We used to have our office on Great Clarendon Street," the man, Edward Launcey, said in a jovial voice. "But it got so expensive we moved out here years ago. Now you've been out of the workplace for some time, I gather?"

"Yes." Harriet swallowed again. Her mouth was so dry. "Eleven years."

Someone made a tutting sort of noise but Edward gave her a kindly smile. "Do sit down." He indicated a chair at the other end of the table, making Harriet feel as if this was more of an interrogation rather than a friendly interview.

Which is what it ended up being. It only took her about two minutes to realize, despite her cram session on the Internet yesterday, she was woefully unprepared for this job. She didn't have any contacts in the relevant field. She didn't know what trends in academia were hot. Even the business she had been in, marketing fiction for a small publishing house, had moved on miles and miles since she'd last worked in London.

She tried to rally and offer some insights, but her brain felt as if it were full of cotton wool. When Edward had asked her a question about how she would come up with an "integrated digital plan" for a specific title, Harriet had stared at him miserably. When she'd last worked in publishing, ebooks had been something of a joke.

"Lovely to meet you, Harriet," he said when the interview had thankfully come to a close. He extended a hand which Harriet cringed to shake, since her own was icy and damp with sweat. "We'll be in touch."

"Bugger, bugger, bugger," she muttered under her breath all the way down in the lift and then out to the car.

That couldn't have gone worse. Well, actually, yes, it could have. She could have been sick all over the conference table or Edward Launcey's polished brogues. She could have frozen up completely. She could have done any number of things which would have made it a catastrophe, but she'd certainly done enough, wittering her way through her nonanswers, to ensure she didn't get the position.

She was still in a grumpy mood, only just managing to stave off proper despair, when she drove in to Willoughby Close. The house was quiet and empty as she came inside, but she could hear laughter from out back. Slowly, Harriet walked to the French windows and looked out at the idyllic scene of her three children and Jace playing with the puppy in the garden.

Harriet paused as she surveyed the scene, drinking it in. Chloe was crouched down in the grass, the sunlight gilding her wild blonde curls in gold, as the puppy trotted around, sniffing. Mallory was trying to entice the puppy with a ball, her face alight with laughter, and William was tackling Jace. Fortunately Jace seemed like he could handle it.

Smiling, Harriet opened the French windows and stepped outside.

"Mummy!" Chloe looked up, beaming. "We've decided on a name!"

"Have you? Not Darth Maul, I hope?" Although the puppy *was* becoming her nemesis.

"No, Daisy, because…" Chloe faltered, wrinkling her nose. "Because…"

"Because she ate those little daisies," Mallory explained, pointing to the miniature daisies that littered the lawn, "and then sicked them all up over Jace's boots."

"Oh, no." Harriet looked askance at Jace. "I'm sorry…"

"It washed off. And she seems better now, wee little thing that she is."

"Daisy." Harriet smiled at the puppy that was now running rings around all of them. "I like it."

"How did the interview go?" Jace asked with one of his slow smiles.

Harriet tried for a laugh. "It was terrible. I won't be getting that job, sadly."

"You never know."

"Sometimes you do." She sighed and stretched, trying to shake off her gloom. "I'm going to change and then why don't we have lunch out here in the garden?" She smiled at the children—Chloe was delighted and Mallory looked mildly enthused, William indifferent. *Win.*

"Do you want to stay for lunch, Jace?" she asked, hoping he wouldn't think she was coming onto him.

Although Harriet imagined a lot of women came on to Jace. She and Ellie had talked about how disconcertingly sexy he was.

"It's like ODing on chocolate," Ellie had said. "Too much of a good thing."

Jace shook his head. "I need to get on. Lady Stokeley's expecting me to mow her lawn."

"How is she doing?" Harriet asked.

"Fine," Jace answered with a narrowed look, and Harriet suspected Lady Stokeley hadn't told him about the cancer.

Had she told anyone? And more importantly, had she decided to start with the chemo? Harriet hoped so. She promised herself she'd look in on her tomorrow.

Jace said his goodbyes to the children and Harriet walked him to the front door. "Thanks again for watching my three," she said as he took his leave. "You were a lifesaver."

"Always happy to help." He nodded towards number three. "You might be getting another neighbor soon."

"Oh? Who is it?"

"Can't say. She's keeping a low profile at the moment."

"Sounds intriguing."

"We'll see." With a smile Jace waved and left, and Harriet turned back to her children and puppy—who, of course, had done a wee again.

Chapter Sixteen

T HE WEATHER HELD for the second week of the holidays, so Harriet was able to boot everyone out to the garden for hours at a time. They sowed seeds and planted flowers and ate every meal they could, lounging in the grass, drinking in the sunshine.

Miraculously everyone seemed to be getting along—mostly. The occasional squabble broke out, of course, but was thankfully, usually silenced pretty quickly. It was hard to be cross when the sun was shining and a puppy was frisking about.

During the week, Harriet also painted the children's bedrooms, allowing Chloe her beloved elephants, which did look like gray blobs—and that was being generous. She didn't care about interior decorating, though, or having the house look like something out of a style magazine. She just wanted it to feel like home. And slowly, slowly, it was starting to.

The Friday before school started again Harriet got a letter in the mail, ominously thin, marked Oxford University. She opened it alone in the kitchen, with the children out in the garden with the puppy, her heart starting to beat its way up her throat, which was not all a pleasant a feeling.

Dear Ms. Lang, We regret to inform you…

The words blurred before her eyes. It was stupid, of course, to be disappointed. It was utterly absurd. She'd known she wouldn't get that job. She'd accepted that she wasn't remotely qualified. And yet… part of her had obviously still been hoping, for her to feel this crushing disappointment now. She'd been so hoping, so counting on, things finally starting to go her way. Everything to.

But of course everything wasn't. And it was just one job, and she'd looked at the classifieds tonight, but… Harriet took a deep breath. It still felt hard.

The children burst through the French windows like bullets from a gun. "Daisy keeps weeing!"

"I know," Harriet said tiredly.

Daisy had been a wee machine since they'd brought her back from Wold View Farm. Harriet stuffed the letter back in its envelope and then tossed it in the recycling bin.

"No, I mean, *really* weeing," Mallory said, her tone serious. "Every few minutes. And she's whimpering a bit. I think she has some kind of infection."

"Oh." Harriet glanced down at their little puppy that, now that she was looking at her properly, seemed more than a bit woebegone. As if to prove the point, Daisy whimpered and then did a tiny bit of wee. "Oh, sweetheart." She crouched down to stroke Daisy's little head. "I think you're right, Mallory."

Which meant a trip to the vet... and the only one Harriet knew was Tom Roberts. A kindly receptionist offered her an appointment that afternoon, and so an hour later Harriet had bundled kids and puppy into the car and was driving towards the veterinary surgery's off the high street.

"Will Daisy be okay, Mummy?" Chloe asked tearfully as the puppy whimpered and weed—again. Even William looked anxious.

"I'm sure she'll be fine. She probably has a urinary tract infection, poor thing."

"What's a urinary tract infection?" William asked.

"She has to wee all the time, *duh,*" Mallory snapped. Her oldest daughter was, as usual, choosing to act angry rather than afraid.

"Listen," Harriet said as soothingly as she could. "Daisy is going to be fine." She glanced down at the puppy nestled in the foot well of the passenger seat, and felt a tug of sympathy as well as a pang of guilt. She'd been getting annoyed with Daisy when the poor thing had some infection—and she knew how much one of those hurt.

Tom Roberts's surgery was in a pretty little cottage of Cotswold stone, with the sitting room converted to a pleasant waiting room and the back rooms of the house into an office and examining room.

Mallory kept Daisy on her lap with Chloe cooing to her

while Harriet nervously flicked through a magazine and William drummed his heels. She didn't know how she felt about seeing Tom Roberts again. Of course, he was a professional, and this situation was entirely different from the dinner party at Colin's house. Not that anything had even happened at that party.

They'd chatted awkwardly, that was all. But she still felt nervous—and, yes, she could admit it—a tiny, *tiny* bit excited. For what, she couldn't—or wouldn't—say. Daisy was most likely going to wee on her and at least one of her children would do or say something awkward. There was nothing whatsoever to be excited about.

A few minutes later Tom appeared in the doorway of the examining room, a wide smile on his face.

"Harriet. Nice to see you again."

"Wait, what?" Mallory said, her voice sounding sharp and loud.

Chloe blinked slowly, looking from Tom to Harriet. "Mummy, do you know him?"

"We've met." Harriet rose from her seat. "Thank you for seeing me—us—on such short notice."

"My pleasure." Tom touched her shoulder lightly as she squeezed past him into the examining room. "But my recollection was that you didn't have a dog."

"We got one rather unexpectedly—"

"It wasn't unexpected," Mallory interjected. "We'd been on a waiting list for eight months."

"Yes, well, I'd forgotten about that part," Harriet said as lightly as she could. "Anyway, this is Daisy, and I think she has a UTI."

"Does she? Poor thing." Tom crouched down to Daisy's level and gave her a friendly smile. "Let's check you out, sweetheart."

William craned his neck to view the proceedings. "How are you going to do that?"

Tom looked up with a smiling glance. "Easily enough. I'll get a bit of her wee."

"She wees all the time," Chloe confided. "But not much comes out."

"It certainly sounds like a UTI."

What an enlightening conversation this was. Harriet raised her eyebrows. "Is there anything I can do to help?"

"Well, maybe. Let me see if I can get a sample the regular way. If not, I'll need you to hold her still while I insert a needle into her bladder."

That didn't sound like much fun for poor Daisy and so Harriet stood back, shepherding the children against the wall, while Tom crouched down with a clean vial and waited for Daisy to do her business.

He really was quite good looking, Harriet couldn't help but notice. Thick, wavy hair—a little long, admittedly, but still quite nice. And warm, brown eyes the color of toffee, and a nice smile. A nice butt too, since she was looking.

Harriet let out a startled *oof* as she received a sharp poke in the ribs from Mallory.

"You're *staring*," her daughter hissed, with a meaningful nod towards Tom's posterior.

Harriet blushed. And then felt a twinge of shame, followed by a surge of defiance. All right, yes, she was staring. Ogling, even. But why shouldn't she? She and Richard were separated. She was doing her best to move on. She might not have got that job, but she could get other things.

And what a naughty thought that was. Not a particularly appealing one, but still.

"Got it," Tom announced, and held aloft a vial with a few drips of wee inside. "Now to test."

Mallory scooped up Daisy as Tom took a reagent strip. "Yes, it's exactly what it looks like," he said. "A UTI. I'll prescribe a course of antibiotics and she should be as right as rain in a couple of days." He aimed a smile at all three children. "So no need to worry."

"Thanks," Mallory said with genuine relief. Daisy squirmed in her arms.

"Right, yes, thanks." Harriet gave him a distracted smile, conscious of how his attention had turned from the children to her.

"I'm going to take Daisy out to the car," Mallory announced. "I don't think she likes it in here."

"Okay, but wait—" Before Harriet could say anything more Mallory marched out, followed by Chloe and William, leaving Harriet alone with Tom.

If she hadn't known her daughter better, she would have thought she'd done it on purpose. Although she *did* know her daughter, and Harriet had more than a sneaking suspicion that Mallory had done it on purpose... for some nefarious reason of her own.

"Thanks," Harriet said again, and then cleared her throat, the universal signal for *this feels awkward and I don't know what to say.*

"I'm glad I've seen you again," Tom said. "I was feeling badly about the other night. I think I really put my foot in it."

"No, no," Harriet said hurriedly, "I was overreacting. I know I was. I'm legally separated from my husband. If it's not common knowledge, it probably should be."

"Oh." Tom looked startled, and then pleased.

Belatedly Harriet recalled that they hadn't actually talked about Richard. And now Tom probably thought she was letting him know she was available.

"I know how hard it is," he said. "Been there, done that, unfortunately."

"Right." Harriet managed a smile.

She didn't know Tom's story at all, but she didn't feel that he could equate hers with his. He was divorced, a done deal, his marriage in the dust. She definitely wasn't there yet. Then she remembered the set look on Richard's face when he'd spoken about still seeing Meghan. Maybe she'd be there one day. One day soon.

"But if this doesn't freak you out," Tom was saying, and Harriet clued back into the conversation, having the sinking feeling that she'd missed something important. "Do you want to come to dinner sometime? Or go out for a meal? Just as friends, of course, since I know it's probably too soon for you…"

Harriet's mind spun. "Umm…"

"Just an idea," Tom said, half-mumbling, and Harriet realized it had taken a fair amount of courage for him to ask.

"Sure, why not?" she said impulsively. Why shouldn't she go out with a friend? Richard certainly had. "I'd love to."

They exchanged mobile numbers and a few minutes later Harriet headed for the car, catching Mallory shooting her a look that managed to be both smug and suspicious. Harriet raised her eyebrows back at her, all innocence. It wasn't as if it was a date. And if it turned into something vaguely date-like… perhaps that would be no bad thing.

THE REST OF the weekend was a manic frenzy of trying to locate uniform and PE kit, get the house somewhat tidy, and do a supermarket sweep for lunch box necessities. In between sorting mismatched socks and digging out lunch boxes that hadn't been cleaned in two weeks—William's still possessed a festering yogurt pot—Harriet scoured the want ads and wondered if she could be hired as an administrative assistant to the faculty of chemistry at Oxford.

"Why not?" Ellie said when she asked her how she'd bagged a decent-paying job at the university. "You have transferrable skills."

"Do I?" Harriet wrinkled her nose. "I don't actually think I do. I can't type better than the average emailer, and the only computer programs I know are Word and a little bit of Excel."

"Oh." The look on Ellie's face was almost comical. "Hmm…"

"The world has moved on so much since I was in the workplace," Harriet confessed. "I'm not sure I'd even be able to do half the things I did back then. Everything's different, more advanced, and I never did keep up with technology." Mallory rolled her eyes whenever Harriet asked her help to figure out some app or other on her phone.

"There's no harm in applying," Ellie encouraged, and while Harriet wanted to agree with her, she had her doubts.

Applying took a lot of work, tweaking her CV and ago-nizing over the cover letter, but most of all it meant having hope, no matter how little. And the trouble with hope was that disappointment usually followed.

"I'll think about it," Harriet said, but the deadline was Monday and she let it pass.

On Sunday night she steeled herself to look at her bank balance and then shuddered. The rent was due next week and there wasn't enough in there to cover it. Child benefit, unemployment, and dwindling savings did not let a family of four live in the Cotswolds for very long.

She rang Richard, reluctantly, because she hated talking about money, and she really didn't want a fight.

"Harriet." He sounded pleased. "How was your week with the kids?"

"Fine. We worked on the house."

"How's the puppy?"

The children had all regaled him with tales of Daisy the last time he'd called. "She's getting there," Harriet answered. She wasn't weeing as much, at least. "Richard, I don't have enough money in the bank account to pay next month's rent."

Richard was silent for a moment. "How much do you need?" he asked, and with a jolt Harriet realized he must be feeling the pinch more than she'd thought. Ever since they'd lost the house, they'd made an informal arrangement where Richard deposited money into her account every week or so to cover her and the children's needs. It had always been enough, if only just. She'd assumed, terribly naively, she realized now, that wherever it came from, there was more. Not much more, granted, but enough to cover their basic costs.

She'd lost a lot, but she hadn't yet had to deal with there not actually being enough to live off. To keep a roof over their heads and some food in their fridge.

"Four hundred pounds to cover the rent," she said. "And another thousand pounds or so for food and petrol and bills for the month." Richard was silent, and Harriet's stomach twisted painfully. "Richard…?"

"I'm sorry, Harriet, I don't have it."

She sank onto a kitchen chair with a thud, truly shocked though perhaps she shouldn't have been. She'd *known* they were poor. Just not this poor.

"You don't have a thousand pounds?" she whispered.

The children were all upstairs in bed but she still felt the need to pitch her voice low. *A thousand pounds.* It was a huge amount, but at the same time it seemed paltry. She'd spent more than that on the stupid Swedish stoneware, which she'd more stupidly broken. Why hadn't she sold it all on eBay? She was officially an idiot.

"I don't," Richard answered steadily. "I'm sorry. With rents on two places and all the normal bills and nothing much coming in—"

"What about your freelance work?"

"That barely covers my rent."

She felt true panic seize hold of her. She'd never actually been in this situation before. Even when they'd been first married and been what they'd then considered poor, they'd had *enough.* They'd gone out to eat in restaurants on occasion. She'd bought clothes, admittedly cheap stuff. They'd certainly paid their rent.

But now… mentally Harriet catalogued everything she'd spent money on in the last few weeks. Daisy, for one. Five hundred pounds! Yet she couldn't regret buying her. Already, even with the weeing problem, she'd brought so much joy to the children's lives. And then there had been paint supplies and Daisy's kit, and she'd taken all the kids out for pizza… everything had seemed negligible, but it all added up to a fair amount. An amount she really could use now. All along she'd known they were poor, of course she had, but she'd still thought there had been a tiny bit of cushion. Something to keep them from being totally destitute.

"So what am I going to do?" she asked Richard, even though distantly she was realizing this wasn't as much his problem as it was hers. She could earn money just as well as he could. Maybe not as much, but something.

"I can deposit enough to cover the rent," Richard said. "And you can put everything else on a credit card for now."

Her stomach squeezed. "I don't even have a credit card anymore." After they'd maxed out their top-tier Platinum cards, Richard had cut them all up. No more living on credit. Besides, their credit now sucked.

"I have one. I'll send you a joint card in your name that you can use."

"But how will we pay it off? When are we going to get more money?" When was *she?*

"I'm trying, Harriet." Richard didn't sound just tired; he sounded defeated.

And Harriet felt more sympathy for him then than she had since first picking up that damned phone bill.

"I'll get a job," she said, aware that their roles were, for this moment, neatly reversed. "I promise I'll get a job this week."

Richard was silent. "It would help," he said at last.

After she'd rung off Harriet sat, staring into space, wondering how money had come to dominate her thoughts, her life. She'd thought they'd hit rock bottom financially but it appeared there was further to fall.

Guilt needled her as she thought of Richard's flat in Bexley. What was the rent on that place? A thousand pounds a month, probably, or something like that. If he moved back in with them, they would save a lot of money. But did he even want to move back to Wychwood-on-Lea? And what about his job search? *What about Meghan?*

The questions were still circling around in her head as she walked the children to school the next day. She'd offered to take Abby with them, so Ellie could have a stress-free commute, and it cheered her to see Mallory and Abby walking along, chatting. It cheered her even more when Mallory didn't peel off as soon as they reached the school gates to join the in girls, her old friends. She stayed with Abby, her head held high, while her former friends shot them looks and laughed behind their hands. That didn't cheer her, but at least Mallory didn't seem to mind too much.

On the other side of the school yard, Sophie was chatting with Cheryl Dennison, highlighted-blonde heads bent close together. Harriet looked away, and made direct eye contact with a mum she sort-of knew, a fellow parent of a year four.

"Hi," she said, because to not say hi when she was staring directly at the woman seemed rude.

"Hi." The woman—Helen, she recalled—gave her a shy smile and then ambled over. All the children had gone off to their classrooms, so Harriet was alone. "How are you?" The question sounded genuine rather than snide, and so Harriet answered it honestly.

"Better than I've been recently."

"I was so sorry to hear about your house." Helen grimaced, and Harriet managed a smile.

"Yes, well, at least someone else is enjoying it." She glanced at Cheryl, who was walking out of the school yard with Sophie. Both of them were dressed in high-end Lycra, no doubt intending to hit the gym. She had officially been replaced.

"Still, it's hard."

"Yes." Harriet refocused on Helen. "Yes, it's been really hard," she said frankly. "I loved that house." *I loved my life.*

Helen took a step closer to her. "We left London because my husband didn't get the promotion he thought he was going to get," she said in a low voice, as if confessing something shameful. "We had to sell our flat... we'd just bought it, thinking he was going to get the job. When he didn't..."

"I'm sorry. That must have been tough." Harriet appreciated the confession.

She understood the instinct to hide it, or anything that

tarnished the glossy perfection of your life as seen by others. How many other people, like Helen, like her, were faking it? Acting like it was all perfect when it so wasn't?

"We should get a coffee sometime," she said impulsively, and Helen smiled.

"I'd love that."

Was it really that easy? Harriet mused as she started to walk out of the school yard. She'd spent the last two months feeling isolated but was it really that easy to vault over the chasms that seemed to separate her from everybody, and just be real and open and friendly?

Harriet turned to walk into school and inform reception that her children would not be taking any after school clubs this term. It was one small way she could economize, and she'd decided that mini iPad club for Chloe was not actually necessary, and William could play football with his friends on the green instead of being drilled by a grumpy coach.

"So all of your children are quitting the after school clubs?" the receptionist, Mrs. Jamison, asked, thin eyebrows raised in what seemed like censure.

"Yes, I'm afraid so. Maybe in the autumn we'll start again." She could not imagine what the autumn would look like at this point.

"May I ask why? Are they not to your taste anymore?"

Harriet had forgotten how frosty Mrs. Jamison could be, so unlike the cuddly Mrs. Wendell, who job-shared with her. "It's not about taste," she said, deciding recklessly to be as frank with Mrs. Jamison as she had been with Helen. "It's that I can't afford them."

Mrs. Jamison's mouth opened silently. Perhaps she hadn't heard the gossip, or perhaps no one realized just how dire Harriet's situation truly was. Even she hadn't.

"So like I said, maybe in the autumn."

She left the office, taking a deep breath of fresh air to steady herself. Being honest was liberating, but it still left her feeling a little wobbly.

"Are you looking for a job?"

Harriet looked up to see a mum she only vaguely recognized coming out of the office. She was definitely from the other side of Wychwood-on-Lea, the side with council houses and homes turned into flats. The side Harriet hadn't even ventured into much after six years in the village.

"Umm… yes?"

"Just heard you talking in there about the clubs," the woman said with a nod to the office. "And if you're looking for a bit of work, my job's going. I've got to leave it to take care of my mum. She's poorly."

"Your job?" Harriet felt as if she was missing half of the conversation.

"Dinner lady at the school, five lunchtimes a week. It's decent pay and it works around the school run. I know they're desperate to fill it because I've got to leave straight away. Have a think, anyway."

She smiled and walked out, leaving Harriet practically

gaping. *Dinner lady?* She pictured herself standing behind the metal counter, her hair held back in a net and one of those little white paper hats on her head as she doled out scoops of instant mashed potatoes. She pictured the children seeing her, recognizing her, and then telling their mothers.

She could not be a dinner lady.

But as she walked back to Willoughby Close the idea kept rattling around in her head. Did she have the right, not to mention the luxury, to be so snobbish? What was wrong with being a dinner lady? It was good, honest work, it was local, and it fit in with the school run. She might not be using her degree or doing something she could brag about, but surely she was beyond those kinds of concerns at this point?

Or did she still have further to fall?

Harriet opened her front door, surprised to see an envelope that looked like it was made of thick, expensive parchment had been dropped through the letterbox. Her name was written on the front in spidery handwriting, and when she opened it up she saw it was from Lady Stokeley.

Dear Harriet, If the offer still stands, I would much appreciate you driving me to Oxford for my treatments. Please call on me to discuss the arrangements. Sincere regards, Dorothy.

Chapter Seventeen

THE JOHN RADCLIFFE Hospital was heaving on a Tuesday morning. Harriet peered through the rain-spattered windscreen—the glorious weather had broken and a persistent, misting drizzle had fallen for the last twenty-four hours, leaving her feeling permanently damp.

And what a twenty-four hours it had been. Her life had sprung into surprising gear. First she'd called on Lady Stokeley, finding her in the sitting room, looking small and somehow shrunken huddled under an old tartan rug.

"I'm so glad you've decided to go ahead with the treatment," she'd said, and Lady Stokeley had sighed.

"I'm not entirely sure it was the right decision, but I was never one simply to give up." She gave Harriet one of her shrewd, narrowed looks. "If that was the case, I would have got divorced years before Gerald had died."

Which was a loaded statement if there ever was one, but marriage and divorce wasn't a subject Harriet felt courageous enough to broach with Lady Stokeley at that point.

"You certainly don't seem like someone who gives up to

me," she'd said. "So when is your first appointment?"

The appointments were every weekday at ten o'clock, leaving Harriet with just enough time to get there after the school run, and get back to Wychwood-on-Lea before her shift at the school as dinner lady—for, after speaking with Lady Stokeley, she'd rung up the school and been hired that same afternoon.

When she'd told the children, they'd been nonplussed, but then Mallory had given her something resembling a smile and a nod, which Harriet deemed as approval. It seemed her children weren't going to be too embarrassed seeing their mother in a paper hat, doling out cafeteria food.

"I'll pay you," Lady Stokeley had said when Harriet had made arrangement to collect her the next morning. "For your time as well as your petrol."

"Oh no, you don't have to do that—"

Lady Stokeley gave her a severe look. "I might not have to, but it is entirely sensible. The petrol alone will cost you, and it will take several hours every day. Shall we say seven pounds an hour?" Which was a little less than the national living wage, so Harriet didn't feel *quite* so bad. "And," Lady Stokeley added, "I'm sure you can use the money."

"Can you spare it?" she'd dared to ask, and Lady Stokeley's snow-white eyebrows snapped together.

"How impertinent," Lady Stokeley said, drawing herself up. "Of course I can afford it."

Which made Harriet wonder why she didn't splash out

on some heating, at least, or better food. But those were questions she did not have the courage to ask.

So now, here she was, searching for a parking space, with two jobs rather than none, and the prospect of making if not decent money, then maybe enough.

With a gusty sigh of relief, Harriet pulled into a miniscule space, sucking in her stomach to squeeze out of the door and then jogging to the pay and display. She'd dropped Lady Stokeley off at the hospital's main entrance but she was worried about leaving her for too long. The old lady still had plenty of spirit, but she'd grown frailer in the last few weeks, her clothes hanging off her thin frame, her face more deeply creased than ever.

The chemo treatment, at least, was short and simple—after taking her blood pressure, the nurse gave her a cup of water and a pill to swallow. Then Lady Stokeley waited for ten minutes to make sure there were no adverse effects, and then Harriet took her home. Afterwards Harriet stopped at the chemist's on the ground floor to get Lady Stokeley's antinausea prescription, and then she went to get the car.

"So, now what happens?" she asked when they were back in the car and she was turning out of the hospital, heading for the A40.

"Now I wait to feel awful." Lady Stokeley waved a bunch of pamphlets she'd been given. "There are plenty of side-effects, it seems."

Harriet had a look at the pamphlets as she boiled the kettle for a cup of tea for Lady Stokeley back at Willoughby Manor. *Living with Lung Cancer. You and Chemotherapy. When You're Neutropenic.* It all sounded rather horribly grim—and it made Harriet wonder if it really was worth it. What would Lady Stokeley do if she became truly ill, here on her own? Jace looked in on her, as did Abby, and a care worker came in three times a week for about an hour each time. But added up, that still was a negligible amount of time. What if Lady Stokeley needed more care than Harriet or anyone else could offer her?

She took the cup of tea upstairs, pausing on the threshold of the bedroom. Lady Stokeley had already fallen asleep, her face pale, one thin hand resting by her cheek like a child's.

Harriet tiptoed in and put the cup of tea on the table next to her bed. She never liked leaving her alone, and now more so than ever, but she didn't really have much choice. She was due at the school in twenty minutes.

Half an hour later, Harriet was in the huge school kitchen, tucking her hair into a net as the head cook, Ruth, bellowed orders to two sub-cooks who were scurrying around, looking demented. The place smelled strongly of tikka masala, as the main dish was a curry, with a pervasive, underlying odor of boiled cabbage, even though cabbage hadn't been served since before the holidays. Harriet suspected the smell never went away. She'd need to shower after this.

For her first day, she was serving out rice from an enormous vat, which seemed simple enough. Each child got one scoop. No one got seconds until a bell was rung. It felt like the army, or perhaps prison.

And then the soldiers or prisoners, however she wanted to look at it, came into the cafeteria in a jostling, screeching stream, making her question whether it was going to be as easy as she'd thought.

Harriet thought she'd had quite a bit of experience with children, even with groups of children. She'd manned plenty of bake sales, led toddler groups, donned the ever-important teacher's voice when needed. But she had not manned the lunchtime barricades, flinching as children pushed and shoved, shouted and screeched.

And the *rush*. Lea Primary was a relatively small school but the children kept on coming, thrusting their trays forward, looking bored or surly or mildly interested that someone they recognized was wielding the scoop.

And rice was *sticky*. Harriet found she had to clang the ladle quite hard on the plate in order to get all the grains off, but after umpteen scoops the ladle was half-filled with rice when she tried to place a scoop on someone's plate, meaning a child only got a half-scoop, and drama ensued. And then the vat was empty, and Harriet had to run around breathlessly, burning her fingers as she tried to lug another vat of rice over to the waiting—and ever-lengthening—queue of hungry children.

By the time the year sixes had helped stack chairs and then run out for playtime Harriet was exhausted. She smelled of cabbage, curry, and sweat—and the sweat was hers.

She helped tidy up the kitchen and dining areas, spritzing and wiping down tables, every muscle in her body aching. She had an hour to kill, hopefully making herself presentable, before she was back at school for the pickup.

"You did well." Ruth gave her a craggy smile as Harriet put away the cleaning supplies. "I wasn't sure you had it in you, but you did well."

"I wasn't sure I had it in me, either," Harriet said with an answering smile, and then dragged herself back home.

Daisy was yipping madly as she came in the house, and Harriet let her out of her crate, smiling as the puppy gave her playful nips. Then she switched on the kettle and sank into a kitchen chair, deciding she needed a cup of tea before she attempted to rid herself of the smell of tikka masala.

"How did it go?" Ellie asked that evening when she collected Abby from Harriet's after work. It was an informal arrangement that seemed to work out well—Abby and Mallory hung out most days, playing with Daisy or walking the Matthews's enormous beast of a dog, Marmite.

"It was utterly exhausting," Harriet answered. "And tell me the truth—do I still smell like a cabbage?"

Ellie leaned forward and took a sniff. "Maybe a little bit," she said with a laugh.

Harriet rolled her eyes. "I washed my hair twice. I suppose I'll have to get used to smelling like a roast dinner."

"Could be worse," Ellie said with a laugh. "You've come a long way, Harriet."

And Harriet knew she had.

That evening, after the children were in bed, she decided to call Richard. The hiring had happened so quickly that she hadn't had a chance to tell him about her gainful employment.

She was curled up on the sofa sipping a glass of wine when she called him, and it wasn't until she heard his voice that she realized she'd actually been kind of looking forward to the call.

"Harriet." Richard sounded tired but pleased to hear from her. "How are you?"

"Proud," Harriet answered. "I earned forty-two pounds today."

Mentally she shook her head at herself. She'd once spent that much during one visit to Starbucks. Easily.

"How did you manage that?"

Briefly Harriet told him about her two jobs. "I know it's not much," she said, "and I'm only making minimum wage part-time." When she said it like that, it didn't sound like anything at all. "But it's still something," she finished, sounding a bit defiant.

"It is, it definitely is. And I'm glad and proud of you." He paused, his tone softening. "I know it's not easy, managing such a huge step down."

"It isn't, but it's easier than it was."

They were silent for a few seconds. Harriet wanted to say something more, something about how she'd changed, how she looked back on the person she'd been and wasn't sure she actually liked her anymore. That she understood a bit more what Richard had been trying to tell her back at the pub.

And yet... it felt like too much risk. What if Richard said, *"Yeah, thanks, but you're still not quite what I want"*? And what if he got a job? If Richard found a job... if they could move into a decent house together... maybe not Wychwood House, but something bigger and nicer... would she? If she could send Mallory to Ellerton, and get Cobbler back, and rejoin the Soho Farmhouse, would she? Would she be friends with Sophie again, reigning once more as Yummy Mummy Number One?

"It won't be for long," Richard said. "I promise. I've got an interview next week."

"You do? A proper interview?" This was news.

"Well, it's more like a pre-interview, but I feel good about this. It's with a start-up firm that likes to take risks. They're a bit edgy, and they don't mind the fact that I have a colossal smudge on my CV."

"That's good."

"And. if I get it, you can quit the dinner lady job, hand in your notice for that place."

Which made her feel... strange. "And we'll go back to the way things were?" Harriet asked. "I thought you didn't like that." She paused. "Didn't like *me.*"

Richard sighed. "I didn't mean it quite like that."

"Maybe not, but it wasn't working, was it? Our life. I realize that now." Even if she still wanted parts of it back.

Richard sighed. "It still could work," he said. "I believe that." Now he was the one to pause. "Do you?"

"Maybe," Harriet said, and it felt like a big admission. She shifted on the sofa. "I should go," she said after what felt like an endless silence, the only sound their breathing. "School tomorrow and all that."

"Right. Shall I come up this weekend and do something with the children? We could take the puppy out, give you a break…"

"They'd love that, I'm sure."

"Okay."

More silence. More awkwardness. Would he call Meghan after this and describe the conversation? *I'm not even sure if it's worth it anymore…*

Harriet closed off that line of mental torture. "Bye, Richard," she said softly.

As she disconnected the call a text pinged in.

"How about Friday for dinner? –Tom."

Chapter Eighteen

I T WASN'T A date. Harriet had made that very clear to her children, who were rather nonplussed about the whole thing, and to Ellie, who was watching them at her house while she went to Tom's for dinner and had looked both intrigued and smug when Harriet had told her where she was going. Harriet had even told Lady Stokeley on the drive into Oxford, when she'd asked if she had any plans this weekend. Harriet had blurted out about the dinner, and how it wasn't a date, and Lady Stokeley had raised her thin eyebrows and quite eloquently said nothing.

Now it was seven o'clock on Friday evening and she was due at Tom's in half an hour. What to wear? Harriet felt she needed to make a bit more effort than her usual skinny jeans-and-floaty-top combo, but definitely not too much. Would adding a chunky necklace and lipstick do?

"You're spending a lot of time getting ready," Mallory grumbled as she slouched into Harriet's bedroom.

"Not really." With effort, Harriet turned away from the mirror where she'd been scrutinizing her reflection. She hadn't had her hair done in months, and she'd used to get it cut, styled, and highlighted every four to six weeks. Was she really that gray?

"So this isn't a date," Mallory said, bouncing on her bed. "What is it then, exactly?"

"Dinner with a friend." Harriet reached for her lipstick.

"Dad wouldn't like you having dinner alone with a guy."

Then maybe Dad shouldn't have cozied up to his secretary.

"Dad and I are separated, Mallory. He doesn't get a say in this."

"And if you're having dinner with someone else, then you're probably going to get divorced, right?" Mallory lifted her chin, her bold look contradicting the telltale wobble of her lower lip.

With a sigh, Harriet put down her lipstick. "I don't know what's going to happen. Nothing's been decided, and Dad and I still have a lot to work out. In any case, you seemed like you were pushing for me to go out with Tom. You left us alone in the examining room, didn't you?"

Mallory looked away. "I wanted to see what would happen. I didn't think anything actually *would.*"

Typical. "And nothing has," Harriet assured her.

"Except that you're going on a date."

"Mallory."

Twenty minutes later, Harriet managed to extricate herself from both children and puppy and was walking down the high street towards Tom's flat above the surgery. The evening was mild, the sky turning lavender with shreds of silvery cloud, the village quiet and peaceful on a Friday evening in May.

Nerves jumped and writhed in her belly and started fluttering up her throat. This might not have been a date, but it felt like one—too much for her peace of mind. As much as she'd told herself she needed to move on, wanted to feel attractive and valued again, wanted to try something, all she felt now was sick.

With a hand that was not quite steady, Harriet knocked on the door of the surgery, and Tom opened it almost immediately. "I was waiting," he explained at Harriet's slightly startled look. "So I could take you upstairs. To my flat," he clarified quickly, and Harriet gave a little laugh. She wasn't the only one who was nervous.

Upstairs Tom's flat was cluttered and cozy, with a living room with two squashy sofas and what looked like a hurried effort to appear tidy. Newspapers and books were stacked in haphazard piles and there were coffee rings on the low table between the sofas, but it was a homely and pleasant space, if clearly a bachelor's pad.

"Something smells delicious," Harriet said brightly.

She still felt nervous, every exchange sounding clumsy and awkward. Tom reached for her light coat and they had a bit of a tussle trying to get it off.

"It's spaghetti bolognaise," he said when he finally relieved her of her coat. "The only thing I can really make, I'm afraid."

Richard was a good cook. Harriet had a sudden, piercing image of him making pancakes on Saturday morning when Mallory and William had been little. He'd worn her apron, which had looked ridiculous, and flipped the pancakes spectacularly high, making the children scream with laughter. But he'd been able to cook properly—when they'd been first married, he'd go to the Chinese market and get all sorts of exotic ingredients—lemongrass, fermented black beans, Sichuan peppercorns. He'd toss things into a wok willy-nilly and always come up with something delicious.

"That sounds lovely," Harriet said, realizing the silence had gone on a second too long. "I'm always up for some pasta." She sounded inane. She felt inane, and she knew she needed to loosen up.

"Wine?" Tom asked, and she nodded with relief.

"Yes, please."

With a glass of wine in her hand and Tom occupied at the stove in his little galley kitchen, Harriet felt marginally better.

She wandered to the window overlooking the courtyards and tiny gardens backing onto the buildings on the high street. "So what made you choose to live in Wychwood-on-Lea?" she asked.

"I liked the look of the place," Tom replied with a smile and a shrug. "I was driving through one day, on the way to my parents near Oxford, and I thought it looked quaint. The kind of place you'd see in a series on the telly, you know?"

"Pictured yourself as Dr. Doolittle?" Harriet teased, and he let out a little laugh.

"Something like that, I suppose. What about you?"

"Similar story, really. When I was expecting our third child we decided we should move out of London—that's what everyone was doing—and we toured the area and liked the looks of Wychwood-on-Lea. Quaint without being too twee or tony."

Tom arched an eyebrow. "You don't like tony?"

"I didn't want to be rubbing shoulders with celebrities or people who think they're far more important than they are." And yet she had, perhaps, without realizing it, become like one of those people.

She had an image of herself at the open house Christmas party she'd thrown a few years ago, watching everyone with narrowed eyes, assessing outfits, salaries, social status without even realize she was doing so.

"Is it too early in the evening to ask what happened?" Tom asked and Harriet refocused, startled.

"What happened…?"

"With your husband." He glanced back down at the stove, intent on stirring the sauce.

Yes, it was too early. In the evening and in their friendship. It felt rude to say as much now and so Harriet stalled, taking a sip of wine.

"We grew apart," she said after she'd swallowed. "Like a

lot of people do. What about you?"

"Sarah left me." Tom spoke flatly, with an edge of pain to his voice. "For someone else, unfortunately."

"I'm sorry."

He shrugged. "We got married young, maybe too young, just out of university."

Which was when she and Richard had married, twenty-five and fresh-faced, full of idealism and hope. "And what happened?"

"We settled down into a routine, as you do. I was finishing my clinical experience and Sarah was working as a teacher in a rough school in London. We hardly ever saw each other, and we were scraping by on a pittance."

"Yes." Harriet's throat had gone tight.

The details were different but the story felt the same.

"We were also trying to have kids," Tom said. He glanced at her, wry and uncertain. "Sorry, I'm offloading. Is this too much information?"

"No." She tried to smile. "I'm interested."

"It wasn't happening, and the doctors couldn't figure out why. I think secretly we blamed each other. In any case, it added to the strain and it started to feel like a relief to spend more time apart. Longer nights at work, seeing friends separately on the weekends."

How many times, when Richard had rung her to say he was working late, had she felt a little treacherous frisson of relief? She hadn't even acknowledged it to herself, had presented a martyred but slightly annoyed air to Richard, as if he was inconveniencing her but she'd manage...

She was ashamed of herself. In so many ways.

"It all sounds a bit familiar," she said to Tom. "Unfortunately."

"Right. It happens to plenty of marriages, doesn't it? I didn't see the affair coming, though. That kind of blindsided me."

"Yes." As far as she knew, Richard hadn't had an actual affair.

The emotional stuff counted, of course it did, and yet... It *was* forgivable, wasn't it? And if it was, what did that even mean for them?

"Did the two of you ever talk about getting back together?"

"No, that never came up, sadly. I found out about the affair through email. Sarah had already left."

Harriet grimaced. "Ugh. Sorry, that's rough."

"Yep." Tom smiled, trying to rally. "But it was over a year ago, and I'm trying to move on, so..."

"Right. Can I help with anything?" Tom handed her a Caesar salad kit and Harriet set about assembling it. Their little heart-to-heart was clearly over, and she was relieved to have got off so lightly. Tom hadn't asked any probing questions and he didn't seem likely to now.

"How's Daisy?" he asked as he ladled out sauce and Harriet brought the salad to the table.

"Fine. Doing much better, thanks to the antibiotics. I'm hoping she'll be trained soon."

"She seems like a real sweetheart."

"Yes, she is a cutie. And the children love her. I wasn't sure about bringing a puppy into the chaos that is our home, but it was definitely the right choice."

"A pet can be a great healer."

"How come you don't have one?" Harriet looked around the flat just to check there wasn't some animal hiding somewhere.

"We had a dog," Tom said as he poured them both more wine. "A Labradoodle. Sarah treated it like our child, which I suppose was understandable considering our circumstances. When we divorced she took the dog. She was more attached to him than I was, so I agreed."

"Ouch." It all sounded pretty awful, and yet that was what happened with divorce, wasn't it? People divided things up.

They steered the conversation to more innocuous topics then, and Harriet finally started to properly relax and even enjoy herself. It was nice to chat, and she had to admit it was nice to feel Tom's admiring glances, the low level of flirt he kept going. Was that terrible of her?

After a dessert of a shop-bought apple tart they ended up on either end of the sofa, finishing the wine and chatting some more. The sun had set and the room was dim, and the mood was… something.

It had been a long time since Harriet had dated. A long time since she'd felt flutters in her stomach, and these flutters weren't entirely the good kind. Actually, she felt kind of nauseous.

Tom leaned one arm across the back of the sofa, his fingers inches from her shoulder. In the dim light, the moon just starting to appear in a twilit sky, she could catch the glinting gold strands in his hair. She inhaled the scent of his aftershave, something citrusy and unfamiliar. It all felt romantic, and yet... not.

"So, dinner lady," Tom said, smiling.

She'd already told him about her new job, and Tom had laughed when she'd regaled him with horror stories of children who didn't like what was on offer, or the boy who had burst into tears when Harriet had accidentally flicked a piece of macaroni in his face.

"Yes, it's not all that bad. The timing works out really well and I actually like being in with the children." She'd also found a surprising camaraderie with the slightly terrifying head cook, Ruth, and her two overworked minions.

That afternoon, at the end of the week, they'd all kicked back with a cup of tea and had a chat. Ruth, Harriet discovered, had a husband on disability and four teenaged sons. Elaine and Tiana, the two women who worked under her, had similar burdens—Elaine with a mother with early onset dementia, Tiana with a fifteen-year-old daughter who'd just announced she was pregnant. In comparison Harriet's problems paled.

"Do you think you'll look for something else?" Tom asked.

Would she? It made sense. "I suppose," Harriet said after a pause. "Eventually. But I'm not in a rush. I just started, after all." And, in a weird way, she actually liked what she did.

No, it wasn't using her brain in the way she had eleven years ago. And no, it didn't pay very well. But it felt like a necessary step in the journey she had never expected—or wanted—to take.

"Well, it sounds like you've had quite a few hard knocks," Tom said with a smile that made Harriet's stomach start fluttering again, this time in a mixed way. It felt nice to have someone look at her with so much warmth and approval. Someone who was single and interested and present.

"As have you. Hopefully we're not too battered."

"Hopefully." Tom shifted on the sofa and his fingers brushed her shoulder. Harriet jerked involuntarily.

Tom smiled self-consciously and shifted a bit closer. It had been twenty years since Harriet had been on a date with someone she didn't know, and that someone had been Richard. Even so she recognized the look in Tom's eyes, the expectant hum in the air.

She froze, unsure what to do. How to feel. Then she thought of Richard and his kisses with Meghan. Technically, he'd said, he'd started it. So why shouldn't she? Even up the score a little?

It wasn't the best reason to kiss somebody, especially when that somebody wasn't her husband, but Harriet was curious. And, yes, even the tiniest bit excited. It wasn't quite desire, but it was something. She shifted closer too. Tom's pupils flared—message received. Harriet held her breath.

Tom smiled a slightly self-conscious, wry smile that Harriet couldn't decide if she liked or not. It looked a little too deliberate. Then he leaned forward, his hand drifting down to her shoulders. Harriet closed her eyes.

It all felt choreographed somehow, far more complex and less natural than she would have liked. And then—lips. The feel of them on hers was another jolt and, this time, a bigger one. They were so... unfamiliar. Dry, thankfully, and soft, no problems there. His hand tightened on her shoulder. He angled his body closer.

Harriet didn't move, didn't respond. She felt as if she were standing on the other side of the room, watching this play out with a kind of distant curiosity.

Then Tom nudged open her mouth with his tongue—and *eww*. She didn't want his tongue in her mouth. It was slimy and wet and—ugh. She didn't want to be kissing him. At all. The realization was both instantaneous and overwhelming. She drew back.

"Sorry," Tom said quickly, as if he thought she might be grossly offended. "I thought..."

"It's fine." Sort of. She'd just complicated what could

have been a nicely simple situation. Harriet took a deep breath. "I'm not sure I was ready for that, though." She knew she wasn't.

"That's okay. I mean, I'm patient."

"Okay." Harriet knew he would be waiting a long time. A very long time. "I should probably get going." She rose from the sofa and Tom did as well.

"Maybe we can do this again?" he asked. "The dinner part, at least?"

"Yes…" Harriet heard the note of hesitation in her voice. "Yes," she said, a bit more firmly. "I think so. Maybe." And then wondered what she was agreeing to, and why. Moving on didn't have to involve dating quite yet, and certainly not kissing.

Tom didn't try to kiss her goodnight, not even on the cheek, which was a good thing. Harriet wasn't sure how she would have responded to that. As it was, they did the awkward hug dance back and forth for a few seconds before they both fluttered their fingers and then Harriet was released out into the now-chilly night.

Whoa. She wasn't at all sure she wanted to do that again anytime soon. And yet… what *did* she want to do? It was the never-ending, unanswerable question.

Her phone buzzed in her pocket, surprising her. The number wasn't one she recognized, and with trepidation— fearing a call from A&E or worse—she answered.

"Harriet? It's Colin. Colin Heath."

"Colin…" Harriet knew him, of course, but she had no idea why he'd be calling her. "Sorry, is something wrong…?"

"A bit," Colin said, and he sounded uncharacteristically grim. "It's Richard."

Chapter Nineteen

HARRIET STOOD IN the doorway of The Drowned Sailor and squinted as she tried to see through the press of bodies. Wychwood-on-Lea's high street might be quiet, but at nine o'clock on a Friday night the pub was hopping. Rock music blared from speakers positioned above the bar, but Harriet could barely hear it over the raucous laughter and boisterous guffaws.

Colin hadn't told her much over the phone—only that he'd stumbled upon Richard at the pub, received an earful, and then realized Richard was far too drunk to go home by himself. Richard had rattled off Harriet's number, and here she was.

"Harriet!"

Harriet turned at the sound of her name and saw Colin waving from the back of the pub. She shouldered her way through the crowd, looking around for Richard but not seeing him anywhere.

"He's in the gents," Colin said when she'd finally made it across to him. "My mate's with him. He's not in good shape,

I'm afraid."

"Oh, dear." Harriet couldn't remember the last time she'd seen Richard drunk. In university, perhaps.

"Hat." She turned to see Richard staggering out of the WC, one arm loped around the shoulders of someone Harriet didn't recognize. *"Hat,* you came."

"Colin rang me, Richard."

He looked terrible, hair rumpled, face flushed, shirt untucked. And he reeked of beer and, yes, vomit. She took a step back. Richard burped and covered his mouth, or tried to.

"Sorry," he muttered.

Harriet looked at Colin, who shrugged. "He can't drive."

"I realize." She felt exasperated and unsure, but underneath it all was a strange sort of affection. "Come on, Richard," she said. "You can come home with me."

His face lit up blearily. "Really…"

"Yes, really. What else am I going to do with you?" With a sigh she took his arm and practically frog-marched him out of the pub.

The cool night air seemed to rouse him a little, and he straightened. "Sorry about this, Hat."

"You haven't called me Hat in a long time." Besides that one unfortunate mention when he'd first told her they were broke.

"I know," Richard said. "You haven't been Hat for ages."

"Let's not get into all that now. I need to get you home."

"I like the sound of that."

"Don't," Harriet said, but something fluttery was going on in her stomach. Again.

They walked in silence down the high street, and then turned off onto the narrow, darkened lane that led to Willoughby Manor. Under a pale, crescent moon, the manor house was dark, its crenellated towers thrusting into the night sky. Richard stumbled on the rutted road and she took his arm, his shoulder pressing against her. It was the closest they'd been in months. And he definitely did smell.

Back at the house the children were, thankfully, asleep, as was Daisy in her crate, and Ellie was curled up on the sofa, watching telly. Her eyes widened rather comically as Harriet came in with Richard's arm around her shoulders.

"What…"

"It's a long story," Harriet said. "But thanks for watching the kids. Any trouble?"

"Not at all. Mallory's still stirring upstairs, I think. I turned her light off at half past nine."

"Okay." Harriet extricated herself from Richard and he stood there, smiling goofily and swaying slightly.

"Right." Ellie looked from Harriet to Richard and back again, eyebrows raised in silent query.

"Thanks," Harriet said meaningfully, and with a knowing grin Ellie moved off. The door closed and with a deep breath Harriet turned around. "Right. I'm not letting you sleep on my sofa without a shower."

"Okay."

"I'll make you some coffee. The bathroom's upstairs—be quiet, for heaven's sake. The last thing I want is one of the kids seeing you."

"Would that be so bad?"

"Yes," Harriet snapped, on edge now. "It would. First of all because you're drunk and you reek, and second, because it would confuse them, and that's something none of us needs." Even if she was already starting to feel confused.

"Sorry," Richard murmured, repentant, and then headed upstairs.

"Brush your teeth while you're at it," Harriet called. "There's a spare toothbrush in the medicine cabinet." She heard the bathroom door click shut and she went to boil the kettle.

She tried to sift through her feelings as she spooned coffee into the cafetière and got out two mugs, but gave up after a few minutes because it was just too hard. Rescuing Richard from The Drowned Sailor on top of her evening with Tom, as well as that semi-awful kiss, left her feeling too unsettled to figure out what was really going on underneath the disquiet.

The coffee made, she checked the mirror by the front door to make sure she didn't have something stuck in her teeth and that her hair wasn't frizzing too badly. Good on both points, although why she was bothering when Richard had smelled like a brewery, she didn't know.

Realizing his clothes would still smell, Harriet went upstairs and dug out an old shirt of Richard's she wore as pajamas and a pair of his track bottoms that had somehow found their way to Willoughby Close. She left the clothes outside the bathroom, pausing for a few seconds to listen to Richard humming in the shower. Imagining him in the shower, water streaming, *naked*—

She was ridiculous.

The shower turned off and Harriet hurried downstairs.

A few minutes later Richard came down, smelling like soap and toothpaste, his hair damp and curling. Harriet pinned a smile on her face and handed him a cup of black coffee.

"To sober me up?" Richard said with a wry smile, his eyebrows lifted. "Thank you."

"You're welcome." She clutched her mug, holding it in front of her almost like a shield, at a loss now that he was here, showered, smiling, and so very Richard. "So what happened?" she asked eventually. "How did you end up half-cut in The Drowned Sailor?"

"Well." Richard moved to the sofa and after a second Harriet followed. "I stopped by here first."

Surprise rippled through her. "You did? Why?"

"To see the kids." A pause as he sipped his coffee, averting his gaze. "To see you."

"Why?" Harriet asked again, dumbly.

She sat down on the sofa with a thud, and Richard sat on

the other end. Just as she and Tom had done earlier. She'd entered *The Twilight Zone* of relationships.

"I wanted to give you something." He let out a little, uncertain laugh and then went to fetch something from his coat. Harriet watched him, baffled.

"It's nothing much," Richard said as he fished something out of the coat's pocket. "Here." He handed her a bundled up T-shirt and Harriet shook it out, letting out a little laugh as she saw the logo on the front. *I Survived the School Dinner Rush.*

She'd forgotten how he used to make her T-shirts—*I Survived the School Disco, I Survived Ten Years of Toddler Group.* It had been a joke between them, one she'd forgotten about.

"Thanks," she said, and carefully folded the T-shirt back up. "That was thoughtful. I have a lot more of them to survive, though."

"And I'm sure you will." Richard sat back on the sofa. "I really came here tonight because I wanted to. Because… because I miss you, Harriet. I realize I haven't said that, not up front. I had more fun chatting with you on the phone for five minutes than hours with—"

"Don't," Harriet cut him off, acid in her voice. "Don't talk about Meghan now, please."

Richard looked down at his coffee. "I miss you," he said again, quiet now but no less heartfelt.

"So you came here and found I was out…"

"With Tom. Who the hell is he?"

"Daisy's vet. We're just friends, Richard. Acquaintances." She thought about making a cheap shot about his friendship with Meghan, but somehow she didn't feel like it right now.

"Mallory was acting like it was a date."

"Of course she was." Harriet leaned her head back against the sofa, her mind spinning as if she was the one who had downed several pints. "We are legally separated, you know."

"I never wanted that."

"I know. You wanted to have your cake and eat it too. Quite a lot of it." She lifted her head to give him a direct look. "Are you still seeing Meghan? And please don't give me the spiel about how you were never seeing her that way. You know what I mean."

"Yes, I do." Richard's steady look back was just as direct. "And I'm not. Not so much as a text. I told her that we couldn't be friends anymore. I'd already come to the decision, but hearing that you were out with some guy, even if it was just as friends… it made me furious." He gave her an apologetic grimace. "I wanted to punch him, and you know I'm not a punching kind of bloke. But it also made me realize how unfair my friendship with Meghan was to you, Harriet. I don't think I quite saw it that way before, but trust me, now I do, and I don't ever plan on talking to her again."

Harriet's breath came out in a rush, surprised and a little wary by this easy victory. "Okay."

"My marriage is far more important than a friendship that never should have happened in the first place. I was stupid, Harriet. Completely stupid. I don't know how I came to be in the place I was, but I did."

Here was the groveling she'd been craving for so long, and yet now she didn't know what to do with it. "I know what you mean," Harriet said after a pause. She felt as if she were carefully edging around a vast and gaping emotional pit. "I feel like I'd become someone else without realizing it. Someone I don't really like, actually. And I know you didn't like her, either." It still hurt to say that.

"But I love you." He looked at her seriously, unblinkingly. "Do you believe that?"

"I'm not sure what that even means, or who I am anymore. Can I find myself at age thirty-nine? Do I have to?"

"I'll find you." Richard shifted on the sofa, closer to her. "I want to find you. Can we try again, Harriet? Properly? Please?"

Harriet's fingers clenched on the stem of her wineglass. No evasions anymore, just bold questions and hard truths. Emotional risk. "How are we meant to do that, exactly? You're in London and I'm here."

"I come here two or three times a week. We can see each other then."

Which meant...? Harriet's stomach started fizzing. It had been so long since she'd been touched or kissed, not counting tonight's clumsy experience with Tom. So long since she'd felt comfortable and safe and desired and *loved*. She missed that. She missed it a lot, but she still wasn't sure she and Richard could recapture what they had. But perhaps they could try.

"Maybe," Harriet said slowly. "But at this point, Richard, I don't even know what that would look like." Or feel like.

"How about I take you out on a date? Dinner at a nice restaurant."

"We can't afford it."

"Fine, dinner at The Drowned Sailor. Or McDonald's, if you'd rather. We go out and we have fun and we get to know each other again. Because it's been a long time, I think, since either of us felt like we knew the other person. Since we knew ourselves."

"I know." Harriet tucked her knees up and wrapped one arm around them, hugging herself close. They were in agreement about that, but she still felt uncertain. Afraid. "And then what?" she asked.

"Then we see what happens. I'm hoping to get this job I told you about. We could be living in Wychwood House or something like it in a few months."

"Really?" With a flicker of surprise Harriet realized she wasn't quite as pleased about that as she would have expected.

"It's still on the market. I could knock them down to a million five, I bet."

It made her head spin. She was earning minimum wage and counting pennies at the supermarket, and now he was talking about buying one of the most expensive houses in the village? "Do you really think it's in our price range?"

"With my signing bonus we could manage it. And I want you to be happy, Harriet. I want us to be happy."

The trouble was, Harriet didn't know if Wychwood House would make her happy anymore. Once upon a time she'd pinned all her hopes, all her ambitions, on the beautiful house in the country and the idyllic life to go along with it. Once upon a time.

Now? Now she felt she didn't know anything anymore.

"It can all happen for us, Harriet," Richard said, his tone sounding so sure, so promising. "We can get back together; we can live in the house you've always wanted. We can send Mallory to Ellerton, even. Just give me a chance to make it all right."

How could she deny him a chance? And the picture he was painting *was* seductive. A life of ease and comfort again, but they would have learned and changed from the experience. Better and better. She wouldn't turn back into the person she'd been, shallow and image-obsessed without even realizing it. She certainly wouldn't spend the way she had. The children could have a big garden, and a pony, and all the afterschool activities they wanted. Holidays in Provence, skiing in Verbier…

Life could be perfect. So why did she feel so uneasy?

"Let's take it one day at a time," Harriet said finally. "To begin with."

"Fine, let's start with tomorrow. How about I spend the day with you and the kids?"

"I was going to visit Lady Stokeley in the morning." After five days of treatment Lady Stokeley had to be starting to feel the effects, and Harriet wanted to check in on her.

"Okay, then I'll watch the kids while you do that. After that we'll do something together. A walk in the woods, maybe, and a picnic?"

"I think it's meant to rain."

"Harriet." Richard looked affectionately exasperated, and Harriet managed a small smile.

"I'm scared, Richard," she said quietly. "That's the truth."

"Scared of what?"

"Scared of trying. Scared of it not working out between us, and the kids and I are left in an even worse place emotionally, even physically. I know this doesn't seem like much," she added, gesturing to the house, "but we've settled here and everyone seems to be doing okay. Doing well, even. Mallory's made new friends and so have I and I don't want to upend it all for something that's not a sure thing." What if she moved out of Willoughby Close and then it all fell apart again? She wasn't sure she'd be able to recover a second time.

Richard flinched a little, and she knew she'd hurt him with that remark. "Nothing in life is a sure thing."

"No, but…" Harriet let out a gusty breath. "Some things are more sure than others."

"You don't trust me."

"Should I? You lied to me for six *months*. You embarked on an affair, yes, I know, only emotionally, more or less, but *still*. I know I'm partly to blame for the train wreck our lives had become without us even realizing, but I don't think I abused your trust." She held his gaze. "Did I?"

Richard looked away before resolutely turning back to her. "No, you didn't. I'm the one who lied, in a lot of different ways, and for that I am sorry. Truly sorry, more than you could possible realize, I think."

"What freelance work have you been doing?" Harriet asked abruptly. Richard looked startled.

"Nothing much…"

"Tell me, Richard. I want truth between us, in everything. No more evasions. No more lies."

"I'm tutoring in history and economics," he said. "For GCSE pupils."

"Oh." What had she been expecting? Not that, certainly.

She realized she'd been afraid he'd been doing something risky with investments and finance. Something that could set them back even farther, or blow up completely. Again.

"Do you enjoy it?" she asked.

"It's fine. Doesn't make much money, but…" He shrugged. "It pays a few bills."

He'd studied history in university, and when they'd been

first years Harriet remembered him talking about becoming a teacher. Dismissively, because there was no money in it, but with a tiny hint of longing.

"So?" Richard pressed. "You said you wanted to take it one day at a time. How about tomorrow, then? We'll start there."

Was there any reason, any reason at all, to say no? Harriet tried to imagine the children's reactions when they learned they'd all be spending the day together, happy families cobbled together. Was she setting them up for disappointment? Setting herself up?

"Okay," she said at last. "Tomorrow."

Richard grinned, his whole face transformed by lightness and joy, so much so that Harriet had to smile back. Felt a little skip of excitement inside, even.

"You won't regret it, Harriet," he said. "I promise."

"It's just a picnic," Harriet answered as she uncurled herself from the sofa. "And remember, it might rain." She didn't know whether she was speaking metaphorically or not.

"Then we'll have a picnic in the rain." Richard took their coffee cups into the kitchen and Harriet stood there, watching him rinse the glasses in the sink, realizing how much she missed having someone in her life. How much she'd missed him.

Then Richard turned and saw her staring. In a single second the mood changed from affable to something far more intense. Harriet's breath caught in her throat. She wasn't ready for this.

"Harriet..." He walked towards her, heat simmering in his eyes.

Harriet felt as if she were caught in a snare, unable to move. He stood before her, gazing at her so steadily, with so much certainty. How he had arrived at such a sure place so quickly? She still felt beleaguered by doubt.

And yet... that look. She wasn't immune. Excitement and anticipation made her stomach turn over. She was still holding her breath.

Richard reached up and brushed a strand of hair from her face. His fingers touched her skin and she shivered. It had been a long time since she'd been affected like this. Since *he'd* affected her like this.

"Do you know," she said, her voice sounding wobbly, "I can't actually remember the last time we had sex."

Richard laughed softly. "Maybe it's time for a reminder, then."

"No, Richard." She made herself sound firm. "One day at a time, remember?"

"I know." He brushed his fingers down her cheek. "But I've missed you, Harriet."

"Have you?"

"Yes. I wish you would believe me." He brought his hands up to her shoulders, his fingers curling around them. "Please believe me," he whispered, and started drawing her towards him.

And Harriet went, because part of her—a large part—didn't even want to resist. And yet as her lips parted in anticipation of his kiss, she remembered that the last person he'd kissed was Meghan. And even though she knew she was hurting them both she stepped back.

"I'm not there yet." Her voice trembled. "Not yet," she said again, and wrapped her arms around herself.

Richard looked gutted but after a second he rallied, nodding slowly. "Okay. Sorry, I shouldn't have rushed things."

"You can sleep on the sofa." Harriet turned away, trying to compose herself. She felt scraped raw, by everything. "I'll get some sheets and blankets. Why don't you let Daisy out for a wee?"

Blindly she went upstairs and rummaged through the linen cupboard. When she came downstairs Richard had resettled Daisy in her crate.

"She's a sweet little thing."

"Yes. The children love her."

She proffered the sheets and together they made the sofa up, both of them working in strained silence. Harriet felt as if she should apologize, but she didn't.

She tucked the blankets into the side of the sofa and then stepped back. "There." She pictured Mallory coming downstairs in the morning and skidding to a surprised halt at the sight of her father lying there. "What are you going to say to the kids?"

"I won't get their hopes up too much, if that's what

you're worried about."

It was. "Okay." She let out a breath. "I hope Daisy doesn't disturb you too much. She whimpers sometimes, in the night."

"I'll be fine."

Harriet nodded and then, with nothing left to do, turned and headed upstairs. As she turned the corner she heard Richard's voice, soft and sad.

"Goodnight, Harriet."

Chapter Twenty

HARRIET WOKE TO sunlight streaming through the windows, the sound of laughter, and the smell of pancakes. Dread seeped into her stomach, which seemed an unreasonable reaction to so many positive things.

And yet... *I won't get their hopes up too much.* What had happened to that promise?

Quickly she showered and dressed, pausing to slap on some makeup and make sure her hair was behaving itself. It wasn't as if she were actually making an effort. Not exactly.

Downstairs, happy chaos reigned. Richard was at the stove, with her pink apron on over the trackie bottoms and T-shirt he'd worn to bed, just like in the old days, flipping pancakes high. In fact one had, judging by the grease stain, hit the ceiling.

The children were surrounding him, Mallory slouched on a stool, pretending to look bored, William jumping up and down and occasionally tackling Richard for no apparent reason, Chloe hugging his legs. Health and safety regulations be damned, Harriet thought in bemusement. The pan on the stove close to Chloe's head was smoking.

"Good morning."

"Mummy!" Chloe turned to her with delight. "Look who's here."

"I think Mum knows, Chloe," Mallory said in a well-duh tone.

Harriet gave her a look, and Mallory shrugged and raised her eyebrows, clearly wondering what was going on. And what could Harriet tell her? Already this felt complicated.

"And he's making pancakes," Chloe continued, blissfully oblivious to any undercurrents. "I'm having mine with golden syrup. Lots of golden syrup."

The bottle of syrup, Harriet saw, had tipped on its side and the sticky contents were now oozing out. In her rose-tinted memory of Richard's kitchen sessions, she'd forgotten what an absolute mess he made. Men definitely could not multitask.

"How lovely," she said, and Richard quirked an eyebrow at her, his smile a little questioning.

Harriet smiled back, a working of her mouth that didn't feel quite real. She didn't know how to feel. Didn't know whether she should go with this, and all the joy Richard seemed to be bringing to the children, or hang back a little, stay a bit cool. A little safe.

"Mummy." Chloe ran over to tug on her shirt. "You're going to have a pancake, aren't you?"

"I suppose I will."

"You always like Daddy's pancakes." Chloe was heart-breakingly earnest.

It was impossible not to see how excited she was about having her parents together, her family whole.

"Yes, I've always liked them," Harriet said dutifully, and righted the bottle of golden syrup.

They ate the pancakes crowded around the table, and Harriet tried not to notice what a bomb-site the kitchen had become—splotches of golden syrup everywhere, pans left grease-spattered on the stove top, flour and icing sugar dusting everything.

The mess didn't matter. She knew that. What was important now was that they were together, that William was laughing and Chloe was on Richard's lap, and even Mallory was smiling. They were happy, and they were a family. So why did she still feel uneasy?

"Right," Richard said to the children when they'd finished the last of the pancakes, along with the golden syrup. "Why don't we clean up while your mum visits Lady Stokeley?"

"What? Oh." Harriet stared at him in surprise.

He really was making an effort. She left them all clearing the table, William balancing too many plates and Chloe drawing patterns in the spilled icing sugar. She promised to be back in an hour, and Richard suggested they all go for a walk since it was, despite Harriet's warnings last night, not raining.

"A walk?" Mallory said with deep suspicion. "Why would we want to walk anywhere?"

"You're not a teenager yet so enough with the attitude," Richard said good-naturedly. "And you're not taking your phone."

It felt good to have someone else help to shoulder the burden, Harriet reflected as she walked down the drive from Willoughby Close to the manor house. The sky was a pale grey, with darker clouds on the horizon. It wasn't raining yet, but it most likely soon would be.

Richard was making a huge effort to help, to be involved, but how long would it last? As soon as he got a job, whether it was this edgy one he was hoping for, he'd be back in London working all hours and she'd be left in Wychwood-on-Lea alone, struggling. Because she had been struggling, even if she hadn't thought so at the time.

She'd been lonely and frustrated, and she'd filled up her life with things that didn't matter. Harriet didn't think she'd do that again, but she didn't want to go back to anything close to the status quo. She didn't think Richard did either, at least not between them. But what about his job? The status, the money, the *stuff?*

The manor house was quiet and empty-feeling when Harriet poked her head round the massive front door. "Lady Stokeley?"

There was no answer, and so after checking in the downstairs room Lady Stokeley used she tiptoed upstairs and tapped on her bedroom door. There was no answer, and feeling uneasy and a bit invasive, Harriet cracked it open.

Lady Stokeley was lying in bed asleep. Her face looked paler and more wrinkled than ever, her body seeming tiny and frail beneath the worn satin coverlet.

"Lady Stokeley?" Harriet whispered, guilt needling her.

She'd left her after her last chemo treatment two days ago, and hadn't checked back to see if she was coping. From what she'd read online, a patient started to feel the effects of the chemotherapy around now.

Lady Stokeley's eyes fluttered open and it took her a moment to focus on Harriet. "Hello, my dear," she murmured, her voice a raspy thread of sound.

"Hello." Harriet smiled. "Can I get you anything?"

"A bucket, perhaps." Lady Stokeley sighed and her eyes fluttered closed again. "I'm afraid I've been rather ill."

"From the chemo…"

"It would appear so. I was hoping to avoid that most unpleasant side-effect, but the antinausea medication I received doesn't seem to help." She smiled faintly, her eyes still closed, and Harriet's heart ached. It was a miserable existence, enduring this all alone in this huge, empty house.

"Would you like a cup of tea?" she asked, because she couldn't think of anything else she could do. "And some toast maybe, with just a little bit of butter?"

Lady Stokeley grimaced. "I don't think I can keep anything down."

"You need to eat," Harriet protested with rising alarm.

She knew enough about cancer to know that keeping one's strength up was vitally important. Lady Stokeley was thin enough as it was. She didn't have any weight to spare.

"Very well." Her lips twitched. "I shall endeavor to eat some toast. Since I've already endured that wretched chemotherapy, I can hardly fall at this small hurdle."

"Good." Lady Stokeley's strength of spirit was an inspiration, but Harriet still worried. How was she going to cope here all alone?

Downstairs in the cavernous kitchen she noted the lack of food—a few slices of bread going stale and one box of UHT milk—with ever increasing alarm. She definitely needed to do a shop. And Lady Stokeley, whether she wanted it or not, needed more help.

Harriet made the toast and tea and brought it back upstairs. Lady Stokeley had fallen asleep again, but she opened her eyes as Harriet came in.

"Thank you, my dear."

"I'm going to stay here until you eat this," Harriet warned. "Every bite."

Lady Stokeley managed a small smile. "I have not had so stern a taskmaster since my nanny insisted I eat my porridge. I've always hated porridge."

"I won't make you porridge, then," Harriet answered as she pulled up the powder puff stool to the side of the bed.

Lady Stokeley struggled to sit up and Harriet leaned forward to help her, conscious of how thin her arms felt, how bird-like her bones, so light they felt hollow.

"You cannot imagine how aggravating it is to be so feeble," Lady Stokeley said once she was upright, leaning back against her pillows, her breath coming out in a shuddering gasp. "So utterly maddening."

"No," Harriet agreed quietly. "I can't imagine."

Lady Stokeley gave her one of her shrewd looks. "You really cannot, you know. Perhaps you think you can, but no one actually believes one is going to grow old. Not like this." She held out one scrawny, claw-like hand, the veins bumpy and blue. "It's shocking, even when it shouldn't be, to see your body wither and, of course, die. Eventually." Her mouth curved up in a smile, her eyes glinting with humor. "Please don't lecture me on how I need to be positive or some such nonsense. I am perfectly entitled to a moment's complaint."

"Of course you are," Harriet answered, and gestured to the plate. "Now eat."

It took forty-five painstaking minutes for Lady Stokeley to nibble her way through a single piece of barely buttered toast. Harriet watched, wondering how to broach what she knew would be an uncomfortable topic. Finally, when Lady Stokeley had pushed the plate away, Harriet said carefully, "Lady Stokeley, have you told anyone about your— diagnosis? And your treatment?"

"I think," Lady Stokeley said, "that it is perhaps time you

called me Dorothy."

Harriet smiled at that. "Dorothy, then. What about your nephew, Henry Trent? Have you spoken to him?"

Dorothy sighed. "No, I have not. And before you tell me that I should, let me remind you, Harriet, that I am in full possession of my mental faculties if not my physical ones, and I have good reason for not ringing my only living relative." She sagged back against the pillows, her eyes closed, that brief diatribe having exhausted her.

"I'm sure you do," Harriet said quietly. "But I'm worried about you here all alone. I don't think it's safe—"

"I am perfectly safe."

"What if you became really ill?" Harriet pressed. Dorothy's eyes snapped open, full of ire.

"I have already been really ill, and I have managed. Now I appreciate you are speaking out of concern, but I do not need your well-intentioned interference in this matter." She took a short, sharp breath. "You are very young, Harriet, even if you don't think you are. I have endured and experienced far more than you have, although I appreciate these last few months have been difficult for you. But the truth is, and will remain, that you know very little of my situation."

That was her told. Harriet couldn't remember the last time she'd receiving such a scolding. She had no choice but to drop the matter. "Very well," she said after a pause. "But may I ask, have you told Abby? And Ellie? Because I think they should know."

Dorothy's mouth compressed. "Very well," she said after a moment. "I will tell Abby when she next visits. I imagine she suspects something already, since I have been so fatigued. Now if you don't mind, I'd like to get some rest."

"Okay." Clearly a dismissal. Harriet took the cup and plate, feeling both chastened and helpless. "Is there anything else I can—"

"No." Dorothy closed her eyes, leaving Harriet no choice but to tiptoe out of the room, closing the door quietly behind her.

Back at Willoughby Close the kitchen was, amazingly, clean, a picnic had been packed, Richard had changed into jeans and a jumper he'd had in his car, and the children were all wearing welly boots, ready for their walk. The gray clouds gathering on the horizon had started to spread, but Richard dismissed them with a shrug of his shoulders.

"If it rains, it rains. We've all got Macs on."

And so they headed out, making for the Lea River, Daisy frisking at their heels, delighted to be out and about, and with so much company.

The day was cool and muggy, the air already feeling damp. Harriet dug her hands into the pockets of her waterproof jacket as she watched William and Richard kick a football back and forth across the muddy ground as they walked. Chloe was skipping ahead, singing, and Mallory, deciding whether she wanted to keep sulking about the confiscation of her phone, walked a little behind.

When had they last had a family walk? When had they last done *anything* as a family? Richard had been gone so much and then when he had been home, Harriet had usually had a laundry list of to-do items for him to tick off, usually involving paperwork or DIY. And when he wasn't doing that, he was holed up in his study, pretending he was doing work when he was probably surfing the Internet or watching his ridiculous sci-fi television programs.

How had they got into such a massive rut? She didn't know whether to be depressed she hadn't realized it, or encouraged that she finally had. And she wasn't at all sure that a couple of burned pancakes and an afternoon walk was going to dig them out of it.

"Mummy, look!" Chloe danced back towards her on her tiptoes, pointing to a line of ducklings in the river, all of them paddling furiously behind their proud mother.

"Aren't they sweet," Harriet said, and smiling down at Chloe, she reached for her hand.

She needed to stop worrying so much, stop second-guessing absolutely everything. She'd just try to enjoy this moment, this day, without wondering where it might lead.

They walked farther down the river than Harriet ever had before, with Mallory only asking for her phone twice and William and Richard kicking the football back and forth, once kicking it accidentally into the river. Richard got it back with a tree branch, and Chloe cheered. Harriet's heart started to lighten. Maybe she didn't need to make this so hard after all.

About half a mile past the bridge that led to the high street and the school, they found a clearing with a fallen tree that looked like a good place for their makeshift picnic. Harriet spread the rug while Richard got out the food and the children mucked about.

Then she sat down and glanced at the offerings, unable to hide her bemusement. Half a bag of stale crisps, two browning bananas, a single juice box, and a couple of slices of ham that looked like it was about to go off. Admittedly, she hadn't had much in the way of food in the house, but what about bread for sandwiches? Or water since they were all thirsty?

Richard looked at the food piled in the middle of the rug and gave Harriet a wry smile. "That's a bit pathetic, isn't it?"

"It's fine," Harriet said bracingly, surprising herself.

In another life, an old one, she would have found a way to show him how annoyed she was. Said or at least thought how if she wanted something done properly, she would have done it herself. All right, perhaps she was still thinking that, at least a little, but maybe having something done properly wasn't as important as she'd once thought.

They divided it all between them—bananas, crisps, ham. They even passed around the juice box, taking sips, save for Mallory, who said that they were all disgusting. As they finished it up it started to rain, big fat drops that promised a good soaking.

Richard cleared away the rubbish while Harriet bundled up the rug, and somehow, even though it was pouring, it felt okay.

"This was the worst picnic ever," Mallory pronounced, but she was smiling.

They walked back down alongside the river to the footbridge, and then down the high street. It was still pouring rain and they were all soaked but nobody seemed to mind.

"How about some proper food?" Richard suggested, and nodded towards Olivia's teashop.

Harriet did a mental calculation of how much hot chocolate and scones for everyone would cost, and then decided this was not the time to parse pennies. "Sounds lovely," she said, and they all headed into the shop, which was thankfully empty, as five people and a frantic puppy would drive even the most loyal customers away.

"Hello," Olivia said in surprise as she bustled out of the back room. "Nice to see you again."

Mallory gave Harriet a suspicious look, clearly wanting to ask how Harriet knew this person.

Harriet just smiled contentedly. "Hi, Olivia," she said. "Cream teas for everyone, I think. And do you mind a very wet puppy in here?"

"Not at all," Olivia answered, now smiling broadly, and she headed back to the kitchen.

Harriet shrugged off her sopping jacket, catching Richard's eye and then sharing a complicit smile that made her insides tingle. In that moment, despite the rain and the pathetic picnic and Mallory's occasional moans, the day felt near perfect, her uncertainties scattered.

As they sat down at two spindly tables, the children already starting to bicker, their clothes lightly steaming and Daisy pressing close to their legs, Harriet wanted to simply keep hold of this moment. To remember it always, to live in it—shining and perfect.

Chapter Twenty-One

HARRIET KEPT HOLD of that perfect feeling—well, almost perfect—for the next two golden weeks of May. Richard spent several evenings a week in Willoughby Close, helping Mallory with her homework, kicking a ball with William, tucking Chloe into bed with her legion of stuffed animals.

Watching him, covertly of course, engaged in all these activities made Harriet realize how much the children had missed him. Not just since January, but for a long time before that. They'd all become accustomed to being without him. And while it was good—wonderful, in fact—to see Richard spending so much time with the children, she wondered how long this honeymoon period would last.

In the evenings when the kids were in bed, he spent time with her. They'd sit on the sofa with a glass of wine or take Daisy out to the garden for a late-night play. They didn't do anything exciting, but it was nice simply to sit and talk, to get to know each other again. It was also strange, because Harriet had to keep reminding herself that this was Richard, her husband, the man she'd shared so much of life with. It felt like meeting someone new as well as slipping into something familiar and well-worn. The best kind of dating, in a weird way, although the stakes were so much higher.

But Harriet was trying not to think about what was at stake. Chloe had asked her several times if Daddy would be moving to Willoughby Close, something Harriet couldn't quite imagine. And Mallory kept giving her speculative and even suspicious looks, but when Harriet tried to ask her how she was feeling about things, she exhaled heavily and rolled her eyes, fobbing her off with some attitude. No real change there, and yet Harriet knew her daughter well enough now to realize she was hiding her fear. She didn't want this to crash and burn, just as Harriet didn't.

Two weeks after that rainy picnic she and Richard were having dinner at The Drowned Sailor, to celebrate the interview he'd had that morning in London. They'd taken to making the slightly down-at-heel their regular, in part to avoid their old crowd—Sophie and Cheryl were now BFFs and had taken to acting, quite obviously, as if Harriet did not exist—but also because people they knew, people like Ellie and Jace, Colin and Anna, went there. And the food, plain and no-frills as it was, was surprisingly good.

"I've got a feeling about this one," Richard said as he poured them both glasses from the bottle of champagne he'd impetuously ordered to celebrate his interview. "They seemed keen, really keen. They liked that I was willing to take risks."

"Did they?" Harriet tried to sound pleased when what she really felt was faintly alarmed. Surely there had been enough risk taking already.

"Yes, their attitude is much more pragmatic. Win some, lose some. That's how it is in this business." His chest swelled, and she saw that old glint in his eye. Finally getting an interview had certainly jazzed him up.

"So when will you find out?"

"Not for a week or two. They might call me in again, talk to some higher-ups…" He shrugged. "It doesn't happen overnight. There are a lot of details to work out, you know."

"Right." It had been nearly a year since he'd worked in finance. "And what about the tutoring? How is that going?"

"The tutoring?" Richard looked at her blankly.

"Yes, the GCSE students you're tutoring in history and economics? How is that going?"

"Oh." He looked bemused. "I enjoy it, actually. I've got a couple of really bright kids, very motivated. And I've always liked history, you know that."

"Yes…" For years she'd bought him a subscription to a very nerdy-looking history magazine for his birthday, and he'd always read it from cover to cover and then kept the issues to read again.

"But it doesn't pay the bills," Richard finished. "Or a new house or anything like that."

"But if it did…" Harriet said slowly.

Richard frowned. "What is the problem, Harriet? I'm going to get another job. I'm going to get it all back."

She'd heard this so many times and, for so long, she'd wanted to believe it. But now she wasn't sure she did. "But I don't want to go back to the way we were, Richard."

"And we won't." He made it sound so simple. "Of course we won't. We're going to be different, Hat, we're going to be better. But I need to do this." He leaned forward, his face intent. "I need to show I can get back on the horse, you know? I can't walk away from it all. I won't." There was hard edge to his voice that made Harriet blink. Had he just given her an ultimatum?

Richard smiled and poured them both more champagne. "And how is your adopted granny?"

"Lady Stokeley?" She still had trouble calling her Dorothy. "The same, more or less." Harriet had continued to drive her to her chemo treatments, and after that first week Dorothy had rallied a bit. She was eating a bit more, and seemed determined to fight on. She hadn't, as far as Harriet could tell, called her nephew, but she had told Abby and Ellie about her diagnosis. Ellie had been tearful and distraught, but Abby had seemed grimly determined.

"If anyone can beat cancer," she'd said, "Lady Stokeley can."

Harriet had to agree with her.

"It's good of you to drive her to Oxford," Richard said.

"She is paying me." Harriet had tried to refuse that first

check, and then Lady Stokeley had simply given her a look, so Harriet had laughed and thanked her—and taken it. Twenty-one pounds was twenty-one pounds, after all, and half of her daily income.

"What happens if you don't get this job?" she asked abruptly and he blinked, looking a bit affronted.

"I'm counting on that scenario not happening."

"I know, but..." Why did the thing she'd once wanted most now feel like something unpalatable, even frightening? The last few weeks had been good, even great in some ways, but Harriet couldn't keep the unease from settling the pit of her stomach, a stone she couldn't dislodge. "But what will happen if you don't?" she pressed.

"Why are you asking?" Richard asked. "Don't you have faith in me?"

"It's not about faith in you, Richard."

"Isn't it?" Richard lifted his chin. "I know I got us into this mess, Harriet, and I told you, I'm going to get us out of it."

Harriet knew there was no point in arguing, not now, when Richard was practically drawing a line in the sand. "I suppose we'll cross that bridge when we come to it," she said.

She realized she was no longer thinking of her life at Willoughby Close as a blip. A bump on the road. She didn't *want* to think of it that way.

"What if..." she began, and Richard leaned over and touched her hand.

"Let's not worry about the what-if scenarios just yet, Harriet. I've got a good feeling about this interview. I really think it's all coming around for us." He squeezed her hand, and Harriet managed to smile back.

Back at Willoughby Close, Richard walked her to her door as if she were sixteen and her father was waiting at the window, twitching the net curtains. Two weeks of dating and they had done no more than kiss, lightly, at the door. Harriet wasn't sure how long she was going to hold back, only that she wasn't ready yet to delve back into those marital intimacies they'd once enjoyed what felt like a very long time ago. Strange, to feel sex was such a monumental step with a man who had bought her tampons and seen her nether parts getting sewn up.

As they reached the little courtyard, now full of flower pots and climbing clematis, Richard said, "I was thinking perhaps we could all spend half-term together, go on a holiday."

Harriet let out a surprised laugh. "On holiday? Where?" Where could they afford?

"What about a camping trip? I think we still have all the gear from that trip we took years ago."

An ill-fated camping trip to Normandy, when Mallory had been a toddler and William a baby. Not a good time to sleep in a tent. Breastfeeding in a sleeping bag was as difficult as it sounded, and they'd taken turns chasing Mallory and rocking William, both of them looking shell-shocked from lack of sleep. Harriet had vowed never to go camping again. Just the thought of sharing such a tiny space with her entire family made her cringe inwardly a little.

"I looked online and there's a place up in the lake district that's pretty cheap," Richard continued. "Beautiful spot, near Ambleside. We always wanted to go there, do you remember?"

Vaguely, when they'd briefly gone through an outdoorsy period, back in university. Harriet had somehow got it into her head that hiking was fun. She'd since learned better. And yet… a holiday. Together. That wouldn't cost too much. It would be a litmus test of their relationship, their strength as a family… and as a couple. And the children would love it. Well, not Mallory. But Chloe and William would.

"What about Dorothy?" Harriet asked. "I need to drive her to Oxford…"

"Could someone else do that, for a couple of days?"

Harriet hesitated. She hated the thought of letting Dorothy down, and yet she was also recognizing more and more that she could not provide all the help an inform elderly lady needed. But *camping*… it really did feel like a test. A grueling one.

"I'll see," she said.

The next afternoon she stopped by Willoughby Manor to ask Dorothy if she could help to arrange another driver for the week. "I think Ellie could do it," she said hesitantly. "She's taking a few days off work. Or Jace…" She trailed off as Dorothy waved a beringed hand, the rings now sliding up and down her thin fingers. She'd lost weight since beginning the chemo, and she hadn't had any to lose.

"I'm sure something can be arranged. I would hardly want you to miss your holiday." Her blue eyes narrowed as she gave Harriet an openly speculative look. "If I am not mistaken, this is a holiday *en famille?*"

Harriet let out a surprised laugh. "Yes… how did you know?" She'd shared very little of her life with Dorothy, despite their many hours together.

"I have my sources." Dorothy leaned back in her seat. She'd made it out to the terrace today, and was sitting in the sunshine, a bit of color in her cheeks. "I'm pleased for you, my dear."

"Thank you. Although it isn't as exciting as it sounds. Camping in the lake district."

Dorothy gave an eloquent shudder. "Something I have never been remotely tempted to do. But perhaps you shall enjoy it."

"Perhaps. We're trying, anyway. To make it work." Dorothy nodded, and Harriet knew she understood she wasn't just talking about camping.

"I found marriage to be a great deal of hard work," she said after a moment, her eyes closed, her face tilted to the sun. "And the work is often necessary at the very time when you least feel like doing it."

"Yes, I suppose that's true," Harriet agreed. She paused

and then dared to ask, "But you were happy, Dorothy? In your marriage?" Suddenly it felt important to know.

Dorothy didn't answer for a long moment. Finally she said, "Young people these days, and I count you among them, set so much store by happiness. You're always asking yourselves, 'Am I happy? Is this making me happy?' as if that is so very important." She let out a rasping laugh. "I cannot imagine how one can determine such a thing, especially amidst such endless analysis."

"You haven't answered the question," Harriet reminded her gently. "But I understand what you're saying."

"Do you?" Dorothy opened her eyes. "I wonder." She sighed, her gaze now on the green lawn rolling out to the yew hedge border. "My marriage was something I am proud of," she said at last. "Because it took work, at times a great deal of work. Because I stayed in it, even and especially when the work was required. At times I was happy, yes, at times I was very happy. But overall, at the end of my life? It's not whether I've been happy that concerns me."

Harriet couldn't help but be a bit shocked by this. "What concerns you, then?" she asked.

Dorothy was silent again, and Harriet didn't think she'd answer. "Oh, the usual claptrap," she said on a sigh. "Whether I've been a good person. A good wife, and sister, daughter, friend. I never had the chance to be a mother, not properly, more's the pity."

"Not properly?"

Dorothy just shook her head. Harriet could tell she was starting to tire, and she decided they'd had enough of a heart-to-heart for the moment, although she would love to know more.

She helped her back inside and settled her in her bed with a cup of tea. She'd done a shop at Waitrose a few days ago so at least Dorothy had plenty of ready-made meals and tins of decent soup, proper milk and not boxes of UHT, as well as a pack of freshly made chocolate croissants—Harriet had seen, to her satisfaction, that two had already been eaten.

Harriet was still mulling over the old lady's words as she headed back to Willoughby Close. Was she too concerned about her own happiness? Her children's happiness? Was she chasing pleasure with an ax rather than living life as it came, accepting the joys along with the sorrows? Maybe happiness was a by-product rather than an end point—and if so, what did that mean for her and Richard?

She supposed right now it meant they'd go camping.

Two weeks later, for the first day of half-term, Harriet was gazing into the back of the Rover, wondering how on earth they were going to fit all their camping kit in it, while Richard attempted to stuff the badly folded-up tent into the roof box. The weather for the lake district was forecast, unsurprisingly, for rain.

"Maybe we should have a staycation," Harriet said, even though she didn't mean it. William was wildly excited to camp, and had been wearing the head torch Richard had found in the mess of their camping gear for the last twenty-four hours, including when he was asleep.

"This is going to be great," Richard said firmly, and then managed to close the lid of the roof box.

Harriet looked up at the sound of a car approaching, her eyes widening at the sight of the cherry-red Mini Cooper convertible speeding up the lane. Richard straightened, squinting at the car as it pulled up in front of number three.

The woman driving the car looked like a cross between Marilyn Monroe and the Duchess of Cambridge. Long, shiny caramel-colored hair streamed from underneath a wildly patterned scarf. She removed her oversized sunglasses to inspect Harriet and Richard, giving them both a rather cool smile.

"Hello," she said after a pause and Harriet managed a smile, shocked by the sight of this movie star type swanning into Willoughby Close.

"Hello."

The woman stepped out of the car, revealing a svelte yet curvy figure that was poured into a pair of designer skinny jeans and a flowing, low-cut top of purple chiffon. The eyes behind the sunglasses were a smoky, purply-gray that complimented her top perfectly. She was utterly gorgeous, super sexy, and Harriet was immediately conscious of every fault and flaw she possessed, from the poochy belly hidden by her loose T-shirt to the gray in her hair and the deepening crow's feet by her eyes. Plus she had a pimple coming out on her chin.

The woman reached into the back of the Mini and picked up a little crate that held a very small dog, the kind one could put in a pocketbook. She turned back to Harriet and Richard with a small smile.

"Are you my new neighbors?"

"What…" Harriet's jaw nearly dropped before she managed to rally. "Yes, that is, if you're moving into…"

"Number three, yes." The woman glanced at the cottage next to Harriet's with a small, wry smile. For a second Harriet was able to look past the woman's obvious glamour and beauty to see something vulnerable and sad underneath. But only for a second.

"Oh, well, then." Harriet gave her a bright smile. "I'm Harriet Lang, and this…" She paused for a second, wondering how much to explain, but then Richard stepped in.

"Richard," he said. "The husband."

"Right. No husband here, I'm afraid." The woman clutched the dog crate closer to her, her smile turning brittle.

There was a story there, but one she wasn't about to volunteer and Harriet was hardly going to ask after two seconds' acquaintance.

"Ava Mitchell," she added, extending one elegant, well-manicured hand. "Nice to meet you."

Chapter Twenty-Two

I T WAS RAINING in the lake district. Hardly a surprise considering the location and the forecast, but enduring rain while in a tent was entirely different from watching it pour from the window of your five-star hotel. Or four or three or two-star hotel. Basically anything that had walls and a roof.

Harriet was amazed she'd managed to forget just how much she hated camping. She'd *thought* she remembered, but the visceral dread that poured through her veins as Richard and William manfully set up the tent—it only took two hours—while she entertained Chloe in the car and Mallory walked around, desperately trying to get mobile phone reception, told her differently.

She really, really, hated camping. She hated the close, cramped quarters, the piles of stuff that got all mixed up, the fug that emanated from everyone's breathing in an enclosed space, even that peculiar tent smell of nylon and damp. She hated cooking on a tiny propane one-ring stove, and she hated eating crouched around the tent, huddled over paper plates of soggy pasta and cold tomato sauce.

Camping in the rain was a thousand times worse than camping when the weather was fine. By the time they'd lugged everything into the tent it was soaked, with no prospect it seemed of it ever getting dry. Going outside was virtually impossible; the campsite was a sea of mud, the block of loos swimming in sludgy rainwater.

They spent an interminable evening all huddled in the tent, the rain drumming down and making the roof sag, absolutely everything feeling chilly and wet, while they attempted to spin out a game of twenty questions until Mallory, with a loud, theatrical groan, said, "Can't we just go home?"

They'd booked for a week.

When the kids had finally, *finally* dropped off and Daisy, who found the whole change of scenery to be equally wildly alarming and exciting, had fallen asleep as well, Harriet stretched out on top of her sleeping bag—which Richard had positioned next to his—and let out a soft, heartfelt sigh. One day done.

"Well," Richard whispered, his hand finding hers in the dark. "This is fun."

Harriet let out a muffled laugh. They were crammed in like sardines and there looked to be no end to the rain. "What are we even going to do tomorrow?" she whispered. They'd originally planned to hike around Tarn Hows but Harriet could not envision taking her children on a hike in the pouring rain.

Richard squeezed her hand. "We'll figure something out."

Morning dawned, barely, gray and drizzling. Harriet crouched by the kettle, spooning instant coffee into a couple of tin cups. Even the granules seemed damp. *Everything* was damp, and the smell of wet clothing—and far too many humans—permeated the air so Harriet found it hard to breathe. Behind her the children huddled in a pile of sleeping bags, Mallory determined to stay asleep and Chloe and William watching an episode of *Shaun the Sheep* on Harriet's phone. One day in and she'd already resorted to electronic entertainment.

"Hey." Richard poked his head in the tent, fresh from the shower block. "The showers are free if you want to go. I'll make a breakfast."

Harriet arched an eyebrow, skeptical as to whether the tent could survive the kind of mess Richard usually generated in the kitchen. He grinned, reading her mind.

"I'll be fine. And I'll clean up, as well."

"When did you become a saint?" Harriet murmured as she dug through the piles of stuff for her towel and toiletry bag.

"Not a saint," Richard said seriously. "Just trying to make up for lost time."

By the time Harriet had showered and dressed, she felt almost optimistic about the day. Yes, it was still wet, but the rain had downgraded into a drizzle she thought they could brave.

Richard had been as good as his word and cleaned up all the breakfast things, leaving a bacon buttie for her along with a cup of coffee.

"So, shall we attempt Tarn Hows?" Harriet asked as she finished her breakfast.

Mallory groaned and William fist-pumped the air. "Yes!"

It continued to drizzle as they set out, optimism as yet unflagging, for Tarn Hows. Although it was one of the area's most visited spots, only a few hardy-looking souls joined them on the mile and a half amble around the lake. Even in the misty grayness, the view was beautiful, the tranquil tarn surrounded by conifers, the hills and fells a stunning backdrop worthy of a postcard.

William and Chloe skipped ahead with Richard while Harriet fell back to keep Mallory, who had abandoned any hope of getting mobile reception, company, Daisy trotting at their heels.

"How are you doing?" she asked, and Mallory gave her one of her looks.

"Okay."

"I know camping most likely isn't one of your favorite things in the world, but we're all together and the scenery is stunning."

"Yup." Her daughter was clearly in monosyllabic mode. Then Mallory surprised her by asking, a note of uncertainty in her voice, "What's going to happen?"

Harriet didn't pretend to misunderstand. "I don't know, Mallory. We're taking things one step at a time."

"It seems like you guys are back together."

"I suppose we are," Harriet answered after a moment's reflection. "In a way."

"What does that mean?"

She gave her daughter a lopsided smile. "It seems your parents are dating again."

"Ew. Gross. Don't ever say that again."

Harriet laughed. "Okay, I won't."

They walked in silence, avoiding puddles, the rain starting to come down harder. By the end of the walk they would be well and truly soaked. "So what happens when you go from dating to being, like, married again?" Mallory shot her a look to express how distasteful she found the whole concept of dating in relation to her parents. "Will Dad move into Willoughby Close?"

It was a thought that had been circling around Harriet's mind, finding nowhere to land. "I don't know," she said slowly. "If he gets this job he interviewed for... we'll probably buy a house." Why did her stomach sink at this prospect? Didn't she want a beautiful house, and the life to go with it? Was she *crazy*?

"Not our old house, though."

"No, not our old house." And that didn't hurt nearly as much as it had a few months ago. She'd given up that dream, along with a lot of others, and that was no bad thing.

"What house, then?"

"I don't know. One we all like, somewhere in the village, hopefully. Does it matter so much?"

Mallory kicked at the ground, causing mud to splash up and splatter on their jeans. "The thing is, I kind of want to stay at Willoughby Close."

Harriet nearly tripped on a tussock of grass. Startled, Daisy let out an indignant yip. "You do?"

"Yeah." Mallory shrugged. "Kind of."

"Because of…"

"Abby. And Lady Stokeley, even. And Jace. He's been good fun, actually. And just… I like it there. Sort of," she qualified, being Mallory.

"Hmm." Harriet liked it there, too.

And if she was honest with herself, she didn't want to leave Willoughby Close either. But would Richard want to move in? Certainly not if he got this job he was hoping for. He'd be back in million-pound territory, commuting to London, living the high life, working all hours.

Harriet sighed. There was no point making any decisions until Richard found out about his interview. Until something really changed.

They finished the walk around Tarn Hows and then drove to Ambleside to dry out in a coffee shop that, to Mallory's exultation, had free wifi and also allowed dogs. Harriet nursed a latte while Richard played table football with Chloe and William, and Mallory frantically tried to keep up with everything that had happened on Snapchat in the twenty-four hours she'd been away from it. Daisy, exhausted from the longest walk she'd ever taken in her short life, curled up at their feet and promptly fell asleep.

"Hey, Mall." Richard gave his eldest daughter a look, his eyebrows lifted. "Put down the phone and play with us."

Mallory looked outraged. "I need to keep up my streaks—"

Whatever those were. "Come on, Mallory. This is family time." Richard turned to Harriet. "And how about you, too?"

"What?" Harriet looked at him, startled. Their modus operandi in these situations was for Richard to entertain the children while she had a much-needed break. But he'd been entertaining the children a lot, and maybe that was the wrong attitude anyway.

"Okay," she said, and put down her coffee to send a penny ricocheting across the table and score between the salt and pepper shakers.

The last two days of the week the rain finally stopped and the world started to dry out. Harriet had succumbed already and dragged all of their stuff to a laundromat in Windermere to wash and dry it thoroughly, even though everything would just get wet again. When the weather turned they managed two decent hikes, Richard carrying Chloe on his shoulders for the steep bits.

By the last night they were all tired but happy, and Harriet was very much looking forward to sleeping in a real bed. To celebrate, Richard had bought fish and chips from a nearby shop which they ate sitting outside the tent for once, rather than in it.

The night air held a bite although the last, dying rays of the sun as it spread syrupy light over the horizon were warm.

Most of the campers on the site had braved the soggy ground to enjoy the sunshine, and there was a smiling sense of camaraderie as people ate their dinners. Even though there had been some tensions as people queued in the rain for showers and grit their teeth as they shared the water tap, now it was all genial bonhomie.

After dinner the children raced off, even Mallory, to play an impromptu game of rounders with the other kids on the campsite. Harriet settled Daisy and Richard burrowed among the food supplies and came out with a bottle of wine and two plastic cups.

"It really is a celebration," Harriet said as she accepted her cup. "Cheers."

"Cheers," Richard answered, and they clinked plastic. "To us."

The words hung in the air for a few seconds, waiting for a response. Harriet gazed out at Tarn Hows in the distance, now alight with the setting sun, and listened to the children's shouts of laughter. "To us," she repeated, and smiled.

As night fell and the stars came out, the children tumbled back into the tent. Harriet tidied up the last of their dinner dishes, almost but not quite regretful that they would be back at Willoughby Close. It had, despite the rain and the wet and the bone-deep cold even in the end of May, been a good week.

And maybe there was a lesson to be learned here—that even when the circumstances were less than ideal, even when life gave them something they really didn't think they wanted, it could turn out okay. It could turn out great. Like Lady Stokeley had intimated, happiness was a by-product, not an end result.

The next evening they arrived back at Willoughby Close with a mountain of washing and three tired but happy children, plus puppy. Richard helped lug everything in and then put the first load of wash in, something he never would have done in their previous lives.

The children, after seven days of far too much fresh air, instantly plugged in. Harriet didn't mind; last night they'd played rounders until it had been too dark to see.

While Richard continued to tidy up, Harriet let Daisy out into the garden and then popped over to Ellie's to check how the week driving Dorothy had gone.

"It was fine," Ellie said when Harriet came in for a quick chat. "At least, as fine as these things can be. But Lady Stokeley—I still can't call her Dorothy—seems to be doing well. The last day the consultant checked her levels of this and that, I'm not sure what, and he seemed pleased."

"Did he?" Harriet was greatly cheered by this. "That sounds like good news, then."

"I think so." Ellie paused, looking almost guilty. "Actually, I have to confess, I didn't take her to Oxford on the last day."

"Jace did?"

"No… he was gone for the whole day, I don't know where. He seemed a bit secretive about it, but I suppose that's nothing new."

"Then who took her?" Harriet asked with a frown.

"Ava did."

"Ava?" Harriet could not keep from goggling. She'd almost forgotten about their new neighbor, but now that she'd been called to mind Harriet could hardly believe that the sexy glamour-puss with the designer clothes and pocketbook dog had volunteered to drive Lady Stokeley to Oxford, and during her first week of tenancy. "How did that come about?"

"Well… I'd forgotten I had to take Abby to the dentist, and since Jace was away… Ava was outside and saw me running around and asked if she could help."

"Wow."

"She seems nice, I think. Sort of, anyway."

"Okay." Harriet supposed she shouldn't feel quite so stunned. *Don't judge a book by its cover, and all that.* "Well, good," she said. "I guess."

Back in the house, the kids were still avidly attached to

their screens, and Richard had put a third load of wash in.

"Thanks," Harriet said in pleased surprise.

"How has the lady of the manor been this week? Managed without you?"

"Yes, it seems so. She had some tests done on Friday that the consultant sounded pleased with."

"That's great news."

"Yes."

They smiled at each other; the only sound the tinny noise of shooting from William's game on his DS as he sprawled, oblivious, on the sofa.

"I suppose I should get going," Richard said, his hands shoved into the pockets of his jeans.

Harriet glanced at him, his dark hair rumpled, his expression a little rueful, wearing an old rugby shirt and faded jeans, and she blurted, "Why don't you stay the night?"

Richard's eyebrows rose nearly to his hairline. "Do you mean…?"

She didn't know what she meant, only that it felt wrong now, after everything, to have him take the train back to his lonely flat in Bexley. She didn't want that, but what *did* she want?

"I'm not sure," she admitted with a little laugh. "But… I don't want you to go."

Relief flashed across Richard's face. "I don't want to go, either."

And suddenly it felt wonderfully simple. "Then don't,"

Harriet said, and walked into his arms.

He rested his chin on top of her head and she wrapped her arms around his waist, her cheek pressed against his shoulder, savoring the embrace. It felt like the purest communication they'd had in a long, long time.

"What about the kids?" Richard asked in a low voice, conscious of William nearby, his lips brushing her hair. "What will we tell them?"

"I don't know." She doubted William or Chloe would even notice.

As for Mallory... she remembered her daughter's disgust about the prospect of them dating. She didn't like to imagine Mallory's reaction at realizing even more than that might be going on.

"Let's just play it by ear," she said as she nestled closer, "and see what happens."

In the end, even Mallory didn't seem to notice the tectonic shift that was occurring in her parents' relationship. Harriet was kept busy doing laundry and trying to get the household into some semblance of order before school the next day while the children mooched around and Richard got his laptop out and did some work—when Harriet asked what the work actually was, he gave her a bashful grin and admitted, "I'm marking GCSE essays for my tutoring kids."

"Oh." She came over and looked over his shoulder, saw the comments he was making on an essay on Hitler's Germany. "That looks interesting."

"It is, actually." He looked up with a rueful grin. "Makes for a nice change of pace."

"I'm sure it does." It made for a nice change of pace to have the children settled and adult company for the evening. And as for after…

Harriet's stomach flipped at the thought. Seeing what happened sounded incredibly nebulous now that bedtime was approaching.

They spent the next few hours sorting the children's bedtimes out; Richard read to Chloe while Harriet helped William find his PE kit and liberated Mallory from her phone so it could charge for the night. By nine-thirty all was quiet and the downstairs was dim, lit only by a few table lamps. Richard was sitting on the sofa and after a second's hesitation Harriet joined him, curling up on the other end.

She didn't know quite why she felt so ill at ease. Over the last few weeks, they'd spent quite a few evenings on this sofa, chatting… but it had always been with the expectation that Richard would take the train back to London, with no more than a brief kiss goodnight, if that.

Although now that she thought about it, it seemed like an awfully long way to go at ten or eleven o'clock at night. "Did you take a late train," she asked, "before, when you spent the evenings here? You must have got back to London very late."

Richard ducked his head. "I didn't go back to London."

"You didn't?"

"There aren't any trains that late. I kipped at Colin's."

"Colin?" she repeated in surprise.

"We've become friendly, ever since I was sick all over his shoes." Richard grinned. "He offered me a place to stay while I wooed my wife."

She laughed. "Is that what you've been doing?"

"Trying to, at least. Is it working?"

She gave him a look. "You're here, aren't you?"

"Yes." His laughing gaze turned considering, intent. "Yes, I am."

Harriet's heart started to thump. Yes, he was. And the room was dim and the bed upstairs had fresh sheets on it. He was her husband, none of this was remotely new territory, and yet it felt new. It felt startlingly, frighteningly brand new.

"I'm not expecting anything, Harriet," Richard said quietly. "Hoping, yes. Definitely hoping. But I know this part of our reunion is hard for you."

She looked away. "I don't know why, exactly…"

Richard lifted one shoulder in a shrug. "I betrayed your trust. And that is the ultimate expression of trust, isn't it? Sex. Vulnerability. Nakedness."

She let out a wobbly laugh. "Too true. And stating it like that makes me want to freak out. I think your seduction moves could use some work."

"Could they? Let me try again." He reached for her hand, threading his fingers through hers. "I think you're a beautiful, sexy, smart, amazing woman and I want to make love to you very, very badly."

Harriet's throat was dry, her heart beating wildly. "That's a little better."

"Only a little?" He tugged on her hand and she came willingly, nerves jangling, first on her knees and then falling on top of him clumsily. He hauled her against him, his hands on her hips, his lips a breath away from hers.

The feel of his body, lean and hard, under hers was a jolt to her entire system. Legs tangled, hips pressing against his, her breasts crushed against his chest... it had been so *long*. Heat simmered in Richard's eyes and Harriet felt an answering tug in her tummy. Her breath shortened.

"Hi, he said softly, and she let out an uneven laugh.

"Hi."

He kissed her then, long and sweet, far more of a kiss than anything they'd shared in their few weeks of dating. A kiss that went on and on, that promised so much, that melted away her nerves and fears. A wonderful kiss.

At its end, Harriet let out a sigh and rested her forehead against Richard's shoulder as he stroked her hair.

"That was just meant to be a beginning, you know."

"I know." Her stomach tightened at the thought.

They lay there together for a few minutes, the room silent all around them save for Daisy's little snores.

Richard shifted under her and Harriet raised her head. "Am I crushing you?"

"Not at all." His grin was a little bit wolfish. "But I will admit to being a little uncomfortable."

And she could feel how uncomfortable he was. "Perhaps we should go upstairs."

"Perhaps we should."

Her nerves came back in a cold rush as they went upstairs. She'd gained at least ten pounds since January, thanks to lack of exercise and comfort eating, and sexy Meghan was just that. Young, stick thin, with no stretch marks or love handles. But then he hadn't seen Meghan naked... had he?

Harriet spent an inordinate time in the bathroom, brushing her teeth, checking for wrinkles or stray hairs, garnering her courage. Finally, when she couldn't postpone the moment any longer, she opened the door.

In the bedroom, Richard had stripped down to his T-shirt and boxers and turned back the duvet. A single lamp by the bed had been turned on, and the effect was intimate without trying too hard to be romantic. Even so, Harriet had gulped.

She was wearing one of Richard old T-shirts and a pair of pajama shorts, because she'd packed away her few slinky nightgowns when she'd first moved. At that point she'd felt she'd never have had need of them again.

She took a deep breath and closed the door behind her. Richard waited, smiling faintly.

"So here we are," she said.

"Here we are." Neither of them moved. The space between them felt like miles and yet no distance at all. "Harriet," Richard said, "we don't have to…"

Harriet knew what he meant, and she knew he meant it. They could lie in bed together all night long and Richard would respect her wishes, whatever they were. The last few weeks had shown her that. But it seemed stupid, suddenly, to hold back. To act like some shy virgin when she'd once bellowed at this man for pain relief. She had, after Mallory's birth, asked him to buy hemorrhoid cream for her—*and apply it.*

Either she was all-in when it came to her marriage, or she wasn't. She accepted Richard, all of him, or she didn't. And really, when it came down to it, why not enjoy what had, in the past, been a very nice benefit?

"Come here," she said and Richard came towards her, a goofy smile spread over his face, his arms open wide.

Harriet walked into them.

That was the last either of them spoke for quite a long while.

Chapter Twenty-Three

"YOU SEEM HAPPY."

Harriet looked up from the shopping list she'd been doodling on. It was early June and she was sitting in Olivia's teashop, enjoy a latte after the morning school run and wondering, rather dreamily, what the future held.

"I am happy," she said to Olivia.

The last week, since she and Richard had returned from the lake district and reignited their marital relationship—which caused a host of lovely and blush-inducing memories to play through Harriet's mind—had been quite wonderful.

The children had taken Richard's continued presence at Willoughby Close in their happy stride, although, when he'd come downstairs Monday morning, whistling, looking a little too much like the proverbial cat in regards to the cream, Mallory had done a double take and then visibly shuddered. Harriet had poured coffee and avoided her daughter's gaze.

Richard had returned to London that morning, ringing Harriet to say he'd had a request for a second interview with the startup investment firm. Harriet had tried to ignore the queasy feeling that bit of news gave her. She was going to concentrate on all the positives in their relationship—the companionship, the newly restored trust, and yes, the sex.

"How's the dinner lady job going?" Olivia asked and Harriet looked up with a laughing grimace.

"Fine, actually. It's not the most scintillating work but, in an odd way, I enjoy it." She liked the camaraderie with the other kitchen workers, as well as seeing all the children, even if only from behind a lunch counter. And, funnily enough, working in the cafeteria had opened up a whole new range of possible friendships to her—women who didn't have gym club memberships or million-pound houses. Women like her. And women who were the way she had been, mums who had revolved around Sophie's and her circle, but who now were starting to peel off. Harriet almost felt as if she'd birthed a movement. Next weekend, she was planning a drinks night for year one mums at The Drowned Sailor.

"What did you do before kids?" Olivia asked, her elbows propped on the counter.

The café was empty save for Harriet; an elderly woman had left a few moments before with a box of macaroons— apparently she bought them every Monday morning, like clockwork.

"I was in publishing, the marketing side. Seems like a lifetime ago, though."

"Oh? Well, if you're looking for work, I wouldn't mind a bit of freelancing. I don't have a huge budget, mind."

"Freelancing?" Did Olivia want her to waitress?

"I need to boost the profile of this place, now my mother is retiring. If I'm going to be able to afford to keep it open, anyway. Build a website…"

Harriet grimaced. "I'm afraid I'm terrible with the tech side of things. Digital stuff had barely started being an issue when I was last in the business."

"Oh, I can manage the tech side fine," Oliva assured her. "I was thinking more about special events—I want to offer parties, you know, for hen nights or children's birthdays… but I'm rubbish at that sort of thing and I'd need helping organizing and marketing it. Making it fun and different."

"My experience was in publishing…" Harriet began dubiously, although Olivia's ideas had sparked her interest.

"I don't care about that," Olivia answered with a laugh. "It's not your publishing experience I'm after. It's your mum experience. You organized the school fete last year, didn't you? Everyone said how brilliant it was."

"Oh." Harriet let out a laugh, surprised and pleased. That kind of experience she did have, in spades. "Okay. Well, then, yes, I'd love to help you."

"I don't have a lot of money, though…"

"Don't worry," Harriet reassured her. "I'm making minimum wage on my other jobs. I don't think this one should be any different."

After her coffee, Harriet strolled back to Willoughby Close, humming under her breath, feeling happier than she had in a long time. Lady Stokeley had the week off chemo so there were no drives to Oxford, and when Harriet had stopped by to visit her, Dorothy had admitted, gruffly, that the consultant seemed to feel she was responding to the treatment.

"That's really wonderful news," Harriet had enthused and Dorothy had let out a harrumph.

"I suppose, but at my age you become leery of false hope."

"Maybe this hope isn't false."

"We won't know, will we," Dorothy shot back, "until it's too late?"

"And how was Ava Mitchell?" Harriet asked, deciding not to indulge Dorothy's acerbity too much. "She drove you last week? That went all right?"

"I suppose." Dorothy sniffed. "She's quite a glamour girl, isn't she?"

"Very fancy," Harriet agreed. "Did you get along?"

Dorothy glanced at her shrewdly. "I am not your child, my dear. You do not need to fuss quite so much, or so openly. I have, in all of my eighty-six years, perfected most social niceties so I can get along with just about anyone."

Harriet suppressed a smile. "I'm sure you have."

Now, as Harriet turned up the drive to Willoughby Close, she wondered how Ava Mitchell was getting on. She hadn't seen much of her new neighbor save for the cherry-red Mini parked outside.

She should be more welcoming, but she'd been so busy with children, puppy, work, and Richard that she hadn't. Now she decided to knock on the door and say hello.

She had to wait for several uncertain minutes before Ava came to the door, wearing a dressing gown of fuchsia satin, her hair in a glorious, golden tangle about her face.

"Oh. Hello." She looked decidedly unenthused about seeing Harriet.

"Sorry, did I wake you?" It was ten in the morning, but Harriet supposed that was early for someone who appeared neither to work nor have children.

Ava yawned. "Sort of. I was lying in bed wondering if I should bother getting up."

"Oh. Well." Harriet tried for a bright smile. "I wanted to welcome you to Willoughby Close—"

Ava arched one perfectly groomed eyebrow. "Are you the welcoming committee, then?"

"No, not officially." Harriet couldn't quite gauge her tone, whether it was snarky or simply amused. "Anyway, perhaps you'd like to…" She paused, wondering whether she really wanted to invite Ava over. Then she decided she did. "Come for dinner one evening? It's a bit mad at my house, but we'd love to have you."

Ava cocked her head, her gaze sweeping slowly over Harriet, so she blushed. What on earth was she thinking, inviting someone like Ava into the madhouse that was her home?

"Perhaps," she said. "When I've settled in." She paused and then added, as an afterthought, "Thank you for the invitation."

"Oh, well, sure. Okay." That hadn't gone quite as Harriet had hoped.

And now Ava was closing the door, so she had no choice but to step back with a cheery little wave. Harriet walked back to number two, wondering if Ava would ever take her up on her invitation, and also wondering if she wanted her to. The sound of tires on gravel had her turning her head, and she blinked in surprise at the sight of Richard's beat-up Toyota coming down the lane. He'd sold his beloved Beamer along with everything else, back in February.

"Hey," she said as he clambered out of the car, a near-exultant look on his face. "What's up?"

"I got the job!"

"You... did?" Harriet tried to smile.

Why, oh why, did she not feel nearly as excited about this as Richard did?

"Yes, I did. They're really keen to have someone experienced on their team, someone who knows how to take risks."

Harriet refrained from pointing out that, based on previous experience, Richard did not know how to take risks. At least, not successful ones. Clearly that kind of comment would not be helpful now.

"Wow," she said, feeling inadequate to the moment.

"Come on." Richard reached for her hand. "I want to show you something."

"Okay." Harriet got in the car, deciding to ride Richard's wave of success as best as she could. He was happy and excited, and that could only be a good thing. Right?

They drove out of Willoughby Close, and then out of Wychwood-on-Lea. Harriet had no idea where he was taking her, but as they headed down the road towards Burford she started to get a feeling.

"Where are we..." she began, only to have Richard cut her off with a firm shake of his head.

"Wait and see."

Another couple of minutes of driving and then they were turning up the sweeping drive, rolling fields on either side, and towering stone pillars topped by lions in front of them. Richard drove through the pillars and parked on the circular drive, in front of the massive front door.

Wychwood House.

Slowly Harriet unbuckled her seat belt and got out of the car. The house was bigger and more intimidating than she'd remembered—three floors of golden stone, with eight long, sashed windows on each floor.

"Come inside," Richard said.

Harriet paused in front of the house. "Can we..."

Richard brandished a set of keys. "Yes, we can."

"You have the keys?" Her stomach swooped rather unpleasantly. "You haven't..."

"No, I haven't. I had a viewing this morning and the real estate agent let me keep the keys. We'll turn them in after you have a look."

"And then?"

"And then we'll make an offer," Richard said as he unlocked the front door. "The agent thinks the seller will accept a million five. They're desperate, apparently."

Desperate. With a feeling of dread seeping into her stomach, Harriet followed Richard through the now-open door.

"Isn't it amazing?"

She'd been the one who had been excited about Wychwood House, once upon a time, and now Richard sounded thrilled. The foyer was huge, with black and white marble tile, and several sets of double doors leading off it.

"It is amazing," she said, because of course it was. It was enormous and elegant, a dream house of majestic proportions.

"Come and see," Richard said as he opened a set of doors that led to a huge drawing room, a fireplace with a stone-carved mantel on one end. He was like a little boy at Christmas, unwrapping present after present. Harriet didn't have to say much, simply follow where he led—drawing room, dining room, library, second, smaller sitting room. A huge kitchen with an adjoining breakfast room that only looked somewhat more updated than the kitchen of Willoughby Manor.

"It needs a lot of work," Richard said, "but can't you imagine it? And look, two pantries and a boot room, *and* a utility room."

After that they went upstairs, and saw the six huge bedrooms. "There are no en suites," Richard said, making a face. "They've definitely done the minimum of modernizing. But we could turn one of the bedrooms into an en suite, easily, for us. And the top floor could be for Mallory... she'd have her own space, acres of it. We could put a bathroom up there, as well. No more queuing for showers."

The last thing Mallory needed was her own floor. She'd done better sharing with Chloe, forced into socializing with her family rather than retreating into the world of her phone. Richard knew this, Harriet knew he did, and yet he seemed to have a determined blind spot about so many things right now.

"Now the garden," Richard said, and they headed outside. The garden was beautiful—a Victorian walled garden for a vegetable plot, an apple orchard, and a winding stone path through a very overgrown rose garden. It was all so gorgeous, and it made Harriet ache, because who wouldn't want this house? It was incredible. And it came with too high a cost—a cost that had nothing to do with the million five price tag.

"So, what do you think?" Richard asked, and then continued on blithely, without waiting for her answer. "We could put an offer in this morning, when we return the keys. Have the deal done by the end of the week, move in over the summer. We'd have to do it up slowly, I'm afraid. My signing bonus isn't *that* big." He let out a laugh, sounding so happy, and Harriet felt her stomach hollow out.

This was not going to be an easy conversation.

"Richard," she said quietly. They were standing in the marble-tiled foyer, sunshine pouring through the sunburst-shaped window high above. He turned, his eyebrows raised in query, his mind still going a million miles per hour.

"I don't want to buy this house."

"What?" He frowned, her words clearly not computing.

And why would they? For so long she'd made it clear that she wanted their old lives back. Their old house back and, if they couldn't have that, she'd wanted this house. But she didn't anymore. She didn't want any of it.

"I don't want to buy this house," Harriet repeated. "It's amazing and gorgeous and all the rest, but I don't want to go back to the way we were."

"But we won't," Richard said, his expression clearing. "I've told you that. We've learned, haven't we? This has been a good thing for us, in a way, because of how we've grown." He reached for her hands. "Moving into Wychwood House won't change that. It won't change *us.*"

"I like Willoughby Close."

He stared at her in surprise, letting out a laugh Harriet didn't quite like. "Willoughby… are you joking? I mean, I know it's nice enough, but it's a rental, Harriet. A tiny rental."

"You said what a nice place it was before."

"That was when things were different! Come on. Willoughby Close was never meant to be forever, no matter what happened. You knew that."

"Maybe," Harriet allowed, "but we've been happy there." And she wasn't willing to toss that aside so easily.

"And we'll be happy here."

"Will we?" She tugged her hands from his. "Richard, we have just dug ourselves out of massive debt. We've lost our house. How would we even get a mortgage for this place?"

"I've looked into it. We'd need a bigger down payment, but I think the bank would be willing to…"

"It's far too much risk," Harriet insisted. "The mortgage, the updating, even the furniture. We sold it all. We ended that life."

"But I always said I could get it back—"

"I don't want it back. Not any of it. I don't want to live here." She spoke firmly, knowing she meant every word.

"Fine." She could tell Richard was trying not to show his hurt. "I thought you liked this place, but we can look somewhere else. Maybe one of those modern places on that estate in the village…"

"No." Harriet took a deep breath. "There's more." Richard's eyes narrowed as he waited. "I don't want you to accept this job."

The ensuing silence was like the calm before the storm—Harriet heard a bird twitter outside, the rustling of the breeze in the trees. Somewhere a floorboard creaked as the house settled. And still Richard stared.

"What are you talking about?" he asked in a low, even voice that signaled an almighty row was about to happen.

"I don't want you to take this job. It's too risky. A startup firm and one that *wants* you to take the kind of chances that caused this in the first place?"

"Of course you throw that in my face *now*. They appreciate what I have to offer, Harriet—"

"Richard," Harriet continued doggedly, "if it made you happy, I might think about it more. But I don't think this kind of high finance work makes you happy."

His face settled into a deep frown but he stayed silent, listening. Fuming.

Harriet plowed on. "Do you really want to go back to commuting to London, barely seeing the children, or me for that matter? And do you remember what you said about the pressure? It will be even more intense with a firm that hired you to take the risks that got us into this mess in the first place." She held up a hand to staunch his protests. "I'm not blaming you. I see, more than ever, how I added to the pressure and stress. I don't want to go back to being that person, and I don't want you to go back to being the person you were, either. I don't want this house, not with the price tag it comes with… what it would mean for us, as a couple, as a family."

Richard stared at her for a long moment, his jaw tight.

"You tell me this *now?*"

"It took me a while to realize it. To not want what we had. I've changed, Richard, and that's a good thing. I understand it was important to get this offer, to feel validated after what happened, to know you could go back if you wanted to. But it doesn't mean you have to take it."

Richard's jaw was still bunched. "Then what am I supposed to do, Harriet? I've been looking for a job like this for a year."

She took a deep breath. "What about doing something else?"

"What? What on earth am I supposed to do if not this?"

Harriet took another deep breath, feeling dizzy. "What about doing something completely different? You could retrain—"

"Retrain?"

"As a teacher. You love history, Richard—"

"It pays peanuts!"

"Let's forget about the money for the minute."

He folded his arms. "It's kind of a big thing to forget about. In fact, you had trouble forgetting about it for quite awhile—"

"I know, but money never made us happy. It made us comfortable, yes, very comfortable." She would miss their holidays in Provence and Verbier, no question. And the spa days, and the regular trips to the hair salon, and everything else. "But when I first moved into Willoughby Close,"

Harriet continued determinedly, "I kept remembering our early days, at that grotty flat in Camden Town. Do you remember? It was awful, and we furnished it with plastic crates and a futon, but we were *happy.*"

"We were also young."

"If the money didn't matter, what would you rather be? A history teacher or a high-flying finance guy?"

"Hedge fund manager is the proper term, actually," Richard said stiffly.

"Whatever."

Richard blew out a long breath, raking a hand through his hair before he turned away. "I've been working for this for a year. My whole life, really."

"I know you went into finance because your father did. I remember you saying in uni that if teaching paid better, you'd do it—"

"I didn't mean it."

"Didn't you? I know this is radical, Richard, but we've had a lot of radical changes. It's not just about the money, either. It's not really about the money at all. It's about us. What we want out of life. What kind of people we want to be—"

"I don't see how making a million pounds a year could be a bad thing."

"I do. You know how it would be. You'd have to spend several nights a week in London, work some weekends, always be on your phone or laptop. That's how these jobs are. And we'd start to live separate lives without realizing it. We might say we've changed, we'll be different, but how can we really be different when everything else goes back to the way it was?"

"We just can," Richard insisted, but he sounded anguished rather than resolute. "I don't know what else to be, Harriet. This is who I am."

"It doesn't have to be."

He stared at her, his eyes snapping with frustration and even fury. Harriet held her breath and his gaze.

"So is this an ultimatum?" he finally asked. "Become a history teacher or we're through?"

"I don't want to make ultimatums."

"Answer the question," Richard said in a hard voice.

"It's not an ultimatum, not exactly…"

He rolled his eyes. "Brilliant."

"You don't have to become a history teacher, Richard, of course not. I don't care what you *do*—"

"Really? Because you're certainly acting like you do now. You're acting like you care a lot."

"Within reason, I mean. I don't want you to commute to London. I don't want to live a high-pressured life of financial risk and too much money, a life where we never see each other and we build separate existences. Separate friendships."

"I wouldn't do that—"

"I'm not just talking about Meghan. I mean the whole package."

Richard stared at her, his eyes hard, his jaw bunched. "And if the alternative is no money at all?"

"We'll survive. We already are surviving, aren't we? And if you leave the flat in Bexley, that will save us plenty. You could go to school part-time—"

Richard spun away from her. "This is crazy."

"Maybe, but not as crazy as jumping right back into the snake pit we just clambered out of."

Richard remained with his back to her, silent and fuming. This wasn't about money, not really. This was about who they were as people and where they wanted to go—either together or alone. And if it was alone, her heart would break and, far worse, her children's hearts would break. Again. But it had to be better than going back to something that didn't work, not in the long term, not at all.

"Maybe you should think about it," she said quietly.

"Yeah," Richard answered, his back still to her. "Maybe I should."

HARRIET SPENT THE next three days in a ferment of indecision, second-guessing her conversation with Richard, calling herself an idiot, wishing she could gobble it all back. What kind of crazy woman turned down that kind of money? That kind of life? Not to mention poured cold water all over her husband's dreams.

Richard returned to London the afternoon after they'd

seen Wychwood House, and later texted her to say he was "taking some time." Whatever that meant. His absence made the children uneasy, with Mallory darting her pointed, accusing looks and William having more energy than usual, which was saying something. At one point, Harriet had to stop him from using the salt and pepper shakers as drumsticks on his sister's head.

Chloe started following her around, as puppy-like as Daisy, so Harriet tripped over her as she turned from the cooker to drain the pasta for dinner.

"Chloe." She took a breath and clung to her patience. "Out of the way, darling, please. I'm holding something hot."

"Why isn't Daddy here?" Chloe demanded, and then, almost defiantly, stuck her thumb in her mouth.

Harriet felt as if they'd all taken an awful giant step backwards. Rewind three months and here they were. Again. It was a terrible, terrible feeling.

"Daddy's in London, settling a few things about his work."

"What work?" Chloe's forehead crinkled. "I thought he was looking for a job."

"Well…"

"Is that what this is about?" Mallory's head popped up over the sofa. "Did Dad get a new job?"

"Maybe," Harriet hedged, and Mallory's eyes narrowed dangerously.

"Maybe?"

"He's thinking through his options."

"Which *are?*"

"Leave it, Mallory, please," Harriet answered tiredly. "I don't have any answers right now. I wish I did." And miraculously, her daughter left it for once.

The next morning Harriet was still feeling gloomy and wracked by nerves when she picked up Lady Stokeley for her last chemo treatment of the week.

"What's got you in such a dither?" Dorothy asked as Harriet turned onto the A40.

She glanced across to the passenger seat, noting Dorothy's better color. She definitely seemed to have bounced back from the effects of the chemo, which was one shining bright spot amidst the darkness of her own personal life.

"I'm not in a dither," she lied. "Why would you say that?"

"Because you have been in a bad mood all week," Dorothy answered. "And I usually count on your good cheer."

"Oh." Now she felt even worse. "Sorry. It's just… I think I might have made a mistake."

Dorothy arched an eyebrow. "A mistake you can rectify?"

She made it sound simple. "I suppose I could, but I'm not sure I want to."

"Then it doesn't sound like it was a mistake, simply a choice with some unfortunate consequences."

Harriet laughed out loud. "True."

"What was it, then?" Dorothy asked on a sigh, as if Harriet's troubles were sure to be nothing she hadn't heard or endured before.

So Harriet told her the bare bones of it, from Richard's job to Wychwood House to the ultimatum she hadn't exactly meant to give.

"Hmm." Dorothy pursed her lips as Harriet navigated past a construction lorry. "Your mistake was in telling him what to do. Never make a man think his idea isn't a good one. It emasculates him, poor thing."

Harriet suppressed a choking sound of surprise. Dorothy's advice sounded as if it came straight from a 1950s guide to being the perfect housewife.

"I remember when Gerald wanted to turn Willoughby Manor into an adventure park. Thought it would keep the place afloat financially. I pretended I thought it was a lovely idea, and I listed all the work that would need doing... not to mention the elephants we'd have cavorting on the croquet lawn, a helter-skelter in the topiary..." Dorothy shuddered. "Still I acted as if I thought it would be wonderful. Eventually he came to his senses."

"Ah." Considering the state of Willoughby Manor now, Harriet wasn't sure Lord Stokeley's idea had been a bad one.

"It's tiresome, of course," Dorothy continued, "and I'm quite sure it goes against your undoubtedly modern feminist sensibilities, but the fact is men and women haven't changed, not fundamentally." She paused, reflecting. "They've just become better conditioned."

"Maybe so," Harriet allowed. "But what should I have done? Do you think I was wrong to say what I did? About his job, I mean?"

Dorothy sighed. "It is hardly for me to say."

Harriet couldn't recall a time Dorothy had not volunteered her opinion on a matter. "But what do you think?" she pressed.

"I think," she said after a moment, "that if you love a man, then you love him no matter what the circumstances. For richer or poorer and all that." She gave Harriet a shrewd look. "In most cases, it's the 'for poorer' that is the sticking point. Funnily enough, in your situation it appears it might be the 'for richer.'"

Which really made her sound insane. Harriet sighed, wondering if she should phone Richard or even go to London and talk to him face-to-face. Tell him that whatever job he wanted, whatever life he wanted, she would share it with him.

Wasn't that the right thing to do? Why did it not *feel* like it?

Another day passed with Harriet dithering, just as Dorothy had said she was. She tried to talk to Ellie, but Ellie had had some kind of spat with Oliver and somehow Harriet didn't feel like she could burden her with her concerns. She saw Ava once from a distance, getting into her Mini, and didn't think that that was a friendship that was going to develop naturally.

On Friday night she lay on the sofa, staring up at the ceiling and feeling miserable. The children were in bed, and all evening they'd been just as mopey as she was. Chloe had even pulled a few tears, crying noisily when her milk had spilled.

It felt as if everything was going wrong.

Then a knock sounded on the door. Harriet sat up, her heart starting to hammer. It was ten o'clock at night. This was either going to be a very good thing, or a very bad thing. Unless it wasn't Richard at all.

Another knock and she hurried to the door. It was Richard, and he smelled like a brewery. Again.

"Are you drunk?"

"No," Richard answered indignantly. "I had a pint with Colin, that's all. Some spilled on me." He sniffed his jumper. "That's what it is. Can I come in?"

"Okay." She stepped aside, her heart starting to hammer. "Maybe you should just put me out of my misery," she blurted when Richard didn't say anything.

He bent down to scratch Daisy's ears; she'd roused herself at the sound of the knock and now rolled over onto her back, presenting Richard with her fluffy white tummy.

Harriet watched in deepening apprehension as he straightened and looked around the house. The living area was a bit of a mess; she hadn't had the energy to tidy up after dinner, and so William's trainers and dirty socks were by the

TV, Chloe's elaborate pink Lego construction half-formed on the table. There were dirty dishes in the sink.

Slowly Richard surveyed the room, and Harriet started to get annoyed. Almost. She was still holding hard onto hope, even now. Especially now.

"Richard…" she finally said, a pleading note entering her voice along with the exasperation.

"I was just wondering where my desk will go," he said. "Now that I'm going back to school."

"What…" Harriet's breath came out slowly as she blinked at him, hardly daring to understand. To *believe…*

"Does that mean what I think it means?"

"I turned the job down, Harriet."

"But I was just thinking that maybe you shouldn't—"

"What!" He looked appalled. "Tell me you're joking, please."

"Not for my sake," she clarified quickly, brushing at the tears that were already starting in her eyes. "For yours. Because, if this job really is your dream, I don't want to squash it. I don't want to demand something from you that would kill your spirit…"

"Kill my spirit?" A wry grin tugged at Richard's mouth. "Not managing other people's investments won't do that, trust me. But losing you would."

"But you won't lose me," Harriet said. She was properly crying now, tears of pure emotion streaking down her face. "That's what I'm trying to say. I never should have presented it like that. Like some kind of deal…"

"But it was a deal. Two deals, one good and one bad. And after nearly twenty years of making deals, I should know the difference."

Still Harriet felt she had to persist, to make it completely clear. "But you're not the only one who should change or compromise. If the job in London is what you really want, if it will make you happy, we can make this work. I know we can. I'm willing…" She took a deep breath. "Whatever you want. Whatever you need to be…"

"I know," Richard said gently. "You've always been behind me, Hat, even when I was a total screw-up."

"I was just as much of a screw-up." She sniffled, trying to stem the tide of tears. "All I'm saying is, you don't have to become a teacher for my sake, Richard."

"No, I'm becoming one for my own. I did a lot of thinking over the last few days. A lot of hard thinking, because the easiest thing in the world felt like saying yes to that job. The money alone…" He let out a shaky laugh. "I'm still finding it hard to give that up, if I'm honest, but I know it's the right thing to do. Because you were right, Hat. It wasn't making me happy. I was turning into a stressed out, arrogant prat. I knew that, but I thought I could handle it. I needed to, because I wanted to show that world that I was still somebody. Not just turn my back on it."

"You don't have to…" she whispered.

"Why are you crying?" He reached for her, and she went

into his arms, grateful for his hug that she so desperately needed. "Please don't cry. I know I couldn't see the wood for the trees for a while, but I'm seeing clearly now, I promise. And I know life's not going to be easy, not by a long shot. But we'll be together, and that's the main thing, isn't it?"

"That is the definitely the main thing," Harriet agreed, her cheek pressed against Richard's shoulder. She felt so relieved her knees were watery. She swayed and he caught her in his arms.

"Easy there, Hat."

She let out a trembling laugh and then, from the stairs, she heard Mallory's drawl. *"Finally."*

Mallory was standing on the stairs, her arms folded, Chloe and William peeking out from around her. Although Mallory was trying to rock the bored teenager look, she wasn't quite managing it. William and Chloe were grinning like loons.

"Daddy!" Chloe cried, and hurled herself down the stairs and into Richard's legs, wrapping her arms around his knees.

Richard hoisted her up in one arm. "Group hug?" he suggested, and then turned to Mallory and William with a raised eyebrow.

Mallory snorted in disbelief but, with a bashful grin, William came hurtling towards them. His hug was more tackle than embrace, but Harriet took it. She'd take it all.

And then Mallory came, with a deliberate eye roll. "Oh, whatever," she said, and patted them both on the arm before

Richard grabbed her in a headlock and drew her, protesting feebly, into the hug.

Harriet laughed out loud. Daisy was the last to join the circle of love—pressing her little head between Harriet's ankles and wagging her tail frantically. It felt like the most perfect, complete moment of her life—and then Daisy weed on the floor.

"Ew!" Mallory tried to wriggle away but Richard wouldn't let her. She squealed and then she started laughing, and William tackled Richard again, so he gave a startled *oof.*

It was normal life in all its glory, and Harriet wouldn't change a minute of it. Not one nanosecond.

Laughing, Harriet sidestepped the wee and put her arms around her family.

The End

Read Ava Mitchell's story in Kiss Me at Willoughby Close,
out in May 2017!

The Willoughby Close series

Discover the lives and loves of the residents of Willoughby Close

The four occupants of Willoughby Close are utterly different and about to become best friends, each in search of her own happy ending as they navigate the treacherous waters of modern womanhood in the quirky yet beautiful village of Shipstow, nestled in the English Cotswolds…

Book 1: *A Cotswold Christmas*

Book 2: *Meet Me at Willoughby Close*

Book 3: *Find me at Willoughby Close*

Book 4: *Kiss Me at Willoughby Close*

Book 5: *Marry Me at Willoughby Close*

Available now at your favorite online retailer!

About the Author

After spending three years as a diehard New Yorker, **Kate Hewitt** now lives in a small town in Wales with her husband, their five children, and a Golden Retriever.

She writes women's fiction as well as contemporary romance under the name Kate Hewitt, and whatever the genre she enjoys delivering a compelling and intensely emotional story.

You can find out more about Kate on her website at kate-hewitt.com.

Thank you for reading

Find Me at Willoughby Close

If you enjoyed this book, you can find more from all our great authors at TulePublishing.com, or from your favorite online retailer.

Made in the USA
Monee, IL
03 September 2022

13190727R00229